DRAGONS AND ACES

DRAGONS AND ACES SERIES BOOK 1

J. G. GATES

steed

For Melissa
My wings, my fire, my forever.

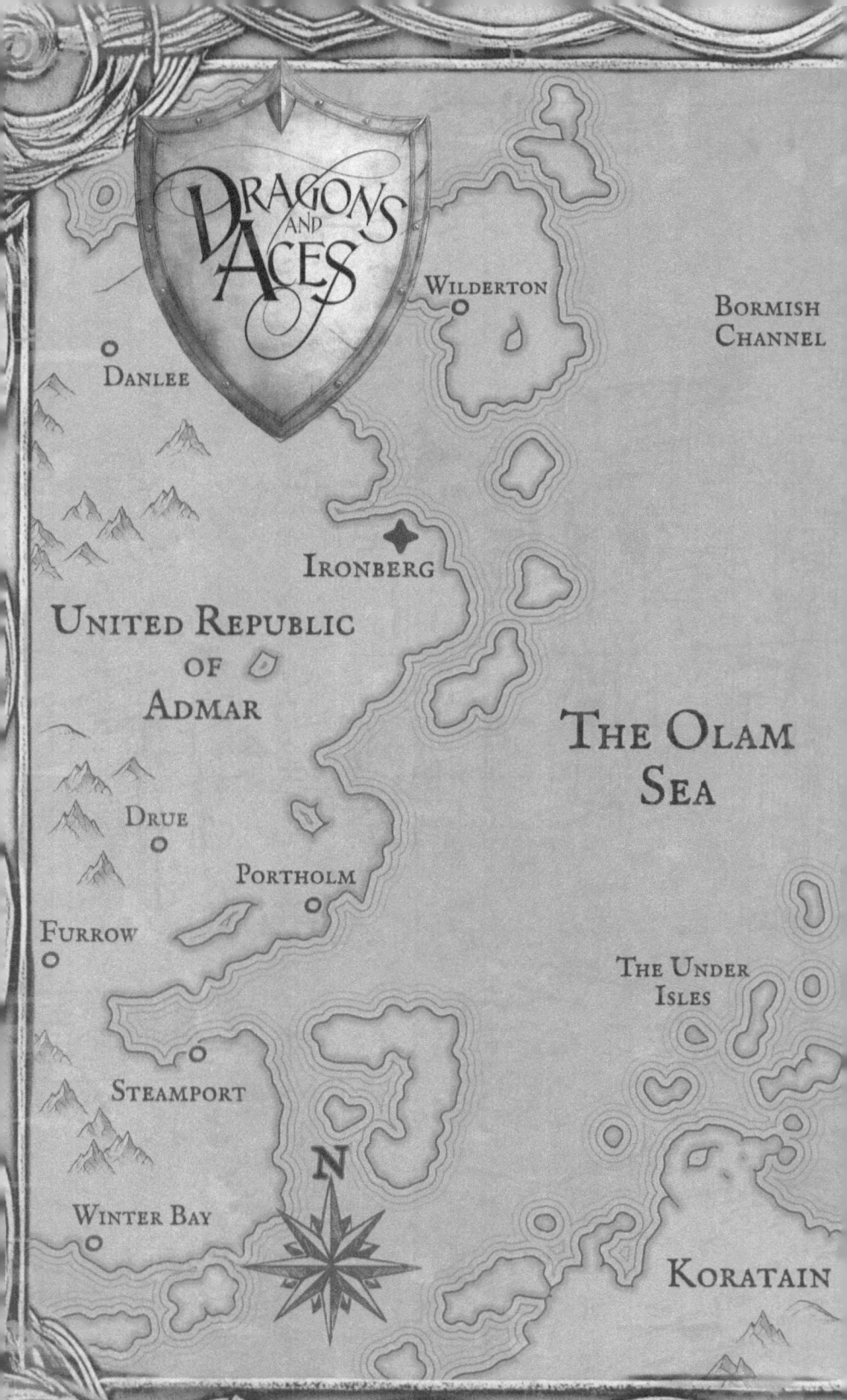

Woe to the city of opal spires
On the evening of three quarter moon
Dragon and machine contended in ire
And brave Irska Paemalla met her doom.

Gray and dim above the seas
Veiled were the skies in fog and brume
Illuminated by cannon and dragon fire
When brave Irska Paemalla met her doom.

Along the shore, the courtiers heard
Roar of beast and thunder of gun
But in the mist, none could behold
What course the terrible battle had run

At last, from the gray they fell in flames
Silver airplane and dragon grand
Like lovers entangled into the sea they sped
Gone forever from mortal lands.

SILVER WRAITH CRASHED AT SEA – A NATION IN SHOCK

by
Kitty Rowley

IRONBERG – The famed fighter pilot code named "Silver Wraith" has reportedly crashed into the Olam Sea and is presumed lost, Air Force officials have confirmed. The Wraith, flying in his trusty biplane, took off with his squadron from McNally Air Base at 4:45PM on Thursday in low-visibility conditions. Though spotters on the ground could see little of the battle, surviving squadron members reported engaging with a group of enemy dragons and facing ferocious resistance. Multiple reports confirmed seeing a silver plane crash into the water somewhere northeast of Rograd Point at approximately 7:10PM, along with a dragon believed to belong to Paemalla, reviled commander of the Maethalian dragon riders. Three other Admite pilots were also lost during the mission.

In a public statement, Air Force officials said, "We believe the Silver Wraith is alive, and will not stop searching until he is safely rescued." But privately, some officials expressed doubt that the highly decorated ace survived the crash. Any rescue mission would be complicated by rough seas, strong currents, and windy conditions known to exist off Rograd Point, as well as frequent patrols by enemy dragon riders.

Though hailed by millions as the premier ace of the URA Air Force, a pilot with more dragon kills than any other, little is known about the Silver Wraith, and his identity remains a closely guarded secret...

1

ESSA

The sky was blue, the sun was warm, my friends were with me, and my sister was dead. It was a perfect morning.

"What will you do if we find her?" Clua asked, sounding out of breath as her pony jogged along behind me.

"Essa would push her back into the sea," Ollie joked from my other side.

Clua was a dwarf, and though her strong arms served her well at the forge, her short legs made riding horses difficult. Her pony had short legs too, and unfortunately my mare, Sisha, tended to gallop ahead. I tugged back gently on the reins to match Clua's pace. My other arm—the one missing a hand—hung at my side, helping me keep my balance just as it did when I rode dragon-back.

"Push her into the sea? Why?" Clua asked. "With her gone, Essa would be the queen's eldest daughter. That means..."

"She knows what it means," Ollie said crossly. "We

agreed we'd have a pleasant ride with no talk of..." he squirmed in his saddle. "Unpleasantness."

Sweet Ollie, my Torouman. He was always protecting me —even from our other friends. I could feel Othura's presence, too. Although she was back at the palace, napping after last evening's flight, a dragon's consciousness was never far from their rider, and I could feel her like a warm blanket wrapped around me. Yet despite being surrounded by friends, I couldn't shake a nagging feeling of loneliness and foreboding. What if Paemalla really was gone?

Then death awaited me too, as inevitable as nightfall...

"Don't worry about my feelings, Ollie," I soothed him. "I have no feelings. Not about Paemalla, anyway."

Feelings... Indeed, I'd felt every pinch and punch and jeer Paemalla had thrown at me over the years. She'd been crueler than anyone had a right to be to a sister who was four years younger, although I suspected she believed her meanness to be virtuous, as if by bullying me she might toughen me up—maybe even enough to compensate for my missing right hand. Whether that tactic had worked was debatable, but her cruelty had certainly made me hate her. And her ruthlessness had served her well as she'd fought her way to the rank of Irska, the top dragon rider of the entire Maethalian army.

Of course, being a bully didn't mean she deserved death at the hands of those treacherous URA machine riders, if that was truly what had happened.

But I didn't really believe she was gone. Paemalla was too stubborn to die. I did, however, relish the idea of being the one to find her crashed, waterlogged, and humiliated. So, we rode on.

Maethalia in the spring was a sight that had inspired

bards since the time before queens, when gods danced in the forests and faerie gazed out from each flower and stone. The sky shone above, a cloudless sapphire vault. The black cliffs to our right plummeted from grassy heights to white froth and dark ocean below. Blooming wildflowers, humming bees, and soaring gulls beset the ancient road, and smells of sea and blossom rode the breeze. A brisk wind pushed the hair from my face and golden sun warmed my cheeks.

But none of the loveliness surrounding me could compare to the beauty of the waterlogged man who suddenly stepped into our path.

Sisha reared, startled, and only through sheer force of will and a mighty squeeze of my legs was I able to keep my seat.

My sword rang from its sheath. Clua pulled out her mace, and Ollie nocked an arrow in his bow.

It took only one glance to see this intruder was no Maethalian fisherman, nor a beachcomber from the surrounding villages. His clothes were soaked and strange. He wore a button-up shirt and tapered olive-green pants, not the normal Maethalian tunic and breaches. He bore no weapons I could see but wore a cloth bag slung over his shoulder.

"Who are you?" I demanded.

The man hesitated. His body appeared well-built, tall, and broad-shouldered. And when he pushed his dark, wet hair from his face, I saw he was young. In his mid-twenties, perhaps—only a few years older than me. A gash on his forehead leaked blood, but that wasn't what arrested my attention. It was his eyes. They were the same blue as the sea below us, dark and deep, and framed by dark lashes most girls in the court would have traded an emerald for. Something in the look of him set me on guard, and I aimed the tip of my sword at his throat.

The man arched an eyebrow, then winced.

"Ow, damn," he muttered, bringing his fingertips to the gash on his forehead. I caught an odd accent to his words.

"The princess asked you a question," Clua dismounted and came forward a step, brandishing her mace.

The stranger's sharp eyes snapped to me once more.

"Princess...?" he breathed.

"Bah. He's witless," Clua growled. "Let's keep going."

"Not witless," Ollie said. "Foreign."

Clua looked back at the man, wide-eyed. "You don't mean...?"

No one said it, but we all knew. This was one of the Admites, from across the sea—sworn enemies of our people. I'd never seen one up close before.

Still holding my sword and leaning the other elbow on Sisha's back for balance, I dismounted and took a few steps towards the stranger.

His eyes were on my right arm. Or, I should say, on the place where my forearm would have been. "You're the one-armed princess. Essaphine Torholt."

I smiled. "See," I called to my friends. "He's not witless at all."

"No, but he *is* insolent," Clua said, moving forward with her mace ready. But I stayed her with a look.

Turning back to the soaked man, I raised my right arm— or what was left of it, as it ended just below the elbow joint.

"Get a good look," I told him. I, too, gazed at the empty space where my forearm should have been. "I can still feel it sometimes, like the ghost of a hand that isn't there. For example, right now it's as if my middle finger is extended."

Clua muffled a laugh.

The man gave a small, cockeyed grin. He was handsome, I saw, square-jawed with fine cheekbones, possessing the sort of masculine beauty even waterlogged clothes, bruises, and a drizzle of blood couldn't erase.

"Your name," I said again.

He cleared his throat and shifted the bag on his shoulder.

"My name is Kit. Kit Rowley. As you've noticed, I'm from the United Republic of Admar, across the sea. I'm a reporter for our largest newspaper, the Ironberg Times. My editor has been in touch with members of your court. I was supposed to do a story about your people—but the plane I was in crashed in the fog yesterday."

Clua snorted. "A likely story."

"Actually, Hoatan did mention something about a visitor from URA coming this week," Ollie said.

"I have papers—" the man reached for his bag, then stopped when Ollie's bow went taut. He put his hands up and glanced at Sisha, who stood pawing the ground with one hoof.

"I don't suppose you'd mind giving me a ride to the castle—Princess?" he asked.

That crooked grin told me all I needed to know. This man was trouble of the worst kind. Fortunately for him, I enjoyed trouble.

I lowered my sword and sheathed it.

"We are known for our hospitality here in Maethalia." I glanced to Clua. "Rope."

She took a coiled rope from her saddlebag and tossed it

to me. I caught it, stepped forward, and kicked the Admite sharply in the back of the knee. His leg buckled, and he fell to his knees, wincing. Another kick sent him face-down in the dirt, and I mounted his back, ready to tie his hands, but he caught my leg and rolled, getting me on my back, his body pressing down on me, his hands on my arms, pinning me to the ground.

We locked eyes, both panting. Slowly, he looked up to find Ollie's arrow tip and Clua's mace hovering dangerously near his head.

"Sorry," he grunted. "Force of habit."

"Same," I said through bared teeth. He had just enough time to give me a quizzical look before I brought my knee up —into his crotch. He convulsed, loosening his grip on my arms. I shoved him off me and he rolled away, groaning.

"He's a surprisingly good wrestler for a bard," I said, rising and dusting off my cloak.

"Hands in front," Clua grunted. The foreigner complied, staggering to his feet and letting her tie his wrists without complaint.

I mounted Sisha. "Get him up behind me."

"We should check him for weapons," Ollie said.

"I'm not afraid of this spirit-burner," I scoffed. "Come on. Let's go."

"Suppose I don't want to ride with you anymore?" the foreigner muttered.

"Suppose I crush your skull?" Clua said, nudging him with her mace.

Limping, the stranger made his way over to Sisha and glanced up at me, a look of plain hatred on his handsome face. "You always crush a man's balls the moment you meet him?"

"Yes," I said.

Clua nudged him again, less gently than before, and he put a foot in the stirrup and climbed up behind me, wincing.

"Hold on," I commanded.

He hesitated for a second, then brought his bound wrists up over my head and down again, so that his arms were around my waist.

"What if he tries to pull you off as we're riding?" Ollie said, his arrow still trained on the man's head.

"Then he'll lose another wrestling match," I said.

"So, I'm a prisoner, then?" the stranger asked.

"Ha. Your bound wrists didn't give you a clue?" Clua chuckled.

"There's paperwork—in my satchel—" he nodded toward a bag still slung over his shoulder.

"There'll be time for that back at the palace," I assured him. "Hold on now, if you don't want to get dumped off on your ass."

His arms suddenly tightened around my stomach, yanking our bodies close with a force that took my breath away. I could feel his strength, his nearness—his anger.

Perhaps I was being a fool. Perhaps he was dangerous. After all, this was a real enemy from across the sea. He might attack at any moment—try to throw me from Sisha's back or strangle me. He might try anything. The thought sent a thrill of fear through me.

But I was a Skrathan. A dragon rider. We don't bow to fear.

And so, I spurred Sisha on and we took off back toward the palace.

2

CHARLIE

If you've never crashed into the sea in a burning biplane, let me just tell you it's one hell of an unpleasant experience. There's the heat, obviously, and the feeling of your stomach flipping over as the plane drops. Then there's the sight of the water rushing up to meet you and a feeling of terrifying inevitability that can only be summed up with two words: *oh, shit.*

After the splashdown, I blacked out—for how long I don't know—and woke to find myself neck-deep in water. My plane was floating, half submerged, nose down and tail up, riding the violent seas of the Bormish Channel like an oversized cork. I cut my way out of my straps, grabbed my emergency oilskin bag from behind the seat, and clambered up onto the tail to wait. One of three things was bound to happen. I would either be rescued, I'd wash ashore, or the plane would sink, taking me to a watery grave.

I spent the night that way, clinging to the plane's tail rudder, riding the swells in moonless blackness. Wind gusted relentlessly, waves crashed all around, and frigid water sprayed over me, freezing my skin and stinging my eyes. I was hungry. Thirsty. Painfully cold and exhausted. It was a hellish night, one of my worst, and there were moments when I almost considered letting go and dropping into the black water just so it would be over.

But when dawn came, I was somehow still there. I was relieved to find myself in the arms of a rocky shoal. Wave after wave shoved the plane toward an unfamiliar coastline of jagged cliffs—and right to the mouth of a sea cave.

I was glad to be near land, but the rocks presented a new danger. To be caught between those cliffs and the crashing waves would be like being between a hammer and an anvil. I had to get off the plane and onto the rocks, but I also had to time my dismount with the precision of a circus acrobat to avoid slipping into the treacherous water.

I watched as one good-sized rock came closer, closer —and I leapt. An especially large swell overtook me at the same moment, smashing me into the stone and sweeping my plane over top of me. Water rushed over my head and body, yanking like a thousand frigid, violent hands, but I clung to the rock, a tenacious barnacle, and somehow when the wave receded, I was still there. I held on as another swell came, then another, each pushing my beloved plane closer to the cliff—and toward the sea cave set in its face. That was good. My guess was these were enemy shores, and having my plane hidden from view might prevent my being discovered.

I watched my plane wash closer to the cave, until with one last swell, the silver wings disappeared into the cave entrance. "Goodbye, ol' girl," I said. "You were a hell of a plane."

The last thing I saw was the name and emblem painted on her tail. The Silver Wraith.

I made my way to shore, jumping rock to rock, and I sat for a long time in the shadow of the cliffs, listening to the crashing waves, watching the mist burn off to a blue sky, and wondering how the hell I was still alive.

It wasn't until a pang of hunger stabbed at my belly that I finally opened the emergency bag, looking inside for rations—and cursed.

Instead of useful things like food, flares, and first aid items, it contained a silky dress, make-up, a reporter's credentials, and a jumble of other random stuff. It was Kitty's flight bag.

I'd just flown my fiancée from her small hometown of Drue back to Ironberg, to the air force base. From there, she'd been supposed to hop a transport flight into enemy territory so she could write her big story about our enemy nation, Maethalia. But the moment we'd hit the ground, the alarm had gone off, scrambling our squadron. I'd gotten Kitty out of my plane, kissed her goodbye while we refueled, then taken to the skies again. Apparently, I'd taken her bag with me.

I groaned and sat back, too irritated and exhausted and hungry to do anything more than stew. My mood darkened.

Our nation would be waking up to the news that the Silver Wraith had fallen. How would people react when they learned I was gone? Would they toll every church bell?

Would they be weeping in the streets? Would the Air Force place the flags at half-staff and wear black armbands on their uniforms?

I thought of the young boys and girls who sent me letters calling me their hero, and of the tearful smile the president had given me last fall when he pinned the Iron Sun on my chest.

Could I just give up? Let our nation's hero waste away shivering on some foreign beach? Hell no. I had to get back home.

But how?

My plane was destroyed. I had no supplies. There was no boat at hand. Swimming the miles of bitterly cold seas back to friendly shores was impossible. I couldn't get home without help. And rescue from these dragon-patrolled shores seemed a bleak prospect. Still, there had to be a way.

In a dogfight, whenever things went against me, I'd find some unexpected way to turn it to my advantage. That's what I had to do here. All adversity held a kernel of opportunity—that's what General Peckham liked to say. What was the opportunity here?

Well... no one from the URA had set foot in Maethalia in over a century. Kitty was to be the first. Perhaps while I was here, I might find a way to get into the capital city and gather some valuable intelligence. Identify targets for future air raids. Learn the secrets of the dragon riders. Perhaps I could even convince the Maethalians to send me back themselves in some sort of diplomatic deal.

Imagine the headlines then: *Our greatest ace, now our greatest spy.*

I couldn't help but smile.

My eyes drifted back to the bag, and I dug out Kitty's travel documents again.

Kitty Rowley, Reporter, Ironberg Times.

Purpose of Visit: Journalism

Approved by: Hoatan Porchain, Minister of Foreign Affairs, Kingdom of Maethalia.

A plan was taking shape in my mind. A crazy plan. It would take a hell of a lot of luck. And cunning. And balls of steel. But if anyone could pull it off, it was me.

A few hours later, I was riding into the famed City of Issastar behind a Maethalian princess. It seemed too lucky to be true. And yet, it had to be. How many one-armed beauties were likely to be galloping along cliff-tops on splendid horses? And if she weren't truly Princess Essaphine, why did the guards bow and step aside for us at each gate and sentry point we passed? Even the girl's friends seemed to treat her with a certain deference.

I watched them with interest. The young dwarf woman had a plain face and short, dark hair, but a wicked humor glinted in her eyes. Her arms, though short, were powerful, and there was a confidence in the way she held her mace and in the sarcastic retorts she gave to nearly every comment from her friends.

The princess's other friend, the one she called Ollie, was harder to pin down. He was clothed in dark blue robes and wore a black cloak speckled with white dots that reminded me of stars in a night sky. His head was shaved except for a strip of hair down the center, which stretched in a long braid down his back, and a long sword hung at his waist, along with a trio of throwing knives. His voice was somewhat high for a man's, and there was an acuity in his sharp, blue eyes. Taking all this into account, along with the deft way he'd handled that bow, I guessed he must be a Torouman, one of the eunuch guards who supposedly kept watch over Maethalian royals—another hint that the girl was truly the queen's daughter.

"Do you always ride along the coast in the mornings?" I asked.

My pretty captor turned her head halfway back toward me. "No. We were searching for my sister. She was battling a squadron of your planes yesterday, and she and her dragon reportedly went down."

"Paemalla? Is that right?" I asked, feigning ignorance. Even back in the URA, everyone knew the name of the lead dragon rider and her terrible dragon, Horban. I'd shot her down yesterday, though I had no idea now whether she was alive or dead.

"Yes," the princess said. "Paemalla."

"Are you a rider as well?"

She snorted. "The term is Skrathan. And yes," she added, more quietly, "I am a Skrathan—though nowhere near the rider my sister is."

Paemalla was a good rider. Of the five lead riders I'd defeated so far, she'd been the toughest to shoot down.

"So, where's your dragon?"

"Resting," she said. "After a night of throwing your planes out of the sky."

She turned her head a little further, and I caught a glimpse of her eyes. They were a hazel of sorts, but there was something kaleidoscopic about them; they contained many more colors than I'd ever seen in an iris before. Her hair held a similar quality. It seemed sometimes chestnut, sometimes auburn, sometimes nearly blonde, changing hues as often as the sun changed its light between drifting clouds. And the smell of that hair, as it brushed my face—I couldn't help but notice—was the most sublime fragrance I'd ever known, nothing like the pungent perfumes Ironberg dancing girls wore. Essaphine smelled of sunshine, sea air— and wisteria, when the flower's scent wafted through open windows on the breeze of a springtime night.

She was small, but not frail. Short, but possessing an energy and exuberance that far outshone her physical frame —as evidenced by the fact that she'd already knocked me into the dirt.

And the way she'd ridden her horse now, galloping along the edge of the cliffs with the wind in her hair...

The Maethalians claimed to be more than human, to have descended from a race of elves long departed from the world, to have magic in their blood. It was a claim the people of our nation scoffed at. But looking at Essaphine, I couldn't help but wonder if it might be true.

If so, it only made the Maethalians even more dangerous.

The thought reminded me of my peril. I was riding into the heart of enemy territory, a place where if they learned my true identity, I'd find my head on a spike as fast as a mousetrap snapping. And yet I couldn't help but gape in wonder as we passed the gates and entered the city.

The terrain was hilly, and the buildings seemed a part of the earth itself. Homes were half buried in knolls, with walls and doors and windows emerging as naturally as moss or stone. Shops sat built into massive trees, some of which towered above, with windows peeping out of them, at a distance as high as any brick tower in Ironberg. But where URA cities paved over and built upon nearly every inch of earth with hardly a tree in sight, here the buildings seemed as much a part of the earth as a stone or a fern. And yet the city seemed no less vibrant or populous than Ironberg. On the contrary, all manner of unusual-looking people bustled everywhere. Merchants pushed colorful carts, shouting out their wares. Warriors in green cloaks strode along, grim-faced in their gleaming armor, gloved hands resting on sword hilts. A tall, too-thin man grinned at us with a mouth full of shark's teeth, a strange, magical glow emanating from an object in one of his hands. Several short folk—like Essaphine's friend mounted on the pony beside us—had formed a quartet, sitting outside a pub and playing a merry tune on pipes and drums. Children screamed and laughed, chasing one another among the throng. A woman in what looked like a dress of glimmering leaves walked past, holding skewers of steaming meat and vegetables, and I nearly slid off the horse, melting with hunger.

Essaphine must have felt me leaning.

"Don't worry. There'll be plenty of food at Charcain," she said.

Charcain. The ancient citadel of the Maethalian royalty, seat of their power.

How many missions had we drawn up at headquarters with the aim of bombing that storied place into rubble, dropping paratroopers into it, running tanks through it? But every attack we'd tried, the dragon riders had repelled.

What would General Peckham say if he could see me

trotting in on horseback, with my arms around the Princess Essaphine?

Probably that you're a fool about to get himself beheaded, I thought.

And yet I felt pride, too, as I imagined the looks of astonishment on the faces of my fellow pilots when I told them this story at the bar. If I ever made it back to tell them...

Above, a blur of motion caught my eye. A flock of a half-dozen birds darted and spun overhead. They were as large as eagles but moved with the grace, speed, and coordination of starlings. Their colors were scarlet and gold, with long, lovely tail feathers which, as they flew, seemed to dissolve into trails of sparks behind them.

"Do you have phoenixes back in your country?" Essaphine asked.

"No," I said, watching the birds in wonder.

"They are revered here," she said. "They say they can communicate telepathically with dragons—just like we Skrathan can."

So that rumor was true. Very interesting...

I watched as the birds wheeled and disappeared among the rooftops.

Suddenly, the princess pulled back on the reins in front of a low, earthen building with a sign of an anvil hanging out front. The others stopped too, and the dwarf dismounted.

"You don't want to come with us, Clua?" Essaphine said. "It's going to be wonderfully dramatic when I show Mother the foreigner we caught."

I tried not to bristle too much at the word *caught*. Did she not realize I could leap off this horse, run down a side street, and be gone in a second? Yet even as I thought of it, I knew I'd never try it. Being lost in this strange city would gain me nothing, and without the princess's protection, I'd likely be caught and killed within the hour. Already, I was receiving wary glances from the passersby.

"Can't," the dwarf said sullenly. "Borrin will tan my hide if I'm not back on the forge soon."

Essaphine sighed. "I warned you not to take this apprenticeship," she said. "You miss all the fun."

"Better to be useful than fun," Clua said. "Father said when he apprenticed me here—*Clua, the gods granted you a pair of strong arms. I expect you to...*"

The dwarf glanced at Essaphine's missing arm, and there was an awkward moment as her words ground to a halt. With the princess's body so close to mine, I thought I could feel her deflate slightly.

"I mean no offense, of course," the dwarf said quickly.

The princess forced a smile. "Like you could offend me. We've been friends too long for that. Go and be useful. I'll share all the gossip with you later."

And she nudged her horse onward.

Down the bustling streets we rode, the buildings becoming grander as we went, the earthen and wood structures replaced by buildings of white stone. Everywhere, eyes watched us. There were smiles and bows, calls of *hail Princess*, and *long live Essaphine!*

She is well-liked, I noted. *I should jot that down when I have a moment, and also sketch out a map of these streets.* There were so many distractions all around me, but I had to stay focused. Every sight and sound held a wealth of intelligence that might prove invaluable when the time for an invasion came.

At last, we rounded a corner and a vast palace came into

view. My breath stopped in my chest. I'd always imagined the Citadel of Charcain as a gray and sinister place, its turrets topped with rotting heads, its walls stained in blood. But as it rose before me now, I saw walls of swirling white stone gleaming in the midday sun. The stone itself was beautiful, iridescent as the inside of an oyster shell, and delicate spires and buttresses rose in wild spirals of impossible complexity, layer upon layer, in a way that reminded me of the petals of a blooming white rose. Atop its walls, blue flags snapped in the breeze, each emblazoned with the symbol of the country—a white star.

"That's Charcain?" I said dumbly.

"What, that?" she pointed to the palace. "No, it's a fisherman's brothel."

"Essa..." the remaining friend—the one she called Ollie —chastised her, but he was laughing.

"He's our enemy," the princess said. "Can't I at least tease him a little?"

The eunuch glanced at me, a thoughtful, pitying look in his blue eyes. "I would say be kind to him. These moments before your mother gets a hold of him may be the last happy moments he has."

3
CHARLIE

E ven from outside, we heard the screams.

I'd seen plenty of widows come to the airbase to clean out their husband's lockers after they'd gone down, and there could be no mistaking what those wails meant. Still, nothing could have prepared me for what I saw when the massive, brass doors to the throne room swung open.

The room itself was enough to inspire wonder. Its vaulted ceiling rose so high I could barely see it. The walls and columns were made of the same shining, milky-colored stone as the exterior and were cloaked in vines, making the palace seem more like a living thing than a building. On a dais at the rear of the room stood a single throne, also carved of white stone, with a huge, glowing blue gemstone in the shape of a star set atop it. Perhaps a hundred people filled the vast space: knights in gleaming armor and colorful cloaks, bookish scribes in robes of various hues bearing scrolls and quills, beautiful courtiers in fine tunics and ornate dresses...

And at the center of it all lay an enormous dragon.

My breath hitched, and I reached reflexively for the place at my belt where my sidearm would normally have hung, but it wasn't there.

That was okay. I saw now that the massive beast wasn't moving. Its limbs sprawled limp upon the slate floor, and its tattered wings had contracted around its body, like the legs of a dead spider. Its head sat cocked at an unnatural angle, the huge globes of its eyes staring, unseeing, into the world. They still glowed orange, as if lit by a fire within, but already they seemed to have glazed over with the sheen of death.

Laid out next to the creature was a comely, raven-haired woman in dark leather armor and a cloak the color of blue sky. On her right hand was a long, leather glove with an orange gemstone set in its back. An empty sword sheath lay at her belt. Her face was paler than morning fog, her lips blue as delphiniums. And her hazel eyes, like the eyes of the dragon, stared, sightless, at the vaulted ceiling above.

"Paemalla," Princess Essaphine whispered—confirming what I'd already guessed. This was the feared lead dragon rider who had ravaged our squadrons for the past two years. Who had downed over a hundred planes. Who had ripped my friends from the skies. Eddie. Bruce. Dora—and so many others. She was the one the Times had dubbed the Terror of the East, who our president had named our number one adversary.

And I'd killed her.

There'd be another medal for me back home, a free drink waiting at every bar in the country, and probably a parade— if I could just make it back to claim them.

If I closed my eyes, I could almost feel the confetti falling in my hair and hear the Army band playing a jaunty march. But here, the mood couldn't have been more somber.

As if to underline my thought, a wail split the silence, and I saw a woman kneeling next to the dragon rider's body. Paemalla's mother, the queen? No. A woman stood at the foot of the dais, near the dragon's head, arrayed in a glittering golden dress with armored plates at the shoulders and a delicate, jeweled crown upon her head. Her dark hair matched that of the dead dragon rider save for a few additional strands of silver—and I remembered, Paemalla was the queen's niece.

So that had to be Queen Synaeda. Sorceress. Tyrant...

While the kneeling woman sobbed, the queen stood perfectly still and silent, though the look on her face betrayed just as much grief as if she'd been screaming in sorrow.

I could steal a blade from one of these knights. Charge her. Kill her. I'd be the greatest hero who ever lived, I thought. *Except I wouldn't live for long...*

With a sigh, the queen shifted her gaze from the dragon and the dead young woman to us.

"Essaphine," she called. "Where have you been?"

The princess stepped forward and gave a perfunctory curtsy.

The one called Ollie nudged me, and I followed his lead and bowed.

"We rode south, mother, searching for Paemalla," Essaphine said. "I see you found her..."

"A Skrathan search party found them washed up north of here," the queen said.

Both mother and daughter looked to the woman I had killed.

"It was the Silver Wraith?" Essaphine asked, as if reading my thoughts.

"Who else?" the queen said, her voice was low and venomous.

"He'll pay!" the girl on the floor said, sitting up suddenly. Even on her knees, I could tell she was tall. She wore the same leather armor and sky-blue cloak as Paemalla, but her armor was the gray of a cloudy sky rather than the black of a storm cloud, like Paemalla's.

"Peace, Laynine," the queen said. "There will be time for revenge. For now, there is a dragon who must be returned to the fires."

She approached the monstrous beast and placed one hand on its snout. I had never seen a dragon except in the heat of battle. Seeing it so still and so close, with its glittering scales, glinting claws, intricately-veined wings, and massive, muscled body—even I had to admit it was a wonder.

"Farewell, brave Horban," the queen said. "May the fire that birthed you welcome you once more."

With a loud clang and a grinding sound, the far wall of the room suddenly began opening up like a set of double doors. In strode at least a hundred warriors on horseback. Chains were attached to the dragon's limbs, and in moments they were dragging the beast out of the room, leaving nothing behind but a trail of thick, dark blood—and the dead girl.

As the dragon departed, I glanced around and saw that everyone had their hands pressed to their mouths as a sort of salute. Every pair of eyes glittered with tears.

"Poor Horban," Princess Essaphine said, her voice warbly with sorrow.

The one called Ollie took her hand and squeezed it.

As the dragon was dragged away, the court fell into procession behind it, filing out the massive double doors. The mourning dragon rider—Laynine, apparently, joined the procession and exited as well. Only a few remained behind—the queen, a dozen guards, a few courtiers, and us.

At last, the queen's sharp gray eyes fell on me. "And who is this?"

In their mourning over Paemalla and her dragon, everyone seemed to have forgotten me. Suddenly, I drew the focus of everyone in the room.

Princess Essaphine gestured to me. "We found him on the cliffside path, waterlogged. He claims to be a bard—"

"Reporter," the one named Ollie corrected.

"Reporter," Essaphine went on, "from the enemy. He says Hoatan sent for him, and his plane went down in yesterday's storm."

"What say you, Hoatan?" the queen asked.

A portly man with the same long braid and dark blue robes as Ollie swept forward, tugging thoughtfully at his graying, wispy beard.

"Have you any papers?" he asked me.

With a nod, I dug the papers out of the flight bag and offered them to him. I glanced at the princess and found her watching me with interest—as one might stare at a caged animal in a zoo. The rest of the court watched me as well, with what seemed to be varying degrees of hatred and disgust. An awkward moment passed, and I grew increasingly nervous as the man studied the papers. At last, he gave a curt nod and offered them back to me.

"Everything seems to be in order. Kitty Rowley, is that correct?"

"Call me Kit," I said, forcing a smile.

"An odd name," the princess pointed out.

"It was my grandfather's," I said. "He... loved cats."

The queen and the old eunuch exchanged a glance. As their silence stretched, I replayed my words in my mind, and dread washed over me. *He loved cats?* Why had I said that? What the hell had made me think I could be a spy?

"Well," the queen said at last. "I can see we have much to learn about the customs of your people, Mr. Rowley."

Hoatan nodded, and several other courtiers in the room followed his lead. I managed a weak smile and sighed with relief.

"As we discussed, Your Majesty, he is one of the enemy's greatest reporters," Hoatan said. "When we show him our mighty dragon holds and reveal to him how great and beautiful our kingdom is, he will go back and convey to his people the folly of battling a kingdom as grand as ours."

The queen's eyes narrowed. "Perhaps..." she said. "That may have been your original plan, but Paemalla's death changes everything."

The queen's gaze bored into me, as cold as that of a hawk.

"Let me kill him for you, my queen," a voice said. Everyone turned to see a tall, powerfully built young man striding toward us with one hand on the silver hilt of his sword. He had long, green hair and was arrayed in the leather armor of the dragon riders. He knelt before the queen.

Princess Essaphine rolled her eyes. "What bravery," she said. "Braimar is willing to kill a skinny, tied-up scribe."

I glared at her. "Skinny?"

"...While my sister's true killer, the Silver Wraith, flies free," she finished.

"I'll kill *him*, too," the young man declared. "And lay his head at your feet, Princess."

Good luck, I thought, though the fire in the young man's eyes gave me pause.

"We will not kill a man sent to us by our own request," the queen said, and the tension that had built up in my chest unscrewed itself enough for me to take a full breath. "But we could use him to send a message." She walked up to me and traced a finger along my jaw. "Return him with that handsome face of his disfigured by dragon's breath."

"My dragon would happily take off his arm," the one called Braimar said. "Essa found him. Let the two of them match."

The princess gave him a look that could have melted steel—a look, I thought, that contained the sort of intimate hatred reserved for siblings—or lovers. Before I had too much time to wonder about their relationship or to worry about my fate, Hoatan stepped forward.

"Your Majesty, I urge you, let him go unharmed. His descriptions of your wisdom and mercy will further our cause far better than harming him would."

The queen glared at me for a moment longer, her lips quirked to one side in thought. Finally, she sighed.

"Fine," she said. "But who will be his escort? I won't have this foreigner wandering my court unrestrained."

"Your Majesty," Hoatan began, "I would be happy to—"

"No," she interrupted. "I won't have you taken away from your duties."

"Give him to me," the one called Braimar said, giving me a cruel smile.

"Certainly not," the queen said. "I trust Hoatan's wisdom. I will not have him harmed."

"The Gray Brothers, then," Hoatan said. "I'm sure Prelate Kortoi has someone who would—"

The queen ignored him, looking instead to Essaphine. "You," she said.

The princess's eyebrows went up in surprise.

"You found him," the queen pressed. "You will be his keeper while he is among us."

"Absolutely not," the princess said, her voice lowering. "Mother, Paemalla is dead. I am the eldest now. You know what that means, what duty requires me to do."

"Yes, daughter," the queen said. "And I also know what the outcome will be."

I thought I saw the queen's gaze shift to the stump of Essaphine's maimed arm. Fire kindled in the princess's eyes.

"You would give up on me so easily, mother?" the princess asked in a whisper.

The queen returned her glare but said nothing.

The princess's jaw clenched, her lips quivering. "I must train," she said. "I have no time to play nursemaid to some poet!" She spat at my feet, then wheeled and stormed out of the room.

When the door had slammed behind her, both the queen and Hoatan looked to Essaphine's companion, Ollie.

"Handle her," Hoatan said.

Ollie gave a bow. "Of course."

Hoatan gave me a polite nod. "Welcome to our court, Mr. Rowley. I'm sure you will find the experience eye-opening."

I returned the nod. "Thank you for your hospitality," I said.

The queen eyed me once more.

"Put him in the Northern tower. And get some clean clothes on him," she told Ollie, eyeing me with a disdainful frown. "He looks like a rat washed out from the sewer. And let me offer a warning to you, Mr. Rowley. I welcome your presence in my kingdom, but mind yourself. I would not cross a dragon in their time of mourning."

With a flutter of her hand, we were dismissed.

4
CHARLIE

Ollie and two guards led me along a maze of hallways and staircases so intricate I couldn't have found my way back if I'd been dropping breadcrumbs.

So far, so good, I thought.

My plan had been audacious. Crazy, really. I never could have hoped for the princess to find me and bring me straight into the castle. And yet here I was, not only inside but accepted into the court.

I was the world's greatest ace. Would I be known as the world's greatest spy, too? The thought brought a touch of a smile to my lips. That is, until I thought of Paemalla's corpse laid out on the stone floor, blue-lipped and still. One of the perks of being a pilot was never having to see my kills up close. But looking at Paemalla, seeing firsthand that she had been strong and young and pretty, that she had friends and cousins who mourned her... well, it was a hell of a lot different than watching a dragon fall from the clouds, then flying back to the base and getting cheered by the boys when I landed.

I thought of my little brother, Joey, a newly minted infantryman on the front lines. He'd been eager to go, to earn a piece of the glory I'd gotten, although he didn't have the eyesight to be a pilot. Joey would be seeing dead bodies like that all day long, up close and personal. Poor kid...

"You're not very talkative," Ollie pointed out as we walked.

I shook my head. "Just... rattled from the plane crash, I guess."

"Tell me, where exactly did your plane go down?"

"Off the coast. Not far from where you found me."

"How many others were on the plane?"

So, this was a friendly interrogation. Fine.

"Just me and the pilot," I said.

"We should conduct a search, no? Perhaps the pilot survived?"

I shook my head quickly. "No. No, I saw him go down—with the wreckage."

"Hmm," Ollie said. "Perhaps we'll send a search crew—just to be safe."

I wanted to protest, but that would look suspicious.

"That would be good," I said, my mouth feeling dry as I realized how precarious my position was. All it would take was for them to find the wreckage of the Silver Wraith inside that sea cave, and I was a dead man.

Finally, we stopped in front of a narrow wooden door. Ollie opened it and gestured for me to enter. Part of me feared I'd see a jail cell. Instead, the space I found was larger than my one-bedroom quarters back at McNally and was furnished with luxurious carpets and rich tapestries. There was a canopied bed, a fireplace, a bookshelf full of leather-bound tomes, and even a copper bath, which was already filled with steaming water. A large window was open, and I crossed to it to find we were high up—at least two hundred feet off the ground—with a view of the city. Beyond it lay the city wall, and beyond that, to the right, mountains rose in a series of jagged peaks. To the left, a grassy heath led to the sea. Far away to the west and lost in mist, I knew, lay the United Republic of Admar and Ironberg. Home—if I could ever get back there.

I turned back to find the guards had remained in the hallway. It was just me and Ollie, which made me feel better. The eunuch had an easygoing demeanor. He reminded me of a friend of mine from high school, Tommy —a laidback, friendly guy, the sort of fellow everybody loved. Although given the way Ollie had handled that bow, I imagined he was a hell of a lot more dangerous than Tommy.

He had crossed to a small table near the bookshelf and was pouring wine from a glass bottle into a pair of pewter goblets.

"Food will be coming soon, but perhaps this will get you through until then," he said, offering me a cup.

I took it and drank gratefully. It tasted far better than any wine or liquor I'd tasted back home; it had a flavor of honey and coffee mixed with the faintest hint of a fine red wine. Already, my body, chilled by my damp clothes, felt warmer.

"Mmm," I raised my glass appreciatively, then glanced around. "It's a beautiful room. Thank you."

"Of course," Ollie smiled. "You'll find we treat our guests well—so long as they maintain our trust."

"Right." I licked my lips. "Say, I don't suppose you have a cigarette?"

Ollie shook his head. "We don't have such things here. I could perhaps procure you a pipe and some mangar. It's good for creating spiritual visions."

I chuckled. "That's okay. I've had enough spiritual visions for one day."

Ollie strolled to the fireplace and sat in a chair, gesturing for me to take the chair opposite. I sat.

"Yes. A dead dragon," he said wistfully. "That is a rather spiritual sight. And not just any dragon; Horban the magnificent. That sight would be a wonder for anyone," he shook his head, gazing into the fireplace. He leaned forward and, pointing toward the logs with two fingers, muttered a word in a language I didn't understand. The logs flared with fire.

I repressed a gasp of astonishment. All my life, I'd heard stories of the powers the Maethalians possessed. I'd always imagined they were nothing but children's tales.

"How did you...?"

Ollie shrugged. "It's... what is the word your people use for it? Magick."

I sipped my drink. "And that makes you a magician, then?"

"I am a Torouman," Ollie clarified. "We're an order of warrior sorcerers—and priests of the Star Father, technically, though we don't have much in the way of religious duties these days. I was born the same day as Essa and am bound to her as protector. I'm a eunuch, as well. All the brothers of my order are."

I tried not to look too surprised. With his round face, rather shapeless body, and doughy-looking hands, he looked more like a librarian than a warrior. And being a eunuch... that I couldn't imagine. But as I looked at him more closely, I thought I could see a bit of what he was talking about. A shrewdness beneath his civility. A power in the way he gestured with his hands.

"In truth, I'm not the most renowned among my order," he said with a sigh. "Any of us can light a fire. That's a children's trick. There are other Torouman fifty times more powerful than I."

"Hoatan is one, too?"

Ollie nodded. "Yes. He's bonded to the queen."

For a moment, the only sound was the fire crackling and the wind whistling outside the window.

"Your princess doesn't seem to like me much," I observed.

Ollie laughed. "No one likes you much. But that's not so surprising, you're the enemy. And anyway, I'm sure the feeling is mutual after Essaphine kicked your legs out from under you and tied you up."

This forced a grudging smile out of me. This fellow, Ollie, had a sense of humor, at least.

"Essaphine said something about duty. She said she couldn't be my escort because she had some duty brought on by her sister's death?"

Ollie nodded. "The death of an Irska, the lead dragon rider—Paemalla, in this case—triggers a challenge among all the dragon riders to discover the next Irska. The second highest ranked rider was Laynine—who is cousin to Paemalla and Essa."

"Laynine... the one who was on the floor crying?"

Ollie nodded. "She and Paemalla were best friends—and lovers, if you believe the rumors. Her grief will be powerful. Anyway, as the second-highest Skrathan, Laynine would automatically ascend to the position of Irska. But it is the duty of the queen's heir to challenge for the top spot. And Essaphine is the last offspring of the queen. Her brothers and sisters—who were also dragon riders—have been killed."

Most of them by me, I thought with a secret pride.

"So, Essa must challenge Laynine," Ollie concluded and sipped his wine.

"Okay..." I said, processing what Ollie was telling me. It made sense. But it didn't explain the chill that had pervaded the room when the topic of the challenge came up. "What did Essa mean about the queen giving up on her?"

Ollie leaned closer to me, keeping his voice low. "Laynine is the highest-ranked rider, Essa the lowest. In any challenge against Laynine, Essa is sure to fail. And failure means death."

The fire crackled and spat as Ollie's words sank in.

I'd only just met this princess, and so far, she'd treated me like garbage. And yet, something in me rebelled at the thought of her dying—at least before I got the chance to kick her legs out from under her, tie her up, and humiliate her like she'd done to me.

"If she can't win, why doesn't she just refuse to challenge Laynine?"

Ollie frowned. "Impossible. She is a princess and a dragon rider. The challenge is a tradition that goes back to Aulucia the White. For Essa to run from such a duty would be unthinkable."

"Well... she might win," I pointed out.

Ollie shook his head sadly. "There are several events in the challenge that all the riders will participate in, and these are deadly enough, especially for a lowest-ranked rider like

Essa. But the final event of the challenge is a one-on-one duel between Essa and Laynine, and jousting is a critical part of it. With one arm, Essa can't both hang onto her dragon and hold a lance." I saw the slightest tremble in his lips. "Paemalla's death has sealed her sister's fate as well. Essa will die. It's only a matter of time."

Ollie stared into the dark pool of his drink in a long and thoughtful silence.

So, the princess had only a short time to save herself—or die. That would certainly explain why she wanted to spend her time training rather than babysitting me. And yet I wished she'd decided to keep me with her. Watching how the dragon riders trained could provide valuable insights about their tactics—and how to defeat them.

Abruptly, the Torouman stood and went to the window, looking east, toward the mountains rather than the sea. In the distance, there rose a series of green hills that grew increasingly tall and rugged, until at the horizon they became jagged peaks. From a crater near one of the larger peaks, there rose an orange glow. Steam rose in writhing, serpentine tendrils.

I crossed to the window, too, and saw what I at first took for a flock of birds gathering around the peak. But no—at this distance, birds would be no larger than specks. The flying things I was seeing now must be huge... Dragons.

Ollie turned up his glass, gulping the last of his drink.

"I must go. Essa will need me. Do you play Torzame?"

"What?"

"Torzame. It's similar to your game of chess."

"I play chess a little," I said.

Ollie nodded. "Good. I'll have a Torzame board delivered to your room, and I'll teach you the game."

He gave me a final glance from my muddy boots to my messy hair.

"An attendant will be in soon to feed you and get you cleaned up. You've arrived at a very poor time, Kit, but I'll do what I can to aid you while you're our guest. If we could do our part to foster some understanding between our people, perhaps we can help bring an end to this terrible war..."

His words drifted off as he gazed once more out the window at the orange, fiery mountains and the gathering of dragons there. Then, with a nod to himself, he turned on his heel and departed, the door banging shut behind him. The final sound I heard was the clink of the bolt as the guards locked me in.

5

ESSA

All one hundred Skrathan lingered in the sacred encampment. Glowing embers floated through the air like untethered stars in the deepening dusk. Near the place where the ground gave way in a steep downward slope, heat rose, its waves making the world seem unsteady—unreal.

This was Kayumal, the dragon womb, the place where legends said dragons first emerged from the molten heart of the earth and where dragons and their riders returned upon their death. And it was where we would return Paemalla and Horban, once nightfall came.

Until then, it was our lot to wait. The huge, dead dragon lay at the lowest point of the crater, on his back. Paemalla had been wrapped and set upon his belly, in the way that mother dragons sometimes held their young.

All around the dragon, riders had set up tents and blankets. Some had brought musical instruments, plucking out sad melodies on lutes or blowing slow etudes on pipes. Still others sat playing cards or reading or talking together in low voices. Fires had been lit, and the smell of roasting food and woodsmoke wafted on the breeze. On the rugged peaks all around, the dragons waited, some spread out to relax their wings, others coiled like serpents, still others sitting on their haunches like cats and chittering to one another, or else staring into the distance at something no human eye could see.

I wandered through it all like a lost ghost.

Conversations hushed when I neared. Riders averted their eyes from me as I passed. They all knew what Paemalla's fall meant for me. It was like I was dead already.

Though I was hardly aware of having a destination, my feet brought me to the brink of Kayumal, closer than any other Skrathan dared venture, and there I stopped, feeling the rising heat on my face. Below, I could see nothing but roiling, sulphureous smoke that choked me and stung my eyes, but here and there through the miasma I glimpsed the orange of boiling lava—Dragon's Blood, as the old ones called it. Idly, I kicked at the crumbly, dry earth and shale under my boots, sending stones to disappear with a sizzle in the crater below. How easy it would be to inch forward and let the ground give way beneath me, to deliver myself into that womb of fire. It would save everyone so much time— and save me so much suffering. But even as the thought came, I felt the presence of my dragon, Othura, nosing into my mind.

No, Dear Heart. You must live.

I looked up to find her sitting on a peak far above, watching me. Her nose twitched, and her huge, bright eyes blinked slowly. She was a relatively small dragon, and unusually dark for a libran. Whereas most of her kind were the color of a puffy cloud, she was darker, more the deep silver hue of a thunderhead. Yet up on that peak, the fading light glinted off her like sun upon the waves of the sea. She was beautiful.

I will live. For you, Dear Heart, I thought to her, stepping back from the edge. *For as long as I can, anyway.*

"Essa!"

The sound of my name startled me, and I turned to find my Aunt Dreya approaching.

"Auntie," I hurried toward her and let her sweep me into a hug.

If anything might have wrung a tear from me, it would have been her embrace, but I clenched my jaw and managed to keep my emotions at bay.

"Come. We must talk," she said, hooking her arm in mine and towing me away from the edge of the abyss and the other riders. She took me far down the path, into a stand of aspen trees. There, we sat on a pair of stones. She studied me for a moment, and I studied her.

"How are you?" we both asked at once.

What on another day would have elicited a laugh brought forth only the faintest of smiles.

"You go first. I know your feelings for your sister were... complicated," Auntie Dreya said.

"I think... I'll miss her," I said truthfully. Paemalla was always a bully and a tyrant, pulling my hair, mocking me, stealing my treats when nobody was looking. But there were advantages to having a bully for a big sister. She'd have killed anyone who tried to harm me, and everyone knew it. I'd lost an antagonist. But I'd lost a protector, too. Of course, I didn't have to tell Auntie Dreya any of this. She already knew.

Dreya was my mother's sister. In Maethalia, aunts were responsible for teaching their nieces, just as uncles were for teaching their nephews. So, from the time I was four years old, Auntie Dreya had been my durram—my mentor. She'd taught me to read, to fix numbers, to ride a dragon, and to fight. And through it all, she'd been the one person who hadn't taken it easy on me, discounted me, or shown me an ounce of pity, even though I had only one arm. That was the greatest love anyone had ever shown me—simply treating me like myself.

"I think we'll all miss Paemalla," Auntie said.

She had trained Paemalla, after all, just as she'd trained me. She had been the one to help my sister become the greatest Skrathan of us all—before those cursed Admite machine riders had slain her.

Auntie was in mourning, too.

"And now..." Dreya sighed.

Now, things were complicated.

Her daughter was Laynine, my cousin. My mother, being her aunt, had mentored Laynine. And she was the second-highest-ranked dragon rider behind Paemalla.

That meant I'd have to take all the training Auntie Dreya had given me—and use it to fight her daughter. To the death.

"What are you going to do?" Auntie asked.

I frowned. "What do you mean?"

"About the challenge," Auntie said.

I shook my head, confused. "I must enter the challenge and fight Laynine. There's nothing else I *can* do."

Auntie's brows knit, and I thought she was going to cry, but no tears welled in her eyes. Instead, they became hard. She took my hand in hers.

"There are other possibilities, Essa," she said. "You could flee."

"Flee?" I said shrilly.

She glanced toward the other riders back at the encampment and put a finger to her lips. "Yes," she said.

I continued in a hiss. "You would have me run away? To what? Go off to the Doramant and live in some fisherman's shack for the rest of my life? Abandon my dragon? Live in shame, until Lord Natath and his law-bringers find me and put me to death for treason and dereliction of duty?"

Auntie's eyes flashed with emotion. "We could find some solitary place for you, Essa. Somewhere that's pleasant, where Othura could be with you."

I snorted, shaking my head, and started to stand.

We should at least listen to her, Othura urged in my mind, and I let Auntie grasp my arm and pull me back down.

"Isn't it better to leave and live than to stay and die, Essa?"

I looked hard at her. "You've trained me my whole life. Don't you think I have any chance at all of winning?"

"Against Laynine?" Her hesitation felt like a stab, and she seemed to mark the pain on my face, because she quickly added, "Of course, if you did win, it would be a tragedy for me, just as it would be a tragedy if you lost. But let's be honest, Essa. Your mother has trained Laynine well. You know how good she is. Even without your..." her eyes ticked to the place where my arm would have been. "You couldn't defeat her."

I surged to my feet, my face warming with anger.

"Why say that to me?" I demanded, my voice uneven as I held back tears. "Everyone knows I have to fight her.

Everyone knows I'm going to die. Can't you at least let me believe I have a chance?"

"You do have a chance," she said quietly. "You can leave and live."

She's only trying to help, Othura thought into my mind.

"Shut up!" I shouted, pushing her out and wheeling on Auntie Dreya.

"Essa—" she began, but I brandished a finger at her.

"You were the one who taught me duty. Who taught me what it is to be a princess of Maethalia and a Skrathan. To have honor. I thought you believed the things you taught me. I thought you believed *in me.*"

"Essa..."

"No!" She tried to take my arm again, but I pulled away from her. "If this is your counsel, I don't need it. I'll train for the challenge myself. Without you."

"Essa..." she started again, her voice soft and consoling.

"Am I interrupting?"

We both looked over to find Laynine standing a little ways away, watching us. The breeze rustled her cloak and pushed back her short, dark hair. She was taller than me, a fact that had always annoyed me. And in conflicts between cousins, she'd always been the one to remain unnervingly calm—whereas my fieriness had always gotten me in trouble. I could feel the same dynamic repeating itself now as my emotions teetered on the edge of a blade, and she stood watching me with perfect posture and the poise of a Torouman.

"I'll leave you two to chat," Auntie Dreya said. "Think on what I said, Essa," she added, and departed.

Laynine approached me slowly, watching me with shrewd, analytical eyes framed with dark lashes.

"I'm sorry for your loss," she said.

The only response was the whisper of the wind through the crater and the low crackle of magma below. I made myself meet her gaze.

"I know you. I know you're going to challenge me," she said. "But I wish you wouldn't. There's no glory for you in dying. And there's no glory for me in killing my own cousin. Especially one who isn't whole."

Her gaze settled on my missing forearm.

I felt my face reddening, my teeth going on edge.

"You're right," I said. "You'll get no glory by killing me."

And I stalked past her, back toward the pit of fire.

6

CHARLIE

I lay on a rug in the middle of my luxurious prison cell, staring up at the ceiling and deeply questioning my life choices. The first rush of self-congratulatory excitement had passed, leaving in its wake a feeling of doubt and foreboding. What had possessed me to impersonate Kitty? I should have made my way up the coast and tried to signal our spy planes when they flew overhead. Or tried to rescue the Wraith's waterlogged radio and call home. Or made a raft to paddle my way back to Admar. Anything would have been a safer course than this. I was a pilot, not a master spy. How long before they found me out and chopped off my head? Or fed me to a dragon? Or worse?

A knock came at the door. I sat up fast, but before I could stand, the door was swinging open. In strode a figure out of a fairy tale. She was about four feet tall, with antlers like a deer's and legs that bent backwards. Her face had the wrinkly jowls of a bulldog, and her hair was bound in a tight bun atop her head. Strange as she looked, there was a friendly twinkle of mischief in her brown eyes.

"You're a—a—"

"A sprite?" she finished, eyeing me with crossed arms. "The name is Rohree. I've been assigned to care for you while you're with us. And you're filthy. Come on. Off with those clothes."

My eyebrows went up.

"Oh, a shy violet, are you? Fine." She turned her back to me. "There. Now into the bath."

I hesitated only a moment before following her orders, crossing the room, undressing, and slipping into the bathtub. The water was still pleasantly hot, and I found a bar of fragrant soap sitting on the edge. After the brine from the sea, oil from the crash, and dirt from climbing up the rocky cliffs were scrubbed off me, I found a towel nearby to dry myself with and got out and began drying myself.

The sprite still stood facing away from me, tapping one small foot. "Do all you machine worshippers take so long to get prettied up?"

I grunted a laugh. "Are all sprites so combative?"

"As a rule, yes," she said. "Clothes are on the bed."

A light green tunic with a gold-embroidered tree on it and black breeches, along with underclothes and socks, sat neatly stacked. I started getting dressed, then glanced over and caught the sprite girl peeping at me.

"Well, I guess you do have some good attributes," she said.

I pulled my pants up quickly. "Do you mind?"

"Not at all," she shot back with a wink.

I shook my head, unsure whether to laugh or shout at her.

"Here, do you prefer to pretend I'm not here?" she asked, and with a flicker, she disappeared. I stood staring at the place she'd been a moment before, blinking in confusion.

"What's wrong, you've never seen peri turn invisible?" her disembodied voice demanded. "Hurry up and dress. Your escort will be here any second."

"Could you please...? Uh..."

She flickered and became visible again.

"Thanks," I said. "It's just... I've never seen magick before."

She grinned, that mischievous twinkle in her eye once more. "Well then. You're in for quite an experience."

Just then, there came a knock on the door. I pulled the tunic over my head just as two burly guards in full armor entered. I couldn't help noticing the swords and daggers at their belts.

"Where exactly am I going?" I asked the sprite warily.

Rohree shrugged. "I'm just a servant. I can only speculate. But from what I've heard, you're here to learn about Maethalia. Our people, our customs, our culture..."

I nodded.

She glanced toward the window. Twilight was deepening, and in the distance, off to the northwest, an ominous orange glow quavered against the slopes of the mountains.

"If you're here to witness the wonders of our kingdom," Rohree said, "You can't miss the funeral of a dragon."

The sprite and the guards brought me down to a waiting carriage drawn by two dapple gray horses, and we made our way out of the castle via a huge gate. I tried to look out and make note of my surroundings, but out the carriage's windows I could see little except shopfronts and small homes. The carts of craftsmen and traders all seemed to be shuttered for the night. Wherever there was some space, people were gathered in hushed crowds, their gazes silently bent toward the mountains.

We passed beyond the city wall, and the road immediately began sloping upward and narrowing. Soon, it had become a rocky path. Sometime later, we stopped at a guard shack. Some words were exchanged, and we traded the carriage out for some mounts—a tall, brown horse for me and a mule for Rohree.

"Don't suppose you fellas have a spare cigarette?" I asked one of the checkpoint guards.

They only stared back at me with cold, narrowed eyes. They were arrayed like the other guards I'd encountered so far, in armor and cloaks and steel helmets, with swords hanging at their sides and spears in their fists.

No guns. No electricity. No cigarettes. Not a motorcar or an airplane in sight, I thought. But there were dragons. And magick. All the stories about this place were true.

It was too bad I was here instead of Kitty—she'd have been able to write a hell of an article about Maethalia. But then, she probably wouldn't be able to keep a running list of targets in her mind like I was.

The guards and the carriage driver stayed behind as the sprite and I mounted up and rode up the trail.

"Just the two of us, eh?" I said to the sprite.

She grunted in affirmation.

"No one is worried I'm going to try to run off, then?" I asked.

"Go ahead and try," she chuckled. "You won't go far unless you've got wings."

I saw what she meant. Darkness was settling in, and the winding path we took often had a sheer drop-off on one side or the other. It made me envy Rohree for her steed, which seemed considerably more sure-footed than mine, and I held on tight to the saddle horn to avoid falling off. The sprite glanced back at me with mirth in her eyes.

"Never ridden a horse before, eh?"

"I have," I protested. I'd ridden a pony in circles at the county fair when I was ten. And I'd ridden a horse just today, although it had been quite a bit easier with Princess Essaphine to hang onto.

Essaphine... my body tensed at the memory of being pressed against her. I wondered where she was, what she was doing. How she was coping with the fact that, as Ollie had told me, she'd soon be fighting her cousin to the death.

She's just another enemy, I reminded myself. *A magick-worshipping savage.* She was nothing like Kitty, with her career and her college education and her dance hall friends and her rich parents with the rowhouse on Ironberg's North Park.

Still, for some reason, my thoughts kept returning to the princess. The way her sweet-smelling hair had kept blowing in my face infuriatingly as we rode together up the coast. The contempt in her bright, changeable eyes as she'd presented me to the queen. The ache that still lingered in my balls from when she'd kicked me...

My watch had stopped when my plane crashed, but if I had to guess, we'd probably been plodding uphill for an hour and a half when the trail abruptly opened up into a broad valley, gently sloping downward. The sun had disappeared behind the peaks to our left, and darkness swept in. All around, small campfires burned, and the smell of cooking meat reminded me I hadn't eaten in a long time.

We dismounted, and Rohree staked the horses, then led me into the encampment.

Men and women in the gray leather armor and blue cloaks of dragon riders sat around the fires, playing games or passing wine skins or simply talking in hushed, serious voices. Several of the riders noticed me and glared as we passed.

"Have you seen dragons before?" Rohree asked.

I've killed dozens, I wanted to say, but of course that was not the role I was playing.

"Only the dead one today," I lied.

"Well then. Feast your eyes."

I saw no dragons, not at first. Then, I followed the sprite's gaze upward. Silhouetted against the twilit sky, at least a hundred dragons sat, perched on the peaks all around us like gargoyles. Even though they were far away, seeing so many of them together sent a shiver through me.

"Come," Rohree said, ushering me forward faster. "The sun has set. It'll be beginning."

The valley we were in was shaped like a shallow bowl broken in half. At its lowest point, it dropped off into a chasm from which an orange glow emanated. The miasma that roiled out reminded me of smoke from an engine fire, black and thick. It diffused and hung over the whole valley, creating halos around each prick of firelight and giving everything a misty, otherworldly quality. Embers floated and drifted like orange fireflies.

At the edge of the precipice, the dark body of the dead dragon lay sprawled.

We walked downhill and were about halfway to the bottom when a sound came from one of the dragons above. It wasn't a roar, and it wasn't quite a howl, either. It was some combination of the two, mournful and terrifying. Soon, the rest of the dragons joined in, the combined din of their voices echoing off the slopes to form a deafening sound that seemed to vibrate every bone in my body and made the hairs on my arms stand on end.

I started to redouble my pace, but Rohree put out an arm, stopping me.

"We'll watch from here," she said. "This is a sacred rite. There are some who will be angry you're here at all."

Indeed, while most riders had their attention on the dragons, two or three were watching me, their expressions grim and threatening. One in particular, a tall rider with a shaved head, met my gaze, and though I stared back at him defiantly, he would not look away.

Above, a half-dozen dragons swooped from the peaks to land near their fallen leader. Massive chains had been attached to the limbs and wings of the beast, and the dragons grabbed these chains in their talons and took flight again. With effort, they hoisted the massive beast into the air and winged their way out over the center of the crater, the dead dragon's limp form hanging below them.

A chant rose from the riders around us, a series of percussive consonants and sung vowels. Though the words were in a language I didn't understand, I felt their meaning wash over me, feelings of reverence and deep sorrow viewed through the glass of ten thousand years of history and sprinkled with a sheen of terrible, ancient magick. Tears stood out on the cheeks of the riders around me. From back in the city came the sound of bells, a low, dolorous clanging that felt somehow like a heartbeat.

Suddenly, the song of the riders and the howl of the dragons shot up in pitch and volume, forming a harmony, a finale, a scream of anguish. Out over the crater, the dark form of Horban hung in the mist, its form made wavy by the heat rising all around it. A glow seemed to emanate from the dragon's scales and wings, and tiny sparks of light surrounded it like motes of orbiting dust. It was so beautiful I stopped breathing. All I could do was stare in wonder. Then, at the same moment the song reached its peak, the dragons let go of their chains, and Horban the Terrible fell.

The singing and howling and tolling of bells abruptly ceased. The only sounds were the wind and the faint flutter of wing membranes as the beast fell, then a low thud as it hit the magma below. In seconds, the monster's huge body sank out of sight, sizzling as it went. The silence that followed was one of the most complete I'd ever heard. There was not a whisper. Not a sob. Not a shuffle of feet or a cough or the clearing of a throat. Even the wind seemed to have died.

A few seconds passed. The dragons that had served as bearers wheeled and flew back up towards the ring of peaks surrounding us. When they reached them, the rest of the dragons took flight, too, all of them winging eastward together like a flock of massive birds.

As soon as they were gone, the riders began moving as well, turning without a word and walking back up the slope —toward us. Having so many enemies striding toward me at once felt like something out of a nightmare, and I clenched my fists to keep myself calm.

"Let's go," Rohree whispered, tugging on my arm. I

turned and followed her back the way we'd come, my mind reeling with what I'd just seen. I knew the power and majesty of dragons. Almost no one from URA was as intimately acquainted with their claws and teeth and fire as I was. And yet seeing them like this, not as combatants but as mourning, magical beasts... hearing their sorrowful song... seeing the tears in the eyes of the riders...

My mind was far away, contemplating ancient magick and traditions and wonders, when I became aware of an out-of-place sound. Footsteps were coming toward me, and not at the plodding pace of a funeral procession. They were running.

I felt a sudden burning in my scalp—a hand, grabbing my hair. At my neck, a jolt of pain and the cold bite of steel.

I shouted and turned just in time to see the face of the bald-headed rider leering at me, his blade pressing into my neck. Then a foot was stomping into the back of his knee. He fell into a kneeling position with a shout of pain, and an elbow swung in, connecting with his temple with a sickening thud. The bald rider fell to the dirt, unconscious. And there, standing over him and looking me over with wild eyes, was Princess Essaphine.

"You're bleeding," she pointed, and my hand went to my throat. My fingertips came away crimson.

I looked down at the rider splayed out at my feet. Already, two riders were stooping over him, binding his wrists. I looked back to Essaphine.

Her friend Ollie was jogging up behind her. "You saved his life," he said.

The princess looked at me again. "No," she said quickly.

"No," I echoed her. But my fingers went to my neck again. I was no anatomy expert, but I knew where my jugular was. If that knife had cut me a millimeter deeper, I'd have been on the ground next to my would-be assassin, bleeding out.

The princess *had* saved my life. I looked back at her. In this light, her eyes looked dark, the rich, luminous hazel of a polished agate. And they were rimmed with red. She'd been crying.

Ollie was glaring at Rohree. "You were supposed to keep him safe."

"I'm a handmaid, not a bodyguard," she shot back.

"And yet you bring him to an okooram full of riders?" Ollie pressed.

"At Hoatan's command. He wanted him to learn about our culture," Rohree said. "When else could he see the funeral of a great dragon?"

"Enough!" the princess said. "It seems none of you can keep our guest safe." She eyed me. "And clearly he can't protect himself..."

"I could've—" I started to protest, but she cut me off.

"So, I'll escort him back to his room. Come on." She grabbed me by the arm like a naughty child and began tugging me with her up the slope. Ollie and Rohree, grumbling together, fell in behind us.

"See that he's arrested and brought before Hoatan," Essaphine called over her shoulder to the other riders.

"Yes, Your Majesty," the riders both replied, bowing.

We started walking again, but my would-be assassin was coming to. He blinked in momentary confusion, then his eyes found me.

"You have escaped this time, necromancer!" he shouted after us. "But you will not leave this place alive. You'll die. And all your kind will die with you!"

7

ESSA

"Why did he call me necromancer?" the enemy poet asked as I poured a drink for each of us from the bottle of wine in his room.

When I turned back, he arched an eyebrow.

"You know, Ollie did the same thing," he said, taking the cup from me. "You Maethalians may have a drinking problem."

I just narrowed my eyes and took a sip. "*Necromancer* means a sorcerer who can raise the dead."

He dabbed his bloody neck with a handkerchief. "Strange, I don't remember having that power."

"It's not just about spirits. The coal and the fuel, the—" I searched for the foreign word.

"Petrol?" he said.

I nodded. "It all comes from dead things. You burn it. Use its energy to power your machines."

"Yes..."

"It was spoken by our oracles long ago that great evil

will come from it," I said. "The seas will boil. The skies will rage—that sort of thing. It's forbidden. *That which lives must be allowed to live. That which is dead must remain dead.* It's one of the most famous Earth Mother prophecies."

"I see..." He gestured to the chairs by the fireplace, but I remained standing.

Regardless, he went and sat, slouching in his chair and watching me as he took another sip of the wine.

"So that's why you hate us? That's why we're at war? Our technology violates your spiritual beliefs?"

I sighed. "Like a typical Admite, you have reduced a complex thing to idiocy. The prophecy is part of it. You've also desecrated the sacred Isle of Dorhane in your quest for your... petrol. You've murdered dragons and their riders. You've sunk trading ships, wiped out villages. The list of atrocities goes back one hundred years."

"Funny," he said. "I could list just as many atrocities committed by your side. In fact, it would take more than both hands for me to count the number of close personal friends who are now in pine boxes because of you and your dragon riders."

I threw back the rest of my drink and banged the cup down on the counter.

"And yet you are alive now because I saved you back at Kayumal."

His fingers went to the cut at his neck, which was still bleeding. "A favor I never asked for."

"Well, don't worry," I shot back. "Next time someone is about to slit your throat, I'll let them."

"Don't worry about me, Princess. I can handle myself."

"Good," I said.

"Good," he said.

I found my teeth were bared. My face felt hot with anger —and the fact that I'd let this foreigner get a rise out of me only made it worse. I shook my head.

"You're just what I would have expected from an Admite —a fool."

"And you're just what I would have expected from a Maethalian. A—" he hesitated, then said: "Esteemed princess."

"Good catch," I mocked.

He grinned and downed the last of his wine. "You seem to enjoy kicking men in the back of the leg. Tell me, do you know any other moves?"

"Keep it up," I snarled, "and find out."

I wanted to take the bottle and smash it over his smug, foreign head. Instead, I turned and stormed toward the door.

"Sorry about your sister," he called after me.

I paused and half turned to him, anger boiling in my veins. "Do you always have to have the last word?" I demanded.

He didn't answer, just gazed at his wine glass. I gave a huff of exasperation and went to leave. Just before the door clapped shut, I heard him shout: "Yes."

Rohree was pacing in the hall where I'd bade her wait. When she saw me storm out of the room, her eyes went wide.

"Everything okay?" she asked.

"Bind up his neck. Or cut it the rest of the way off, if you prefer. I couldn't care less," I snapped, and breezed off down the hall.

Half an hour later, I lay against Othura's flank, staring up at the stars. After leaving the stranger in his room, I'd called Othura with my mind, and she'd met me in the palace courtyard. Together, we'd flown to one of our favorite places, a grove ringed with standing stones that sat on a lonely hilltop about a half mile southeast of the castle. Now, we lie together, warm despite the chill night, gazing up at the scattered glints of light above. Thoughts shot between us like shooting stars, but when we were together like this, our minds open to one another, it was hard to tell whose thoughts were whose.

I felt it when you met him. The beating of your heart.

My heart is always beating.

You know what I mean, Dear Heart. It beat faster.

Your heart would beat faster, too, if you came face-to-face with an enemy.

I don't know. The heart of a dragon is slow to excite. The heart of a human girl, however...

A human woman, *thank you very much. And if my heart beat faster, it was excitement at the thought of killing him. He's insufferable.*

Her response didn't come in words, but I could tell she was scoffing.

Anyway, it doesn't matter. You saw what happened tonight. Someone will kill him before long if he stays here. He's as dead as I am.

Unless...

Unless what?

Unless he had the protection of a Skrathan.

What, you mean me?

Didn't your mother ask you to escort him during his time here?

She did. All the more reason not to do it.

Everyone is right some of the time, Dear Heart. Even the queen. You did save his life today. According to the old code, that makes you responsible for him, at least until—

Until he saves my life. I know the old code. It's called old *for a reason. No one follows such traditions anymore.*

The Skrathan do. Dragons do. Your mother does.

Ugh, you're tiresome!

I gave Othura a playful whack on her side. The blow would have felt lighter than a kiss on her tough hide, and my attempt at defiance only drew a warm laugh out of her. I sat up and turned so I could see her face. Her dark gray body lay stretched out in the grass, the ends of her forked tail flopping in the air like the lazily wagging tail of a dog. Her orange eyes met mine, her expression quizzical and amused.

Do you truly think I should be this stranger's protector? I'd have thought you would have me spending every moment training for the challenge.

Othura chuffed. *Training that much would only leave you exhausted. And besides, in spending time with this enemy, you might learn something that will be useful once you've won the challenge and become Irska.*

Irska. Head dragon rider. The one responsible for leading the Skrathan into battle. Could I fill that role, even if by some miracle I won the challenge against Laynine?

Although I'd participated in years of training and overcome many difficulties, I'd only just been promoted to the top one hundred riders, and I'd participated in just a few actual battles. Even in those, I'd been on patrol duty or held in reserve. The stories other riders told of facing the enemy aces with their terrible flying machines and deadly machine guns were just that for me—stories—whereas Laynine had flown into battle nearly a hundred times. She was better. More experienced.

And—I glanced down at my missing arm—*Laynine was whole...*

Anyone but a fool would see how hopeless it was, me trying to defeat her.

I could run, like Auntie said. But where would I go? And who would I be if I left my whole life and identity behind?

I sighed and leaned back against Othura again, petting her hard, pebbly scales.

You're the only one who thinks I can actually win, you know.

Who thinks we *can win,* she corrected, then her head swung toward me on her long neck, and she nuzzled me with her snout. *Maybe I am the only one who believes,* she said. *But I'm usually right.*

She winked one huge, fiery eye. I laughed, hugging her big head and stroking her snout the way she liked.

But suppose you're right. Othura went on, serious now. *Imagine we're not going to win. Wouldn't you like to have some fun in the time we have left?*

Fun... with that irritating foreigner?

And yet, Othura was my bonded dragon. I couldn't lie to her any more than I could lie to myself. There was something about that poet Kit that intrigued me. I thought about the scandal it would cause, the queen's doomed daughter parading through the city with a handsome enemy on her arm.

How much trouble could a girl get into with five weeks left to live? There was only one way to find out.

8

ESSA

"I've decided to accept your task and escort the necromancer poet during his visit," I announced.

Mother stood holding the edge of her stone scrying bowl, gazing into the dark water. She flinched at the sound of my voice and glanced up at me. It was late. Mother was clad in a nightgown with her hair falling about her shoulders, and we stood in one of her private chambers near the throne room, with only Hoatan and a pair of her personal guards present. Sounds of revelry could still be heard drifting up from the dining hall below, where the courtiers lingered over their post-funeral feast.

"How kind of you to decide to follow your queen's command," Mother said.

For a moment, my mind reeled, trying to think of something to say that might please her. She had just lost her favorite daughter, of course. She had every right to be bitter. But I was her daughter, too.

"I unseated Thaxan in the melee the other day," I said. I

hated what I heard in my voice, the echo of a little girl seeking her mother's approval.

"And did someone unseat you?" she asked.

I sighed. "Yes. Still, I was sorry you didn't come to witness the competition."

"The challenge will begin soon," Mother said, gazing into the black water again. "I will have plenty of opportunity to see your exploits."

"Good," I said. "It has been some time since you've attended any of our trainings. I think it would do the riders some good to see you. For morale. The war wears on their spirits."

Mother did not look up from her dark pool. "I did not ask for your advice, Essaphine."

"No," I agreed. "Paemalla's advice you might have asked for, but not mine."

"Cease your moping," she muttered, leaning closer to the dark, still water. "It's unbecoming of a princess."

Biting my lip with frustration, I thought of turning and walking out of the room, but something drew me the other way. Closer to Mother. My eyes searched the basin in front of her, but I saw only her reflection in the dark water.

"What do you see in that water all day?" I asked.

"Many things," she whispered.

For an experienced sorceress like Mother, scrying could yield all sorts of visions. Over the years, she'd foreseen plagues in far-flung villages, witnessed raids happening in our fishing towns, and identified criminals. According to legend, if you looked long and deeply enough, you could even see other realms, both demonic and divine. It was both the danger and the reward of scrying. It was a great advantage for our kingdom's military to have a queen whose scrying power was so strong, but it also posed a personal risk. Throughout history, some had gone mad from scrying's allure. Whenever I saw Mother like this, lost in her visions, it made me worried for her.

"What are you looking for?" I asked. "Paemalla's ghost?"

At this, mother did look at me—fiercely.

"She will be in the Westerlands, where heroes go," she snapped.

"Not in this world of stone and shadow."

A hero... cruel Paemalla?

I wanted to argue. To pick at Mother. But I could see pain as well as fury in her eyes. As much as Paemalla had tormented me, she was Mother's daughter. Her favorite. And the pain of her loss was real. I should cease needling Mother when she was in such a raw state. So I nodded, relenting. "Of course. She *was* a hero. I'll leave you to your scrying." I addressed Hoatan now. "Is there anything in particular you'd like the poet—"

"Reporter," Hoatan corrected. "They write down important events like our bards do, but with far less artistry."

"Reporter..." I corrected myself. "Anything you'd like me to show him while he's here? And anything you want me to conceal? Obviously, we don't want him to witness any of the secrets of the dragons, or—"

"Show him everything," Mother said, still staring into the pool.

I frowned, certain I must have heard her wrong. There was no way they'd want me to reveal our secrets to our enemies, surely.

"Everything?" I repeated.

Hoatan came forward, linking arms with me and leading me back toward the door.

"Yes," he said. "Show him everything. Withhold nothing. That's part of the plan. You see, only when our URA adversaries understand our full power will they see that their attempts to defeat us are futile. By living as one of us, this reporter will come to see how wrong and perverse the ways of his own people are. The truth is, Maethalia is the greatest and brightest kingdom the world has ever known. Show him the beauty of our land. The magick of our people. Let him witness our power and fall in love with us."

I nodded slowly, beginning to see the wisdom of Hoatan's plan. After all, who could experience the majesty of a hundred dragons in flight and not be moved to wonder? I shouldn't have been surprised. There was wisdom in all Hoatan's plans— which, I supposed, was why he was Mother's chief advisor.

"Very well. I'll show him everything and withhold nothing," I said.

"Good girl," Hoatan agreed, patting my hand.

I turned back to Mother, thinking she might walk down with me as I made my official challenge for the position of Irska. But she still stared into the scrying bowl's black depths, and the words to invite her died in my throat. What was the point? She wouldn't hear me anyway.

I left the room and, with a smile, Hoatan slammed the door behind me.

Wind whipped across the green in front of the Hatchery. Gray wisps of cloud scudded past above, dimming the moon then revealing it again, casting the world by turns in darkness then in light. Othura and I stood side-by-side before the challenge basin. It was similar to Mother's scrying bowl, I now realized—a shallow, hammered copper basin ancient beyond reckoning and filled with dark dragon blood. I took my mark from the small pouch on my belt and held it between my finger and my thumb. Each rider had a mark like this with their name on one side in old elvish and an image of their dragon on the other. If two riders cast their mark into the pool together, it meant they were challenging one another to a duel, and they would then have to fight to the death. But if just one rider put their mark in, it meant they were challenging to become Irska, and an elaborate two-month-long competition to choose a new leader would begin.

I squeezed the coin in my hand, gazing at the still, thick dragon's blood. *There's still time to change my mind,* I thought. As if I truly had a choice...

I felt Othura, then. No words were spoken, but she made her presence known, like a mental hug. Slowly, I reached out, holding the coin over the basin.

Someone is coming, Othura said, an instant before a voice said, "Wait."

I turned to find Braimar striding toward me. My ex-boyfriend. The last person I wished to see tonight—or any night. He was dangerously handsome, tall with long hair, perfect cheekbones, and hypnotic eyes that always seemed to be searching mine. But I knew him too well to be charmed by him anymore.

Don't you think you should talk to me, Essa, before doing something so rash?

He spoke to me telepathically through our dragons—a

mode of communication far more intimate than I liked to share with him.

"Speak to me aloud, please," I said.

He brushed long green hair from his face with one hand.

"Alright," he said, speaking the word with exaggerated slowness just to irk me. He held up his own token. "Let me challenge Laynine on your behalf."

"Why would I do that?"

"Because then in the final battle it will be her and me. I can win. And then I can hand the title over to you."

My eyes narrowed. "And what makes you think I need a champion?"

I could almost feel him trying not to look at my missing arm. Focusing on my eyes. He sauntered nearer. Too near. He loomed over me, his body almost against mine.

I never said you need one. But perhaps you want one?

"I told you, get out of my mind," I snapped.

He smiled. "As you wish."

I had intended this to be a private moment between me and Othura. But of course, Braimar had to turn up and ruin it. She seemed just as irritated about it as I was, because her tail had snaked over until its forked end rested near Braimar's feet. A flick of that tail could have broken his ankle —or his balls—and we both knew it. He shuffled backward a step.

"The challenge is my duty and my decision," I said.

"Perhaps," Braimar said. And before I could react, his hand jerked, tossing his mark at the challenge basin. I felt my heart stop, my eyes go wide. The world seemed to dilate and slow as I watched the coin flipping toward the basin. If Braimar made the challenge and defeated Laynine, he could become Irska. Not only would I be humiliated and lose my honor, I'd also be under Braimar's control. And I knew from experience how bad that could be. The mark spun through the air, toward the basin... I reached up to grab it, but it was too high, arcing over my head.

"No!" I gasped.

There came a whoosh and a sound like a whip cracking as Othura's tail came around and slapped the coin away. She let forth a low growl as the mark glinted, flying off into the night. Without further hesitation, I turned and dropped my own mark into the basin. Immediately, the water glowed a deep red and began steaming and boiling.

It was done. All the dragons would feel the magick and know a challenge had begun. I felt a tremendous relief, as if a suit of heavy armor had been stripped from me.

I turned back to find Braimar watching me quizzically, his head tilted. He didn't appear angry, exactly. But there was something else in his eyes I found even more frightening.

"Shouldn't have done that," he said.

Othura growled, crouching right next to me. But Braimar didn't look at her. His eyes met mine and lingered, as if he could lick me with them. Then he turned and stalked off into the night.

9
CHARLIE

The curtains in my bedroom were open, and a slant of morning light shone across the items laid on the table in front of me: the contents of Kitty's oilskin flight bag. I'd begun my search hoping against hope to find a loose cigarette. I'd only given the bag a cursory search the first time, and I thought perhaps she had half a pack stashed away—but I'd found much more than that.

I'd known Kitty for a year and a half. I had been her fiancé—the word still felt strange—for only a month, but I felt I knew her pretty well. I'd expected to find make-up and chewing gum, nail polish, and perhaps a magazine or two, along with the ever-present leather notebook she used to write her articles. And those things were there, along with the travel visa and photoless ID I'd already put to use. But what else I found surprised me.

There were two maps—one of the entire kingdom of Maethalia and another of the city of Issastar, where I now sat. On the back of the city map was even a detailed floor plan of the palace itself. I also found a strange, leather-encased box with a lens on one side and a button on the top. Perplexed, I pried a hatch off the back. Inside, I found film and realized what I held was a remarkable camera, so small it could fit in the palm of my hand. I could have used it to photograph targets and documents—no doubt that's what it was intended for—but unfortunately, in prying off the back like an idiot, I'd already spoiled the film.

Still, my curiosity was piqued. I searched the emptied bag again and discovered a false bottom. Beneath it were four more items. The first was a metal lighter which bore the unofficial insignia of the URA special forces: an elephant's head wreathed in flame. The second item was a small flashlight. The third, a .38 caliber revolver. The fourth, a folded-up, handwritten note bearing four words:

Report via the Prelate.

I set these items on the table before me and sat for some time, looking at them and pondering what they could mean. I knew little about the newspaper business apart from what Kitty had told me as we chatted together over dinner or lounged in bed. But it seemed to me these items pointed toward a mission somewhat removed from writing a simple news story, even one that involved a trip into enemy territory.

Could my Kitty be keeping secrets from me? Could she be a spy?

And who was this prelate the note spoke of?

A sudden knock at my door made me start.

"Coming," I called, sweeping all the stuff off the table and into the bag again, then shoving it under my bed just as the key turned in the lock.

I expected to find Rohree there when the door swung open. Instead, it was a pair of guards, different from the ones who'd been with me the night before but no less imposing.

"You're to dress and come with us," one of them said. He was a few inches shorter than me but twice as broad, with a crater of a scar over one brow. My eyes ticked from the sword at his waist to the other guard who stood behind him, his mail-clad arms crossed.

"Of course," I said, forcing a smile.

After I'd dressed, they brought me down to a small carriage. One of the guards thrust a burlap sack into my hands.

"To break your fast," he said, before swinging himself up to the driver's seat.

"Don't suppose you have coffee?" I asked.

The two guards exchanged a glance. "What's coffee?" one of them asked.

"That's what I was afraid of," I sighed, climbing into the carriage.

I jounced along in the carriage for what must have been half an hour, nursing a caffeine headache and eating my sack-breakfast, which consisted of a sort of honeyed biscuit and a soft, mild cheese. There was also a drink in a stoppered glass bottle, which I sniffed suspiciously before finally deciding it would be much easier to kill me with one of the swords or daggers everyone carried than by poisoning. Whatever the drink was, it was oddly tasty, a mixture of lemon and lavender with a strong, herbal aftertaste. But I found it left me alert and well satisfied.

The boys back at the base will be eating their biscuits and gravy and those hockey-puck sausage patties and getting their morning briefing, I thought. *Probably hatching a search plan for me. If they haven't given me up as lost already...*

The thought of everyone weeping into their coffee over me gave me a chuckle—which made my bladder ache. I'd rushed out the door without relieving myself. I winced as the wheels banged over another bump and leaned out the window.

"Excuse me, pal, where are we going?" I called.

"The Cauldron. Where the dragons train," the guard grunted, pointing ahead. "We're here."

The Cauldron was a great valley, miles across and ringed with slate-gray peaks, like an open mouth full of broken off teeth, and the entire valley floor was comprised of a vast, round lake. At its edges, the water was pale and clear as a cut aquamarine, but as it deepened toward the lake's center, it got darker and darker, giving the whole valley the unnerving look of a giant eye.

And the dragons—my god, they were everywhere, soaring above in a great, roiling flock. Some darted and feigned and snapped at one another, others moved together in synchronized formations like massive starlings. I'd seen

dragons aplenty, but I'd seen them from the air, maneu-
vering around me while I was flying at a hundred and
twenty miles per hour. Watching them like this, from the
ground, their grace and speed were astonishing. I watched
one, a green one with an orange belly, turning flips and cart-
wheels in the air, changing direction with the agility of a
bat. A gray one flew straight ahead with a speed that, I was
sure, would have outpaced my trusty Sackman Comet
handily.

They were so numerous I couldn't count them, though I
guessed there had to be a hundred up there, dragons of all
sizes and shapes and colors, crisscrossing and wheeling,
climbing and diving, roaring and whipping their tails. Occasionally, one would blow a plume of flame so powerful that I
could feel the heat from the ground.

The beasts weren't only in the air; they were on the
ground, too. Some lazed in the sun with their eyes closed.
Others sat looking at their riders, conferring, I guessed, with
the silent, telepathic connection the beasts and their
masters were supposed to share. Still others lingered at the
lake's edge, extending their long necks to sip from the water.
A mid-sized black dragon lay on its back while a female rider
rubbed some sort of balm on its belly. It was the type the
boys called scorpions, and I eyed its tail stinger warily.

All in all, it was an awesome and frightening sight.

I heard footsteps and turned to find Princess Essaphine
approaching. She wore tight-fitting, gray riding leathers
with metal plates at the shoulders and a short, sky-blue
cloak. A helmet with a visor of glass or crystal sat atop her
head. Her black boots came up to her knees, and a long
sword hung at her waist. With her hair tied back beneath
her helmet, her eyes seemed even more prominent than

they'd been yesterday. Now they were a grayish green and filled with intensity. She looked so striking, my breath hitched in my chest.

"Shouldn't you be writing, poet?"

I looked down at my empty hands. She was right. A reporter ought to be taking notes. My second day as a spy, and already I was stumbling...

"Of course," I dug into the oilskin bag for Kitty's notebook and pen. I took them both out and waggled them at the princess. "Here we go," I said, flipping the notebook open and clicking the pen, poised to write.

The princess frowned. "You necros. Even your quills are machines... Well, I have some bad news. My mother has convinced me to be your tour guide after all. So, you'll be stuck with me while you're here."

At her words, I felt an odd sort of relief—a blooming, giddy heat kindling in my chest—something I'd hardly felt since being a kid on winter holiday, though I had no idea why I should feel that way. Sure, she'd saved my life. She'd also kicked me, tied me up, and abused me.

But it didn't matter if I hated her. Having a princess and dragon rider for an escort could give me access to valuable information.

I gave a small bow. "I'm honored, Your Majesty."

"You should be," she said with a wry twist of her lips. "I don't take in every handsome stranger I find on the side of the road."

"Just most of them," Ollie muttered, sauntering up to us, and the princess shot him a glare.

"Let's start your education then, shall we?" Essaphine said to me, tilting her head to glance over her shoulder. As she did, one of the dragons divebombed us from above. I was about to duck for cover when it pulled up and landed delicately behind Essaphine.

Steep dives and short landings. I should jot that down, I thought, but before I could, the dragon swung its long neck around until its face hovered inches from mine. The eyes it fixed on me were the size of cantaloupes and glowed orange like bowls of fire, but to my surprise, they didn't look reptilian. They were almost like human eyes, inquisitive and full of intelligence. Still, I couldn't help but notice the grinning mouth full of ten-inch-long, knife-sharp teeth. The dragon's face came closer until its muzzle was against my chest.

My god, it's going to eat me. I held my breath. My full bladder ached, wanting to release. But the dragon did not bite. Instead, it inhaled, an impossibly long breath, as if it were trying to suck my soul from my body. When it was finished, it pulled back, looked at me one more time, then swung its huge head around to look at Essaphine.

Some silent exchange seemed to take place between them, then the princess said, "Oh, stop." Then, to my surprise, she bopped the dragon on the nose like a naughty puppy.

Legend said riders could talk with their dragons telepathically, but I'd never really believed it—until now.

"What did it... say?" I asked, trying to keep my voice steady as adrenaline pumped in my veins.

"She says you're handsome and prime for mating," Essaphine said, arching an eyebrow. "Is that true?"

"Uh..." I glanced at Ollie for some cue as to how I should respond, but the eunuch only watched, amused.

The princess laughed. It was only a small one, but it was a lovely sound. It felt real, somehow, very different from the braying of the dance hall girls back in Ironberg, and from Kitty's bored giggles.

The laugh of a dragon rider is a real laugh. Perhaps I'll write that down, too, I thought, though it didn't seem a proper observation for a news story.

"Essa!" someone shouted. A trio of riders strode toward us. For a second, I was on guard after what had happened last night, but one glance at their faces told me they were friendly. The impression was confirmed when one of them —a short woman with curly red hair- swept Essa into a hug.

"So sorry about your sister, love."

"I'm not," Essaphine said with a bitter smile. Then added, "I mean, of course I *am*, but..."

"But she was a mean ol' cooter," a tall, gangly rider said. The female rider slapped him on the arm, but I could see she was repressing a smile.

Mean or not, I killed her, I thought, with a glance at Essaphine's dragon. The beast continued to watch me with those huge, unnervingly thoughtful eyes. Would it tear me apart if it knew? The thought sent a tingle of fear through me—which made my bladder ache again.

"And who's this?" Essa's red-headed friend strode up to me, nearly nosing me like the dragon had. She was no more than five feet tall but strongly built, with pixyish features and dark blue eyes. "Is this the necro everyone's been talking about?"

"Yes," Essaphine said. "He's a famous poet."

"Uh—reporter, actually." *Ace,* my inner voice corrected.

The dragon cocked its head at me.

My god, I thought. *If it can communicate telepathically with its rider, what if it read my mind?*

I supposed I'd find out soon enough. If any dragon here

knew I was the Silver Wraith, no doubt they'd bite me in half without a second thought. But the beast made no move to attack. It just kept watching me.

Essaphine was talking. "...Hoatan sent for him. I'm to show him around so he can go back and tell the enemy how grand our kingdom is."

"They have Essa doing diplomacy now? Gods, we're all pegged!" The tall, awkward fellow joked. He was an interesting character. His hair looked as if he had cut it himself with dull scissors, and the hem of his uniform tunic was tangled up in his belt. He must be the lovable cutup of the bunch. Every squad had one.

They all laughed at his joke except the third friend, who crossed their lean, muscled arms. I couldn't tell immediately whether this one was male or female. They were of average height, with dark caramel skin, a shrewd, high cheek-boned face, a coif of black hair slicked into a ponytail, a single dangly earring, and charcoal smudged around their eyes to create a rather menacing look.

"You'd best behave yourself while you're with us, Poet," they said, one hand on the hilt of their sword. "Dragons devour their meals, bones and all. If one took a fancy to you, there'd be nothing left for Hoatan to send back to your kin."

"Stop it," Essaphine chided. "I'm protecting him, not feeding him to dragons." She glanced at me, "Unless I absolutely have to..."

Essaphine made formal introductions. The tall, awkward fellow was Dagar, the short, fiery young woman was Pocha, and the one who'd threatened to feed me to a dragon was Lure. Ollie, I already knew.

Behind the princess, the gray dragon chuffed. "And you've met Othura," she added, stroking the beast's head.

Somewhere, a horn sounded, ringing off the peaks around us, and the dragons answered with a roar so loud it seemed to shake the ground beneath my feet. Deftly, the princess jogged up her dragon's tail as if it were a ramp and dropped into the saddle.

"We're about to begin," she said. "Watch closely, poet. You're about to witness the might of dragons."

10

ESSA

At the sound of the Thurn Horn, all the dragons lined up around the shore of the caldera. They were on edge, pawing the earth with their claws, whipping their tails, and making the low, growling *hoom* in the back of their throats, a sound like the purr of a cat which denoted pleasure and excitement.

Othura seemed less excited than most. She stood stock-still, staring up at the only dragon still flying: the massive akmerus, Tryce. And on his back, her cloak whipping against the gray sky, rode Laynine. While Tryce hovered, slowly beating his wings to remain aloft, my cousin shouted down to us.

"A challenge of dragons has been called. I, as the highest-ranking flyer, will conduct the ceremonies, and I will act as Irska until the final act of the challenge is completed."

And when it's completed, Essa will be Irska, Othura said in my mind.

I appreciated her words, and I tried to project confidence back to her, but doubt hung over me like a shroud. My eyes kept returning to the water. It was cold and it was deep. It also hid many submerged rocks lurking just beneath the surface. Today, every rider would be falling into that water except one. And if history was any indication, not all of us would survive that plunge. I'd participated in four melees before. I'd been the first one knocked off my mount three of the four times. All it would take would be to fall in the wrong place, strike a rock, and it would all be over.

And this was only the first game of the challenge. They'd get harder—and deadlier—from here.

Did I have any chance at all of making it through this challenge alive?

My gaze drifted down to the stump of my right arm...

I should just listen to Auntie. Flee. Find some village where no one knows me. Become a fisherman's wife. But what would become of Othura? Our bond could never be severed. What would she be—a fisherman's wife's dragon?

No. I was a princess. I was a Skrathan—even if I wasn't the best. And I was the eldest of the royal line, now. I'd be queen one day—or I would die. There could be no running away. No pretending to be someone else. The only path was forward, even if it left me broken on the rocks.

"The first act of the challenge is the melee," Laynine went on from above us. "The only rule is that you remain above the caldera. The last rider still on their dragon wins."

With these words, Tryce shot skyward, azure wings thudding with incredible power. Up, up, up he climbed, to a greater height than Othura and I had ever reached, and there he opened his jaws and blew a crackling web of lightning across the sky. Akmerus were among the largest of the dragon breeds, and Tryce was the largest and strongest akmerus alive. The lightning he released was so powerful it lit up the day with a brightness far stronger than the sun's, making me wince even from the ground.

Show off, Othura snorted.

She hated Tryce. Most of the dragons did, especially the females, who he was always trying to mate. But there was no denying that he was the biggest and the best, now that Horban was dead—at least while Mother's dragon remained in hibernation.

You know I can hear you, Othura turned her eyes on me, fixing me with her orange glare.

If you don't like pessimism, get out of my head, I shot back.

Othura growled. *Your pessimism may get me killed. Our lives are bound, remember? If you don't believe in us, who will?*

No one, I thought, though I tried not to project it to Othura. Pessimism again... Or was it simply rational fear? Too often, they amounted to the same thing.

I hated when things got testy between Othura and me. It felt as if I were fighting a part of myself, like stabbing my own leg.

But there was no time to make up with her. The Thurn Horn blew again, and the riders all scrambled onto their mounts. The melee was beginning.

Othura surged upward, her wings making a powerful *whump, whump, whump* that seemed to beat in time with my thundering heart. Though the caldera was nearly a mile across, it still felt overcrowded. Everywhere we turned, there was another dragon, their claws or fire or snapping jaws striking for us. There were also the lances to worry about. Every rider had one—every rider with two working arms, that is. It was impossible for me to hang on to my saddle grip—a necessary thing when riding a weaving, dodging dragon—and hold a lance at the same time. So, I didn't have one. That meant I had to rely on Othura alone for our attacks.

Fortunately, Othura was good.

She wove expertly through the chaos, dipping under a slashing claw from a two-headed geminus, rolling away from a blast of flame from a green sagittan. We came up behind someone riding a brown capran, approaching so stealthily they didn't see us yet.

Now! I told Othura, and she blew. Like all libran dragons, she didn't possess the ability to blow fire. Her power was wind, and she opened her mouth now and unleashed a blast of air. The force of it spun the massive dragon around, and the unsuspecting rider, who'd been angling to attack a golden leonin, lost their seat and pitched off to fall, screaming, into the water below.

That wasn't the first rider to fall. Already, a half dozen had made the plunge into the freezing depths. Several had grabbed onto their dragon's tails and were being towed back to shore. Another was being hauled into one of the rescue boats that floated on the lake, ready to help the injured. One Skrathan, I saw, had already landed among the rocks. His dragon was bowed over him, bellowing a terrible, mournful roar.

All these sights passed before me in a flash, then we were tilting and building speed again.

Ahead, I saw a crackle of lightning. Laynine.

Maybe we should pick off some of the lesser riders first,
Othura suggested.

No, I thought back. *That's what she expects. We take
her now.*

Already, this was the longest I'd survived in a melee. If I
didn't challenge Laynine now, I probably wouldn't have the
chance. And I desperately wanted to show her, and everyone, that I was a threat.

Othura knew my mind, and I felt her redouble her
efforts, speeding ahead.

Then, wings blotted out the sun. I glanced up to see a
massive gray dragon above me.

It's Cronin! I warned, and Othura rolled on her side just
as a blast of flame came down upon us from above. Othura
folded her wings and dropped like a stone, dipping out of
range of the fire before rolling and opening her wings again.

My hand and arm ached from holding on while sideways.
My heart beat so hard it felt louder than the wind in my ears.
We'd nearly flipped, and the thought of going upside down
always stirred panic in me, ever since the fall where I'd lost my
arm. But I forced myself to think of Othura, not my own terror.

You okay? I asked.

Fine, Othura's voice came back in a snarl.

Dragon hide was much tougher than human skin and
was generally resistant to flame, although taking a direct
blast never felt pleasant.

We were out of Cronin's range now, so low now that
Othura's wingtips skimmed the water.

Look out. Laynine's minions are coming now.

I looked up and saw she was right. Cronin, Romia, and
Kramat, three of Laynine's best friends, were circling us like

buzzards. I looked for my friends, but the only one I spotted was Dagar on his leonin, far off and beset with attackers. I was on my own.

Romia came first, her scorper darting in, then wheeling away and whipping its tail stinger toward us. Othura blasted wind at her, shoving her away so that her tail stinger passed harmlessly a few feet from my face. Dagar's carcer struck next, swooping in on us with its crushing, pincer-like front talons. Othura banked and pumped her wings, building speed, pulling away.

More lightning blinked, catching my eye. Laynine was ahead of us. If we could just break away, we could catch up to her, and—

Fire erupted around me. I snapped my head left to see Cronin and his dragon speeding into us. Romia hadn't really been trying to catch us; she'd been steering us back toward her wingmate. The realization had hardly sunk in when Cronin's lance caught me, a blow to the ribs that knocked all thought and breath out of me.

Then, I was falling.

11
CHARLIE

Ollie stood at my side, biting a thumbnail and watching the dragons wheel above us. We were both watching one dragon and one rider in particular.

"Her dragon moves well," I said, then silently cursed myself. Would a reporter make a judgment about the combat ability of a dragon? I doubted it. True, there were viewing stations along the coast where Admites could drop a nickel into a slot and watch through a huge set of binoculars as aces and dragons battled over the sea. But Kitty would never have made a pronouncement about a dragon's maneuverability. *Be more careful,* I chided myself.

But if Ollie noticed anything amiss, he didn't show it.

"Othura is one of the best at dodging," he said. "She's had to be. If she weren't, she and Essa wouldn't have lived this long."

"Why doesn't the princess have a lance?" I asked.

Ollie looked at me sidelong, a hint of mockery in his raised eyebrow.

"She has only one arm," he said. "Even with the special saddles riders have, their legs alone aren't capable of keeping them in place through all their maneuvers. They have to hold on with one hand. And Essa's other limb isn't capable of holding a lance."

I frowned. "But couldn't there be some sort of prosthetic made?"

The eunuch glanced at me. "A what?"

"Prosthetic. A fake limb. They can make them with hooks, or hands, or even pincers that—"

"We don't worship machines as your people do," Ollie said, a sharpness in his tone that silenced me for a second.

I watched the dragons darting and moving once more.

"Why doesn't her dragon blow fire?" I asked.

"She's a libran," he said, then noticed my blank look. "A wind dragon. They don't breathe fire. They—"

As if on cue, Essaphine's dragon opened its mouth and a whirlwind burst forth. It turned a much larger dragon around, sending its rider flying into the lake.

"That was impressive," I said. I'd never seen a dragon in combat using such a technique, but my guess was it would be hell on a plane's vertical rudder.

"Are they rare?" I asked.

Ollie nodded. "Not as rare as some types, but fairly rare. There are only a few Skrathan riding them currently. Remind me, and I'll deliver a few books on dragons to your room."

"I would appreciate—"

"Uh oh," Ollie whispered, interrupting me.

Above, three large dragons were descending on Essaphine and Othura. I felt my heart beat faster. I recognized these dragons and their riders. I'd fought them. They were three of the best. And they were all closing in on the princess.

"He's above you," I muttered. "Dive, dive, dive."

Essaphine seemed to see the dragon above her—but another was behind her, winging her way fast.

"Watch your eight!" I blurted.

The rider swooped in, his lance blasting the princess from the saddle. Ollie gave a cry, and I held my breath as the princess fell what had to be at least three hundred feet. The world seemed to hang in silent suspension for a terribly long moment as she fell, then there came the crash and the explosion of spray as she hit the water.

Ollie ran to the lake's edge, and I followed him, both of us staring across the water with our hands shading our eyes, waiting for the princess to come up. Only she didn't.

"The lance..." I started to say, but Ollie cut me off.

"They're blunted," he said. "Still, the impact... and if she hit a rock..."

We both stared across the water.

"There!" the Torouman pointed, and I saw the princess's head emerge. She took a breath and began paddling haphazardly toward the shore. I found myself breathing again as well, though I hadn't realized I'd stopped. Othura swooped in, dropping her tail into the water. The princess grabbed it, and the dragon began towing her back toward the shore.

"She's okay," Ollie said, a hand over his heart.

I looked at him. "You really care for her, don't you?"

"Of course. She might as well be my twin sister." He bent over and put his elbows on his knees. "Ugh. I might retch."

Now that I knew the princess had lived, my analytical mind had returned.

"There are more trials like this?"

Ollie nodded. "Twelve in total, leading up to the final challenge."

I shook my head. "She can't compete when everyone else has a lance and she doesn't. It's too much of a disadvantage."

"I'm sure she would agree with you," Ollie said, spitting into the dirt.

A stack of spare lances lay on the beach nearby. I picked one up.

"God, it's heavy. Solid wood?"

"Ash," Ollie nodded, shading his eyes again and watching as the princess made her way toward shore. "Riders train for years to wield them. The princess is so slight, she can barely hold one even with her good arm."

I hefted the lance one more time. The thing had to be at least twelve feet long. With a frown and a grunt, I dropped it on the pile with the rest, then I turned back to the lake.

The princess was reaching the shore now some distance from us, and three women in pale green robes surrounded her. She was nodding to them and gesturing to her side.

"Should we go over?" I asked.

Ollie shook his head. "The healers are not to be disturbed. Essa will come to us once they've checked her over."

We turned our attention to the sky once more. Many riders had fallen since the princess had taken our attention. Only perhaps two dozen remained, among them Laynine and the three who had defeated Essaphine.

Those four dragons and their riders were the most powerful and skilled, and we watched as they systematically eliminated the others one by one. Essaphine's friend Dagar and his golden dragon were already out. Her friend Pocha soon followed. Lure, on a mighty purple fire-breather with ram's horns, put up an impressive fight. Together they knocked off five riders—including one of the four best— when Laynine swept in. Her dragon stunned Lure's with a crackle of lightning, then changed direction and slapped Lure out of the saddle with a whip of its tail. Lure went skipping and tumbling across the water, nearly to the shore, but emerged again fast, alive and cursing.

My attention returned to Laynine. I'd seen that dark blue dragon of hers before. In fact, she was the one who'd taken down a friend of mine, Edith, only a month earlier. But I'd never seen her dragon use lightning before.

So, they're holding that in reserve. Interesting.

Laynine and her dragon were good. Not only powerful, but clever. Calculating. Strategic. From what I could judge, they were even better than Paemalla and her dragon had been. And that would spell trouble for my squadron.

"Is it true what I've heard, that the lead dragon can communicate telepathically and give orders to the others?" I asked Ollie.

He eyed me. I knew the calculation he was making. He didn't wish to give away any valuable secrets that might wind up in the Ironberg paper. But he was also under orders from the queen to share information with me. I'd have to thank her later...

"Yes," he said.

I looked back across the lake. Only Laynine and two of her three companions remained. Together, the three sailed down to alight on the water like ducks. The other two riders leapt off into the water, leaving Laynine the last one still mounted. A horn sounded, and a cheer went up from the shores, followed by shouts of *Laynine, Laynine, Laynine!*

Here was a danger. With a leader like her, these dragon riders might be able to tip the scales of the war. Laynine was the strongest rider, and her dragon was the most formidable —that was clear.

But what if she didn't win the position of Irska? What if, instead of Laynine, a weaker rider were to win the challenge? What if the very *weakest* rider won?

My eyes went to the princess again. Her armor was removed, revealing a wet bodice as the healers ran a bandage around her ribs. The sunlight seemed to shine upon her like a halo, and droplets of water hung in her hair like diamonds. Even in pain, in defeat, her face looked radiant, like an image I'd seen in a dream and tried to hold onto upon waking.

A pretty face concealing a wicked heart, I thought, remembering her kicking my legs out from under me.

I hated her, sure. But I could use her.

A plan was forming in my mind, a gamble so outrageous that its chances of working were slim, its dangers immense. But if it did work, it might just win the war and make me the biggest hero in URA history.

I would help Essaphine defeat Laynine and become Irska of the Maethalian flyers.

Then, I would destroy them all.

12

KITTY

Kitty's high heels clicked as she walked through the administrative office at McNally Airbase. As she swayed down the aisle, she heard typewriters cease their clicking, conversations fall silent, and young officers' chairs creaking as they leaned over, nudging their buddies to watch her pass.

So, the new form-fitting business dress she wore was a winner. That was good to know, she thought with a smile.

I'm heading in to meet with the general of the entire nation's Air Force, one of the most powerful men in the world. And he's going to be eating out of my hand like a puppy.

She could never have imagined this life when she was just a party girl living it up in the dance halls of West Ironberg. Actually, that wasn't quite true. Kitty had always known she was meant for greatness, whether that meant starring in moving pictures or dancing onstage or something even greater. She'd had a belief in herself that rivaled the faith of the most fervent saints. The only question had been, how would her greatness be achieved? Getting her job at the paper had been a start. But she had a feeling the next big chapter was about to begin.

The General's aide, First Lieutenant Michaels, saw her coming and sprang up from his chair like a jack-in-the-box, folding the newspaper he'd been reading in half and snubbing out his cigarette. He almost saluted her before he caught himself and gave her a small, awkward nod instead.

"Miss Rowley," he said. "Right this way. The General is expecting you."

She fell into step beside him. He cleared his throat and brandished his folded-up paper.

"I was just reading your latest article about ammunition production in Danlee. Fascinating."

Kitty gave an airy laugh. "Yeah, the president of that company pestered me for months to write that article. He finally sent his private car to take me to his private train to get me down there."

"Sounds glamorous," Michaels gushed.

Kitty wheeled on him. "Glamorous?" She twiddled her fingers in front of his face. "Look at these ink-stained fingers. I tell ya, it doesn't wash off. The article came out alright, though."

"Yes," Michaels pushed his glasses up his nose. "It got me to take my old cans down to the recycling depot, I'll tell you that. The idea of running out of raw materials for ammo is pretty concerning."

Kitty favored him with a smile. "We all have to do our part," she said.

They had reached a frosted glass door with the name General Peckham stenciled on it. The lieutenant gave a brisk knock, then swung the door open.

"Kitty Rowley, sir," he announced.

The general rose from the chair behind his desk. "Yes, yes. Send her in. You stay too, Lieutenant."

General Peckham was a broad man with a silver crewcut and a nose like an eagle's beak. He cut an impressive figure with his perfect posture and a chest full of medals, but Kitty noticed as she got closer that he wasn't as tall as he first appeared.

There were three other men in the room. One was a Lieutenant Colonel—Kitty didn't remember his name. The second was an elegant-looking man in a black suit who she knew very well indeed. Edward Langford, of the Secret Intelligence Bureau. The third fellow was a pilot. He was tall, with the long legs of a stork and a movie star's face, complete with sleepy blue eyes and a thin moustache. They were all smoking, and the room was filled with a faint bluish fog.

"Gentlemen," she said with a curt nod.

The ace nearly squirmed with longing at the sight of her. God, how she loved having that effect on a man. He left the desk he was leaning on, approaching her.

"Kitty, right?" He took her hand and kissed it.

"That's Miss Rowley to you," she shot back, smiling.

"Ms. Rowley," Peckham gestured to the man. "Meet our new Silver Wraith, Major Carter Blaize."

She looked at the general sharply. "So, we're sure Charlie is gone?"

"Unless he's one hell of a good swimmer," Peckham sighed. "And if he is, I expect he'd have swum back here by now. But we can't let it slip that he's dead, you understand. The Wraith is a hero to people. If they thought he was gone, it would be a blow to morale."

"So... you're going to let them think he's still alive..."

Kitty bit her lower lip, thinking. The brass had never let the papers publish Charlie's real name and had only allowed him to be photographed with his goggles and flight helmet on. This, they had claimed, was for his safety, to prevent an enemy spy from trying to assassinate him when he was off duty. It also allowed Charlie to move about in public with anonymity, rather than getting mobbed by fans and photographers everywhere he went. Kitty had always taken these explanations at face value. But perhaps this had been the plan all along. If Charlie died, they could replace him. He was expendable. And if Carter Blaize crashed, they'd just replace him, too. It was rather heartless. But then, that was war.

She glanced at Edward. His cold blue eyes stared back at her, unblinking, and he gave a barely perceptible nod. That was all it took. She had her orders.

"Of course, we could use your help to pull off this little ruse," the general said.

Kitty had been photographed with Charlie when he was in uniform, and it had been publicized that she was the Wraith's fiancée. People liked knowing their hero was a regular fella with a gal waiting for him back home. And of course, the notoriety, along with her weekly column, had made Kitty the star she was.

It was a shame, though. Charlie had been a decent guy. She might even miss him.

She eyed Major Blaize. She remembered the name, now. Charlie had hated him. He was a good pilot, second only to the Silver Wraith himself. But Charlie had thought he was a brash prick and had said so on more than one occasion. Seeing her on Major Blaize's arm would have made Charlie sick.

But Charlie was dead, wasn't he? A girl had to move on.

She already had, in fact, she thought—feeling Langford's eyes lingering on her.

She smiled at the general. "Of course. Anything for the war effort."

Carter chuckled lecherously, grinning at her like a fool.

"Excellent," the general said. "Michaels, get the photographer down at the hangar and have him snap a few photos of Miss Rowley with Captain Blaize—I mean the Silver Wraith—in front of his plane. Welcoming him back from the mission, kissing, that sort of thing. The sooner we dispel the idea that the Wraith is dead, the better."

"Yes, sir," Michaels said, scribbling in a notebook. He opened the door, and everyone filed toward it. Michaels exited first, followed by Blaize and the general. Before Kitty could go, Langford caught her arm, turning her around in the empty office.

"A word, Miss Rowley?"

He pushed the door shut behind her. Then, his lips were on hers. Snarling. Licking. Biting. He was a biter.

His hand went to her breast, squeezing, sending a shock of pain through her, but also longing.

When he pulled back, he was holding a metal vial up in front of her. She knew what it contained without looking. A rolled-up message. And within that, a smaller glass vial—of blood.

"You'll pass this to the contact in Torrey Square at nine-fifteen tonight," he said. "And I'll come to you at midnight. Wash yourself first and be wearing nothing."

She gazed into those hypnotic eyes of his. He wasn't handsome, not the way Charlie was. But there was something intoxicating about him. Something inevitable, like the feeling of an oncoming storm. For half a second, as he stared at her, the entire world seemed to crumble to a single point of infinitely dense blackness. There was only her and Langford. No airbase. No war. No Charlie. Nothing.

"Yes, master," she whispered.

Then Langford was opening the door and ushering her out of the office, back into the world of light.

13

ESSA

Rohree brought the enemy poet to the stables shortly after dawn. He'd been handsome when I met him at first on the road, but he looked far better now, washed and combed and dressed in a proper Maethalian tunic and cloak rather than his strange foreign clothing. I still felt like a crumpled piece of parchment after yesterday's fall. The healers had looked me over and assured me I'd suffered no serious damage—although the bruises, they said, would be mighty. Still, under the stranger's gaze, I couldn't help but feel oddly self-conscious, as if I were broken in some way I wasn't quite aware of, and I brushed a strand of hair out of my face nervously.

He smiled and bowed.

"Your Majesty," he said in that low, strangely accented voice, all choppy consonants and oddly stretched vowels.

I laughed at him. "Do you think you're talking to my mother?" I asked. "You may call me Essa."

His brow wrinkled. "Just showing due respect, your—I mean, Essa." He looked rather adorable when he was disconcerted. I decided to keep him in that state as much as possible today, just for fun—and, perhaps, to see how he would respond. My own little war.

I looked to Rohree. "Has he been giving you any trouble?"

"Far less than you usually do," the sprite sniffed. She'd been my personal attendant for many years and knew better than anyone what a brat I was. I didn't doubt Kit was a dream compared to me.

I turned back to the enemy. "I thought today I might give you a tour of the city. Would that please you?"

"Sure," he nodded. "Thank you."

"Excellent," I said, mounting Sisha. "Let's go."

"On horseback?"

I arched an eyebrow. "I don't think you're ready for dragon back just yet, do you? Besides, it's forbidden for foreigners to ride dragons."

He glanced around. "Is there a horse for me?"

I repressed a smile. "One horse worked fine for us last time," I patted Sisha's haunch behind me. "Up you go."

Rohree gave me an amused but reproachful look as the reporter clambered up awkwardly behind me. But once he was in place, he surprised me by wrapping his arms tightly around my waist and pulling my body against his with a force that made my breath catch. I glanced back to find his face only inches from mine, a teasing smile on his lips.

"Don't want to fall off. *Your Majesty,*" he said.

The smile he gave me was bold. Teasing. Ferocious. It took a few seconds for me to remember we were only inches apart.

"No, indeed," I said. "It would be a shame to lose you so soon. We only just found you."

I gave Sisha a nudge and we surged away, leaving Rohree shaking her head in our wake.

Issastar was a large city made up of six major districts. It held so many wonders it would have taken weeks to show Kit them all, but I made a good start. We started at Downcity, where I took him on a walk along Sand Crescent. I showed him how to find the best seashells along the water's edge and how to pick out sea relics—bits of carved marble that are the remnants of the lost city of Eoshad, which sank during the second elven civil war three eons ago.

"Here," I said, placing one in his hand. "They say they're lucky."

"They're part of a city that blew up?" he asked. "How lucky can they be?"

"I never thought of it that way," I laughed.

He showed me how to fling rocks and make them skip across the water. Apparently, I learned, it's all in the wrist.

Next, I took him to the wharves. The tide was coming in, and we sat on an old dock with our toes in the water and watched the white-sailed fishing boats and the gray-sailed warships, and the silver-hulled merchant ships coming into port.

"I haven't sat here and watched the ships come in since I was a girl," I said, closing my eyes to enjoy the sun on my face. "My Auntie Dreya used to take me here. In Maethalia, aunts teach their nieces and uncles teach their nephews."

"Did you come here often?" he asked.

"We did before my accident. After that, Auntie felt I needed extra training, so there was no time for frivolous things like trips to the bay."

I opened my eyes to find him staring at me.

"Sorry. I was just..." he blinked and looked away quickly.

"Imagining how you might strangle me and become a hero to your nation?" I asked, nudging him with my shoulder.

He smiled. "Something like that. Actually, I was noticing your necklace. Is that—?"

He reached for the stone that hung on the silver chain around my neck. Instinctively, I slapped his hand away—far harder than I meant to. He pulled back, his eyes hard.

I wanted to apologize, but stopped myself. *Better to be cruel than weak.*

"Never touch a rider's dragon stone," I said, my fingers going to the necklace's smooth gem. I glanced down at it. Beneath the stone's gray-blue surface, its power swirled and glowed, like sunlight glowing behind clouds.

"Is it... magick?" he asked.

I smiled, trying to lighten the mood again. "It's only the beginning of the magick you'll see here in Issastar," I said. "Come. I have more to show you."

I took him to the fish market next, where the mongers shouted prices in three different tongues and tossed fish back and forth and did tricks with their sharp knives as they cut fillets for their patrons. For lunch, I bought him a strip of kotash, sweet and salty dried fish that sailors eat on long journeys, and a jar of jinjin, the fermented juice of the prickle fruit from the faraway Under Isles, which sailors use to get drunk. In fact, we each drank a jar of jinjin, which perhaps wasn't the wisest thing to do.

You're in the company of an enemy, I reminded myself. But the poet didn't seem much like an enemy today. His questions seemed more the sort a curious little boy would ask, rather than a shrewd scribe.

Do you have pirates here?

Do you like to sail?

Have you ever been seasick?

They say there are merfolk in Maethalia. That can't be true, can it?

This last question prompted me to take him to see the Downcity merman. Ever since I was a little girl, the merman had been there, sitting each day in a wooden tub outside the crab fishers' warehouse with a bucket set out in front of him to collect coin from out-of-town visitors who'd come to the city to see the sights. He was still there, but he looked older and shabbier than he had when I'd last seen him. His beard was longer and grayer, his eyes more distant. But when he took up his pipes, the tune he played was as lively as ever.

I sighed, saddened to see this icon from my childhood looking so bleak. "He looks so lonely," I said, half to myself. "You can tell he's broken. It's a shame he isn't a woman."

Kit glanced at me. "What do you mean?"

"It's just too bad he's not a woman, so he'd be stronger," I explained.

Kit blinked. "Because women are stronger than men, you're saying?"

I met his glare. "Of course. It's well known. Why? Is that not known in your country?"

Kit shook his head. "Well... I've known plenty of tough, smart women. But back in Admar, the men do the working and the fighting and the women mostly cook and clean and take care of children. Of course, there are career girls..." Here he trailed off for a moment. "But mostly they rely on their husbands. Because the thinking is, men are stronger."

I laughed. Then I laughed harder. The silent spasms of mirth shook me until I had to bend over and rest my elbows on my knees.

"Oh my," I said, wiping tears from my eyes. "I think we've just discovered what's wrong with your country, my friend. Push a squirming human out of your genitals or fight a female Skrathan in the war ring, then tell me about how men are stronger than women—if you still have the breath to speak. Ha. Wow. Your country is run by men..." she laughed again.

"Alright. Maybe we should settle this with a pull-up contest," Kit joked. Then he glanced at my missing hand and stopped himself, clearly realizing his mistake. I watched with amusement as the color drained from his face.

"Fine. A one-armed pull-up contest," I said. A low tree branch spread over us. I stretched up and grabbed it with my one good arm. Then, using all my strength, I pulled myself up until my nose touched the branch. I managed to do it two more times before dropping back to the ground, trembling and already beginning to sweat. Several people around us applauded.

Kit stared at me with something like wonder. Then he shook his head. "Fine. You win. Women are stronger," he said—ending the conversation with a hint of a smile.

We both turned back to the merman. "Now come on. Is he real? Or is that tail fake?"

"Tug on it if you don't believe me," I scoffed. "Why would his tail be fake?"

"So people will put money in his bucket."

I frowned at him. "Why would having a fake tail make people give him coin? He'd be a liar."

"There are all sorts of swindlers like that in Canal Square in Ironberg," he said. "There's a woman who pretends to have three legs, only one of them's made of papier-mache. And another fella has trained his dog to lie down and act sick, so people will feel bad and toss him a few pennies. And there's another one, a little short woman who pretends to be a lost child, and she—"

I grunted. "Well, we Maethalians are not as deceitful as you necromancers," I said. "He is a real merman. I've been coming here to watch him since I was a girl. Watch. He's getting ready to call the birds."

Just as I spoke, the old man took out a set of smaller, more high-pitched pipes and played a sad tune. From all around, seagulls came, wheeling and cawing, to land near him. Some splashed down in his tub with him, others roosted on his head or shoulders, or on the dock nearby.

"They say he lived on the shoals off Rograd Point," I said. "When the war began, his people were all driven away and scattered. He's the only one left."

I watched the poet watching the merman.

"Poor guy," he said at last, and dug his hand into his pocket, but it came out empty. "Hah. I forgot. No wallet."

I reached into the pouch at my belt and gave him a silver. He took it and dropped it into the merman's bucket. The old piper gave him a nod.

"Very interesting," I said when we were walking again.

"What?"

"To see that you're charitable. You necros are supposed to be nothing but robbers and pirates and crooked merchants."

"Well, some of us are," he said with a smile. "Just not me. I still don't get the *necros* thing, by the way."

"You use machines, which are inanimate objects brought to life," I explained. "And to make them and fuel them, you use petrol, which is derived from the dead. It is a form of necromancy. And it is written that such things will one day bring disaster upon our people—and upon all the world."

"Right. Motorcars and planes are pretty handy, though."

I eyed him. "You would choose convenience over morality?"

"Depends on what day you ask me," he joked, then sighed. "When you put it that way... I guess not. But good luck convincing the car companies and railroads and airlines that they're wrong."

"I don't have to convince them," I stopped walking and turned to him. "I only have to convince you."

"That's why I'm here, isn't it? You convince me your way is right, then you send me back to convince my people."

I nodded.

"And what if you can't convince me?"

"Then you're an idiot," I said. "Maybe I'll slap a fake tail on you and put you in a tub next to the merman. You could bring in a few coins that way, I imagine."

He gave me a thoughtful smile. "You're not what I expected from a dragon rider."

"No? Why not?"

"Well... you have a sense of humor, for one."

I shrugged. "Every time a Skrathan flies, death flies with us. You either cry or you laugh."

He nodded. "I understand."

At those words, an unexpected anger rose in my chest,

along with an image of Paemalla laid out on the stone floor —and of the brothers and sisters and friends I'd lost before her. "*Do you* understand, poet?"

"I'm a reporter, technically—"

I interrupted him. "You risk paper cuts and ink-stained fingers. A rider risks—" I brought the stump of my right arm up between us, holding it in his face so he couldn't help but look at it. "Everything."

I waited for him to look away. Everyone looked away from the shiny, rounded, scarred stump where my forearm ended. Only he didn't look away. He looked right at it, then into my eyes.

"I'm sorry," he said, his voice low with sincerity.

He meant that he was sorry for insulting me, I guessed. But it felt like more than that. It felt like he was sorry about what had happened to my arm. To me. And in all these years, no one had ever said that to me. They ignored it. Or whispered about it. Or joked about it. Or babied me. Or pitied me. But nobody, not once, had ever simply looked at my arm and said, *I'm sorry*.

Tears welled in my eyes. The poet didn't look away. Instead, he came closer, as if he might reach out to me, embrace me, comfort me, but I turned away fast, wiping the tears away and hoping he hadn't noticed them.

"Come," I said, fighting to keep my voice even. "There is more to see."

We tied Sisha to a hitching post and made our way up the Jagged Stair and into the neighborhood called Belltower, or Jordamtor in the old tongue. There were many sprites about performing errands for their masters, their antlers making the lanes of Highmarket look like a thicket of twigs. Dwarves bustled about, too, their rings and golden necklaces and brightly polished chainmail glinting in the midday sun, the air pleasantly scented with the musky perfume they favored.

A hush fell over the square, and I turned to see people hurrying out of the way as the sound of tromping boots and jangling mail drew near. I stood on my tiptoes and craned my neck to see a troop of warriors in wicked-looking black armor marching toward us, carrying a banner of plain black.

"Who are *they*?" Kit asked.

"Lacunae. Warriors of the Gray Brotherhood," I said, distaste wrinkling my nose as I watched them march past.

"I've heard of them," Kit said. "Our boys in the trenches are terrified of them. I've never seen one up close..."

I could tell from his expression that he was impressed, and not a little dismayed by their presence. Which wasn't surprising. The Lacunae had that effect on everyone with their massive stature, narrow slitted helms, dark cloaks, and general aura of bleakness and death.

"No one likes them," I admitted. "But they're necessary. The crown's army would have folded long ago without them. That's why Prelate Kortoi, leader of the Brotherhood, has such power."

"Prelate Kortoi?" he asked, as if startled by the name.

"You've heard of him?" I asked. The thought that Kortoi's fame extended across the sea was disconcerting.

"Yes," he said. "The prelate... I'd like to meet him one of these days."

I frowned. "I can't imagine why. But perhaps we can set up an introduction, if you want..."

The Lacunae had marched on, and in their wake, the crowd returned to their business.

"Come," I said, shaking off the dismal feeling the Lacunae had left behind. "I have more delicacies for you to sample."

We purchased a snack of sausage and honey rolls from an elvish-looking waif at a food cart, then hiked up and sat on a stone bench overlooking Oerl Spring. The spring had been dammed up in centuries past to form a lovely reservoir of clear water, and from its west end the Falls of Cheselie dropped over two hundred feet. From here, we could see the Dragon Hatchery, the palace, and almost the entire city of Issastar.

Off to our left, the two towers that gave the Belltower district its name stood looking down on it all.

"What's the story with those?" The reporter asked, pointing up at them.

"Those are Sytor and Ertor, the two towers. They were supposed to represent the Earth Mother and Star Father who came together to beget the elvish race hundreds of eons ago. The one that is broken off is Sytor. It was supposedly destroyed by a raid of rival dragon riders thousands of years ago, before Aulucia the White united all riders under one banner. Ertor still remains. The bell in it rings when danger threatens the city, and watchers sit there night and day, watching for enemy war machines coming across the strait."

"Your people still worship them, don't they?" the reporter asked. "Earth Mother and Star Father?"

I nodded. "Star Father gives us things like magick, scrying, mathematics, and poetry. Earth Mother is responsible for the forests and fields and springs and seas. And love—physical love."

As I spoke those words, I was surprised to feel warmth flooding my cheeks. The stranger watched me so intently. No one had looked at me like that in a long time, not even Braimar.

Was it a sort of bravery that made him look at me so? Was it defiance? Should I be offended? Or flattered? Or...? I was overthinking. *Stop.*

"So, you have just the two gods?" he was asking.

I blinked, shrugging off my previous thoughts. "Not exactly," I said. "Everything has its own spirit, every rock and stone and tree and star. But it is Earth Mother and Star Father who bring these different beings into relationship with humans."

"That's a very succinct description of an entire religion," the reporter said, licking honey from one of the rolls off his thumb. "Well done."

I laughed. "Oh, there's a great deal more I could get into. The daemons of abyss and negation. The lineages and traits of the twelve houses of dragons. The One-Hundred Saga. The Nine Forbidden Acts. The high and low magicks. How much time do you have, poet?"

He smiled. "Well, I haven't seen any flights leaving out of Maethalia to take me back home, so I imagine I have a lot of time. And remember, I'm a reporter, not a poet. You can call me—uh, Kit."

I returned his smile, but mine was cold. "You have time. I do not... The challenge looms over me. By the way, what did you think of our first challenge event yesterday?"

"Impressive," he said.

"More impressive than your country's flying contraptions?" I pressed.

His expression was smug. "Impressive," he said again. "But I'm biased, I think."

Naturally, it would take more than one demonstration of dragons' prowess to make him recognize our superiority. Still... his response annoyed me. I tried to change the subject. "Tell me about your country's religion."

He gazed out across the city and sighed. "Not much to tell, really. We have just the one god. Zero magicks."

"And your god, he is both creator and punisher, yes?"

"Right," he said. "In the afterlife, the good get eternal salvation, the bad get eternal suffering. Pray to the fellow upstairs and he's supposed to listen and help you. And then there's his daughter, Sophi, who came to earth and was enslaved for twelve years. She whispered secret wisdom among the slaves, then, on the day she was to be executed for her insubordination, the chains on the wrists of all the slaves transformed into water, and they were freed. She became a mist and floated up to heaven in front of a cloud of a thousand witnesses."

"That sounds like a powerful magick,"

He yawned. "If it really happened. It was three thousand years ago, after all. Who knows? Say, that market down there doesn't have coffee or cigarettes, does it?"

I shook my head. "I don't think so. I don't know what those things are."

He groaned.

"But wait. Go back," I pressed. "You sound skeptical. Do you not believe in your god?"

He'd been turning a pebble between his finger and thumb. He threw it now, sending it skipping down the path.

"I should," he said. "I've been luckier than most. But some of my biggest prayers were never answered. And Sophi's great wisdom hasn't done much for me—most of it was about giving money to the poor, and I've never had a hell of a lot of money to give, to be honest," he shrugged.

I tutted. "You're a faithless poet."

He looked at me. "My faith is in myself. And..."

I leaned in, waiting for his next words, but he hesitated. I could almost see the thoughts shifting behind his eyes, as if he were building up to say something important. Then, he looked away, across the lake.

"And...?" I prompted.

He looked serious. "Listen. About your challenge. What if I told you I could help you defeat Laynine?"

I felt my eyes go wide. Nothing he could have said would have surprised me more than that. "I'd say what everyone says about you foreigners is true. You're mad fools." I laughed, but he was not laughing. "What would a poet from the land of necromancers know about flying dragons?"

"More than you might think." He leaned close to me, conspiratorial. "There is a way for you to win. But you'd have to trust me."

I felt anger rising in me. Despite the occasional annoyance, Kit had been a pleasant enough distraction so far. Now, he was mocking me—like everyone else. It was a reminder of who he really was. An enemy. A foreign agent. Whether his words were a sick jest or some perverse attempt to sabotage me, I wanted no part of them. And worse, they gave me an aching feeling in my chest. The unease and hurt and dread he'd momentarily distracted me from began to seep in again, like water from a spring.

Abruptly, I got to my feet. "Just because I've shown you a little kindness, you take me for a fool?"

He looked flustered. "What? No—"

"I would *never* trust you."

"My apologies, Princess. I only—"

"Silence!" I snapped, in a voice that sounded frighteningly like Mother's.

"I have neglected my training today. Come. I have to get you back to your room."

Your room—more like your prison cell, you cur, I thought. *I'll leave you there for a week and see if you dare to mock me then.*

His mouth hung open as if he would say more, but I turned on my heel and strode away toward the Jagged Stair, leaving him to keep up or be left behind.

14
CHARLIE

I spent the next three days confined to my room. Surly guards brought me three meals each day, but I did not see the sprite, Rohree. On the second day, I received a basket of books with a note saying they were from Ollie, but he didn't come in person, either. Inside the basket, I found two volumes on the history of Maethalia and one on the twelve types of dragons. Those were the only instances of human contact I received.

As the hours stretched long, I paced, by turns cursing Essaphine for locking me up and cursing myself for angering her. Things had been going so well. We'd smiled together along the seashore like a pair of lovers. We'd eaten and drunk. We'd laughed. And then, like a fool, I'd screwed it up. All I had to do was gain her trust, and I'd utterly bungled it. In the silence, I replayed each word, each look we'd exchanged in excruciating detail, until I decided I was fixating on her a little too much and tried to place my attention elsewhere. But no matter whether I was doing pushups or thinking through air combat scenarios or wondering what Kitty was doing, my thoughts kept coming back to the princess, like a homing pigeon returning to its own nest.

Aside from the books, my only source of entertainment was staring out the window, and I did so for hours. Young knights trained in the courtyard below each morning and I studied them, making notes on their techniques with sword, spear, and mace so I could report them to headquarters. In my boredom, I even took a long candlestick off the table and practiced some of their moves.

In the distance, off in the mountains, I could see the dragons and their riders training for the next phase of the challenge, whatever that might be. Yet they were so far away they looked like birds in the distance. The worst part was I knew Essa was training, too. And I knew if I were there, I could help her.

As I paced and pondered and muttered curses to myself and gazed at the dragons far away out the window, my predicament came into greater focus. The queen had placed Essaphine as my protector and escort. The princess could either open all the doors in the kingdom for me or leave me locked in this room. She could probably even tire of me and order me killed. I had to win her back, to gain her trust and keep it. To do that, I had to have something to offer her. But the only thing I could think of was the very thing she'd rejected—help in winning the challenge.

And yet when I offered that help, it must have seemed an empty gesture. I was supposed to be a reporter, not the greatest ace in URA history. I couldn't reveal that secret; to do so would mean death. But I needed something, some gift, some gesture, that would demonstrate my goodwill was genuine and the help I offered was real. And halfway through the third day, the solution came to me.

The more I thought over my plan, the more convinced I became that it might work. When Essaphine saw what I had to offer, saw how I could help her—saw that I was in fact the only one in the kingdom who *could* help her—she was bound to trust me.

And so, I waited for nightfall.

Dinner arrived, a bowl of delicious, creamy fish soup, biscuits, and a salad of greens, along with a pot of strong tea, which partially assuaged the ache in my head from the lack of coffee.

I ate well, wrapped up the biscuits in a napkin, and added them to my oilskin bag. Beyond the open window, the sunlight was fading, bathing the world in the cool purple of twilight. I leaned out the window and peered down along the stone wall of the palace. Though stones jutted out at regular intervals, the wall was utterly sheer. The wind blew hard enough to push the hair from my face and furl the banners on the turrets.

Step one of my plan: climb down this tower in the dark. Steal a horse. Escape the palace.

I gazed again at the dragons wheeling in the distance.

"I sure wish I had a plane," I muttered. Then I sat down to wait for night to come.

Two hours later, I clung to the side of the castle wall, a chill wind buffeting me, darkness obscuring my vision. Peering out the window, it had seemed that the stone face of the palace was uneven, with plenty of jutting stones. Once I stepped out, however, it became plain that each foothold was no more than two inches deep. Already, my hands ached and my calves trembled as I fought to hang on. To make matters worse, the cloak I wore fluttered annoyingly, catching the wind like a sail, and I cursed, wishing I had my leather flight jacket on instead.

When I thought of the deadly drop below, my heart thudded fast and my hands trembled. And yet I found a smile growing on my lips. This was an ability I'd taught myself in pilot training, a special sort of alchemy. For me, adrenaline became fuel, electricity. The closer I was to death, the stronger and more alive I felt.

Kitty had once suggested I might benefit from visiting a psychotherapist.

I was perhaps a third of the way down when the rain started, just a drizzle at first, then a pelting torrent that made the rocks slick. I'd made vertical dives locked in the claws of fire-breathing beasties and my heart hadn't pounded this much. But having gone this far, there was no going back up. My hands and arms burned. My calf muscles trembled. I lost track of how many times I nearly slipped and fell to my death. But through it all, I kept moving methodically downward.

I must've blacked out, because the next thing I knew, my boots were hitting the ground—terra firma!—and I fell to my knees, overcome by gratitude that I hadn't ended my spy career as a red splatter.

But there was no time to celebrate. I had to be back by dawn, and there were many miles of travel ahead of me.

The good news was, since the tower my room was in abutted the palace's outer walls, I'd been able to shift to my right as I descended and come down not inside the courtyard, but outside the perimeter of the walls. It was a security flaw. They should never have put me in that room—but doubtless, no one imagined their prisoner-guest would be foolish enough to scale down two hundred feet of sheer rockface.

Before darkness fell, I'd looked down at the streets and alleyways from above, sketching a mental map of the city. Now, I traced my way along the path I'd planned out. I guessed it was around nine PM, and light shone from the windows of pubs and inns and houses, illuminating my way, though I kept to the shadows as much as I could with the hood of my cloak pulled up. I very much doubted anyone had seen me climbing down the wall in the rain. Still, I couldn't quite shake the feeling that someone was watching me. I glanced over my shoulder, but each time I saw nothing but empty streets and drizzle.

As I passed a stable behind an inn, I paused. Having a horse would make my task much easier. But stealing one presented its own risks. I might get caught. I didn't know what the punishment for horse-thieving was in Maethalia, and I wasn't keen on finding out.

So, I hurried ahead on foot. At the city gate, a pair of guards sat in a booth at the bottom of the tower, playing cards and sipping from bottles, paying little attention to the few people passing by. I held my breath as I strode by the booth, but they didn't give me even a single glance.

Once outside the city wall, I stopped pretending to be on a casual stroll and began jogging. The rain let up and stopped and the clouds peeled back, revealing a canopy of stars so brilliant I nearly stopped to gawk up at them. The night sky here was far different than in Ironberg, where the factories and foundries and power plants kicked out smog night and day. The stars shone like scattered diamonds against a sheet of black velvet, and I repeatedly found myself tilting my head back to look at them before admonishing myself. This was a race against the dawn; there was no time for stargazing.

By my calculations, it was at least eight miles along the coast to the place where my crashed plane lay. I'd been a middling track runner in high school and had kept up with it through flight academy. I'd still dash off three or four miles when I could, just to keep in shape. But eight miles was further than I'd gone in a while. And I'd have to keep a keen eye out for the spot where the Silver Wraith waited, a place I wasn't sure I'd recognize in daylight, much less in darkness.

Still, I felt good as the miles dwindled beneath my churning feet. The air held the sweet musk of rain and sea. The trees and grasses swayed, and a warm wind dried my clothes. The moon came out, nearly full and bright as a searchlight, and I ran with a feeling of triumph in my heart, as if my crazy plan might actually work.

At last, off to my right, I spotted a familiar landmark—a large elm tree—and my steps wound down to a halt. The tree was so huge it would have taken five men holding hands to make a ring around it. From the looks of it, the thing had been struck by lightning at some time in the past. Its trunk was blackened, and it was bisected into two halves, and yet it still lived. I remembered leaning against it when I'd finished my climb up from the beaches below. This was the place. Now, I—

What was that?

A sound, like a foot scuffing on dirt, turned me around, and I squinted into the darkness, listening. A full minute must have passed, but I saw no movement in the woods or on the path behind me.

Finally satisfied, I turned and waded into the grass, making my way toward the scorched tree and past it, to the edge of the cliff. The sea spread before me, its tranquil, white-capped waves glistening in the moonlight. And yet, in the distance I heard a low rumble like thunder. Mortars. Bombs. The front. The night was so clear I almost imagined I could see the Island of Dorhane, where the knights of Maethalia and the soldiers of the URA battled one another night and day. Perhaps my fellow aces were there even now, participating in a nighttime bombing run.

And my little brother, Joey. He'd enlisted and was supposed to be shipping out just as I left. Was he in those trenches now, facing the spearmen and the flaming arrows and the dark mages of Maethalia?

But there was no time to worry about him. Below and to the right, a black gap in the cliff face grinned up at me. All around it, waves burst off jagged rocks in explosions of foam. In that cave, the Silver Wraith waited—and that's where I had to go.

I dreaded another precarious descent, so I felt relieved when I found a narrow path leading down to the water. From there, I made my way along the rocky shoreline until it ended in a great slab of dark stone that marked the edge of the cave entrance. When I'd left the plane here, the tail had still been visible from this point. It was hard to tell in the darkness, but it looked like the plane was gone now, and I felt a pang of worry that it had perhaps washed away or had been broken up by the crashing waves. But I'd come this far. I had to know for sure.

Hopping from stone to stone, I made my way toward the sea cave. Waves crashed on the rocks around me, sending up great plumes of freezing spray.

I leapt onto a small rock at the same time a large swell came. The water rose to my knees, and I felt the push then suck of the water, its flow almost enough to wash me off the rock. I crouched, steadying myself, and the swell passed, leaving my heart beating fast in its wake. I just had to keep my footing, that was the main thing. Get knocked off these rocks, and I'd be washed into the heaving ocean, never to be seen again, or else dashed into the cliff face.

I tried to focus, to concentrate all my energy on each leap and each landing. But my mind kept wandering.

I thought of Essaphine and wondered what she'd think if I disappeared from my room and never returned. *She'd think nothing. You're her enemy. You mean less to her than a chunk of gristle stuck between her dragon's teeth.*

I thought of Kitty.

What was she doing now? Was she crying? Mourning? Broken up with grief at my loss? Or had she just resumed the life she'd had before me, nights at the dance halls, days on the reporter's beat, glamorous dinner parties on the arms of rich men...

No. She'd be crushed that I was gone. At least I hoped so. Not only for the sake of my own ego, but also so that her editor wouldn't try to contact Hoatan to reschedule her visit to Maethalia. If that happened, I'd be finished...

I jumped again, but another swell came, its crest slapping me like an icy hand, disrupting my landing, then clawing at me, trying to wash me away as I clung onto the rock with both hands.

I scrambled back to my feet after it receded.

"Focus, dammit," I grumbled to myself. I looked down to find my hands were bloody, cut by barnacles. My clothes were soaked and I was shivering. The cave entrance still loomed a good fifty yards away. I looked back the way I came, thinking that this was my chance to turn back. It would be far better to return soaked and bedraggled but alive than to be drowned on this godforsaken beach. But I'd come this far...

On I pressed, redoubling my pace, jumping from rock to rock without pausing to think. I found my rhythm, and my constant exertion chased away the chill that had left me shivering. Soon, I was passing beneath the edge of the cave mouth, leaving the moonlight behind. I paused on a particularly large, flat stone, took the flashlight from my pack, and shone it into the dark. To my surprise, light shone right back at me, making me shade my eyes. It was the Silver Wraith's reflective fuselage. The cave wasn't as deep as it had seemed, and the plane had been pushed to the back of it. Both her wings on the left side had been snapped off, and she sat pinned to the bottom by the heavy engine in her nose while her tail rested against a stone shelf, jostled by the waves. It was better luck than I'd hoped for. With renewed energy, I bounded forward, stone to stone, until I was standing on the rocky shelf where the plane rested.

The first objective was almost comically easy. A spring-loaded clip was attached to the tail, which was right in front of me. I unclipped it and put it in my bag. The next task would be far more difficult, and to do it, I'd need the tool kit under the pilot's seat—which was now beneath the surface of the water.

Better not to think too much about it, I thought, as I stripped my shirt off and set my bag aside toward the back of the stone shelf. *Just jump in and go.*

My body convulsed as I hit the cold water. As I surfaced, my mouth salty with brine, a swell shifted the plane. The edge of the cockpit banged into me, leaving my head aching and ringing. I gulped a breath and dipped under again, groping blindly in the dark water under the seat for the hatch where the small tool bag was stowed. Somehow, I got the bag loose and, cradling it under my arm, brought it back and clambered up onto the stone shelf. I took out a utility knife and turned back to the plane, still catching my breath.

For the next step of my plan, I'd have to cut through the doped, painted fabric of the plane's fuselage, remove one of the long aluminum stays that gave the plane structure, and somehow get out of the cave again with it.

I hazarded a glance toward the cave entrance. It looked smaller than when I'd first come through it. For a moment, I stood staring, perplexed. Then I realized what it meant. The tide was coming in. If I didn't work fast, I'd be trapped in here and drown. Fantastic.

Despite my aching head, cut hands, and shivering body, I moved with renewed purpose, locating one of the aluminum stays and cutting through the fabric along it. After that, I used a hammer and screwdriver to get it loose from the wooden ribs that held the stays together. When I was finished, I held a fifteen-foot-long, squared-off aluminum tube. I slung the oilskin bag containing the clip over my shoulder and looked at my silver steed once more.

"So long, old friend," I told her.

Then, holding the aluminum stay like a spear, I began making my way, rock-to-rock, back toward the entrance of the cave. The tide had risen so high I had to duck when I came out, and I tried not to think about what would have happened if I'd been any slower in my task.

My return trip along the beach and up the cliff-face path was a blur, but I somehow found myself back up on the path where I'd first met Essaphine. The moon, nearly set, hid behind the trees, and I had to use the flashlight to locate the road. Once on it, I began trudging ahead, the stay making a metallic ringing sound as I dragged it along the path with me. The miles passed in a weary fugue until, at last, Issastar and the parapets of Charcain rose before me, dark shapes against the night sky.

I must have looked more dead than alive as I made my way back through the city gates, but the guards who had been playing cards earlier could still be seen through the window of the guard house, asleep in their chairs.

Another security weakness to note...

As I passed through the gates, I heard a footstep behind me and turned to look back. A man in a dark green cloak with three long scars along the left side of his face strolled behind me, perhaps two hundred feet distant, one hand on the hilt of his sword. Could this be the person I'd heard following me in the night?

I felt a pang of worry, but the man moved without a sense of urgency, and he seemed to pay me no mind as he turned down an alleyway and disappeared. I exhaled in relief and kept moving.

I took a few wrong turns before locating my destination. Sunlight had begun melting into the eastern horizon, and the streets were waking up with activity when at last I came to the door of the blacksmith shop and knocked. I expected a dwarf. Instead, a huge man opened the door. He had black hair, a thick black beard, dark skin, and a hard expression in his eyes as he looked at me.

"Sorry. I may have the wrong place. Is Clua here?"

The man glowered at me once more, then turned his head and bellowed into the room behind him.

"Clua! A customer."

There must have been living quarters attached to the shop, for I glimpsed a kitchen behind the man, with a pot of food cooking over a fire. The smell of it made my stomach lurch with hunger. Then the dwarf girl was there, elbowing past the big man. When she saw me, her eyes widened.

"What...?" she said, looking me up and down.

I'd forgotten how I must look—wet, dirty, cut up by barnacles... I felt a drizzle of dried blood in my hair where I'd banged my head. But none of that mattered now.

I held out the aluminum stay.

"Clua. I need you to help me save the princess's life," I said.

15
ESSA

I was at the Hatchery, saddling Othura for the day's challenge when Ollie found me. "We need to talk about your reporter."

"Ha," I said, cinching up a strap. "You mean my prisoner?"

"He escaped."

I wheeled on Ollie. "What? His door was guarded."

Ollie held up a hand, trying to still me. "Don't blame the guards. He climbed down last night."

"Impossible!" I exclaimed. "A squirrel couldn't have climbed down from there."

"And what's more, he climbed back up just before dawn," Ollie grinned at my shocked reaction. "It would appear he's extremely spry for a scribe."

"But... why? Where did he go?"

"I'm not clear on that yet, but you know me. I have ways of finding out. Of course, the simplest way would be to ask him."

"So ask," I said, turning back to work on the saddle.

"I thought perhaps you might like to ask," Ollie suggested. "After all, he seemed to take a shine to you during your tour of the city, from what I've heard."

That was one of the infuriating and valuable things about the Torouman. They had spies everywhere.

"I do not wish to see him," I snapped, hating the petulance in my voice.

"That's understandable, but your mother charged you with him. And just yesterday she was asking Hoatan how Kit was liking our city. I put him off for now, but..."

I sighed. Hoatan was the head of the Torouman order. Ollie's superior. Crossing Hoatan could get Ollie in trouble, just as it would be trouble for me to disobey or lie to my Irska. I didn't want Ollie to face punishment on my account.

Ollie is right, Othura said in my mind.

You always take his side! I shot back.

Because he's always right, Othura said.

I shook my head, irritated.

"You need to let the reporter out," Ollie concluded. "At least for the day. Let him attend the challenge. Your mother will see him out and about, and then you can do with him what you wish."

Those last words sent a cascade of impure thoughts through my mind. Stars, I needed to find a boyfriend. It had been a long time since Braimar...

But Ollie was probably right, as usual.

"Very well," I sighed.

Rohree met me outside the foreigner's door.

"Your Majesty," she curtsied. "Forgive me for being here. I've left him for the guards to care for the past few days, just as you said. But when they told me what state he was in this morning... he came back at dawn, you see—"

"I know," I grumbled, reaching for the door handle.

"Um—he's bathing," Rohree said, stopping me.

I frowned. "Well, get him out. I have plans for him today. What's this?"

She held up a bundle of cloth.

"New clothes for him. The ones he came back in were ruined, cut up, and bloody. And can you believe he climbed down and back up? I hardly think any of the Skrathan could pull off a feat like that."

I gritted my teeth. "If he could do it, any Skrathan could." I took the bundle from her. "I'll deliver these."

"He is in the bath."

"So you said," I replied. "Thank you, Rohree. That will be all."

She sucked her teeth. "It's improper for you to go in there while he's indisposed, Your Majesty. I mean, I hardly blame you. He is quite the specimen. Just see you don't cause an international incident. I once heard of a—"

"That will be all," I said again, and Rohree curtsied and turned to go—though I had no doubt she'd double back soon enough to put her ear to the door. That was the way of life in court.

I entered the foreigner's room, locking the door behind me and placing the key in my pocket to prevent another escape.

Inside, it was cozy and humid, the air infused with scents of mint and eucalyptus.

The poet lay in a copper bathtub, a washcloth over his eyes.

"Thanks, Rohree," he called when he heard me enter. "Be a dear and leave the clothes on the chair, would ya?"

I did drop the clothes onto the chair, then I meandered slowly to the tub.

"You seem awfully comfortable giving orders," I said. "One would think *you're* the princess."

The poet snatched the cloth from his face and looked at me, blinking. His hands disappeared into the water, and I imagined he was covering himself, although the suds made the act unnecessary. Still, I found myself wondering what his body looked like under that water. His face soon distracted me from my musing, though. Removing the cloth had revealed a nasty bruise and gash on his forehead.

"Your Majesty," he said, composing himself.

"I heard you went on a little jaunt last night."

"News travels fast here," he said with a tight smile.

"Where did you go?"

"I visited your friend Clua."

That derailed me for a moment. It wasn't at all what I'd been expecting to hear.

"You risked your life scaling two hundred feet down a sheer stone wall in the rain to go and *visit Clua*?"

"Well, the door was locked," he said.

He was playing the wise-fool, thinking himself clever. Fine. I'd play his game.

I pointed at his face.

"Did Clua do that to you?"

He chuckled. "No. I bumped my head."

"And if I talk to Clua, she'll have the same story?"

He shrugged. "I can't imagine why she wouldn't."

Could he be trying to woo Clua? Why else would he risk his life to sneak out and meet her? The thought left an uncomfortable tightness in my chest.

My eyes narrowed. "And when you scaled down the tower, did Clua catch you at the bottom?"

"No," he said. "I did that all on my own."

"Why?" I demanded.

"She and I are preparing a surprise for you, if you must know."

"A surprise for me?" I repeated dumbly. "What is it?"

He leaned on the edge of the bathtub, revealing a surprisingly muscled arm.

"If I told you," he said slowly, "it wouldn't be a surprise."

I stared at him for a long moment, letting Othura's intuition flow through me. I felt her sniffing the air, plumbing as far as she could into the stranger's mind.

After a moment, her voice came to me: *He speaks the truth. But he is hiding something. He is more than he appears.*

That was obvious. Whoever heard of a poet who could scale towers? I crossed my arms, watching him.

His gaze met mine, then, after a moment, he looked away, clearing his throat. "If we don't have other plans today, I thought it might be nice to meet the prelate."

These were the last words I'd expected to hear from him, and they hit me like a slap of cold water.

"The prelate? Prelate Kortoi?"

"Sure," he said, giving me what, for most women, must have been a disarming smile.

But though I was on guard before, the mention of Prelate Kortoi truly made my hackles rise.

"What do you know of Prelate Kortoi?"

He lay back in the bath, put his feet up on the edge. "Not

much, really. I've just heard talk of him back in Ironberg. Heard he was a fellow I should meet."

"If you don't know about him, I'll give you a primer. Kortoi is the chief of the Gray Brotherhood, head priest to the Gods of the Void. His Lacunae are dreaded warriors and his Brothers are mages powerful in the dark arts."

"Gods of the Void." Kit yawned. "That sounds ominous."

I found his casual air maddening.

"The Gods of the Void—and the power their priests possess—are indeed ominous. They've probably killed thousands of URA soldiers since the start of the war. That's why I wonder that you should be so excited to meet him."

"You don't seem to like this prelate much," Kit said. "What's the problem? Do his gods not play nicely with your gods—the Earth Mother and Star Father?"

I glared at him. "Kortoi's gods are as old as time and as hungry as the worms of the earth that eat the flesh of the dead. The gods of the dragon riders are gods of sun and rain, plants and flowers. Earth and life. The gods of the void stand for eternal oblivion. Both exist. Both are real. Both are necessary. We require Kortoi to maintain communion with those dark forces. To keep equilibrium. It's true, there are times when he and my mother are at odds over certain issues. The priorities of the spirits of the abyss are not the same as those of the living. But Kortoi is loyal, if that's what you're asking. And he is certainly no friend to the URA."

Kit scratched his chin. He'd been clean-shaven when he arrived, but the stubble there was growing thicker—which lent his fine features a ruggedness that suited him infuriatingly well.

"I don't have to meet him. It makes no difference to me," he said.

I sighed. "I'll introduce you to Kortoi. You should know that dragons aren't the only formidable power in Maethalia. But we have other plans first. Get out and get dressed."

I tossed a towel to him. He caught it deftly, then paused, waiting for me to turn away. When I didn't, he smiled.

"Are you going to watch me, Princess?"

"If I want to, I can. This is my kingdom."

I expected him to give me a snappy retort. Instead, he stood. I glimpsed strong vein-lined arms, square shoulders, chiseled abs—and a manhood that made my breath hitch in my chest before I spun, turning to face away from him.

I hadn't expected that he'd really stand up...

My face flushed, my heart was beating nearly out of my chest, as I stood there, listening to the soft sound of the towel caressing the moisture off his body.

"I'll wait outside," I muttered, bolting for the door.

My mind should have been on the day's trial as I rode Sisha out of the city and up the trail toward The Cauldron. Instead, it was on the poet. On his arms, which were wrapped around me and his body, pressed against my back. Arms I'd glimpsed slick and moist and hot from the bath...

Stop, I chastised myself. *Focus.*

Othura's presence nosed its way into my mind. *What did you expect, making him ride with you again?*

I expected to tease him. To drive him *crazy. Not myself.*

But apparently, distaste and distrust didn't prevent attraction. Good to know.

A warm feeling of amusement flooded over me. Othura was laughing at me.

"Shut up," I grumbled.

"What?" the poet said.

"Oh. I was just talking to Othura. Sorry, sometimes I forget if I'm speaking out loud or not."

"I always thought that was a faerie tale," Kit said. "The whole dragon / rider psychic connection thing."

"It is," I said. "And faeries are meticulous historians, so of course it's accurate."

"Right..." he muttered.

We topped the hill, and the Cauldron appeared before us. Most of the other riders and their dragons were already there. Others were soaring in now, alighting on the lakeshore. Riders shouted greetings. Dragons, excited for the competition, snarled and snapped at one another. Othura was there, too, curled up on a broad, flat rock like a snake sunning herself.

"Remind me why we're coming in on horseback while all the other riders are arriving on their dragons?" Kit asked.

"Normally, I would ride Othura up here," I said. "It's much faster. But foreigners can't ride dragons, remember? It's forbidden. And since you've proven untrustworthy, I figured I'd better accompany you."

"Untrustworthy? Me?" he feigned hurt.

I turned in the saddle and glared at him again.

"Yes. And until you tell me truthfully the reason you snuck out, I shall continue to hold you under suspicion. Is that clear?"

"Clear as glass," he teased in a low whisper that reminded me how close we were—mere inches separating our lips. I turned away again fast.

The Thurn horn sounded at that moment, signaling for the riders to get ready, and I coaxed Sisha into a gallop. "See. You've made me late," I snapped.

"What's today's trial?" he shouted over the clatter of hooves.

"The Thimble Race," I called back to him.

"Is it as dangerous as the last one?"

"More dangerous," I said, reigning Sisha in and dismounting.

"What do you have to do?" he asked.

But I was already jogging over to Othura, running up her outstretched tail as if it were a ramp and dropping into the saddle.

"I'll tell you all about it afterwards—if I survive," I said. Then Othura leapt, pumping her wings, and we were in the sky.

16
CHARLIE

My journey to the sea cave and back had left me beaten and exhausted, but I still felt illuminated with electricity as I watched Essaphine wing skyward to join the flock of dragons.

"She's brave. You have to give her that," a voice said, and I turned to find the eunuch, Ollie, coming to stand at my side.

"She is," I agreed, as together we watched the dragons diminish into the distance.

"But then, you're no stranger to adventure yourself, are you?" Ollie asked. "I heard about your night out."

I studied Ollie's face, but it showed no sign of emotion, good or ill.

"Word really does travel fast in this place," I said.

"There is a saying. There are three things you can never keep a secret from: yourself, the wind, and the Torouman. And of course, Clua went to me immediately. She'd never do anything concerning Essa without my blessing."

He must've seen the look of alarm on my face because he clapped me on the back.

"Don't worry. Your secret is safe with me. Anything done to help the princess is a virtue in my book. Still, I have questions. Did no one help you get out of the castle? Did you truly scale down the wall?"

"I did," I said.

"And where did you get the items you gave Clua? I've not seen metal like that before."

"From the wreck of the plane I arrived in," I said.

The eunuch arched an eyebrow. "I thought that was lost at sea."

"It is now," I lied. "It had been lodged in the rocks, but when I pulled the stay free, it fell into deeper water."

Ollie nodded thoughtfully. "Why take such a risk? You could have fallen in. You could have been caught—and the queen's guards are far less understanding than I. Why risk yourself to help a princess you barely know?"

I couldn't tell him the truth. *I'm helping her because she's weak. Because she's the worst rider you have. Because if she leads the Skrathan, I'm pretty sure we can crush them.* But I had no other excuse ready. Damned if I wasn't a terrible spy.

"Unless..." Ollie went on slowly. "Unless you're in love with her."

My eyebrows went up and I blinked, my mind leaping to catch up with his words. Part of me wanted to laugh in his face at the suggestion. Me? In love with Essaphine? The girl had been nothing but demeaning and insulting ever since I'd arrived in Maethalia. She'd kicked me, tied me up, imprisoned me. And yet, I found my heart beating surprisingly fast at his suggestion.

"In love. With—with her?" I stammered.

Ollie gave a low laugh. "Well, the attraction isn't hard to see for those who are looking. And, of course, the princess has her charms."

The gears in my mind were turning. The Torouman was shrewd. He'd need an explanation why I was helping Essa. Perhaps being in love with her was the cover I needed. I blinked, trying to wrap my head around the new role. "Is she not in some sort of relationship?"

Ollie shook his head. "Others have stayed away from her over the years, perhaps because she isn't whole, or because she might become queen one day and must be sanctified— or because they were simply scared of her. All except Braimar."

Braimar. The green-haired bastard. I didn't like him when I first met him. Suddenly, I liked him even less.

"The two of them dated?"

Ollie cocked his head. "Dating isn't a word that is used in Maethalia. But there was a courtship between them when more of Essa's siblings remained alive, and it seemed as if she might not become the queen's heir. Some even hoped they might marry and solidify the bond between the crown and the Gray Brotherhood."

"The Gray Brotherhood. That's Prelate Kortoi," I said.

Ollie smiled. "Ah, you have done your homework. Yes. Braimar is Kortoi's nephew, which, in the traditions of our people, means that Kortoi is his durram, his teacher and mentor."

"And the bond between Kortoi and the queen needs solidifying?"

Ollie glanced over his shoulder. There, against a cliff face, stood a tower of stone so like the rock it abutted that I'd never noticed it before. In the tower, there was a balcony where a host of finely dressed people sat. It was the perfect vantage point from which to watch any contest taking place in The Cauldron, and, though it was hard to tell from here, I felt sure one of the spectators seated there must be the queen.

"Neither side acknowledges any animosity," Ollie said quietly. "But Kortoi and the dark gods he serves have their own purposes, that is known. The queen and her allies work constantly to keep the Gray Brothers from becoming too powerful. And yet, the crown requires their Lacunae knights and their dark mages to maintain the war effort on Dorhane. It is a complex dance."

"I guess so," I said, rubbing the growing stubble on my chin. It explained the instructions to report via Kortoi. Perhaps this prelate was working against the queen more actively than Ollie knew... "And whose side are you on?" I asked.

The eunuch looked offended. "The queen's, certainly. The Gray Brotherhood is all about negation. No sweets. No sex. No butter. No song. They care for nothing but the secrets to be found in black, starless skies and beings who whisper at the bottoms of wells. Demons, phantoms, and incubi. Their path offers power, certainly, but they're far too morose for my taste."

"Sounds like it," I said. "Still, I'd like to meet this Kortoi sometime. Newspaper readers love a good boogie man."

Ollie looked troubled. "I'll talk to Hoatan. If he thinks it's a good idea, perhaps it can be arranged. But if it does happen, don't take the meeting lightly. The Brotherhood has strange powers. They've been known to hypnotize the unwary—and worse."

I nodded. "Thanks. I'll be careful."

But my mind was back on Essaphine again. The last dragons had disappeared over the edge of the Cauldron and were out of sight.

"Tell me about this challenge," I said.

"The Thimble Race? It is one of the greatest challenges riders face. According to legend, two riders—an Irska and his second—once fell in love with a royal seamstress, and they were at odds over who would marry her. The queen, rather than doing the sensible thing and asking the girl who she preferred, devised a task. She placed a thimble on the highest peak of the Yrdam Mountains. The first rider to return with it would get the hand of the seamstress. Both riders set out from the Cauldron in a vicious race through the mountains, each using all his powers to reach the thimble first and return to here to claim his bride."

"Which of them won?" I asked.

Ollie chuckled. "Neither. Their dragons were found at the bottom of Bellu Gorge, their claws buried in each other's bellies, their jaws locked onto each other's throats. They say the bones are still there, turned to stone now, if anyone cares to risk their lives to clamber down and look for them."

I gave a low whistle. "And that's what Essaphine's doing now?" I asked, my eyes on the empty sky where the dragons had disappeared.

Ollie nodded gravely. "There are enough thimbles for each rider now, but not every rider lives long enough to retrieve theirs and bring it back. I don't know if the god of your people answers prayers, reporter. But if he does—and if you truly care for Essaphine—now would be the time to pray."

17
ESSA

I could feel their eyes on me as we flew out of the Cauldron. Kit's. Mother's. Ollie's. All the noble court who'd gathered to see us off... All of them wondering if I, in particular, would make it back alive. Their attention made me nervous, and worse, it annoyed me.

But once we'd soared through the gap, into the mountains, there were no more stares. No more pity. No more judgment. There was just the wind in my hair and the rhythmic thump of Othura's wings, the slanting sun glistening off the snowcapped peaks and the stones and treetops and white-foaming brooks that shot past below.

The wind is ours, Othura said in my mind, and I smiled.

The wind is ours, I thought back to her, our own little mantra.

No matter the danger, no matter the difficulty or the odds we faced, any time we took wing together, joy awaited us. All the nerves and worries shrunk into a pin-prick point, like a mote of dust, and were lost behind us, until there was only me and Othura and the sky.

Fish leapt and flashed in the stream below. Mountain goats standing on their ledges brayed as our shadow passed over them. Kelmoon, the great mountain eagles that were the royal bird of our house, ceased their gliding and darted away as we approached. I smiled. It was a beautiful spring day, we were flying, and I was free.

That is, except for the many dragons and their riders who wanted to kill me.

No sooner had the thought passed through my mind than a great, orange-bellied sagittan shot out from behind one of the nearby mountain peaks in an explosion of snow, its massive jaws open, its fore-talons grasping. Instinctively, Othura banked away to create space, then looped back, ready to fight—though her odds of overcoming the much larger sagittan in a grappling contest were grim. Instead of attacking with tooth and claw, the sagittan took a heaving breath and blew fire. Othura pulled up sharply, bringing her body vertical so that her belly and wings shielded me from the worst of the flames. Still, the heat was so much that it nearly made me pass out and lose my grip on the saddle horn. I immediately smelled burned hair as the wisps that poked out of my helmet caught fire.

The dragon flew at us, all slashing claws and gnashing teeth, but Othura folded her wings and banked right. It would have been ideal to roll—if I could go upside down. As it was, we dropped sideways, evading the attack, then Othura popped her wings open again, swooping away.

Her voice snarled in my mind: *That traitorous, faithless, coward...*

Traditionally, in the Thimble Race, dragons did not use their greater powers—fire, ice, lightning, wind or venom. The course itself, winding among mountain peaks at high speed, was dangerous enough, and dragons usually confined their attacks to jostling one another, knocking wings or occasionally hazarding a claw slash or a bite. To attack us with fire was bold and underhanded. That other riders were so eager to knock me out of the challenge showed how certain they were that Laynine would end up as Irska, and how desperate they were to win her favor.

But if they were willing to use fire...

Take them out, I told Othura.

She waited until the sagittan was banking, then swooped toward them and breathed wind. It came out with a hiss, a blast of air strong enough to form a whirlwind. The enemy dragon was nearly sideways as it turned, and the wind caught its lower wing and twisted it, causing it to crumple. With a roar of surprise and fury, it dropped. Flailing desperately with its one good wing to slow its fall, it spiraled downward and hit the slope below, sending up a mighty puff of snow.

"Yes!" I shouted.

Big dragon, big crater, Othura said with a dark laugh.

You're brilliant.

You can say that once we've returned with a thimble, she said, turning to get us back on course.

Her words sobered me. Taking out one opponent was fine. But there were a hundred more miles to fly and over ninety more dragons waiting to take us out. I'd have felt better if Lure, Dagar, and Pocha were with me. But since we'd gotten a late start, they were probably far ahead by now. We'd have to make it on our own.

Othura's intuition tingled suddenly within me, and I glanced back to find three riders flying in a V formation coming up behind us—probably trying to decide whether we were worth attacking. Then suddenly, like a flock of star-tled birds, they banked and scattered. I craned my neck to look back over my shoulder and immediately saw why.

A huge green dragon was approached, moving closer with each beat of its broad wings. It was an ugly and mighty beast with two horned heads and two sets of wicked, protruding teeth. A geminus. And I knew too well whose dragon it was.

Braimar was coming.

If he comes at me with a lance, be ready to dive. Maybe we can find a low canyon Zaman is too big to fly through, I told Othura.

I didn't have to tell her to be careful. Two heads are better than one, they say—and that was especially true when one of the heads could grab you with ten-inch teeth while the other roasted you with fire.

No words came back from Othura, but I felt her agree-ment, plus something else. Anger. Determination. A hard-ening of her will. Part of it was the protectiveness she always felt for me, but that wasn't all. Zaman and Othura had nearly become mates at the same time Braimar was wooing me. There was a lot of history there. A lot of bad blood.

We might die in this race. But we were both determined that it would not be Braimar's doing.

They were closer now, just a few dragon lengths back.

Get ready, I told Othura, adjusting my grip on my saddle horn.

But instead of coming at us with lance and claw, Zaman came up beside me, giving us a wide berth.

He wants to talk, Othura said, her distaste clear.

Riders could communicate with their dragons using their minds, and dragons spoke with one another telepathically, too. Hence, riders could communicate with one another using their dragons as intermediaries. But dragons did not speak human language. Their communications actually came in the form of feelings, impulses, and nudges to direct a rider's attention. With time, this communication became so natural and precise that it felt like words, so that when Othura and I communicated now, my mind automatically translated it into something that felt very much like human speech. But at its heart, dragon communication was much more intimate than that. And neither Othura nor I were eager to have that sort of intimacy with Zaman and Braimar. I could feel Othura's reluctance as she shared Braimar's thoughts with me:

Hey, Little Bird.

Eat shite, I shot back.

I felt his amusement. *Come on. Let's fly together. Like old times.*

I fly alone.

So I see. Where are your friends?

I don't know. Up ahead. I got a late start. But I'm sure if you attack me, they'll show up fast enough.

Why would I attack you?

I don't know. Perhaps to solidify a pact with Laynine? Most of the riders seem to be clamoring to show their allegiance to her.

A great horn of a mountain peak thrust up between us, and our dragons glided apart to go around it, then drifted back together. I also saw, out of the corner of my eye, the three dragons I'd noticed before were coming up behind us again. There were two more up ahead that we were closing in on. Any of the five could attack us at any time. I couldn't let Braimar distract me. We had to remain vigilant.

Can you blame the other Skrathan for siding with Laynine? Braimar asked. *Akmerus are powerful dragons. Who would want to face off against Tryce and his lightning?*

I must, if I want to live, I told him.

Not necessarily. There might be another way.

And what would that be?

Your aunt spoke to you of it.

What? Run away and live alone and in exile somewhere?

No. Not alone, he said. He wore a rider's helmet, and though I couldn't see his eyes, I knew they were looking at me, the same deep green as Zaman's scales.

In that moment of distraction, as I pondered Braimar's words, the dragons behind us shot ahead, and the two ahead of us doubled back, closing on us in a coordinated attack.

Othura waited until the last instant, then banked and wheeled, darting out of the way so that the dragon before us and the one behind us slammed into one another. They fell in a tangle of wings. Turning hard, we came up behind one of our other pursuers, a big brown capran. Othura caught the end of its tail, chomping down on it so hard the dragon shrieked.

Ahead, mighty Zaman caught the neck of one of the attacking dragons in his jaws and worried it, shaking the rider off. She fell, screaming. Zaman's second head blasted another dragon with a tremendous plume of fire that left its wings smoking and its rider howling in pain. The remaining attacker retreated, dipping toward the ground fast.

Meanwhile, Othura still held onto the tail of the big capran. It kept turning, trying to snap at us with its jaws, but Othura would not let go, so both dragons kept swirling in circles. The other rider—I recognized her as a female from the noble house Cardum—tried to jab me with her lance. I tried reaching for my sword to parry her strikes, but the centrifugal force of our circling was too strong. Let go of the saddle horn, and I'd be flung off. So, all I could do was lean forward or backward to dodge the lance tip. Once, twice, thrice I made her miss, until the fourth jab caught me in the shoulder of my missing arm. Pain shot through me like boiled water being poured into my veins, and I cried out.

The feeling was transmitted to Othura, who opened her mouth in a roar of agony, letting go of our opponent's tail. Free now, the capran turned and pumped its wings, going for Othura's neck. I saw it coming, saw what was about to happen—but I was powerless to stop it. With a lance, I could have struck the capran in the head, defended Othura. But I couldn't hold a lance. All I could do was watch as the capran's jagged teeth sped toward us. Then, seemingly out of nowhere, Braimar was there. His lance caught the rider in the helmet, sending her cartwheeling into the open air. Her dragon gave a hiss of alarm and dove, breaking off its attack and trying to catch his rider before she hit the ground.

Othura banked, resuming our original course, and Zaman winged up beside us.

You okay? Braimar's question came through Othura.

Of course, I shot back, although in truth I wasn't sure. My shoulder throbbed and my armpit felt soggy with blood.

We flew in silence for a few wingbeats.

What? No thank you? Braimar asked. Even through the

layers of translation, I could still feel his teasing, his flirting, even his smug self-satisfaction.

I didn't ask for your help.

And yet I offered it. That should say a lot.

It says you are arrogant and entitled.

And without my help, you would be dead.

And I'd rather be dead than accept your help again.

I leaned forward and Othura took the cue, pumping her wings, pushing us faster. A geminus like Zaman might be big and strong, but he was no match for a libran when it came to speed. We pulled away from them.

I'm just going to follow you, Little Bird, Braimar called after us. *I'll be watching.*

For a time, there was only wind and silence, mountains drifting past below and clouds drifting past above against a pale blue springtime sky. The pain in my shoulder had settled into a dull ache, and the bleeding, fortunately, seemed to have slowed. My thoughts wandered. Part of me did feel grateful to Braimar for saving my life. But there was another part that would have felt better lying broken at the bottom of a ravine than to owe gratitude to anyone—especially him.

You know who his uncle is, Othura said—as if I needed reminding that Braimar was not to be trusted.

But I'd wasted enough time thinking about him. He was behind us now, and we had a race to win.

At that moment, a shadow eclipsed the sun. I looked up

to see a huge, ocean-blue dragon emerge from a peak to our left. Laynine. Was this an ambush? I tensed, ready to break into action and fight back. But Tryce didn't swoop down and attack. Instead, he passed over us, paying us no heed.

Laynine had her thimble and was already heading back to the Cauldron.

My teeth ground together in frustration. I imagined my mother standing and applauding as her dear apprentice flew back triumphant—with me still nowhere to be seen.

That would be the entire future. Laynine crowned in glory. Me, non-existent.

Less than five weeks... that was the time I had left, assuming I survived until the challenge's final trial. The question was, what would I do with that time?

My philosophical thoughts disappeared as the shadow above us returned.

Laynine had seen us. She'd doubled back.

Othura! I warned—too late.

Tryce's triple-barbed tail whipped downward, encircling Othura's body, then yanking like a cracking whip. Othura shrieked, tumbled, and fell—and I fought to hang on without enough breath in my lungs even to scream.

18
CHARLIE

It was strange, the way I held my breath, searching the horizon for a first glimpse of Essaphine and her dragon. I told myself it was because I was standing next to Ollie, who clasped and unclasped his hands and paced continuously. I knew from my time in the pilot's barracks: nerves could be contagious.

Plus, of course, my plans depended upon the princess surviving.

Laynine was the first to return, which didn't seem to surprise anyone. Her arrival was met with polite applause, and the assembled court watched as she dismounted her dragon and walked over to the queen's box. She knelt and offered the thimble up on the palm of her hand. A white bird flew down, took the thing in its beak, and flew it up to the queen. The queen held the thimble aloft to another round of applause from the crowd.

"Your performance brings me honor, my durrah," the queen said.

"Durrah means student," Ollie whispered to me.

"Because Laynine is her niece, the queen has mentored her since she was a young girl."

"Who does the queen favor in the challenge?" I wondered aloud. "Laynine or Essaphine?"

Ollie gave me a dark look. "The queen would never answer that question. Essa would certainly say she favors Laynine. She's always been jealous of her cousin. But then, it's not uncommon for a daughter or son to feel jealous of their mother or father's durrah. And with Essa being maimed and Laynine being whole, I think their rivalry has a sharper edge than most. Still, it must be hard for the queen. She will lose either a beloved niece or a daughter."

I looked at Ollie.

"There's no way they can both survive the challenge?"

He shook his head.

"Essa is the initiator of the challenge, and Laynine is the Irska. Assuming they both make it through the challenge's trials, the final event will be a one-on-one duel—to the death."

As I processed this grim information, I looked around again, trying to channel my inner reporter and be observant.

Below and to the left of the queen's box, I noticed that several black tents had been erected, one large and three smaller.

"What are those?" I asked, pointing.

"The pavilions of the Gray Brotherhood," Ollie said. "They are made of a fabric so that the prelate and his acolytes can see out, but others can't see in.

"Ah, here comes another..."

Two dragons were coming. Ollie pointed up at them.

"That is Kramat on the dark red carcer and Romia on her black scorper, friends of Laynine's. You can identify the dragon types both by their color and by some of their physical characteristics. See the stinger on the tail of the scorper? And carcers have those crab-like foreclaws rather than the usual talons."

I jotted these facts down in my notebook, beaming inwardly at the praise my commanders would give me when I shared my intelligence report. It was also worth noting: not only did Laynine win, but her allies also came in second and third, further reinforcing how dominant she was, and underlining the need to keep her out of the top spot.

The next rider to come drew cheers and shouts from Ollie and quite a few other members of the court. It was Essaphine's friend, Lure, on their purple aran. Lure dismounted with a backflip and strode up to the foot of the queen's box with such swagger that several of the noble girls pretended to faint.

A string of riders began arriving after that. I didn't recognize any of them, and Ollie seemed to pay them little attention.

Perhaps five minutes later, a pair of dragons broke the horizon, and Ollie gave a cheer.

"That's Dagar on the gold leonin and Pocha on the teal piscean," Ollie said. "Friends of mine and Essa's."

Ollie cheered, and I clapped politely as both riders landed and presented their thimble to the queen. Then, our attention turned back to the horizon. Riders were arriving in a steady stream now—but not the princess. Ollie chewed his thumbnail.

"Often, riders are attacked along the way, or ambushed when they land to collect their thimble," he explained. "Because the course is so spread out, riders often become isolated, which makes it a perfect time for their rivals to take them out."

Already, a few of the dragons had come back riderless, and on the far side of the beach, I could hear the friend or family member of a lost rider wailing.

"Come on, Essa..." Ollie whispered, staring at the horizon.

He wasn't the only one muttering. All around us, an uneasiness seemed to have stolen over the crowd as everyone scanned the ridgelines ahead of us, waiting.

More dragons came, more riders presented their thimbles. Still, Essaphine did not appear. Footsteps approached, and I turned to find Dagar, Lure, and Pocha coming toward us.

"Did you see her out there?" Ollie asked.

Dagar shook his shaggy head. "She started behind us."

"Do friends not fly together?" I asked, the words coming out more sharply than I'd meant them to.

All three riders looked at me with surprise.

"Back home, the pilots stick together," I explained, my tone softening. "Fly in formation..."

"We fly in formation," Lure said with narrowed eyes. "But not in the Thimble Race."

"It's meant to test a Skrathan's speed," Pocha explained. "To slow down would dishonor your dragon."

"Still, some help others..." Dagar said, sounding a bit guilty as he gazed toward the mountains.

"Or attack others," Lure added.

Just then, one of the largest dragons I'd seen so far broke the horizon, a two-headed monster that I recognized from past battles. The pilots in my squadron had nick-named it Double Trouble, and it had killed several of my good friends. Just seeing it made my blood roil with hatred.

"Braimar survived," Dagar said, not sounding too pleased about it.

"Unfortunately," Lure added.

Pocha jumped up, pointing at the sky. "Essa!" she exclaimed.

I followed the gesture and saw the princess and her steed were indeed there, flying in the shadow of the much larger dragon.

"And she's with Braimar," Lure said darkly.

"Who's Braimar again?" I asked.

"Nephew of Prelate Kortoi," Ollie said. "Foremost rider of the Gray Brotherhood."

"And Essa's lover," Dagar added.

"Ex-lover," Pocha and Lure snapped at once.

I felt a strange, nervous fluttering feeling in my chest as both dragons landed and their riders dismounted and strode toward the queen. I recognized Braimar now, with his height and broad shoulders and long, green hair showing out the bottom of his helmet. I'd seen him the first day I arrived. I didn't like him then. I liked him less now.

Essaphine walked beside him toward the queen's box, moving like the breath of her dragon, like wind across a wheat field, all grace and power. I also noticed a dark stain of blood down her right side.

Braimar knelt and offered his thimble toward the royal box. The white bird took it, and he stepped aside.

It was Essaphine's turn. But instead of kneeling, she remained standing. She and her mother locked eyes, and some conversation seemed to pass between them, though no words were spoken. She held up her thimble, but the white bird remained perched on her mother's shoulder and did not fly down to her.

"Isn't she supposed to kneel?" I muttered, but no one answered me.

An awkward stretch of time passed with the princess holding out her thimble and the queen glaring down at her daughter, the white bird remaining perched on her shoulder. At last, Essaphine dropped the thimble into the dirt, turned, and walked away. Members of the crowd gasped and murmured to one another, and her friends exchanged rueful glances.

"What just happened?" I asked Ollie.

But he didn't answer. Everyone just watched in a tense silence as the princess mounted her dragon and flew away.

19
ESSA

"It was reckless," Ollie said, pacing the room.

"I'm a dead girl. Why shouldn't I be reckless?" I asked.

Dagar chuckled. He, Lure, and Pocha sat at a table in the corner of my suite, devouring a platter of roast chicken and cheese. I sat on my bed, wincing as Rohree blotted at my shoulder wound with witch oil.

Ollie threw his hands up in frustration. "You want to be reckless? Have a tryst with a courtier. Spend the night drinking on the wharves. But don't insult the queen."

"She's my mother," I pointed out.

"Exactly," Ollie said. "So, we know just how ruthless she can be. And insulting her in front of the entire court is just..." he shook his head.

"All I did was refuse to kneel," I tried to sound dismissive, but the truth was, I knew what I'd done. Throughout history, there were many who had suffered greatly for lesser infractions than mine.

Maybe refusing to kneel was just a petty act of rebellion.

Maybe I was jealous of Laynine and how Mother favored her. And when Laynine had come back and knocked me from the sky... If Braimar and Zaman hadn't swooped in to catch us and break our fall, I'd be dead. Had Mother counseled Laynine to do that, to end me now, before the final challenge came? I didn't know. But the fact that it even seemed like a possibility had given me all the fuel I needed to hate Mother.

And standing tall in front of everyone, refusing to kneel and seeing that look on Mother's face... it had felt good.

Ollie's cheeks were getting red with frustration.

"Essa—"

"Look, Ollie. I get it. Your job is to keep me safe, and I'm making that job harder. The problem is, I'm really starting to have trouble caring. Ow—"

Rohree tugged the thread as she stitched my wound. "Hold still then," she grumbled.

"You might just have to decide to let me go," I said, turning my attention back to Ollie.

My friends in the corner looked up at me as one in a way that almost made me laugh. Ollie straightened up, his face going pale now instead of crimson. "Never," he said. "Never."

"Oh, Ol," I took his hand and squeezed. "You're too sweet, really. I'm sorry you got saddled with a broken egg like me. You should have been paired with Laynine. Then you'd be like Hoatan one day."

Don't get defeatist, Othura said in my mind. I nudged her back out and closed my mind to her thoughts.

"I don't want Laynine. I don't want to be like Hoatan," Ollie said, kneeling in front of me. "And I won't let you give up on yourself."

"None of us will," Pocha put in.

"I'm not giving up. I promise. I'm just..." I searched for the right words. What was I doing? Letting go? Releasing all my dreams, all my hopes for the future? Changing my skin like a molting dragon hatchling? Becoming something else? I didn't know how to explain it, but I wasn't giving up exactly. I was giving up on a specific idea of what my future would be. And it didn't feel like an ending. It felt like a new beginning, somehow. I just didn't know *what* was beginning.

Probably my afterlife...

Regardless, I had a sense of something coming. Something new, vast, revolutionary, and somehow hopeful, like the feeling in your chest on the first warm day of spring.

I sense it too, Othura said, wriggling back into my mind again. *It scares me. But it excites me.*

Rohree finished tying off her sutures, nodding in satisfaction as she snipped off the thread. "There," she said. "At least we can say this wound isn't the one that will do you in."

It had been a shallow one—lucky for me.

"What about Braimar?" Lure said, and all eyes snapped to me.

"What about him?" I asked.

Lure arched an eyebrow. "Don't play dumb with us, Essa. We've known you too long for that. Braimar helped you. What does he want?"

"I know what he wants. It's between her legs," Dagar said, and Pocha slapped him on the arm.

"He offered to run away with me," I said as casually as possible. Everyone gaped at me.

"Yikes," Dagar said.

"That's so romantic, though!" Pocha exclaimed.

Ollie crossed his arms, thoughtful. "Anytime Braimar does something, I always look to his durram. Why would Kortoi want Braimar to run off with you...? I'll tell you. The queen is almost out of her childbearing years, which means the nobles will soon begin pressuring her to put the crown aside. There are only two more of the royal line, you and Laynine. If Braimar takes you away and defiles you, you have no chance of becoming queen."

"I have basically no chance of becoming queen anyway," I pointed out. "Because I'll probably be dead. And there would still be Laynine."

"There would," Ollie agreed. "But with you gone, and Laynine as the Irska, she'd be only one bad flight away from leaving the throne empty. And you know who would be the first to sit his arse on that empty throne..."

"Kortoi," Lure said, venom in their voice.

"Or Lord Natath," said Pocha, "with Kortoi behind him pulling the strings."

"Exactly," Ollie nodded.

I flipped my hair. "It is possible Braimar is just enchanted by my beauty."

"Possible, but unlikely," Dagar grinned.

I took a wad of bloody bandage and chucked it at him. He ducked it, laughing. Dagar was always teasing me like a brother, and I felt suddenly overcome with love for the misfits in this room. In the whole court and the whole kingdom, these were the handful of people I knew I could trust. There was no way I could have lived without them.

"The question is, how do we turn Braimar's advances and the queen's ire to our advantage?" Ollie mused.

I rose, patting him on the shoulder.

"I'll leave you to ponder that, wise councilor," I said. "Tomorrow will be a busy day of playing hostess. I plan to take our poet friend to see the Dragon Hatchery."

"And to see Kortoi," Ollie said. "He's requested an audience with our guest. And Kit asked to see him, too."

I rolled my eyes. "Ugh. How has the prelate's fame made it all the way across the sea?"

"I'd like to know that, too," Ollie said. "It makes me uneasy. But perhaps we'll learn more when they meet. Hoatan has asked me to observe their audience closely."

I nodded. "And so you shall."

20

CHARLIE

The morning after the Thimble Race, Rohree woke me, fed me, and bade me get dressed.

"And be quick about it," she said. "The princess is waiting."

My head throbbed for want of coffee and a cigarette, but I dressed as speedily as I could, grabbed the oilskin bag with my notebook inside, and followed the sprite.

One arm of the palace grounds extended toward the sea, and as I followed the sprite down the stone path, the manicured gardens grew more wild. Tangled brambles and vines replaced the roses and hydrangeas; rocks and boulders replaced the perfectly trimmed lawns. Off to my right rose the waterfall Essa and I had stood atop during our tour of the city. Its falling plumes filled the air with a pleasant mist and left a rainbow hanging against the sky.

The path ended in a building so ancient, at first I took it for a hill overlooking the sea. When I looked closer, however, I saw that it was in fact a hill-shaped stone building, four or five stories high and very broad, made of vast slabs of wine-colored granite, with windows the shape of a cat's iris. Strange runes and carvings covered the walls, though most had been obscured by moss and lichen. I'd never known magick before, but just seeing the place sent a flicker of electricity down my spine that seemed unnatural —in a most exhilarating way. But that was nothing compared to the feeling that went through me when I saw Essaphine standing near the entrance, waiting for me.

She'd shed her leather armor in favor of a blue dress the color of forget-me-nots. In the morning sun, her changeable hair took on the color of hammered gold. She stood with the perfect posture of a dancer—or a royal—but her eyes were cast down in a way that made me think at once of the queen her mother was and the little girl the princess must once have been. The wind off the sea whipped her hair and her dress, giving her the look of a figure on the prow of a ship, or a car's chrome hood ornament.

I didn't realize I was staring until Rohree nudged me from behind.

"Go on, then."

I approached Essaphine, one thumb tucked into the strap of the oilskin bag slung over my shoulder. I neared her, but her eyes remained trained on the ground. It allowed me another moment to stare at her. I found myself wanting to memorize the curve of her cheek, the shape of her nose, the bow of her lips.

So, you can slap it later, right? I reminded myself. *Because she* is *the enemy. And the minute you're not useful, you can be damn sure she'll feed you to that silver dragon of hers.*

This voice of reason in my head sounded alarmingly like Kitty's, which was a jarring reminder that I was, in fact, engaged. All this was a role I was playing. And at my earliest convenience, I would fly back to this place and bomb it to dust.

Still, for now, I had to play the part, and I approached her.

"What are you looking at, Your Majesty?" I asked.

She pointed, and I followed her gaze to the dirt. Ants were swarming from a hole in the ground, carrying pieces of leaves to and fro.

"The ants," she said absently. "I envy them."

"You'd like to have legs the size of an eyelash?" I teased —probably because I was looking at her eyelashes. God, they were so long.

She smiled. "I never imagined your people could be funny," she mused. "With your bullets and your tanks and your olive-colored uniforms. You seem like a very unfunny people. But you're funny."

"Thank you?" I said.

She gestured to the ants. "What I mean is, the ants always complete their work. Always do their duty. Even if a foot is about to trample them, they won't step out of line. They are perfect, even until the moment they are crushed. I have never felt perfect."

Her hand went to the stump of her arm, hugged it to her body.

Several times, I had wanted to ask her what happened to that arm. Was she born that way? Was it an accident? But she looked too vulnerable now. I was afraid if I asked her a question that personal, she'd clap shut like a book and I would lose this moment.

"Congratulations on the Thimble Race," I said.

"Thank you," she said. "But I'll have to do better than that if I want to live..."

Her eyes found mine. Today, they were a pale gray, like a rain cloud when the sun is trying to burst through.

"Come," she said, brightening. "I have dragons to show you."

The princess led me through a triangular hallway so narrow we had to walk single file. Torches flickered on the walls on either side, rustled by an ever-present wind that made the hollow, eerie sound of a seashell pressed to one's ear. Just when I'd begun to imagine we'd be walking through an endless series of tight spaces, we emerged onto a landing overlooking a vast hall, at least twice as large as the "A" hangar at the McNally Air Base. Dozens of dragons filled the space. Some were snuggled together, dozing. Others wrestled and snapped at one another like puppies or prowled like jungle cats in the Ironberg zoo. A series of arches lining the far wall opened toward the sea, and dragons were constantly leaping out to take flight or swooping in to land.

"This is where the dragons come when they're feeling social," Essaphine explained. "Below us are seventeen stories of catacombs. Each dragon has their own chamber— a series of interconnected caves overlooking the sea. Supposedly, the place was constructed by the first riders and their dragons over ten thousand years ago."

I gave a low whistle, my eyes ranging up to the ceiling, which was shaped like an inverted step-pyramid. I searched for words, but there was really nothing I could say. I was looking upon a wonder of the world.

The princess gave me a mocking smile. "What? You're not jotting down any verses."

"I'm a reporter," I reminded her. "No verses, just facts. And at the moment, I'm a bit lost for words..."

A great, purple beast took flight and wheeled overhead. It gave forth a burst of flame, lighting up the whole room and sending a wave of heat washing over us.

"Although a place like this might inspire me to write some poetry..." I said.

Could a well-placed bomb on the roof of this building collapse the whole thing? Bury the dragons? End the war? That was the sort of note I was really considering jotting down.

"Come. I'll show you Othura's chamber," Essaphine said.

I followed Essa down a broad staircase to the floor of the hall. The smell of dragon hung in the air, a bouquet with notes of ammonia, vanilla, and wood smoke that was peculiar but not entirely unpleasant. More worrisome were the beasts frolicking and lumbering all around us. Most were so large that a misstep could easily have hurt or even killed us. We made our way to the center of the room without incident, although two or three dragons did turn their huge eyes on me in a way that made me decidedly nervous. A round hole in the floor loomed ahead, and as we reached it, I saw a spiral staircase leading downward. It was so small in the scope of the entire room that I hadn't noticed it from above, but it was wide enough that the princess and I were able to descend side-by-side.

I thought I'd be relieved leaving the ruckus and chaos of the dragon social hall behind, but the hike down this dark stair made me more nervous still. I was in a dragon lair. The princess could lead me into any chamber, ask a dragon to devour me, and I'd be gone in a heartbeat.

The temperature dropped as we descended, and the roars and shrieks were replaced with a ponderous silence underscored by the constant howling of wind and a breathless hush that made my hackles rise.

"I thought I might get my surprise today," the princess said. "The one you and Clua are preparing?"

I hadn't heard back from the dwarf yet. I could only hope she was truly working on the gifts we'd planned for Essa...

"It's not quite ready yet," I said. "Soon..."

"That's too bad," she said. "You've piqued my curiosity. What gift could you give me that would be worth risking your life?"

"You'll see." I cleared my throat, ready to change the subject. "So, you and that fellow Braimar are allies, then?"

Judging from the ferocious look the princess gave me, it was the wrong thing to say. "What makes you say that?"

"Well, the two of you came over the finish line together. And..."

"And Ollie said something, didn't he?" She shook her head. "Braimar and I were sweethearts once. Some men think what was once theirs is theirs always."

"But you don't... feel that way about him anymore?"

Essaphine wrinkled her nose. "If you outgrow a shoe, do you keep wearing it, or do you throw it away?"

I smiled. "So, he's an old shoe, eh?"

"Not at all," she said. "Old shoes smell better."

We both laughed, and the sound seemed to wash away the foreboding I'd felt a moment before.

We continued our descent, the staircase opening up periodically to reveal huge hallways running off to either side. At the third such opening, we exited the stairwell and proceeded left, down the hall. On our right, we passed a series of doorways, each of which revealed a huge chamber that was open on the far side, overlooking the sea, so that if it were viewed from the other side, I imagined the place must look like a vast honeycomb.

Some of the dens we passed were empty. In others, dragons slept, the sounds of their snoring at times enough to vibrate the stone underfoot. A few of the dragons we passed sat on their haunches like dogs, gazing out of their caverns at the sea.

"So, this is where dragons live..." I wondered aloud.

"When they're not knocking your country's planes from the sky or torching your soldiers on the battlefield—yes," she said. "Have you ever seen a dragon's egg?"

She gestured to one of the chambers. Covering its floor was an array of oblong eggs, each about the size of a large cantaloupe. There were many different colors and textures, some speckled, some striped with swirled patterns like a snail's shell, others as plain as a common chicken egg. A narrow aisle with piles of eggs on either side went down the center of the room, and Essaphine led me down it.

"You could make a hell of an omelet," I said, taking it all in.

Essaphine gave me a look, but I didn't miss the curl of a smile at the edge of her lips. "Female dragons usually lay one egg per day," she said. "And there are a lot of dragons here."

"How many?" I asked, knowing this was a question the military brass would surely ask me.

"A hundred and fifty, at least," she said. "Although only a hundred are bonded to riders."

I heard a grunt and saw two men clad in gray robes working at the end of the chamber, where it opened up to the sea. As I watched, they each picked up an egg and tossed it off the cliff. A second later, I heard the eggs crack on the rocks below. The men stooped, picked up another egg each, and chucked those off as well.

"What are they doing?" I asked.

"Making the omelets," Essaphine teased, then knelt over one of the eggs, beckoning me down, too.

"See?" she scraped a thumbnail over the shell. A dark substance sloughed off, building up on her thumbnail and leaving the eggshell bare.

"It's Egg Blight. A fungus," she said. "It infects all the eggs laid here and kills the baby dragons within. The tainted eggs must all be destroyed to keep the infection from spreading."

I looked up to the men toiling at the edge of the room again, frowning as they hurled another pair of eggs onto the rocks below.

"That's why the hatching grounds at Rograd Point are so important," she went on. "There are only two places in the world where dragons roost and lay their eggs. Here and there. And only the ones hatched there survive."

I suddenly understood why the Skrathan had fought so ferociously over that rocky peninsula on the northern shores of the Isle of Dorhane. Maybe the brass already knew about the hatching grounds there—but if they did, I hadn't heard about it.

Take Rograd Point, destroy the eggs there, and the dragons will go extinct, I thought. The intelligence I was gathering right now was top-notch. I could almost feel the general pinning a medal on my chest.

"Sad to think of all these dragons dying," I said, nodding toward the gray brothers chucking the dragon eggs. Part of me even meant it. As much as I hated the creatures, their majesty was undeniable. And there was something about Essa's dragon, Othura, that I liked. "Isn't there some way to wash the fungus off?"

The princess gasped. "You know, in the ninety years we've been dealing with this problem, we've never thought of that. Thank the Star Father you came here to share your incredible wisdom with us simple people!"

"Okay. You're being sarcastic..." I muttered.

The princess smiled, nudging me with her shoulder. "Well, at least you understand sarcasm. It's more than I can say for my mother, the queen. Come, poet," she breezed past me, back toward the hall. "There's more to see."

I followed the princess into a chamber that was smaller than some of the others we'd passed, but also cozier. It was the only room we'd passed that had human décor. Rugs lay upon the floor and art on the walls. One painting depicted fancily dressed courtiers at a ball, another of a pair of dragons soaring together into a sunset sky. Another was a whimsical portrait of three cute puppies.

At the center of the space Othura lay, her long body curled upon herself like a coiled serpent, her chest expanding and diminishing with slow breaths. She seemed to be sleeping, but when I looked again, I saw her orange eyes on us. As we entered, she lifted her head and gave us a look filled with every bit as much intelligence as a human's.

"I've missed you, too, my love," Essaphine approached Othura's gray head and stroked her between her huge orange eyes. In all my life, I doubted I'd ever get used to seeing someone acting affectionate with these killing machines. As if she heard my thoughts, the dragon looked to me. Her eyes narrowed.

"Well, why not bring him here?" Essaphine said. "I'm supposed to show him all the most impressive places in the kingdom. This place is awfully grand, don't you think?"

The dragon huffed.

"Is she really talking to you?" I asked.

The dragon's tail had reached up and idly wrapped itself around the princess's arm, the way two girlfriends might hold hands.

"Of course," she said. "And she can hear my thoughts, too. I was just speaking aloud for your benefit, to be polite. But dragons don't speak words in the same way you and I do. It comes through as feelings, at least at first. But the more time a dragon and their rider spend together, the more precisely you're able to interpret each other's communication, so in the end, the communication feels like speech, and it's just as accurate. More accurate, really."

I rubbed my chin. "More accurate than speech? How?"

The princess shrugged. "Well, speech often does a poor job of conveying emotion. Imagine seeing someone beautiful across the room. You feel drawn to them. You want to speak with them. You feel suddenly like you'll die if you don't make the leap and talk to them. And yet, along with that sense of longing is an equal feeling of dread that they'll dismiss you. This comingling of emotions ignites a feeling of excitement that seems as if it will set your insides on fire. It takes a lot of human words to convey a feeling like that. But a dragon can convey such a feeling to their rider in an instant."

I nodded. "It must be an incredible sort of intimacy to share a mind with another being like that."

"It is," Essa said. "And that's one of the reasons your country will never defeat ours. Your aces may be skilled. They may even love their planes. But a machine can never love its operator. It is written: the living will always defeat the dead. That's why our dragons will defeat your war machines in the end."

Tell that to my Sackman Comet when I'm strafing these cata-combs with my machine guns, I thought.

The dragon's orange eyes narrowed again. She gave a low growl.

Involuntarily, I shuffled back a step.

"What is it?" I asked.

The princess stroked the dragon's tail, watching me just as intently as her beast was.

"Othura says you are unconvinced. And you're hiding something."

I opened my mouth to speak, but could find no clever words. What use was there in lying to a creature that could catch glimpses of my thoughts? I wondered if real spies—like Kitty—were warned not to keep company with dragons for just this reason.

"Don't worry," the princess went on. "Dragons are very intuitive, but she can't read your thoughts the same way she can mine. Your secrets are safe."

"I have no secrets," I lied, giving a wan smile. "Just an overwhelming desire to not be eaten."

"No secrets at all?" Essa tsked. "That's disappointing. Anyway, I wouldn't worry. For some reason, she's taken a liking to you."

"What about you?" I asked.

For a second, she looked startled by the question. Then she cocked her head, a ghost of a smile on her lips. "I haven't made my mind up yet."

Just then, I heard the sound of a low bell ringing in the distance. Then, a horn sounded, this one deeper than the one that had played during the challenges at the Cauldron.

"The Theyrune horn." The princess's brow furrowed.

"What does that mean?" I asked.

But she was already running up Othura's tail and leaping onto the dragon's back. "We are called to battle. Return to your room. I'll find you later. Go back up the way we came."

Before I could answer, Othura leapt out of the cave and into the air. With a flap of her wings, they were gone, leaving me alone.

21

ESSA

Battle. Its song hummed in my blood, its fire burned in my belly, its lightning crackled through my mind. I felt Othura's excitement too, the battle lust of a dragon, a restless, inexorable desire to sow destruction.

We landed, and I was off Othura's back before she'd even stopped, running into the barracks. Shrugged into my armor, pulled on my boots and gloves, strapped on my sword, and donned my helmet. I skipped the lance rack—no need for one of those—and hurried out to the courtyard where the other dragons and their riders waited.

I'd flown into battle before, but Paemalla, mindful of my royal blood, had always been careful with me, keeping me in reserve, assigning me to the rear guard, or sending me to patrol the coast, where the enemies' ships and planes rarely reached. But today might be different. Until the challenge was complete, Laynine was the highest-ranking Skrathan, which meant she was the acting Irska. She'd likely put me in the vanguard, in the most dangerous assignment possible, hoping that some enemy fighter plane would do her a favor and cut me from the sky.

That was the danger, but it was also an opportunity. Othura and I would fight well and triumph. And when the rest of the riders witnessed us in battle, a few might even decide to support me over Laynine.

I strapped Othura's war saddle on then mounted her, and we both waited with restless excitement as the other riders finished their preparations and mounted. At the center of the courtyard stood an ancient mound where the Irska would stand to give her orders. Laynine was there now atop Tryce, and Braimar was with her, the two of them conferring together.

He was the second-highest-ranked rider, the Irska's Right Hand. It was natural that she'd be consulting with him before the battle. Still, it made me wonder. Just yesterday, Laynine had tried to kill me, and Braimar had saved me. Now, they were talking together like friends... or conspirators.

Could her attack during the Thimble Race have been a trick? Perhaps Laynine only pretended to try to kill me so Braimar would have the chance to swoop to my rescue. But if so, why?

You know why, Othura said in my mind. *It's what everyone has been pushing you toward. Marry you off to Braimar, send you away... and save your life.*

Right, I thought back. *And get me out of the way. With me gone, there would be one less Skrathan and one less royal to worry about.*

And yet, maybe I should go. Braimar was handsome. He was a powerful Skrathan, and he'd always been protective of me. I could do worse.

But I just couldn't imagine myself running away.

Finally, Braimar nodded, his geminus bearing him away, and Laynine sat tall in her saddle and blew the Theyrune horn once more, bringing the assembled riders and their dragons to silence.

"Listen well," Braimar barked. "As acting Irska, Laynine will give the battle assignments."

Laynine opened a scroll and began booming out names.

"Vanguard: myself, Braimar, Cronan, Romia, Lure, Kramat, Dagar, Pocha..." she continued, listing off at least forty names, but mine wasn't among them.

"Rear guard..." she listed off another forty names. Each time her lips parted, I expected her to say *Essaphine*. But my name never came.

By the time she said, "Coastal guard..." I was shaking with fury. And still my name was not among the thirty or so listed.

My fist clenched so hard my whole body trembled. I felt Othura growling beneath me.

"If I did not read your name, you are to remain here in reserve. You will receive a call through your dragon-mind if you are called into battle. Now fly!"

As one, the dragons took to the air in a wild clapping of wings.

This won't stand. Stop her! I told Othura, but there was no need. Already she was bounding ahead, weaving her way through the chaos of whipping tails and thumping wings as I held onto the saddle horn, fighting to keep my seat. She sprang forward and grabbed Tryce by the tail, tugging him back toward the ground. With a snarl, the beast wheeled on us. Othura, though much smaller, didn't shrink away. She stood even as Tryce put his forehead to hers, both dragons growling at one another.

"What are you doing?" Laynine demanded.

"You dare to leave me behind?"

She sighed. "Cousin..."

"Don't!" I shouted. "Don't pretend there is love between us. You're afraid I'll distinguish myself in battle. Admit it."

Laynine's eyes flashed with emotion, but it was Braimar who came up beside her and spoke.

"Distinguish yourself in battle? Essa, you can't even hold a lance."

The pity in his voice opened up a pit of emotion inside me that felt like roiling lava.

"I'll fight you," I shouted. "In a heartbeat."

He barked a weary laugh, shaking his head. "Essa... be real."

"Fight me," I said. "And see how real I am."

"Enough!" Laynine shouted. "There is a real battle at hand. I won't have you two squabbling like children. And I won't waste royal blood, either. Essaphine, you're to remain here. That's final. Follow us and you'll face the brig, just like any other Skrathan who defies orders. Braimar, with me."

And with that, Tryce took wing. Braimar gave me one more look, an expression dripping with pity. Then he clapped the visor of his helmet down and took to the air, leaving me to watch them fly away through the blur of angry tears.

22

CHARLIE

I stood alone in the dragon's den, watching at the edge of the cave entrance as other beasts left their roosts, flew upward, and disappeared back over the cliff face, heading, I guessed, for some gathering place where the riders would put on their armor and get their orders.

I squinted out at the horizon then, imagining for a moment that I could hear the buzzing of plane engines in the distance. Then the wind changed, and the sound was gone.

A battle. There was going to be a battle, and I wasn't in it.

I felt strangely left out.

But I wasn't a pilot today. I was a spy. And I found myself in a unique position. I was alone in the Hatchery, the inner sanctum of the Skrathan's power. It was a chance I might never have again. With renewed energy, I turned from the sea and made my way back into the hallway from which I'd come, trying to decide what would be the most useful thing to do. Should I sketch a map of this place for use in a later raid? Commit some act of sabotage? Search for secret weapons or documents? Assess the place for structural vulnerabilities?

But I was no engineer or demolitionist; I would be of little use figuring out how best to destroy this vast stone edifice. And I'd seen nothing to indicate a cache of weapons, maps, or papers nearby...

Think. You can't let this chance pass by without doing something.

And then it hit me. The power of this place didn't lie in some hidden information or in the stone of the building itself, impressive as it was. It was the dragons. That's what I had to learn about.

Quickly and quietly, I made my way back up the hallway to the egg chamber. The workers who had been inside were gone, and I heard their voices moving away up the hallway. I crept into the room, looking left and right, but found no one inside, neither man nor dragon. Everyone was off preparing for battle. And why should this place be guarded, anyway? These eggs were to be destroyed. I might as well be walking into a trash heap.

Quickly, I unslung my oilskin bag and knelt. An array of eggs lay before me, of varying colors and sizes and patterns. There was no telling which would be the most useful for our scientists to study—assuming I could get the thing back home, somehow. So, I just grabbed the first egg that came to hand, a mid-sized, pinkish one that sparkled slightly as the light hit it, like a chunk of rose-colored granite. It was surprisingly heavy as I lifted it, slipped it into the bag, and stood, hurrying away.

I had just emerged from the entrance when a voice called my name.

"Kit!"

I'm caught, I thought, my heart stuttering in my chest.

But Ollie was smiling as he strode up to me, his robes swishing.

"There you are," he said. "Rohree said I would find you here. Prelate Kortoi has summoned you. It's time for your audience."

I don't know what I expected, but this wasn't it.

Maybe it was the name. The Gray Brotherhood had always sounded so ominous. And yet, I sat now in a high-ceilinged conservatory surrounded by windows. Outside, butterflies wafted between flowers in a lovely garden filled with varieties of flowers I'd never seen before. All around the room were interesting oddities. Samples of dead birds and bugs in glass jars. Heads of taxidermized creatures. Several human skulls decorated in gold leaf. On the walls were star charts, anatomical diagrams of all twelve dragon types, and detailed sketches of plants and naked people. There were also several paintings in the new, brutalist abstract style that was all the rage in Ironberg currently.

It hadn't taken long to get here, even on foot. The Gray Brotherhood had their own walled compound about a quarter mile outside the city. It consisted only of an outer wall and a single tower, the architecture of which was blocky and jagged and dark. Its grim, square turrets were a marked contrast to the town's nature-inspired shops and dwellings and the palace's smooth, sweeping white walls.

From the outside, the keep's black stone had looked bleak and forbidding, and so I'd been pleasantly surprised by the cozy atmosphere that greeted me within.

The couch I sat on was of soft, fragrant leather, and a smiling man in a gray robe set a tray before us. On it was a generous cup of black liquid and a tray of cigarettes. I picked up the mug and sniffed.

It was coffee! At just the scent of it, the pounding headache I'd dealt with for days seemed to ease. I sipped. It was delicious.

"Oh, God. Thank you," I said. The robed man bowed, then turned and departed.

"They don't talk," Ollie said when he was gone. "The Brothers take a vow of silence, all except the prelate and his top brothers. Oh, and I'd go easy on that coffee if I were you. The Brothers are known for adding potions to guests' drinks. It can affect the mind."

I gazed into my coffee cup dubiously. It was tasty, but now that he mentioned it, I did notice a strange, faintly sweet aftertaste. And there was a feeling, too. An odd effervesce that roiled through my stomach and seemed to rise up to my head; I wasn't sure if I would vomit or float up to the ceiling. Grudgingly, I set the coffee aside and lit a cigarette.

The copper-clad doors creaked open, and a lady and two gray-robed men entered. The woman was tall, with fine cheekbones and long black hair. She wore a black velvet robe tied with a black belt studded with diamonds, like stars sprinkled across a night sky. Many rings glistened on her long fingers. Her fingernails were long and her pale skin was unnaturally smooth, perfect and still, as if made of wax.

It wasn't until the figure drew close that I looked at the

facial features more clearly and realized it was, in fact, a man. The low voice, when the figure spoke, confirmed it.

"So, this is our esteemed guest from across the sea," he said, gazing at me with dark eyes that glinted strangely—like the eyes of a forest animal reflecting firelight.

Ollie stood, and I followed suit.

"Prelate Kortoi," Ollie said with a small bow.

"Good Torouman," the prelate said amiably, then his attention turned to me. Up close, I could see how tall he truly was—a head taller than me, at least, and skinny as a stork. But the thick veins that crisscrossed his hands hinted at physical strength.

"A stout fellow," the prelate said, looking me up and down. "No wonder his nation has fought so bravely and for so long. And yet I hope one day soon we may call one another friends."

I nodded, taking a drag off my cigarette. "That's very kind of you," I said. "I appreciate the hospitality."

Something I said must have pleased or amused the prelate, because his already excessive grin grew even wider.

"Ah, I've just remembered something. Joman!" the prelate called, and one of the brothers entered. "Please take our friend Ollie and show him the Steinman. Then wrap it up so he can take it with him."

He leaned to Ollie conspiratorially, looming over him.

"I've procured a gift for the queen. At great expense, I might add. A painting. You've heard of Steinman?" he asked me.

"Uh. Yeah," I lied.

"One of Ironberg's greatest living artists. We disagree with the Admites about many things, but their art is fantastic.

Steinman's work in particular truly captures the spirit of the void. I know you won't mind delivering the gift to the queen on my behalf, since you'll be heading back to the palace anyway..." the prelate said to Ollie, gesturing toward the doorway.

Ollie hesitated for a beat, then gave a smile that seemed forced. "Of course, Prelate. I'd be honored." He began moving toward the door. I went to follow him, but the prelate stopped me with a hand on my chest.

"Mr. Rowley, please stay. The Torouman can manage the painting, I'm sure. But we so rarely get visitors from across the sea. Stay and chat."

He gestured to the couch. Ollie gave me a grudging look, as if he hated to leave me alone with the prelate, but after a moment's hesitation, he turned and followed the Gray Brother, and the door shut behind them with a click.

The prelate and I were alone.

"Well, well. Kitty Rowley," he said. "Such an interesting name. I'm happy Hoatan was able to bring you here. I'm a great fan of your reporting."

From the folds of his robe, he took a newspaper and handed it to me. It was an edition of the Ironberg Times, dated yesterday. On the cover was a photo of a pilot in a flight helmet and goggles kissing a girl in front of a familiar-looking plane. The headline read THE SILVER WRAITH FOUND SAFE.

What...?

I stared at the picture again. Sure enough, the plane looked exactly like my Wraith, which was now at the bottom of a sea cave. And the girl kissing the pilot... was Kitty. My fiancée.

I swallowed hard.

"Marvelous work ethic you have," the prelate said. "Even I have trouble being two places at once."

He reached out with one long finger and tapped the byline of the article. BY KITTY ROWLEY, it read.

I felt suddenly cold and hot at once. My head spun—from the spiked coffee or from panic, I wasn't sure which.

"Has the queen seen this?" I asked.

The prelate took the paper from me and turned toward the hearth. "Oh, no. I'm quite sure I'm the only one in Maethalia with a subscription to the Ironberg Times." Chuckling, he tossed the paper into the fire. In an instant, flames were consuming it. "It can be our little secret," he said.

"So you're... on our side?" I whispered.

"Sides? I am a priest of the void. Gaze into the depthless darkness long enough, and one realizes there are no sides. No good and evil. No male and female. No strong and weak. There are not even living and dead. All are one. Ripples on the great sea of non-being."

"Oh. Okay," I said.

The prelate picked up on my sarcasm and laughed. "You're a cynic. I like cynics. Tell me, who are you really?"

I hesitated, wondering how much I should tell this man. But it was clear already that he knew enough to be my undoing. Lying would only risk angering him and put me in further danger.

"I'm a fighter pilot," I said. "My plane was damaged and I crashed into the ocean near the coast. I happened to have Kitty Rowley's documents onboard, so I decided to pose as her."

"Brilliant," the prelate clapped his hands, his many rings glinting. "And already you've wormed your way into the queen's inner circle by way of the princess. That's really impressive work, Kit. Or should I say, Charlie?"

The sound of my real name jarred me. But that wasn't what bothered me most. It was the prelate's voice, I realized. It didn't match his face. Though he looked no more than twenty years old with skin that was smooth, even milky, his voice had the rumble and crackle of an old man's.

The prelate wandered to the mantle and took up a brass figurine of a biplane. He held it up, considering it.

"Yes, I know who you are. Charlie Inman. The ace of aces. The famed Silver Wraith."

"Well, not anymore," I said. "Looks like I was easily replaced."

The prelate turned back to me, his too-wide smile replaced with a mocking pout. "Of course. The void contains all abundance, every possible permutation of life and destiny. We are all infinitely replaceable, Charlie. Even me. But still, you have done well. And you might do so much more."

My hand drifted to my pocket. "In Kitty's papers, there was a note that said to come to you. With any reports."

I took one of Kitty's lipsticks out of the bag. It contained the notes I'd made so far. Sketches of Charcain. Targets. Ideas about how defenses might be overcome. The location of the hatching grounds on Dorhane. Information about dragons and dragon riders, all written on tiny pieces of paper which I'd rolled up and stuck inside the lipstick's cap, just in case this moment presented itself.

The prelate took the lipstick and slipped it into his robes.

"I'll see this gets delivered. We should plan to meet once a week, you and I. I'm sure you'll be glad to come back for more of my coffee and cigarettes. You'll find no one else in the kingdom with such Western-style luxuries. And some find mine especially addictive."

I glanced at the cigarette in my hand. Most of it had burned down to ash while the prelate had been talking, and I hadn't even noticed. I took a final drag then stubbed it out in an ashtray. "I'll certainly come back if Essaphine lets me. She's my escort while I'm here."

The prelate took my hand in his and patted it, as if he were comforting a child.

"Don't worry, Charlie. She won't be around long enough to stand in our way for long. She'll be joining the void soon."

I guessed he meant death, though it was a hell of a creepy way to talk about it. I considered telling him my plan. If I got my way, Essa would live—in fact, she'd be Irska. But something in those sparkling, dark eyes of his stopped me.

He might be an ally—but that didn't mean I could trust him.

Instead, I just nodded.

He brought my hand to his mouth and kissed it. His lips were so cold they sent a shiver through me.

"Charlie. The Silver Wraith. Crashed. Gone. Think of this like an afterlife, Charlie. When you're dead, anything is possible."

His dark eyes bored into mine, hypnotic, bright with some avarice I didn't understand. Then footsteps were coming toward us. Instinctively, I jerked my hand from his as the doors swung open, revealing one of the Gray Brothers.

"The Torouman is eager to depart," he said.

The prelate smiled, the mouth of his once more seeming too wide, like the maw of a shark.

"Of course," he said. "We are done here. But I'll see you again soon, Kit. I think we're going to be great friends."

Outside, Ollie hustled me away from the black keep. He held a wrapped-up painting under his arm and had a scowl on his face. As we walked, he kept looking over his shoulder, as if he expected them to be chasing us. I had to admit, the hulking, black-armored Lacunae guards made me a bit nervous, too.

I tripped over a rock and went down hard on my knees. Cursing, Ollie caught me under the armpit and hauled me up.

"You alright?" He demanded.

"Fine," I said, the word coming out slurred.

"Curse those Brothers," Ollie said. "I told you not to drink the coffee."

"Sorry," I muttered. "I was craving coffee and a cigarette for days, though."

"And now you got them," Ollie said. "But at what price?"

It didn't seem like a terrible price, honestly. I only felt a little buzzed. Although perhaps I'd been a bit less guarded with the prelate than I should have been... Now that I was on my feet, Ollie was hurrying me along again.

"Where are we going?" I asked.

"To Essa. She needs me."

"Is she hurt?"

"No. They didn't let her fight. And she's furious about it."

"They didn't let her fight? Why? Because of her arm? Or because she's the princess?"

He didn't answer; he just kept hurrying along as I struggled to keep up.

I squinted at him. "How do you know?"

"Othura told me."

"Wait. The dragon can talk to you, too?"

"You're just a font of questions, aren't you? Yes. Anyone can communicate with a dragon if the dragon wills it. Especially a Torouman who is sworn to protect that dragon's rider. Now hurry up. The dragons are returning."

We entered one of the palace courtyards and found Essa sitting astride Othura and gazing up at the sky. Above, the Skrathan and their steeds were returning one by one. Some dragons were injured, the webbing of their wings in tatters, or dark bleeding holes in their thick hides, courtesy of my friends' 10-millimeter guns. None of those who landed paid us any mind. Some riders tended to their dragons, along with green-smocked medics who hurried out from a round barn, pushing handcarts filled with medical supplies. Others threw their steel helms to the ground in frustration or gathered together in small groups with their comrades, talking in low, angry voices.

"Look," Ollie pointed at a shape so large it blotted out the sky as it passed over us. Three stout dragons held another dragon by its wings and tail.

As they flew in, I saw the beast had two heads. If I was learning my dragon types correctly, it was a geminus.

"Braimar," Essa whispered, watching as they set the beast down in the middle of the courtyard.

One of the dragons carrying the geminus belonged to Laynine, I saw. Braimar sat behind her in the saddle, and as they alighted, he leapt off and ran toward his dragon's twin heads. One was very still, a mass of dark blood and torn flesh, with a glint of white skull exposed. But as his rider approached, the other head rose and gave a heart-wrenching bellow. Then it dropped to the cobblestones again, and Braimar fell to hugging it and weeping.

Laynine had climbed off Tryce and stood watching Braimar's sorrow, her face twitching with some unreadable emotion—anger or sorrow or pity.

Murmurs rifled among the riders as they watched Braimar's anguish, and a general feeling of foreboding and unease seemed to settle on the entire square like a mist.

Othura took a few paces toward Laynine, and Essa cleared her throat.

"What happened?" she called.

Laynine turned to us, her eyes hard. "It was the Silver Wraith."

Essa recoiled. "Impossible. He died with Paemalla."

Essa's three friends were landing. The one called Lure shook their head grimly. "There's no question. It was him, silver plane and all."

The hell it was, I thought, my mind returning to the article the prelate had shown me. Running a fake news story was one thing. But the brass had really painted another plane silver and sent an imposter up in my place? The thought of it stung my pride.

"They baited us," Laynine said. "Their planes made a sortie and were nearing the hatching ground. We swept in and broke their formation, had them scattered and on the run. We pursued them, hoping to pick off the stragglers before they made it back to their base. Then, they sprang a trap on us. There were more flying machines than I've ever seen. And the Wraith was among them. He—"

From the center of the courtyard, there came a horrific

roar. The geminus seemed to have realized that his twin head was slain. It nudged its other head with its snout again and again, then gave a blood-chilling roar and blew a blast of flame into the sky, bright as a second sun.

"We'll kill him," Braimar shouted, a terrible, haunted look in his eyes. The blade of his drawn sword glinted in the dragon's firelight. Both man and dragon flailed, blind with mad rage, sword and flame flashing so wildly that even the other dragons and their riders backed away. Braimar's eyes went to me.

He pointed his sword at me, its tip trembling.

"We'll kill them all!" he bellowed, stumbling toward me. "You tell them. WE'LL KILL THEM ALL!"

He began running toward me, his sword raised. This wounded dragon turned toward us, too, dragging its dead head with it, leaving a trail of gore behind.

It opened its mouth and sent a blast of flame toward us. Othura leapt in front of me and reared up, shielding me with her fire-resistant underbelly.

"Get on," Essa shouted, offering me her hand as I clambered up into the saddle behind her. Then Othura was flapping into the sky, bearing us upward as Braimar's dragon blasted flames after us.

Below us, Ollie was fleeing on foot. Skrathan were scattering, giving Braimar's mad dragon a wide berth.

Many of the Skrathan seemed more concerned with me and Essa than Braimar, though. From below, I could hear their outraged shouts.

She's taken a foreigner on dragon back.

No!

Look!

It is forbidden.

The queen will hear. There must be justice!

Braimar's dragon pumped its wings frantically, trying to pursue us despite his horrific injury and blasting fire into the sky. Braimar screamed after us like a maniac.

"Go!" Essaphine shouted, and Othura wheeled and bore us away.

It was only a short flight, a hop over the roof of a hall and into a nearby courtyard. Essaphine slid off Othura's back, and I followed her down, my heart still beating fast. I'd faced plenty of angry dragons, but the madness and hatred in Braimar and his dragon's eyes left me shaken.

Essa and I stood looking one another up and down, as if making sure the other was okay. I realized what I was doing with a start and looked away. She did the same, turning to pat Othura's flank.

"You okay, love?" she asked, and the dragon nuzzled her.

"I hope you don't get in trouble—for flying me," I said.

Part of me couldn't believe I'd actually been on the back of a dragon. What the hell the boys back home would say to that, I could hardly imagine. But the flight had been so brief, it had left me wanting more. I could imagine soaring on Othura's back out over the sea, into the mountains, across the dark, wild forests of Maethalia...

Essa just gave me a grim smile. "Don't worry about me, Poet. I'm the naughty daughter. There's no trouble this place could offer that I haven't gotten into already. Come on. Let's get you back to your room."

23

ESSA

I spent the whole next day in training. After all, I had a life-and-death trial ahead—and I'd wasted too much time playing tour guide already. It had been a day of flying and fighting and running formation drills. I always loved time spent in the sky with my friends, and I had moments where I felt I was doing well. And yet, each time I saw Laynine and her dragon, with all their grace and speed and skill, it felt as if a cloud drifted over the sun and I remembered how dire my position was. Even with two hands, I couldn't match Laynine. And I had only one...

Worse, I spotted my mother on a balcony, watching us, and I knew she was communicating with Laynine. Training her. Teaching her. Preparing her—to destroy me.

Afterward, I sat eating dinner in the barracks, chewing a tough bit of stewed lamb and sulking as my friends chattered together, when Rohree entered. She handed me a note.

Meet me at the old stables at six,

and bring your poet. I have a surprise.
-Clua

It was a cryptic message, to be sure. And intriguing.

"Go fetch the foreigner," I told her. "And bring Ollie as well. He'll be doing his evening reading, but drag him out of his chair by the ear if you have to."

"With pleasure," the sprite said.

I summoned Othura, who was cranky to be interrupted in the midst of her post-training meal, and in less than half an hour, we were arriving at the appointed meeting place.

The stables were a huge, old, ramshackle building that sat about a half mile outside of town. It had been used to house the cavalry's horses until, about seventy years ago, they were moved to a newer and more defensible facility within the city walls. Since then, the building had fallen into disrepair, a haunt for owls and squirrels. But its old walls were still sound, its roof mostly held out the rain, and its secluded location in the middle of the woods made it an ideal spot for clandestine meetings. Ollie, Clua, and I had been coming here since we were children.

We found Clua waiting at the south end of the barn, in an area that had once been used for repairing tack. She smiled as we approached with a self-satisfaction that made me even more curious.

"Clua," I hugged her in greeting. "What's going on?"

"First of all, don't blame me." She glanced at Kit. "Blame your poet. It was all his idea."

He gave me the same smug look Clua had a second ago. All this was starting to make me very nervous.

He nodded to Clua. "Let's show her."

The dwarf went to an old worktable and pulled a cloth off, revealing a long, unusually slender lance and a metal object about the size of a fist with leather straps on it and a clip of some sort on one end.

I stared at the objects, confused. "What...?"

"Pick up the lance," Kit suggested.

Warily, I did as he asked, walking over, grabbing the lance by the middle of its shaft and hefting it. Most dragon lances were so heavy I could barely lift them with my one good arm. This one, I was able to lift easily. It had to be less than half the weight of a standard Skrathan's lance.

"What is this?" I asked.

"There were some materials from my crashed plane that I thought might help you," he said. "Aluminum for the lance. The clip to use in place of a hand so you can keep yourself in your saddle. With these, you should be able to fight just like any other Skrathan."

He stepped over to the table, hefted the lance, and sighted down it, eyeing its straightness. He gave Clua an appreciative nod. "Excellent workmanship."

"That's where you went," I said to Kit. "When you climbed down out of the tower. You were going back to your plane to get the materials so you could make these...?"

Kit picked up the other object, testing the metal clip. It was a "D" shaped loop of metal. When he pushed the moving part of it back and released it, it snapped back into place, forming a solid ring once again. I could see immediately how it would work, replacing my missing arm and attaching me to the saddle horn in the same way other Skrathans held on with their hand.

The possibilities these items presented were beginning to dawn on me, and along with them, hope.

I picked up the lance again and looked to Clua.

"It's light. But will it hold up to battle?"

"I took the squared-off metal tube he gave me and shielded it in wood and dried dragon hide to give it stiffness," the dwarf nodded. "It's as strong as a normal lance. Stronger, probably."

"Help me get the hand on."

Clua helped me strap on the false arm.

"I modified your saddle so it has a place to clip onto," she said. "Let me show you."

I mounted Othura, and Clua unscrewed the saddle horn. Beneath it, I saw, she had fashioned something like a leather cup. Within the cup, a steel ring was affixed, which the clip attached to. I tugged at it and it held fast. I could have hung upside down from it easily, and it would not have let go.

"Clever work, Clua," I said to my friend, hardly able to keep back a smile.

"Well, it was him, really," she nodded toward Kit. "The materials he brought me are like nothing I've seen before."

"The Noble Council won't like it," Ollie said. "And neither will the queen. It will be too much like a machine for them."

"It's just a clip with a steel spring," Kit objected.

"Yes," Ollie said. "But as I told Clua, the materials were made with machines. And the clip is pushing the edge of what is allowed."

"Wait," I wheeled on Ollie. "You knew about this?"

He smiled. "I am your Torouman. It's my job to know everything. I let Clua finish the project because it might help you. Now, I'm not so sure."

"So what if the clip is a sort of simple machine, or if it was made by machines?" Kit said. "If it helps you to function as if you had two hands, isn't it a good thing?"

"People have been cast in the dungeons for less," Ollie said.

"Not princesses," I pointed out.

Kit shook his head. "I don't get it."

"It's part of our religious teachings," I told him. "If allowed to exist, machines will lead our people and our world to ruin. That which does not live must not live. So it is written."

For a moment, a crestfallen look passed over the stranger's handsome face. Honestly, it was adorable.

"*But*," I went on, "it may be a risk I'm willing to take. My question is, why would you do this for me?"

The poet hesitated, running a hand through his hair. It fell back into his eyes in a way that was surprisingly charming. "Because I want to help you."

"Why?" I demanded.

"Because..." he hesitated again. "Because though our people may be enemies, I see good in you. I think you'd be a good Irska. At least you deserve a fair shot at getting the job, right?"

I watched him, staring as intently as Mother gazing into her scrying bowl, as if I could probe his soul.

"And for that, you scaled down a palace wall in the rain? And walked for leagues through the night? And risked being slain by the guards as you snuck out of the city? To give me a *fair shot*?"

It wasn't only my eyes boring into him. Othura had swung her head in through a window and watched him as well, with the astute attention of a dragon.

He does want to help you, she whispered in my mind. *But he's hiding something, too.*

The poet squirmed a little under our scrutiny, but his eyes remained fixed on mine.

"Take these gifts," he said. "And let me train you. You can beat Laynine. And I can help you."

A laugh rose up in me, equal parts amusement and bitter cynicism. But the earnestness in his eyes killed my laughter.

"*You* train *me*?" I demanded. "What do you know about flying?"

He put a hand on my shoulder. With Othura's keen senses aiding mine, I felt a breathless electricity in that touch.

"Just trust me," he said.

Our eyes locked. Something passed between us as real and as potent as any communication between human and dragon. The moment stretched and the world seemed to blur. Clua, Ollie, and even Othura seemed to fade until there were only the two of us. Me and Kit. I realized I was trembling.

When I finally found my voice, it came out a whisper. "Alright, Poet. If you're such a dragon expert, come and fly with me."

I put on the false hand device Clua had made me, clipped it into the saddle, and bade Rohree hand me the lance. Kit climbed up behind me and wrapped his arms tight around my waist.

"It is forbidden for outsiders to ride dragons," Ollie reminded me. "If someone sees you—"

"They can go to hell," I finished for him.

Ollie accepted my words with a sigh, and for a moment, I pitied him for his lot in life, destined to talk sense to a headstrong fool like me. But I was beyond caring what others thought. And the wind was calling.

With a gallop and a leap, Othura bore us into the air.

I'd taken Kit up on Othura once before, but it had been only a brief, low flight to get him away from Braimar's wounded dragon. This was a real flight, and some sadistic part of me couldn't wait to terrify Kit—and to humble him, a little.

I'd given rides to plenty of first-timers before. Children from the city who watched us Skrathan with wonder, dreaming of a chance to ride a dragon, or old women who had spent all their lives watching us fly without ever getting the chance to do so themselves. I'd even taken a few cocky knights who thought they were brave enough to fly dragon-back—and most of those I'd dropped off with piss in their pants. I knew how people reacted when they rode a dragon for the first time. Before takeoff, they'd be nearly bouncing with excitement. Then we'd take to the air, and they would go still. By the time we were as high as the treetops, they'd be hanging onto me as tight as a bear trap. And the moment I'd do my first maneuver, even something as simple as a leviathan turn, they'd be trembling like a leaf in a storm.

And so I waited, all my senses attuned, to feel the poet go through those stages as he rode behind me. Only he didn't.

Before we took flight, he was still, not jittering with excitement. As we took wing, he remained relaxed. As we flew higher, his arms at my waist did not tighten around me, though I was aware of his legs clenching, as a proper rider's would, against Othura's sides. I urged Othura higher, then higher still, waiting to feel Kit's breathing get shallow, to feel his arms begin to quake. But they did not.

He's a natural rider, Othura said.

There's nothing natural about an Admite being comfortable on dragon-back, I thought back. It was the sort of thing the priestesses would have proclaimed a sign—the foreigner who can ride dragons. But if it were a sign, what could it portend? That was a mystery, and my mind worried at it like a tongue nudging a sore tooth.

To distract myself from the unease, I decided to try the lance, leading Othura toward a grove of pines on the eastern slope of the hills and tilting at treetops. I'd hardly used a lance on dragon back, but I remembered my training as best I could, rising in my stirrups, squeezing with my knees, keeping my upper body loose, keeping my eyes on the target, and—

I missed. A growl of frustration rumbled out of me.

"Aim a little low," the poet said in my ear. "That way, when Othura flaps her wings, it will bring you up to the target, not lift you over it."

"I know how to use a lance!" I shouted back at him.

But as Othura banked for another pass, I did as he suggested, dropping the lance point a little lower, and—

Pfff!

The treetop exploded in a burst of pine needles.

We tilted and banked, aiming for a second treetop.

Pfff!

My lance tip found that one, too, then a third one.

"Yes!" the poet shouted behind me.

The weapon felt good in my hand. It felt agile, manage-able in a way the standard lances never had. But there was another way lances were useful: as massive wands for focusing a dragon's breath power. I tried that now, urging Othura toward a rocky promontory jutting off a hillside. I focused my energy on the lance, and as I did so, I felt the dragonstone necklace resting against my chest grow warm.

Now, I told Othura.

She did as I asked, exhaling a small whirlwind that whisked along the treetops, stirring leaves and pine needles. I aimed the lance at the rocky outcropping and called upon the power of the dragon stone. Sure enough, the whirlwind veered obediently, hitting the hillside and sending stones rumbling down the slope below us. Of course, I could control wind somewhat without a lance using the dragon stone, but this was better. More precise.

I gave a shout of triumph.

"Impressive," the foreigner said in my ear. I glanced back to find a devilish smile on lips which were, I realized, very close to mine. I gave the smile right back to him, turning forward again.

He's a bit too cocky, I told Othura. *Let's see if we can humble him a bit.*

I felt her amusement as she snapped her wings taut to her body and dove, dropping into the valley like a stone.

At last, Kit's arms around my waist tightened. I felt his body pull against mine from behind. Even through my leathers and even with the wind, I could feel the heat of him against me.

"Hold on," I breathed.

Just before hitting the valley floor, Othura pulled up so hard my heart dropped into my belly. Then she was winging upward again in a vertical climb that left Kit nearly hanging off me, his grip the only thing preventing a long plummet and a grisly death. At the top of the climb, Othura suddenly banked and dropped again, her rear talons skipping off the slope of the hillside.

"You won't lose me that easily," Kit said in my ear. There was a smile in his voice that made me smile, too.

He's a tough one to crack, Othura pointed out.

Then we'd better try harder.

Othura dove below the canopy of the treetops. Limbs jutted out at all angles, assailing us like a thicket of lances, and Othura expertly dodged each one, tilting her wings or tucking them to fit through tight spaces, banking and wheeling to avoid tree-trunks.

I could feel Kit breathing faster behind me, his chest rising and falling against my back. I could almost feel his heartbeat thumping in time with mine, both our bodies lost in a dance of exhilaration and adrenaline and pure, feral joy. We burst out of the woods at the Cauldron and found ourselves in the open. It was dark, and the black lake glimmered with moonshine and starlight. Othura glided over the mirror surface of the water, her wingtips sending up tiny splashes, her tail tracing along the surface of the water, leaving a pattern of ever-expanding ripples behind us.

Kit held me tight now, though it wasn't fear I sensed from him, but something else. Life. Longing. And I found myself arching my back against him like cat against an outstretched hand.

I turned my head and found his face there. My lips brushed the stubble of his cheek—and for a fraction of an instant, I felt what the priestesses called *one*. One with the stars. One with the sky. One with Othura, and the night wind, and the moonlight.

One with Kit.

My body felt alive with his nearness, full, aching, bursting. I turned and faced forward again fast, my heart racing.

"We fly well together," he said, his voice so low and soft he could have been speaking inside my mind, his lips so close I felt his breath on my cheek.

So close... Too close.

Othura, take us back, I thought. *Now.*

24
CHARLIE

It was afternoon, and I'd spent the day locked in my tower room, waiting for Essa to come and thinking of the flight we'd shared the night before. Rohree the sprite had come and brought breakfast and lunch, but she'd shared no news about when the princess might come—either to train or to tour me around the city.

And so, I found ways to pass the time. In the morning, knights were training in the courtyard below, and I studied them, taking more notes on their combat techniques. I read my book on the twelve types of dragons and took notes on those, too. When I grew tired of that, I did some push-ups and squats. As afternoon shifted toward evening, I was so eager to get out that when a knock came at the door, I nearly ran to answer it. But instead of Essa, I found Ollie there, holding a bottle in his hand and a wooden box under one arm.

"May I?" he asked, and I stepped aside, letting him enter.

He set the box on the table and set about uncorking the bottle.

"I promised to teach you Torzame," he said. "I thought you might like some entertainment."

"Where's Essa?" I asked, startled and a little embarrassed by the eagerness in my voice.

But if the Torouman noticed, he didn't let on. "Busy. Laynine called a mandatory training for all Skrathan today. Come, sit."

He poured us two glasses of jinjin and set about explaining Torzame.

At a glance, it looked quite a bit like the chess game I was familiar with, except the board was triangular and there was a set of red pieces in addition to the black and white ones. And along with the normal king, queen, pawns, knights, rooks, and bishops, each side also had four winged pieces which, of course, represented dragons.

"Torzame is the sacred game of the Torouman," Ollie explained. "They start us off playing it at six years old, and we play at least one game daily, even as adults."

"So, my odds of beating you are slim," I said.

He laughed. "Perhaps. But it is a game every person should learn. And there is no way for you to understand the politics of Maethalia without understanding Torzame."

"Why's that?" I asked, sipping my drink.

"Torouman are the chief advisors to the royals. Torzame is critical to our philosophy and our worldview, which, in turn, informs our advice to those we serve."

"The queen and Essa..." I finished, and Ollie nodded. "What about Paemalla? She must've had a Torouman. And the other brothers and sisters Essa had who've also died as riders..."

"They all had Torouman," Ollie agreed. "Paemalla's has returned to the Torouman temple and headquarters at

Empra for a time of mourning. The others live simple lives here in the city, serving as scholars and advisors. Once a Torouman's royal has died, their time of direct service to the crown ends. Now, let me explain the game."

As I'd expected, the gameplay did resemble chess, with the addition that after their own turn, each player also got the chance to move one of the red pieces. The result was a game that felt far more chaotic and unpredictable than a normal game of chess—and I wasn't much of a chess player anyway. Ollie beat me in short order, and I downed the rest of the drink and reset my pieces to play again.

I was bad at Torzame, that much was clear. But as we continued to play, I noticed the red pieces added a dimension that helped me think in a more complex way, and I began to understand why the Torouman valued the game.

"Triangulation is one of the Torouman's core principles," Ollie explained. "Most people think in simple terms. Black and white. Good and evil. Right and wrong. Me and my enemy. But the Torouman always seeks the third path. The third thought. The third power. One analogy we use is a person trying to smash their way through a stone wall. Push as hard as you can, you still can't break through. But..."

"The Torouman would climb over," I surmised.

Ollie smiled. "Or use a ladder. Or hire someone to build a door. Or ask whoever was on the other side to toss over whatever it was we wanted. Or get a dragon to break the wall for us..."

"Ruthless cunning," I said.

Ollie raised his glass. "We prefer to call it wisdom."

"And what game are you playing by coming to visit me?" I asked.

He picked up a piece, considering it. "No game. I'm just

trying to figure out what sort of piece you are. A pawn... or a dragon."

He suddenly tossed the piece at my face—hard—and I caught it. It was one of the winged ones, I saw. A dragon.

"You have fast reflexes for a scribe," he observed, then downed the rest of the drink and stood. "Keep the board and the bottle. I'll come and play with you again when my schedule allows."

"I appreciate it," I said. "It can get a bit dull in here. Do you have any idea when Essa—?"

"If I were to guess, I imagine she'll visit this evening. I think she may have taken a shine to you."

"And how do you feel about that?" I asked.

Ollie's eyebrows went up.

"You've been her companion since childhood. You're sworn to protect her." I shrugged. "You must have some feelings toward her?"

The Torouman smiled. "See, the game is already working. It is very Torouman to ask how I feel about you growing closer to Essa. First off, I am a eunuch. I have no romantic feelings for Essa—or anyone. Second, I like you. And I want Essa to be happy between now and the end of the challenge. My concern is not for her, reporter, but for you."

"For me?"

He turned to gaze thoughtfully out the window. "Another Torouman concept is the scales." He held out both hands palms up. "On one side is your value if kept alive— namely, the article you may write. On the other side is the danger you pose as an enemy in our midst. You must make sure people see your scale balancing correctly."

"So... the queen has to like me."

"Not just the queen," Ollie said. "The nobles. The Gray Brothers. The Skrathan. Even the Torouman. A court is not a game of chess, Admite. It is a game of Torzame. Triangles are everywhere. And it can be deadly."

25
ESSA

"Well, poet, I like the lance and the clip. But I'm still not convinced a poet can teach a Skrathan anything about flying a dragon," I said.

"I'm not a poet," Kit reminded me with a smile. "I'm a reporter."

We were in the graveyard, about three miles from the palace. It was early, but already the spring morning felt pregnant with a growing heat. One could almost taste the dew in the air, could almost feel the flowers unfurling and stretching beneath the strong bronze sun.

As I'd instructed, Rohree had spirited Kit out of the palace early, while the pre-dawn darkness could hide him from curious eyes. It was a risk, bringing him here when so many tongues were already wagging about him sneaking out of the palace and riding with me on dragon back when Braimar attacked. And I was already ignoring a summons from my mother, who'd been demanding an audience ever since I'd refused to kneel when I offered her my thimble.

But the funny thing about being a dead girl was, I didn't

care how others perceived me. And I was highly curious about what Kit thought he could teach me about flying. Part of me felt ready to laugh in his overconfident face. But another part of me hoped there might really be some knowledge hidden behind those dark blue eyes of his.

He took a slow lap around me, looking me up and down.

"Well, the first thing is to relax," he said, putting his hands on my shoulders. "There's a lot of tension in your body when you fly. Probably it was because you were holding on so tight with your hand. Now that you have the clip, you should be able to stay looser—which will make your reflexes faster."

I looked to Othura, who tilted her head, the dragon equivalent of a shrug.

Shut up, I told her.

"What else?" I asked.

"Well, from what I've observed, it's clear many of the dragons are larger and more powerful than yours. No offense," he added with a glance at Othura.

She gave a low growl.

"*But,*" he went on, "Othura is more maneuverable. One move you could use is a half eight."

"Which is?"

Kit searched the ground for a moment, then picked up a twig shaped like a lower-case "t"—or a dragon with wings. He also picked up a second, somewhat larger stick.

"See, if another dragon is pursuing you, you pull up, like this, flip over, and then turn upright again."

"I can't fly upside down," I said.

"With the clip you can. And it's just for a second, before you rotate upright again. See, it will put you in a position right above the enemy rider. If Othura wanted, she could take their head right off as she flew over them. Or, if it were a URA pilot, you could shred their upper wing."

I crossed my arms. "How does a poet know such things?"

Kit hesitated only an instant. "My older cousin was an airplane mechanic and pilot. He did the mail runs out of Danlee. Sometimes, I'd go with him. He was even an Air Force pilot... for a while."

"And you had no desire to follow in his footsteps? Become a pilot yourself?" I pressed.

"Me?" He shook his head. "Well... I thought about it. Every kid in the URA does. But my talent is for words. It would be a shame to waste a gift like mine."

"I have yet to read any of your writing." I crossed my arms, studying him. "Perhaps you'd write an ode for me, one of these days."

He smiled. "An article, you mean. I'm a reporter, Princess. No odes for me. Just the facts."

"So you say." I arched an eyebrow and looked to Othura. "A half eight, eh? Let's try it. And you, poet—you can ride with me. That way, if I fall off, we both fall."

Aren't you going to tell him you're scared of going upside down? Othura asked.

I am not scared, I shot back. But we both knew that was a lie. I'd been terrified of it ever since I was a little girl—ever since the accident. It was one of the main reasons I'd remained stuck at the bottom of the Skrathan roster even as my other flight skills had increased. But for the moment, as I climbed into the saddle, my desire to prove something to Kit, and to myself, outshone my fear.

Even if you keep your seat because of the clip, he may fall off and die, Othura pointed out as Kit climbed on behind me.

If he did, we would know he was telling the truth, that he was nothing but a writer. But...

I have a feeling he won't fall, I told Othura.

My hand clip snapped into place. I had to admit that was a marvelous improvement, whatever the noble council might say when they found out.

"Let's try it first without the lance," Kit said. His tone was all business, but his lips were so close to my ear again, his breath sending tingles through me.

I sort of hope he falls off, I told Othura. I gave my legs a quick squeeze, and she took her cue, galloping forward and launching into the air.

"Now, when you start the loop, make sure you're looking up, not just forward. You want to spot your target early and lock onto it with your eyes. It's a loop and a twist. Here, you can try it on this treetop. First you fly over it, then..."

A lightning-struck tree towered in the middle of the cemetery. Fire had scorched its trunk black, but there was a tuft of green on the top where it was trying to come back to life.

Resilience, I thought. Such a tree deserved respect. It would be a worthy foe.

We made for the treetop and shot past it.

Othura started to pull up, but I shouted to her in my mind. *No! No. I'm not ready.*

She leveled out, and we continued flying.

"What happened?" Kit asked. "We were supposed to—"

"I know what we were supposed to do!" I shouted. "I'm..." I couldn't finish the sentence.

Suddenly, I felt Kit's hand on my neck. I gasped, tensed. But his fingers were gentle, pressing but not strangling.

"Your heart is beating so fast," he said.

I closed my eyes and exhaled a shuddering breath. Riding a dragon into battle was hard. Vulnerability was harder.

"I'm... scared, alright? Of going upside down. Of flying. All of it. I mean, I love it, too. That's the awful thing. I love it, but I'm also terrified. I have been ever since..."

His hand left my neck, tracing down my back to cinch around my body again.

"You don't have to be scared," he said. "I've got you."

I gave a sharp laugh. "You're hanging onto me! I'm the one with the clip and the stirrups. Let go and you'll fling off like a javelin."

"It's a tight turn. Centrifugal force will keep me in place," he said.

He must've felt the tension still in my body, because he leaned in again and whispered in my ear.

"Do the Skrathan have an anthem? Or a credo? Some mantra you can repeat to take your mind off what you're doing?"

I pondered that.

Your grandmother's saying, Othura suggested.

"There is something," I said. "My grandmother died in the beginnings of the current war. When they were preparing her body, they found a tattoo on her leg that matched a saying embossed on her dragon's saddle. It said, *the wind is ours.*"

"Perfect," he said. "Just as you're going into the loop,

think of those words. Over and over. Let them fill your mind, okay?"

I wanted to say something sarcastic, to throw his help back in his face. But I held my tongue as Othura banked and shot ahead for another pass.

We whipped past the treetop and just as Othura started to pull up in a loop, I whispered it:

"The wind is ours."

Kit's said it too, his low voice in unison with mine, making a harmony that sent a shower of goosebumps over my skin.

We repeated it together:

The wind is ours.

The wind is ours.

The wind is ours.

And the next thing I knew, we were upside down. There was a moment of weightless suspension, then we spun out of it, the treetop whooshing past just behind us.

"We did it!" I said, not even caring about the giddiness in my voice.

"That was great," Kit said. "Next time, let's come out of the loop a little faster and make the dive a little sharper to keep that treetop enemy in front of us."

He didn't fall, Othura pointed out.

No, I agreed. *Not yet.*

In truth, he'd handled the maneuver with surprising grace, his arms on my waist barely tightening.

We made another pass. This time, when we came out of the loop, the treetop was in front of us, and Othura snapped at it with her jaws as we shot past. If it had been a rival rider or a URA pilot, they'd have ended up headless.

"Good," Kit said. "Now let's try it with the lance."

We must've made at least fifteen passes with Kit giving me small adjustments each time before he was finally satisfied. "It's a lot more complicated when you're taking the enemy's movements into account, but this will do for now. Let's move on."

Next, he taught us a maneuver he called the cobra. It involved Othura rearing back mid-flight like a rampant horse. This would stall our forward momentum, causing any pursuer to fly past us.

When we'd perfected that, he showed us what he called a pylon turn, in which Othura would bank so hard her wings were vertical, perpendicular to the ground. When executed with her back to the opponent, it would allow me to attack with sword or lance. When executed with her belly to the enemy, she could attack with claws and teeth.

Of course, there were Skrathan terms and techniques that corresponded to nearly every move the poet introduced. More than once, I rolled my eyes.

This arrogant Admite thinks he invented the sun, I told Othura.

Still, I humored him, curious to see what he would say next. And by the end, I had to admit that with each new move he showed us, he had specific techniques and mechanical adjustments that were different from what Auntie Dreya and the other Skrathan instructors had taught me—and they were helpful. Something compelled me to follow each of his instructions, to show him how perfectly I could do it.

He drove us like a bloodthirsty Irska, bidding us to complete the same maneuver again and again until it was perfect. But there was a delicate balance of nurturing and smugness in him that fueled me both through rage and pride.

"Good girl," he said when I had completed a particularly skilled dive attack.

"I'm a woman," I shot back. "Not a girl."

The teasing grin he gave me only stoked the fire inside me brighter, made me want to try even harder.

When at last we lit upon the earth again, my limbs trembled with exhaustion. Othura, hungry from our morning exercises, flew off to scour the valleys for goats to eat, leaving us alone.

I'd brought a sack of food along for lunch. Now, I shouldered it and took Kit's arm.

"Come," I told him. "I know a picnic spot."

We sat on a flat boulder on the bank of the stream that ran through the cemetery. Since I was a little girl, I had little patience for sit-down meals. More often, I'd breeze through the kitchen, grabbing whatever items looked good while the cooks scolded me. I'd done the same thing this morning, so our lunch was a hodgepodge of items. A couple of stalks of yellow sweet root. A wheel of crumbly white cheese. Brown trail bread. A box of triteberries and a couple jars of honey mead.

First, we both cupped our hands and sipped from the stream, laughing at each other as the wetness drizzled down our fronts. But the water from the mountain stream was brilliantly cold and refreshing, and more than just quenching my thirst, it woke me up.

After we ate, we both lay back on the rock, watching a pair of kelmoon circling in the cloudless sky and waiting for Othura to return.

"What's your city like?" I asked him.

"Ironberg? It's just like this, if you replace the mountains with buildings and the streams with railroads and the mountain goats with assholes."

I laughed. "There are the poetics I've been wondering about." I sat up. "Make up a poem about me."

He pushed up onto an elbow. "You?"

I brushed a strand of hair out of my face, suddenly self-conscious. "I'm kidding. I know, you're a reporter, not a poet. It's only the facts for you. Besides, one can write a poem only if they're inspired."

His eyes met mine. I waited for them to dart away, but they held fast. I felt suddenly bold.

"You inspire me," I told him.

He blinked. "I do?"

I nodded. "I don't know why. Before you came, I felt I was just marching alone on this dreary path... like a sleep-walker walking toward a cliff. And now..."

"Now you're awake," he said, nodding as if he understood. As if he felt the same way.

I smiled. "Now someone is walking toward the cliff with me."

It was his turn to laugh, but it didn't break the tension between us. If anything, it became stronger. "Suppose I don't want to walk off a cliff?" he teased.

I inched closer to him, longing coursing through me now. "Why not?" I asked. "For a moment, you'd be flying."

We were so near now that our lips were almost touching. My hands trembled. My breathing became ragged. Here, on this rock, under the sun—I wanted him.

My hand found his shirtfront, grabbing it into a fist and tugging him toward me, my lips hungry for his. They almost met, came so close I felt his breath. Then he shrugged away, getting to his feet.

A huge, steadying breath wracked his body. He ran both hands through his hair.

"Essa... I have someone... back home."

Understanding crashed into me like a wave. Of course he'd have someone back in Ironberg. I'd just made a fool of myself.

I felt my face going red. And, maddeningly, a lump rose in my throat. Now he'd probably tell Mother I'd thrown myself at him. Not only would I be humiliated, I'd also committed a diplomatic blunder. How could I have been such an idiot? I opened my mouth to say something—anything— to redeem myself, but I had no words.

I was rescued by the sound of hoofbeats coming toward us. I looked up to find Ollie approaching and reining in his mount. Thank the gods...

"Your mother summons you, Essa. She's had me searching all over. You won't be able to put her off this time. Don't come, she says, and she'll send Trag after you." He turned to Kit. "And you, Kit—you have another audience with the prelate."

26
CHARLIE

Essa and Ollie walked me up to the Gray Brothers' black keep. As we approached, the shadow of the tower fell over us, and the temperature seemed to drop ten degrees. The pair of hulking, black-armored Lacunae knights who guarded the gates did not acknowledge us as we approached, and no eyes were visible behind the eye slits of their helms. *Creepy bastards.* As if to underline the point, the wrought iron gates swung open without word or touch as we approached, creaking on their hinges.

"You sure you're okay visiting the prelate on your own?" Essa asked. There was a new coldness in her voice. Could it be because I'd told her about Kitty? But surely that would make no difference to her. A princess—a future queen of Maethalia—would have no romantic interest in me. And yet the glint of pain as she looked away from me seemed undeniable.

Ollie was watching me expectantly, and I remembered Essa had asked me a question. In truth, I wasn't looking forward to being with Kortoi alone. However, as a spy, the chance to interface with my contact again unsupervised was one I couldn't pass up. I already had another set of notes in my bag, ready to deliver.

"It's fine," I said. "I met him once already. He seems like a decent enough fellow."

A spooky bastard was closer to the truth, but I didn't say so.

Footsteps drew our attention, and we looked over to find a pair of figures in light blue Skrathan cloaks with their hoods up being escorted out of the keep by a pair of Gray Brothers. It wasn't until they'd emerged from the gates that I glimpsed their faces. It was Laynine and Braimar.

The lead rider's eyes went wide when she saw us. "Essa."

"Laynine," Essa said. "I didn't know you were friendly with the prelate."

Laynine's face had gone pale, but when she spoke, it was with a measured calm. "Of course, cousin. The Irska of the Skrathan must have friendly relations with all important members of the royal court."

"Of course," Essa said, with an expression that looked more like an animal baring its teeth than a smile.

With a polite nod to me and Ollie, she slipped past us. Braimar followed her, giving me a crazy-eyed glare as he passed. Of course, I refused to look away.

Ollie and Essa exchanged a glance when they were gone, as if mutually acknowledging the significance of Laynine and Braimar being here at the Black Keep. But when he turned back to me, Ollie's usual calm demeanor remained intact.

"I wish I could join you," he said. "But the queen asked me to bring Essa back, and I dare not ignore her command."

"Mind what you tell him," Essa said. "He is a person who will use every scrap of knowledge he has to his advantage. And don't eat or drink anything he—"

"It's fine. Really. I can handle myself," I said.

Ollie nodded, satisfied, but Essa gave me a lingering look as I turned away from them and strode through the gates.

The gray-hooded Brothers said not a word but ushered me inside and into the same sitting room where I'd met Kortoi last time.

I'd barely had a chance to survey one of the ancient maps hanging on the walls when the prelate entered in a swish of dark robes.

"The ace returns," he said grandly. He must have noticed the panic in my eyes as I looked behind him. "Oh, don't worry, Charlie. It's true that there are many ears in this place, but I control all the tongues. Your secrets are safe here."

I forced a smile. The prelate seemed taller than I remembered him, and the glint in his dark eyes wilder. He gestured to a table where a tray of cigarettes, a mug, and a steel coffee percolator like the ones from the airbase sat.

"Please, sit."

I remembered Essa and Ollie's warning, but the allure of the prelate's hospitality proved too much. I sat and lit a cigarette, exhaling a great sigh of smoke while Kortoi poured me some of his strange-smelling coffee. When I sipped it, it was even more delicious than last time.

Only one cup, though, I reminded myself, remembering how lightheaded the stuff had made me before.

I reached into my bag and took out a cork.

"Before I forget, I have another message for you to send back for me," I said, twisting off the upper part of the cork.

I'd hollowed it out and placed small scraps of paper inside it, each filled with notes.

"How inventive," Kortoi smiled. "Certainly, I will pass your message along, just as I did the last one."

I placed the top of the cork back on and handed it over, proud of my spycraft. These notes contained some more specific ideas about how dragons might be defeated based on my observations. It also contained a detailed list of targets within the city along with a hand-drawn map.

"My contacts in Admar were pleased to know you are alive," Kortoi said. "And they are most eager to receive your intelligence. Of course, I share a good deal of information myself, but there are things the Skrathan keep even from me. Alas, the crown doesn't always trust my Brotherhood. Bad blood, I'm afraid. But given your vocation and your access, I imagine there are things you can observe which perhaps my brothers and I could not. Your leaders hold high hopes for what you might accomplish here. And when the time comes, I will be ready to help ensure your safe return."

"I appreciate that," I said, sipping the coffee. It was delicious and filled me almost immediately with a warmth that spanned from my toes to the top of my head, making the world swim.

"It's a nice feeling, eh?" Kortoi said, perhaps noticing the flush I was feeling.

I nodded, sipping again, and my eyelids fluttered closed for a moment. When they opened again, his face seemed closer to mine, his eyes disturbingly large. "This potion is one we use in our rituals, Charlie. It's a little taste of the void. That is what our religion is about, you know—we Gray Brothers. Bringing the void into this world. Here on the earth, we celebrate our little handful of young, happy gods.

But the void is teeming with gods, Charlie. Ancient gods. The vast, night-black spiders who spun the webs that hold the universe together. Minds that never cease thinking. Mouths of endless hunger. Hundreds. Thousands. All of them powerful. All of them hungry. They want to live again, Charlie. They want *bodies*."

I realized my eyes had shut, and I forced them open. The world was spinning so hard I almost vomited. Instead, I laughed. "What the hell are you talking about?"

"You'll see, Charlie. You'll see..."

My eyelids fluttered shut again, but his voice continued, seeming to grow louder in my mind until it displaced every other thought, every other feeling. "Now listen. When you wake up, you may not remember this. But I want you to know. To know, in the back of your mind, where all the greatest and most important knowledge lies. A new day is dawning, Charlie. And when it comes, the wars of men will seem as trivial as a raindrop in the sea. The time is nigh. And you will have your part to play, Charlie. We all will."

27
ESSA

I steeled myself and strode into Mother's great hall with Ollie a step behind. Hearth fires and torches lit the vast space, along with light from the tall windows. In their illumination, I saw the long tables set with an abandoned luncheon. At the far end of the hall, the court was being ushered out, leaving only Mother and a few of her most trusted advisors sitting at the head table.

She cleared the room for me. A bad sign...

It was a long walk up the center aisle of the room to the table where Mother sat, and the only sounds were our footfalls and the hiss and flicker of the torches. At the foot of the dais, we stopped, and I curtsied.

"What do you have to say for yourself?" Mother asked.

"Um... Yay me?" I said.

Her eyes narrowed. "Your humor is ill-suited to the moment, Daughter. Perhaps the foreigner's influence has eroded your sense of decorum. Let me remind you. You disrespected me at the Thimble Race. I hear you've allowed the foreigner to ride dragon-back. Now, I hear he's helping you train for the challenge."

I gritted my teeth, wondering who had told Mother about Kit helping me. Really, it could have been anyone. Or no one. Mother was always scrying, and she had eyes everywhere.

"And what is that *thing* on your arm?" she pressed.

I glanced down at the clip prosthetic. I probably should have taken that off...

My impulse with Mother was always to shout, to fire an arrow back at her for every one she fired at me. In private, I would have done so. But here, now, with her advisors present, was not the place.

Hoatan sat next to Mother, drumming his fingers on the table, his kindly, care-worn face a mask of neutrality. Behind Mother stood Trag, Mother's personal guard, his battle-scarred visage implacable in the flickering torchlight. I gathered myself and took a slow, steadying breath.

"My action at the Thimble Race was rash," I said. "My feelings were hurt because Laynine won, and I knew you favored her. I apologize. As for Kit—Mr. Rowley—yes, I did allow him to ride Othura with me. You asked me to give him every experience of Maethalia I could. How better to convince him of the insurmountable power of our dragons than to let him ride one himself? I was only following your orders, My Queen. And as for his aid—yes. I have accepted help from him. To win the challenge over your durrah, I will need every advantage I can get."

Mother sat back in her chair, swishing the wine in her goblet and frowning at me.

"Putting aside the question of what sort of dubious help

that foreigner could give you... do you truly believe you can win, Essaphine?"

My throat constricted with emotion, but I forced myself to remain steady.

"Do you truly believe I can't?"

Mother sighed. "Come, my daughter. Let's be honest with each other—and with ourselves. Laynine is the best flyer we've had in many years. Better even than Paemalla was, though it pains me to say so. And you are—" She stopped.

"I am what?"

Mother sipped her wine. "You are less than whole."

I brandished my maimed arm.

"I have no arm," I said. "Thanks for reminding me. But I am whole. This is all I am, Mother. All I will ever be. It will have to be enough for you."

"You are enough for me, Essaphine," Mother said. "But you are not enough to become Irska. Try, and you will die."

"Is that not what you raised me for?" I demanded. "To fulfill my duties?"

"There are other duties you might fulfill," she said. "You seem to have taken a liking to the foreigner. Perhaps you could accompany him back as an ambassador. Try to broker a peace with our enemies. Or Braimar—he has expressed an interest in marriage—"

"A married woman cannot be queen," I reminded her, trying to keep my voice from shaking. "And only a rider may sit on the throne. Leave the Skrathan or marry Braimar and I would be abdicating my future crown—to Laynine. But of course, that's what you want, isn't it?"

Mother sighed again. "I want you to live, Daughter."

Hot tears stung my eyes, but I would not let them fall.

"You would have me alive and useless. Alive and failed. Alive and cast aside, exiled, rejected."

"You are too dramatic, Essaphine."

"And you're too cold!" I shouted. "I will win, despite you. And despite everyone in this kingdom who doesn't believe in me."

"The best rider will win. Nothing would please me more than if that were you. But..."

"*But* your precious Laynine and a hundred other riders are ranked higher. I know. I saw her leaving the Brothers' tower today, by the way."

A look of dismay flickered across Mother's face, but she quickly mastered herself. "Just a normal social visit, I'm sure. The Gray Brothers are important allies of the crown. We must keep close relations." Despite her words, Mother's expression remained dark. "I'll ask her about it. But I bid you, think about what I've said to you, Essaphine. There are many ways you can serve your kingdom alive, and none you may serve if you are dead. I want only what's best for you."

There was more I could say. Every conversation with Mother seemed to have the potential to be a circular argument, contentious and unending. But I had the grace to stay silent and curtsey.

"But enough about the challenge," Mother went on. "Tell me how your other task goes. Tell me about the reporter."

"Despite being an enemy, he has been little trouble," I said. "He seems to be eager to learn more about our way of life."

"We want him to go back and tell his people that our culture is superior, our army invincible, our dragons and their riders supreme among all fighters on earth. Is he getting the message?"

"I believe he is," I said.

Mother traced a finger over her lips thoughtfully. She and Hoatan exchanged a glance.

"And has there been any behavior from him that you would consider suspicious?"

I frowned. "Suspicious in what way?"

"Well, he has come here to gather information. The line between a reporter and a spy is a thin one. Have you seen anything to make you think he is... other than what he claims to be? There is a rumor he scaled down the northern-most tower. That is hardly the act of a bard."

I hesitated. Kitty was a bard with nerves of steel. A poet who knew flight tactics and weaponry. A scribe who seemed eager to meet Prelate Kortoi alone...

Though Mother was always diplomatic when speaking of the prelate, everyone in the court knew that the Brother-hood had been gaining in power and influence each season. Their dark acolytes had always been a counterbalance to the royals and their riders, but there were whispers among the commoners that the Brothers could supersede the crown one day. Some of the wealthier citizens had taken to tithing to the Brothers on top of paying their taxes to the crown, just to ensure they were in the Brothers' good graces. Kortoi was, in a word, the most suspicious man in the kingdom. And Kitty had known his name, had asked to meet him...

I opened my mouth, but it was a moment before words would come out.

"I... believe Kit is honest. Or at least as honest as one of his kind can be."

"Good," Mother nodded with a glance at Trag. His

scarred face remained impassive. "You keep showing him the kingdom. We'll keep watching him. You may even continue training with him—although you should take pains to hide that contraption on your arm. I'm rather interested to learn what this scribe thinks he knows about flying. But remember, Essaphine: if he were found to be a spy, he would have to be killed. What I'm saying, my dear, is don't get too attached."

28

CHARLIE

In my dream, I stood with Essaphine on a high hill. The land all around us was barren, windswept, and bitterly cold, but heat radiated from the earth, hot as dragon's breath. In the dream, Essaphine had two hands—not just one—and I held them, gazing into her eyes as if we were lovers. There was something I desperately wanted to say to her, but in the strange way of dreams, my lips wouldn't work, and no words would come out. She couldn't speak either, but there was a sorrow in her eyes that made my heart ache.

There came a cracking sound, and I looked down at my feet. Small fissures were appearing in the rock under us, exposing veins of orange magma beneath the stone. The cracks spread, sundering the rock all around us, then a gap began opening, pulling us apart. The world blurred with waves of heat, and the magma's glow lit everything with an ominous orange light. There was something in the sky, too. Many somethings. I could feel them waiting to swoop down and snatch us up in their rending claws, grab us in their gnashing mouths. Not dragons. They were something else. Something unnatural. But I was afraid to look up and see what they were. I held onto the princess's hands as long as I could as the fissure beneath us widened and pulled us apart, until at last I was forced to release her.

"*Essa!*" I shouted.

The word sent me gasping awake, and I found I'd actually been shouting. Predawn light shone in the window, blue and dim. The fire in my hearth had burned down, and a chill hung in the air, but sweat still beaded on my forehead.

A dull ache throbbed in my head, courtesy of the Gray Brother's coffee, perhaps, and I let my head fall into my hands and breathed slow and steady, letting the anxiety of the dream drain out of me.

Crick. Crick-crick.

It was the sound from the dream, the cracking of the earth. But I was awake... wasn't I?

Or was I going mad?

Crick.

No, that was real. I threw back the covers and rose from bed, standing and listening. When the sound came again, I rushed to the window, looking out. *It must be a bird. Or—?*

There it was again—behind me. I turned back to the room and crept forward, listening harder.

Crack.

The wardrobe. I approached cautiously and flung open the doors.

In the bottom of the cabinet, the stack of blankets twitched. I reached in gingerly and jerked the top blanket away. Then the next one. Then the next.

And I saw it.

The dragon egg. Jagged cracks traced its surface, and

from a hole in its top there emerged glowing orange eyes. Needle-sharp teeth. Slimy bat wings.

I gasped, slamming the wardrobe doors, stumbling backwards and falling.

Heart thundering in my chest, I rolled to my bed, grabbed my oilskin bag from beneath it, groped in the false bottom, and took out the gun. Back to the wardrobe I went, weapon ready.

One, two, three.

I threw the doors open again.

The creature emerging from the egg was no bigger than a squirrel. It sat inside its cradle of broken shell, blinking up at me with big, bright eyes. As I watched, it gave a huge yawn, which would have been adorable if not for the mouth full of sharp teeth.

"A dragon," I breathed. "There's a damned baby dragon in my room..."

A knock at the door startled me so much I literally jumped into the air and slammed the wardrobe shut.

"Yes!" I called in an overly musical voice, rushing to the bed and stuffing the gun under my pillow.

The lock clicked and the door swung open, revealing the sprite, Rohree.

"You're up early," she grunted, carrying a tray of food.

"Yes, well..." I tried to come up with some clever response, but nothing came to mind. The sprite set the food on the table.

"The princess has a full day of training today and wishes for you to join her. She bid me get you fed and ready."

From the wardrobe, there came a sound like a baby's yawn. Rohree looked to me, frowning. I clapped my hands to my stomach.

"Hungry," I said with a broad, fake smile.

The sprite arched an eyebrow.

"Well. I'll leave you to eat and dress. I'll be back to fetch you in half an hour," she said, and left the room, locking the door again behind her.

I exhaled the breath I'd been holding and crept back to the wardrobe, praying what I'd seen before had been imagined, a dream that had strayed into the waking world. But no. There the thing was, clambering out of its shell, now. It had one clawed foreleg and a wing free, both covered in slime. When it looked at me, it cooed a greeting.

"My god..." I muttered, passing a hand over my forehead.

Why had I been so stupid as to steal a dragon egg? Had it never occurred to me what came from dragon eggs? But Essa had said the fungus on them would kill the dragons inside. That's why all the eggs were being destroyed. If I hadn't snatched this one, it would have been smashed on the rocks with all the others. I rubbed my stubbled chin, thinking. This egg should not have hatched. And yet here it was: a baby dragon.

I knelt before it. It was grunting now, laboring, trying to get its other foreleg free.

"We're in trouble, me and you," I said.

What could the penalty for stealing a dragon egg be? Given how sacred dragons were in this culture and given that I was an enemy of the state, such an infraction could very well be punishable by death. And there was no way I could keep this creature a secret in my room. Already, Rohree had almost found me out. There was only one remedy.

I stood and went to the bed, taking my gun from

beneath the pillow again and striding back to the wardrobe. I shut off the gun's safety and leveled it at the dragon.

The thing looked up at me. Aside from their orange hue, its eyes looked strikingly like those of a human baby. *But it's not a baby. It's a dragon. A killer. A little man-eating monster. Kill it. Before it grows up to kill me—or my friends.*

Slowly, my finger squeezed the trigger. Tighter. Tighter.

Those orange eyes locked onto mine... And then I felt it. A feeling in my gut that almost doubled me over. I was... hungry.

And then I felt something else. A warmth. Urine was running down my leg.

I cursed, stopping the piss with effort, then hurrying to the water closet, where I finished. My bladder felt better, but the ache of hunger in my stomach continued.

"What the hell is happening to me?" I muttered, dabbing at my wet leg. I dropped the night gown Rohree had supplied me with back into place and hurried back to the wardrobe.

The little dragon was free of its shell now. And the blankets it stood on, I saw, were soaked dark and smelled of ammonia.

It had pissed. I had pissed.

It looked up at me again, and our eyes met. Again, the feeling of hunger came over me, so overwhelming I almost felt dizzy.

"You're hungry," I whispered, turning my attention to the breakfast tray. As I crossed the room, I shivered, goosebumps breaking out on my arms. I grabbed the small pitcher of milk and went back to the wardrobe. By the time I got there, my teeth were chattering. I saw that the dragon was shivering, too.

"You're cold, eh?"

Grabbing an unsoiled spare blanket from the floor where I'd thrown it, I knelt and wrapped the baby dragon up, cradling it to my chest. It nuzzled in like a human infant with a contented sigh, then opened its piranha mouth as if it were a baby bird. I took the pitcher of milk and poured a drizzle into its maw. It gulped it down eagerly and opened its mouth again. I poured some more, and the pang of hunger in my own belly began to subside.

"Holy hell. I'm mother to a baby dragon," I muttered, pouring more milk into the thing's open jaws. Soon, its eyes were fluttering with sleepiness.

I sat staring at it. I'd never had a chance to observe a dragon so closely. They were truly beautiful, their back scales hard and glittering like gems, their fireproof bellies supple and soft like buffed leather. And all of them bullet-proof. Except... Gently, I held one of the dragon's wings and spread it out. It unfurled, a remarkable piece of anatomy. I took one of the dragon's foreclaws and pulled it back, too. It gripped me with its little talons like a baby holding a parent's finger and sighed in its sleep. There, in the little beast's armpit, was a spot where the back-scales and the tough belly skin met. The skin there seemed thinner. More delicate. More vulnerable. Conventional best practices called for targeting dragons at a 45-degree angle from the back, hoping the bullet would penetrate the gap between the scales. But it might just be time to revise that protocol, I thought. Gently, I placed the sleeping baby dragon back onto the blankets in the wardrobe and sat down to make some notes.

I spent the morning with Essa, training in the sky over the graveyard, teaching her some of my favorite dogfighting tricks. For such a belligerent girl, she was surprisingly receptive to my instruction, incorporating each technique and adjustment far better than the young pilots I'd mentored back home. As surreal as it was sitting dragon back, I grew almost comfortable there, my arms wrapped around Essa's taut waist, our bodies pressed together, leaning into the turns as one, feeling her windblown hair brush my lips.

Through it all, my mind kept returning to the baby dragon. I'd fed it until it had drifted off to sleep, then I'd put it back into his blanket nest in the wardrobe. When I thought of it now, I could still feel it there, blissfully asleep.

What did it mean that I could feel what it felt? It couldn't mean that we were bonded...

As we broke for lunch, Essa's friends arrived, Pocha bearing a basket of food, Lure a picnic blanket, and Dagar a small crate filled with jars of honey mead. I greeted them warily, but soon Dagar was clapping me on the back and putting a jar of mead in my hand. Lure was asking me about women back in Ironberg—a subject that elicited a sour look from Essa—and Pocha was making me a sandwich of ham, fresh bread, and spicy mustard, as if we were all old friends.

"Essa says your cousin is a pilot," Lure said, one eyebrow cocked. "And that's how you know so much about flying?"

I nodded, my mouth full of delicious food.

"You must have observed his moves closely to be able to teach them to another," Lure pointed out.

"Well, I am a reporter," I said. "Observation skills are important. And he used to let me ride with him, sometimes."

My smile faded as a pang of hunger struck my belly— even though I was in the middle of chewing food. The little dragon must have sensed me eating and grown hungry. I clapped a hand on my gut, willing it to stop growling.

"So," I grated out. "Tell me... what it's like to be bonded to a dragon? When you're first bonded—is it pleasant?"

Dagar laughed, running a hand through his messy brown hair. "Ha. Definitely not at first."

"Dragons bond with riders when they are first born, the way baby birds bond to their mothers," Pocha said. "It's like sharing a mind. Imagine being plugged into the brain of a baby."

Shit.

I was feeling a pressure in my bladder. Suddenly, it diminished. Back in my room, the baby dragon had pissed on something, I was sure.

Essa was leaning back on Othura as if she were a huge couch. "Yes, it's hard at first. Dragons don't know human language, so they don't actually communicate in words."

"Really?" I frowned. "How do they communicate, then?"

"It's its own language, really," Essa said. "We call it simnal. Impulses, longings, aversions—those sorts of things —pass between dragons and their riders. Feelings, not words. But as time passes and the bond grows, you begin to experience their communications in such a nuanced way that it *feels* like you're talking in words—if that makes sense."

"Yeah. It's weird," Dagar agreed. "You'll be sitting there holding a conversation in your mind, and it will seem like words are going back and forth. Like, you could sit down and write out the conversation, but then when you really think about it, you realize it isn't words at all. It's... I don't know... something more."

"A shared knowing," Lure said, taking a dragon-sized bite of ham.

I nodded, mulling their words over. "Interesting. Can a person who isn't bonded ever hear a dragon's emotions?"

"No," all four riders said at once.

So, the thing is truly bonded to me. My god... Why did I ever pick up that goddamn egg?

In response to this thought, I felt a wave of affection—a psychic snuggle.

What have I gotten myself into?

"Is there any way to block out the communications?" I asked.

"You can learn to," Essa said. "For example, if you're having a... private moment you don't want to share."

"But most of the time we keep the doors to our minds open," Pocha said. "Dragons are very intuitive. Almost psychic, really. And they look out for their riders. Many riders' lives have been saved by warnings from their dragon when danger was approaching. There is nothing in the world more loyal than a bonded dragon."

"Sounds fascinating," I said casually. "Could I bond one?"

They all laughed uproariously.

"Oh. Are only riders allowed to bond them?" I asked, trying to sound as innocent as I could.

"Anyone bonded to a dragon is a Skrathan by definition," Essa said.

"No foreigner would ever be allowed to bond a dragon," Pocha said. "Only Maethalian nobles are allowed to become riders. And even then, they only choose those who are especially talented."

"Or members of the royal family," Essa added, with a glance at her arm.

"And a few non-nobles are allowed to join if they're extremely gifted, like Lure here," Dagar said.

"Yeah. I'm the token commoner," Lure gave me a smug wink.

I sipped my mead, taking all this in.

"But if a dragon did bond with a foreigner..."

"It could never happen," Lure said, sounding irritated. "But if it did, it would mean death—for the dragon and the unauthorized rider."

Dagar nodded. "Yep." He drew a thumb across his throat and stuck out his tongue, a goofy approximation of death.

Essa was watching me a little too closely for my liking. As our eyes met, Othura brought her muzzle up to Essa's ear, nuzzling her in a way that made me think of a person whispering a secret. Essa nodded, stroking the dragon's nose without taking her eyes off me.

"Well, it's all very fascinating," I said, raising my cup and trying to sound as breezy as possible. "Cheers to the Skrathan."

"Cheers to the aces," Dagar said, raising his cup.

Lure gave him a venomous look.

"What?" Dagar shrugged. "They're brave. They fly and they fight. They're not so different from us when you think about it."

"They fly machines. Necromantic abominations," Lure said.

"I'm not saying I agree with them," Dagar said. "But one day the war will be over and our people will be at peace. Maybe we'll be sipping mead with an ace, just like we are with Kit here."

Lure's expression darkened. "The war will never be over. Not until all the aces are dead. Or all the Skrathan..."

We all took a sip of mead in silence.

"Well, who's everyone taking to the ball?" Pocha demanded after a moment, changing the subject. When no one answered immediately, she frowned. "Come on. We're all going."

"What ball?" I asked.

"The Skrathan Ball," Pocha said. "The queen throws one for her riders every season, but it's an especially big occasion on years when challenges are happening."

"They let us party extra hard—because some of us are about to die," Dagar explained, taking a bite of bread. Pocha kicked him in the shin. "What? It's true!" Dagar protested.

"Well, I've been asked to go by Dirian from Second Formation," Pocha said. "And I've accepted."

"Yay Pocha!" Essa said.

Dagar, I noticed, looked a tad dejected.

"I'm taking Vaini from First Formation," Lure said.

Essa looked to Dagar, who crossed his arms sullenly. "I suppose I'll take Clua again—if she'll go. Last time she swore she'd never come again," he said.

"Dagar drank too much mead and ended up dancing shirtless on a table," Pocha informed me. "Clua was not impressed."

"That new rider in Fifth Formation has had her eye on you," Essa said.

"No!" Dagar grumbled. "She calls me Dagie all the time. That's not my name."

"She's flirting," Essa pointed out.

"Well, that's a poor way to do it," Dagar sniffed. "Better to take a friend. No one else would appreciate the hors d'oeuvres as much as Clua anyway."

"What about you?" Pocha asked Essa.

"Braimar again," Lure answered before Essa could, taking a bite of meat off the point of their dagger. "Every time I see him, he has his eyes on you."

"He may not be up for dancing," Dagar said. "I heard he's taking the death of one of his dragon's heads a bit poorly. It's affecting him," he pointed to his head.

"I'm *not* taking Braimar," Essa said pointedly. Her eyes swept to me. "What about you?"

I pointed to myself, blinking.

She huffed an exasperated sigh. "I've been tasked by the queen my mother to show you all the wonders of our kingdom. I think the Skrathan Ball qualifies."

Lure gave a faint smile. "A bunch of debauched dragon riders acting like it's their last night on earth—because it just might be. I'd say it's a wonder."

"I'd go just for the food," Dagar nudged me with his elbow.

"And the gorgeous dresses and decorations," Pocha said.

Lure stood, holding the picnic basket. "We should leave them to talk about it."

In an instant, Essa's three friends had gathered the remnants of lunch and departed. Even Othura wandered off to sniff along the edge of the forest.

I found myself and Essa standing toe-to-toe and eye-to-eye. She reached out her hand and adjusted the front of my shirt.

"Don't think of going to the ball as some big thing. I just want to bring you because taking a foreigner will make everyone angry," she shrugged, but her gaze left the ground and found its way to my lips.

My eyes dropped to her lips, too. I blinked and looked away.

"I'd be honored," I breathed.

It hit me then: a feeling in my bowels, urgent and roiling. Other feelings swelled along with it. Hunger. Thirst. Claustrophobia. And rage.

The baby dragon was awake.

I pulled away from Essa. "Excuse me. I have to go."

"What? Where?" she demanded. "We're not done training."

"Back to my room," I called over my shoulder.

She looked baffled. "Why?"

"I... have to work on my article!" I shouted, then turned away from her, heading back for the palace at a jog.

I burst into my room and stopped cold, taking in the scene. The bedclothes were in disarray, the canopy pulled down. The curtains were shredded and smoldering. A pile of stinking brown waste and a puddle of urine soiled the carpet. The wood for the fire had been chewed to kindling, as had the footstool.

And the little dragon stood in the midst of all of it, its inquisitive orange eyes on me.

Its scales glistened in the sunlight, a dark gold color with reddish stripes down each of its sides, and I noticed it had the buds of horns on either side of its head. Its short wings opened and closed, as if testing the air, and its claws worked on the slate floor like a cat kneading its bedding. A feeling came from it as distinct as the sound of a gong being rung. It was not a word it spoke, but the communication was clearer than any word could have been.

I'm hungry. Hungry. Hungry!

Impossible. There was no way I could exist like this. I could not hide this creature, not for any length of time. I'd be found out. I'd be killed.

Resolute, I slung my bag off my shoulder and took out the pistol once more, aiming it at the spot between the dragon's large eyes.

Kill the thing. Now, before it grows up. Before it kills your friends. Before it kills you. Do it, this time. Pull the trigger.

It watched me. The thing had been happy to see me when I came in, its tongue lolling out of its mouth, its tail swirling in a way that made me think of a wagging puppy.

Now, I thought I saw sadness creeping into its eyes.

"You won't get anywhere begging," I snapped. "Do you know how many dragons I've shot down? Eighty-nine confirmed kills. I've gotten a damned Star of Valor for it. I'm an ace. Not a... not a..."

Essa's words came back to me. *Anyone bonded to a dragon is a Skrathan...*

But I would be damned if I were tied to a beast like this. I'd rather turn the gun on myself. And I did, pressing the barrel to the side of my head, just to test the idea. The dragon tilted its head, confused.

I clenched my teeth, my finger taut on the trigger.

Then I exhaled, and the arm holding the gun dropped in despair.

"Back in the wardrobe," I said, pointing.

I never expected it to understand my command, much less follow it. But with a flourish of its tail, the little thing scampered to the wardrobe and nestled into the blankets there. I stuffed the gun into the waistband of my pants and wagged a finger at the dragon.

"If you come out of this wardrobe before I get back, I swear on all things holy, my dragon count will be up to ninety. Is that clear?"

It agreed, making a sound like the cooing of a baby. I groaned, closing the wardrobe doors and turning to take in the demolished room once more. As fast as I could, I cleaned it up, bunching up the damaged curtains to hide their rips, tossing the gnawed firewood into the hearth, cleaning up the piss and feces with a towel, and re-making the bed. Then, with my stomach grumbling, I left for the kitchens to steal the beastly creature some more milk.

29
HOATAN

It was nearly midnight, and Hoatan stood at the mouth of the tunnel, staring out at the black, heaving sea. The only light came from the sliver of moon above and the flickering torches on the three ships that made their way toward him. The water in this crescent-shaped bay was calm and deep, and a ledge had been carved at the verge of the water, edged with a crenellated balustrade for ships to tie up to. All was made of stone, and from the sea or the air it looked like nothing more than another tiny inlet on the rocky coastline, but it was, in fact, a secret port large enough to accommodate several one-hundred-foot-long ships. The tunnels, which branched off from here, a combination of hand-chipped stone and natural cavern, went all the way back to the catacombs under the castle. This place had been a haunt of pirates and smugglers since before the days of Aulucia the White. But of course, when the Torouman discovered it, generations ago now, they took pains to secure it—and to use it for their own purposes.

The elders Hoatan had trained under would almost

certainly be sickened by the way the place was being used tonight, he thought. But that was the age-old Torzame, wasn't it? The first directive was always to keep the crown safe, and the most necessary work took place in shadow. It required compromise and uneasy alliances. And often, it involved blood.

"It is a historic day," Prelate Kortoi said, stepping up to the parapet next to Hoatan. "And yet you look stern."

"It is hard to smile with the weight of a kingdom on one's shoulders," Hoatan said. "I expect you can relate."

Kortoi turned to face Hoatan directly and put a hand on his shoulder. Something about the prelate's long fingernails always made him think of a spider's legs. It made Hoatan's skin crawl, but he would not let himself shy away from the touch.

"I know you are uneasy," the prelate said. "But we share the same goals. Protect the queen. Win the war. Put the nobles back in their proper place."

Hoatan nodded to himself. It was the last part that had necessitated the alliance with Kortoi: the murmurs of dissatisfaction among the nobility. The war was taking too long. Trade and prosperity were suffering too much. The queen was doing too little. With Paemalla's death, the predicament only became worse. In the eyes of many in the court, Paemalla had been the queen's last viable heir. Essaphine was damaged and doomed to die in the challenge. Laynine had potential, but if someone as removed as a niece tried to claim the throne, it opened the door for other claimants to come forth, too. Lord Natath's family, in particular, descended from the queen's aunt and would certainly grasp for the crown. Other relatives would clamber to assert their claims, as well. The result would be civil war. Such a distraction from the war efforts against the URA would result in Admite forces overrunning Maethalia.

The rule of the Skrathan would be ended. Queen Synaeda would be overthrown. The kingdom would fall. That was a result Hoatan could not allow.

Countering that threat necessitated an alliance with the prelate. And yet, he could not let Maethalia fall into the hands of Kortoi and his demonic knights and dark mages, either.

That was the path of the Torouman: to balance atop a treacherous path with a deadly drop to either side.

A thudding sound from below pulled him from his thoughts. He looked down to find the first ship docking. Sailors shouted, leaping and tossing ropes. A gangplank dropped into place, and the crewmen, along with a small army of Kortoi's gray-robed monks, began unloading the crates. Mule-drawn carts awaited in the caverns below, ready to take the cargo along the Black Road to the castle to be stored until the moment of need was upon them.

Pray to Earth Mother and Star Father that day never comes, Hoatan thought.

And yet a feeling of foreboding sat in his stomach, twisting itself like a slowly coiling snake.

One of Kortoi's monks hurried up to him bearing an envelope with a wax seal. He bowed and handed it over to Kortoi, who took it with one taloned hand. Hoatan watched as he ripped it open, and his eyes scanned the pages. A low laugh rumbled from his lips.

"What?" Hoatan asked.

"It is from one of our contacts across the sea. I asked them for some information about the princess's esteemed guest."

"Really?" Hoatan said. "The reporter?"

The prelate turned to him, holding up a copy of a URA military ID. The image on it was indeed of the foreigner who had been palling around with Essaphine, but the name on the card was not Kitty Rowley.

"First Lieutenant Charles Inman," Hoatan read. "He's an ace... I must warn the queen."

The prelate shook his head.

"No, my friend. I think not. I have scried into the void and seen this foreigner's face. He is a piece we must not take off the board just yet. He has a part to play. And our game is only beginning."

30

ESSA

Two weeks passed, slow and sweet as dripping honey.

Death remained my constant companion, a specter hovering always in the corner of my mind, growing larger as the final challenge date approached. And yet so many small joys filled my hours that the dread of that final showdown felt small in comparison.

By day, I spent my days training, Kit's arms around me, Othura beneath me, our skills and strength growing with each flight. I'd been riding since Othura and I had bonded when I was ten years old, but as I worked with Kit, I saw that no one had ever taken me seriously as a Skrathan. Aunt Dreya had taught me enough to keep me alive and avoid embarrassing my family, but no more. And though I'd been a willing pupil, I'd never truly applied myself to practicing what she'd taught me. What was the point when others would always be so much greater than I was?

But now, my life hung upon my ability to fly and fight. And Kit trained me as if that life were precious indeed. In

Kit's eyes, I saw a desire burning that mirrored my own—a desire to live, and rise, and conquer. And there was something else in him, too... a strength and a calm. I felt it in his body, pressed against my back when we rode through the sky together; I felt it in his arms as they held me even through the most dangerous maneuvers. Feeling how relaxed he was made me realize how tense I had been in comparison. How terrified. But his calm, his confidence, his fearlessness—they must have been contagious, for I felt them filling me, too. And with every flight, my skill as a rider grew.

I began to fixate on tiny moments between us. His hand on mine as he guided my lance. His fingers on my waist as he pulled himself up behind me on the saddle. The moment in mid-air when I turned to tell him something funny, and he pushed my hair back out of my eyes.

I still felt deep down that I would be doomed when the day to battle Laynine came. And my thoughts ran with obsessive frequency to the pleasure I might enjoy while I was still alive. Pleasure with Kit...

Such things were forbidden to a princess. We were to be pure when the day of ascension came and we took the throne—that was what the noble houses demanded of any new queen. Purity.

And yet...

But what if I never lived to wear the crown?

Should I die without knowing the pleasure of love?

The question haunted me. Each meal Kit and I shared, each ride we took on Othura, each walk we took about the countryside, it was there—a sweet and growing tension.

Don't be a fool. Even if he weren't your enemy, he has someone back home, I reminded myself.

And yet for now, for this fleeting season, I couldn't help feeling that he was mine. I had only to order Rohree to bring him to me, and he was there, my prisoner, my teacher. He spoke with passion about how I might improve my riding, adjust my tactics. How I might win. Become Irska. Become queen one day. It was like he wanted me to win, needed me to win. And his ferocious belief was almost enough to make me believe, too.

And yet he seemed distracted at times. I'd find him gazing off into the distance, chewing his bottom lip, as if listening to some distant voice only he could hear. He'd show up with disheveled hair or looking like he hadn't slept.

"He's a writer. He probably stays up late working on his article," Dagar said once when I mentioned it.

"No! He's up all night dreaming of you, I'll wager," Pocha teased.

He smells of dragon, was all Othura would say on the subject—an enigmatic statement which I took to mean Othura felt the same way about him that I did, that despite coming from Admar, deep down, he was one of us. A poet with the soul of a Skrathan, born on the wrong side of the world. I had only to lock eyes with him to know it was true. He did smell of dragon. And it was a sweet, sweet smell.

The other riders whispered about us behind cupped hands. The court watched us with stony faces whenever Kit and I attended royal feasts. Even Ollie seemed on edge about our growing friendship, his usually jocular, supportive air now peppered with warnings.

Remember, he'll have to leave soon, Essa.

Remember, he's not one of us, Essa.

Remember, he's an enemy.

Several times, I saw Braimar up on the castle walls as Kit

and I walked past below, watching us like a crow. Since his dragon's injury, his long green hair had become a mad tangle. His clothes were soiled. Once, he even shouted at us from atop the wall, a snatch of sing-song-rhyme: *Rider and the writer, he wants to get inside her, bloody, bloody, bloody, they all fall down.* Then he cackled, staring down with eyes like burning coals.

"He's gone mad," Ollie had said when I told him about it. "All the riders are talking about it. His dragon is flying again... but for Braimar to be bonded with two minds and lose one of them? It's hard to say how that might affect a man. I can only hope he recovers. The Skrathan need his strength. He's still the number two rider, after all. And he was a good man, once."

Perhaps that was true. But I looked back on our romance, and all the tender feelings of first love and first disappointment that came with it, with a cold disdain. How could I have loved Braimar when the world contained a man like Kit?

I should not think such thoughts, I reminded myself.

But always my thoughts came back to it: Kit and me.

The ball... Each day drew us closer to it. I chose a dress of sprite-woven fabric that shimmered in the light like a waterfall of gold. I had it altered to fit me. I took more pains in choosing my jewelry and my shoes and my hairstyle than I'd ever taken over such frivolous things. And as I lay in bed at night, I imagined what I would do with my enemy poet at the end of that longed-for night. And what I would let him do to me.

31
CHARLIE

"Listen, I have to go to the ball," I told Parthar. That was the name I had given the little dragon—or rather, that he had given himself. Every time I thought of him, he either brayed a word that sounded like *prarrharrr*—half purr, half growl—or the word came into my mind. Parthar. So that was his name.

The dragon had grown an ungodly amount in a mere two weeks, from a baby that could nestle in my arms like a football to a rollicking beast the size of a small hound. I felt like I'd lost the same amount of mass he'd gained—both from the stress of keeping the dragon secret and from the fact that I gave him at least half of my food—I couldn't ask for more without risking suspicion. Already, Rohree had discovered damage to one of the chair cushions and given me a scolding. Now, she scanned the room with an inquisitive eye every time she entered.

Fortunately, the wee beastie was a quick learner. He knew to hide in the wardrobe whenever someone came to the door—though I knew he didn't like it much—and he hadn't trashed the room since that disastrous first day. Still, I was grateful Essa never came here—because I had a feeling a rider would sense a hiding dragon right away.

Now, as I clipped my cloak on and turned from the mirror, Parthar stood atop the bed's canopy, wings spread like an eagle testing the wind.

"Parthar, no," I said. Too late. The beast swooped down, hitting me in the chest and knocking me on my ass as I caught him. "Parthar!" I scolded him.

He licked my face, his long, forked tongue as gritty as a cat's.

Dragons gotta fly. Gotta fly, Dad, I imagined him saying.

I put a finger on his soft snout. "Baby dragons who are secrets have to stay quiet. Or get their human daddies killed. Got it?" I said, sliding him off my lap and straightening the velvet tunic the princess had gifted me for the dance.

"How do I look?"

He cocked his head, blinking his orange, inquisitive eyes. *Hungry.*

Two-thirds of Parthar's thoughts related directly to food.

I groaned. "I already gave you most of my dinner!"

But no dessert. He looked mournful.

"Dessert is to be served at the dance," I said. "I'll pocket a few sweetcakes for you, alright?"

Promise?

A knock at the door. I felt my eyes go wide.

I promise. Now go! Into the wardrobe. Quick, quick, quick! I thought, and Parthar loped toward the cabinet and leaped in. I banged the doors shut and leaned against them just as the door to the room opened.

Rohree was there, her eyes narrowed.

"Everything alright in here? I thought I heard talking."

I smoothed my hair with one hand. "Just... reading some of my writing out loud," I said. "It helps with catching errors." I was grateful for the time I'd spent with Kitty—it had taught me enough about writing to lie about it, at least. The sprite's eyes drifted to my hands.

"Where are the pages you're reading?"

I pointed to my head. "In here," I cleared my throat. "I've memorized it."

"Good," Rohree said. "I know the princess is most eager to read what you've written. Perhaps you can recite it for her on the dance floor tonight."

A bang came from inside the cabinet.

Quickly, I rubbed my elbow. "Ow," I gave Rohree my most charming smile. "Damn, I'm clumsy. I suppose that's why I'm a writer and not a professional baseball player, eh?"

"And not a valet, either," she said. "Come here. Your cloak is a mess."

I came and knelt down before Rohree, allowing her to straighten my clothes.

"Thank you," I said. "You know, you've been really nice to me."

She glanced from my clothes to my face, and her normally hard eyes softened. "Well... I know what it is to be different, Master Kit. And what it is to be far from home."

"Where is your home?" I asked.

"We sprites are from Koratain, far in the south. It is controlled now by a race known as the sylph. Their culture is great and ancient and they are known throughout the world for their wealth and their trading prowess. But their lord is cruel, especially to sprites. Many of us fled."

"Once we get this war wrapped up, maybe I'll head down there and liberate it for you," I said.

The sprite gave me a sharp look. "With your pen?"

I gave a wan smile. "Well, they say it's mightier than the sword..." I moved on quickly. "So, you're a refugee."

Rohree nodded. "Yes. Well, my people are. Our family left in the days of my grandparents. Maethalia is all I've known. The kindness I've tried to show to you, the royal family has shown to us. And I've served Essaphine since she was a girl."

Thinking of the princess as a child made me smile. "What was she like?"

Rohree gave a laugh. "Naughty. Haughty. Sweet..." she paused, thinking, then added: "And fearful. And lonely. It is hard for a child to be different from other children. And harder still to be a royal. I'll tell you the truth. I've never seen her as happy as she's been these last few weeks."

There came another bang from the wardrobe. My heart stopped beating, and with its failure, I felt the blood draining from my face.

"Is that her?" Rohree whispered.

I didn't understand what she meant. "Her?"

She turned to the wardrobe. "Essaphine?" she called.

Then I understood. "Oh. Yes. Yes, it's her in there. Hiding."

The sprite's mouth fell open. "I'm surprised at you!" she shouted at the wardrobe. "I could tell you fancied him, but... Oh, for the sake of Earth Mother, come out!"

The wardrobe doors banged again but remained shut. Rohree was pushing me aside, grabbing the door handle.

"No. No! She's—she's naked!" I protested—too late.

The sprite flung the doors open, and there sat Parthar, his bright orange eyes blinking with calm satisfaction.

Rohree covered her mouth with her hands.

"A dragon," she whispered.

"Well... yeah," I said.

"A dragon cub."

"He's about two weeks old, yes," I sighed.

"It's..." She wheeled on me. "It's a miracle!"

I frowned, confused. "It is?"

"The eggs laid here no longer hatch," Rohree explained. "And even among those in the hatching grounds at Dorhane, none have hatched in over two years. But... why is he with you?"

"Uh..." I groped for an apt lie, but none came to mind. "It's a long story," I said.

"The princess knows, of course?"

I hesitated.

"I must tell her," the sprite said, rushing for the door. I stepped in front of her and put my hands on her shoulders.

"Rohree, no."

"This is the most important news in all of Maethalia. You truly expect me to keep it a secret from Essa?" She shrugged my hands off.

"Rohree, please, listen," I begged. "The princess has been looking forward to this ball for weeks. And if the challenge doesn't go as we hope, it might be the last one she gets." I shook my head. "If we tell her about the dragon now, she'll have to tell the queen. The court will be in an uproar. And I... Just give us tonight. Please. Just tonight. Then in the morning we'll tell Essa—together."

Rohree's lips pursed. She glared at me, then at Parthar,

who sat among the blankets at the bottom of the wardrobe, sucking his tail.

"To keep such a thing secret would be treason," Rohree said. "You're asking me to risk my life for you!"

"Not for me. For Essa. Just one night." I pleaded. "That's all I ask."

The sprite looked from Parthar back to me and nodded. "You have until midnight to tell her," she said. "After that, I'm going to the queen."

32
ESSA

I t had been two years since I'd attended a Skrathan ball, and I'd forgotten the wondrous beauty of it. The vast cascading flower arrangements. The flickering candles and torches. The magical fae lights drifting in the air like clouds of glowing dust motes. The long tables set with a feast of bite-sized goodies, including some of my favorites, like fig-roasted zyrfish and honey-drizzled soft cheese. The royal knights in their intricately painted armor lined up along the west wall of the ballroom at rigid attention. The pixies flitting among the buttresses, leaving trails of sparkling light behind them. Even the ballroom itself was beautiful with its gold-veined white marble columns and its high, vaulted ceilings, with a diamond-cut crystal dome at its zenith to capture and multiply the moonlight.

"Wow. You hold a ball like this every year?" Kit asked, leaning close to be heard over the music.

"Yes," I said. "As the queen's daughter, I'm supposed to attend, but I rarely do."

"Why not?" he asked, eyeing a fountain of sparkling wine.

"Oh..." I sighed. "I don't like the eyes on me, I suppose."

"I'm not surprised they stare," he said. "You look like a goddess."

I assumed he was teasing and slapped his arm. But when I looked at his face, I saw that his gaze upon me was intent, as if he would drink me with his eyes.

I looked away, blushing. "That's not what I mean," I said. "It's the court. Some are envious. Some judging. Some just hating. All of them scheming."

The breakup with Braimar had also soured me on going to dances, but I didn't want to bring that up—not to Kit.

"You make life as a royal sound awfully bleak," he said.

His easy tone made me laugh. "And you grin as if you'd enjoy crossing the mouth of a volcano on foot. But I have to admit, I feel better walking in here than I ever have before—having you on my arm."

Kit's smile deepened.

"If they're going to talk about you, let's give them something to talk about," he said, and led me onto the dance floor.

At the very center of the room, he stopped, turned to me, and bowed. "May I have this dance?"

I actually giggled—a terrible sound I don't think I'd made since I was a girl. My hand went to my mouth as I tried to stop myself, embarrassed.

"Of course," I said, and he crooked his arm around my waist and drew me close. Then we were moving, swept into the flow of the dance along with everyone else on the floor. His dancing didn't match what everyone else was doing, but I tried my best to follow him, and soon we were gliding across the floor together as one. He moved wonderfully, and I felt as light and graceful and sure in his arms as I did on Othura's back.

I shook my head. "Is there anything you're not good at?"

"Hmm. Well, I'm not great at writing," he said.

"That could pose a problem," I laughed.

"It does," he agreed.

"And yet, the fact that you're a professional at the thing you're worst at speaks highly for your other talents, I'd say. It's pretty impressive."

"The truth is, I'm in awe of *you*," he said.

I tried not to look shocked. "Me?"

"I wish I had a tenth of your ferocity and courage."

"You flatter me," I said, my heart beating faster at his compliment. "Besides, I'm sure you have at least *an eighth* of my courage. You're remarkably brave for a scribe."

"There's being afraid and doing something anyway—as you do—that's bravery. And then there's not caring if you live or die. That's something else."

I looked at him more closely.

"Are you saying you have nothing to live for?"

"I'm saying..."

We moved together, our motion world blurring around us as he considered my question.

"I once felt I would rather die than be nobody," he said at last.

It wasn't the answer I expected. "And now?"

"Now I'm *somebody* who is dancing with Essaphine," he said, as if that were the only thing that mattered in the world.

I felt my face heating, my heart beating faster still.

"If your courage came from being willing to die rather

than be a nobody, and now you're a somebody, then by your logic, your courage is gone."

"That remains to be seen," he said.

I laughed, and so our conversation went on, by turns silly and flirty, and earnest and probing. After a few dances, we stopped and got wine. Lure, Pocha, and Dagar found us along with their dates, and we stood around the wine fountain, drinking and laughing. Kit noticed the pixies, and Lure explained how the little thumb-sized fae lived in the hollows near the Yrdam Mountains and came here on special occasions, summoned by our dragons, to bless us with their light.

"I'll be damned. I thought pixies only existed in fairy tales," I heard Kit say as he gazed up in wonder.

"Then your mistake is believing fairy tales aren't real," Lure said.

I watched as Kit noticed the other bits of magick scattered about the room. The flowering vines that were growing up the columns, spreading and blooming before our eyes. The pool in the center of the room that was really a scrying basin tuned to the beauties of the world, showing images of sunrises on the other side of the Earth—butterflies in flight, beach scenes on distant islands, and schools of brightly-colored fish flashing beneath the seas.

"It's incredible," Kit said, the awe evident on his face as he glanced at me. "It's all incredible."

His hand found my waist and pulled me in to stand side-by-side with him. I was just tilting my head back to take in his scent when I glimpsed a face up in the galleries that looked down on the room. Cold eyes. Pale skin. Tangled green hair. Braimar. Our gaze met, and he bared his teeth like a startled beast and faded back into the shadows.

Kit saw my expression change and frowned. "Essa—?"

He glanced up to the galleries, confused, but before I could explain, one of Mother's guards approached us.

"Princess Essaphine. Mr. Rowley," he said. "The queen would like a word."

Mother sat in her box overlooking the festivities. Prelate Kortoi sat with her, as did Hoatan and Trag. The men looked uncomfortable in their finery, but Mother shone in a gown the bright crimson of a sunlit ruby.

While we were some distance away, Kit froze. I looked back at him, concerned.

"Kit. What is it?"

He nodded toward Mother's retinue. "That man with the scarred face. I've seen him before."

"That's Trag," I said. "He's the captain of Mother's guard —and Hoatan's right hand. What—?"

"The queen is waiting," the guard interrupted impatiently, and I took Kit's hand and pulled him onward, though the look of concern on his face remained.

"My daughter and our esteemed guest," Mother greeted us. "The two of you seem to be getting on well. Are you enjoying the ball?"

"Very much, Your Majesty," Kit said with a bow.

"Surprisingly, yes," I answered.

"And yet I would caution you against too much wine," Mother said. "Remember, the culmination of your challenge is only three days hence, Essaphine. You'll want to make sure you feel well."

"How could I forget?" I said. "And yet you've given up hope for me, have you not? What difference, then, if I decide to drink myself into oblivion?"

"While a person lives, there is always hope," Mother said.

I was ready to snarl back a snarky retort, but Prelate Kortoi jumped in first.

"I believe I am the expert on oblivion here as I am its high priest," the prelate said. "Drinking until one experiences oblivion is one of the great religious rites of my order. I highly recommend it. If you take my advice, come see me in the morning. I have remedies that you will find most helpful."

"Thanks," I said. "I'm familiar with your remedies. I'll pass."

"Essa..." Mother warned.

The prelate's smile didn't waver as he turned his attention to Kit.

"Speaking of which, I have been waiting for you to return to enjoy more of my coffee, Mr. Rowley."

Kit bowed. "Apologies. I've been quite busy."

"So I hear," Kortoi said. "The court is all abuzz with talk of your training with Princess Essaphine."

"Indeed," Hoatan said. "Many wonder what advice a foreign reporter can give to a girl who has trained on dragon back her whole life."

"His cousin is a pilot," I said, unwilling to let these leeches ruin our night by bullying Kit. "He's knowledgeable about a good many things. And of course, there is a simple way any man can give a woman confidence. By believing in her."

Hoatan nodded, chastened.

The prelate grinned, as if enjoying the whole drama immensely.

Mother looked pensive, tapping her lips with one finger. "I should like to read the article you're working on, Mr. Rowley. You will come and read it to the court."

"Well..." Kit cleared his throat. "I'm afraid it's not complete yet, Your Majesty. My research about your kingdom is still ongoing. Really, I've seen enough to fill several books. It's hard to know where to begin."

"And yet you must have begun by now," the queen said. "Certainly, you've written *something*."

Kit gave a faltering smile. "Of course, Your Majesty."

"Good," the queen said. "You will come and read it before the court tomorrow."

"Not tomorrow," I said. "We'll all need a day to recover from the ball, Mother."

She frowned. "The following day, then. In the meantime, I hope you'll both enjoy yourselves. Just remember, Essaphine, the eyes of the kingdom are upon you. If you should win your challenge with Laynine, you shall wear the crown one day—with all the expectations that come with it."

I knew what she meant. Remain pure. Don't sleep with Kit.

"Of course," I sneered as I gave her a curtsey, then I grabbed Kit's hand and departed.

As soon as we reached the dance floor again, the herald shouted, "Laynine of the house Stratos, Acting Irska of the Royal Skrathan."

"Ah, your cousin is here," Kit said lightly.

Laynine entered, looking stunning in a sapphire-colored gown. As we watched, a crush of nobles hurried over to pay their respects to her. An almost comical number of riders got glasses of wine and headed in her direction, each hoping to be the first to offer a drink. A knot of jealousy balled up in my stomach.

"Essaphine."

I turned to find Aunt Dreya at my side. She too looked lovely with her auburn hair pinned up and wearing an agate-colored gown. I brought my fist to my heart in a riders' salute.

"Durram," I greeted her with the deference a student owed her mentor.

"Don't you look lovely tonight?" Auntie said. Her gaze went to the door. "I may be biased, but I believe you and my Laynine are the stars of the ball tonight."

Her words were meant as a kindness, I knew, but bringing her daughter into my compliment did little to dampen my irritation.

Kit came to my rescue.

"As an unbiased outside observer, I agree," he said.

Aunt Dreya looked Kit up and down. "Unbiased... I don't know. You're here on Essaphine's arm, aren't you? I don't believe I've had the pleasure of your acquaintance," she said. "Though I certainly know who you are."

"Kit Rowley," he offered her his hand to shake. She offered hers limp and palm-down, and he took the hint and brought it to his lips.

"In normal course, it would be my place to train Essaphine for her challenge," she said. "But I hear you have assumed the role of durram for her."

I spoke up quickly. "I am sorry, Auntie. You know how much I value your instruction. Perhaps in the next few days, before the challenge, we could—"

She waved off my words. "I have taught you all I know. Perhaps there is some unconventional wisdom our handsome friend can impart that I cannot. But tell me, Mr. Rowley, I hope our Essa has been treating you well during your visit with us."

He gave a low nod. "I couldn't dream of a better hostess."

My Aunt's gaze returned to me, her voice low. "It's not too late, Essa, for what we discussed. The prelate and I have been talking. He has connections all over the world, and has offered several different estates owned by the Brotherhood which would be suitable for a royal of your stature to reside in—with servants, space for Othura to hunt..." She glanced at Kit again. "You could even bring along whatever companions you wished. It could be a good life, Essa. Much better than the war and the constant political jockeying here at the capital. And you'd be far from the prying eyes of the nobles. You'd be able to do, to *be*, whatever you wish."

I rolled my eyes. "I'm sure Kortoi would be happy to be rid of me. It would be one less arrow in the royals' quiver. And for you, it would be one less bump on Laynine's road to the crown. It's what you've always wanted for her, isn't it?"

Aunt Dreya paled. "Essa. You know I've loved you like a daughter."

"And yet, Laynine *is* your daughter," I pointed out. I could feel my cheeks reddening, my eyes burning with pent-up tears.

Dreya glanced around at the nobles watching us. "I'm trying to save your life," she hissed.

"Running away is no life," I shot back.

Taking Kit's hand, I turned and pushed my way through the crowd, tears blurring my vision.

Calls of *Laynine!* And *Irska!* Rang through the ballroom as Laynine's admirers clambered for her attention.

Through the cacophony, Aunt Dreya called after us. "I hope you can talk some sense into her, Mr. Rowley. It seems you're the only one she cares for now."

From over by the orchestra, Dagar spotted us and raised a hand, calling us over, "Essa! Kit!"

But I was in no mood for a chat. Instead, I grabbed a bottle of sparkling wine from a passing tray and tugged Kit after me through a side door, down a short servants' hall, and up a narrow, winding staircase.

"I'm sorry," Kit said as we went. "What your aunt said—"

"It's not her fault," I said, sniffing and blinking back my tears. "It's just this place. Between the royals and the nobles and the Gray Brothers and the Skrathan and the war, it's all just so impossibly complicated. It's like... like a hall of mirrors."

At the top of the stairs, there was a narrow door. I turned the dusty knob and pushed. When it didn't give, I banged my shoulder into it. It creaked, but didn't open.

"Here, let me," Kit said. I stepped aside, and he shoved the door. It swung wide, revealing a low, dim room. It had a pleasant smell of dust and candle wax and coziness, the same smell I remembered from my childhood. I found a candle on a table, and Kit produced a mechanical lighter from his pocket and sparked a flame.

I hadn't been up here in years—from the looks of it, no one had—but the room was just as I remembered it. A space about the size of a servant's bedroom, with bare wood floors with a sloped ceiling. In the center of the room, an ornate brass grate in the floor looked down upon the ballroom below. Muted strains of music drifted up, a sleepy, pleasant sound.

"What is this place?" Kit asked, glancing around.

I smiled. "My hiding place. Well, one of them. It was created when the palace was built as a place for bowmen to watch over the royals on the dance floor below. When I was a girl, Mother used to let me stay up here and watch as the balls would take place below. I'd steal a bunch of grapes and sit here with my dolls, making them twirl and pretending they were dancers on the floor below."

Kit's smile mirrored mine. "Sounds nice."

"It was. Far better than swimming with the sharks down below."

I knelt beside the grate and gazed down. Through the floral-pattered brass, I could see dancers twirling, revelers sipping drinks, the musicians rapt in their playing. Kit came up beside me. I felt the warmth of his body immediately, smelled the scent of him, a smell like warm maple syrup mixed with sun-baked skin and the earth after a rain. The light from below shone up through the grate, illuminating his beautiful face. Long, sensitive eyelashes. A rugged chin. Full lips crooked into a bemused half-smile.

Those lips... my eyes lingered on them too long. And his eyes were on mine. Suddenly, the air in the little room seemed too thin. The world spun as if I might faint.

"Have I ever told you the story of what happened to my arm?" I asked suddenly.

He shook his head. "No."

I handed him the bottle. "Open the wine and I'll tell you."

The wine burned sweetly going down, its minuscule bubbles pleasantly tickling my throat. I handed the bottle back to him. He took a sip, and I tried not to think of how sharing the bottle like this was like a kiss once removed, like the rim of the bottle was transporting my kiss to him and his kiss to me.

"I was five years old," I said, my eyes drifting from his lovely face to the dancers spinning on the floor below, then unfocusing as my mind went beyond all that could be seen to a place of memory. "My mother had taken me flying before on short little hops. Some of my earliest memories are of the wind in my hair. The feel of her dragon's sides moving between my legs as she breathed... the little grumbling sound their breath makes as they exhale. It was frowned upon to take young people on dragon back before they were bonded, but I was persistent. I loved Mother's dragon, Autan—and I begged for years to ride her. Once I tried it, I was always begging for more. To go higher, further, faster. Mother, I imagine, took it as a sign that I was destined to become a great rider. So one day, she relented and agreed to take me on a longer trip. We were to go to the Temple of the Oracle in Umsir, in the mountains. It was a fine day when we set out. Clear skies, a fair, warm breeze. But as we crossed the highest peaks of the Yrdams, a storm front came. It was this wall of towering black cloud.

Mother spurred her dragon on, hoping to reach the temple before the storm hit. And we almost made it. But from out of the clouds, a creature came. It was like a dragon, but skeletal. And its eyes... I'll never forget the eyes. There were none. Where the eyes should have been, there were just two holes, as if someone had scooped bits of storm cloud and placed them in the unnatural beast's eye sockets—a black blacker than midnight. The thing attacked. Mother's dragon tilted to defend itself, but the demonic dragon was more powerful than she expected. It knocked us into a roll. And..."

My throat closed up. I clamped my eyes shut, a dam against the tears that tried to come. Only then did I realize I'd never told this story before—to anyone. Everyone around me already knew it. It had followed me around all my life, whispered from person to person. But I'd never told it. Never spoken of it aloud.

Kit took my hand. His skin was soft, but there was such strength in his grip. I squeezed back. And I continued, pushing each word out with effort, as if drawing a knife from a wound. "I fell. Mother's dragon dove to save me, but I was out of reach of her talons. So, she caught me the only way she could—with her teeth. As she caught me, she was exposed, and the attacking dragon caught her by the neck. We all fell. It was all a blur for me, of course, the shock and terror of it all... but somehow, Mother struck the attacking dragon with her sword and made it release us. Autan was able to get us to the ground safely. But her wound was grave. She had to put herself into a kataal, a healing sleep that can last for a hundred years. And as for me..."

I held up the stump of my arm. "The bone was snapped. The muscles torn and twisted. The artery severed. All they could do was remove it and cauterize it with dragon fire.

After that, it was clear I would never be the great rider my mother was. And without her dragon, she flew no more. Mother lost her youngest heir and her dragon in one day— the two greatest losses one could bear."

"But she didn't lose you," he said gently. "You're still here."

I gave a wan smile. "Not to her. Not in the ways that matter."

"You've never mentioned your father," Kit said gently. "Is he dead?"

I shook my head. "I never knew him. We have only queens in Maethalia. The heads of all the noble houses are considered my fathers."

Kit frowned. "And the dragon that attacked you?"

"It was never seen again," I said. "Nor have I ever heard of another like it. I think many in the court believe Mother went a bit mad that day and imagined it. But I saw it. It was real."

I swigged from the bottle until I had to come up for air. Then I handed it back to Kit, my head spinning.

"So, there you have it," I said. "The story of a broken girl..."

Kit's eyes held mine. Gods, the way he looked at me. It was so direct, so complete, his gaze like the heat of the sun on my face. No one had ever looked at me like that before.

"You, Essaphine Torholt, are the most complete person I've ever met in my life."

I tried to laugh, but it came out part whimper, part sigh. "This from an enemy poet."

"I am no poet," he said. "But you make me feel like one."

His fingers touched my cheek, his thumb erasing a tear, and I couldn't stop myself from nuzzling into his touch. I didn't want to stop myself. Not tonight. Not anymore. When I opened my eyes, his face was close to mine, his lips so near I could taste the sweet wine on his breath.

"You don't want me," I whispered. "I am a dead girl."

"And I'm a dead man," he said. "So this must be heaven."

Then his lips were on mine, our kiss slick and salty with my tears. The first touch was teasing, probing, tremulous with longing. His hand found the back of my neck, pulling me in closer, his tongue slipped between my lips. My fingers slid into his hair, our mouths pressed together, tasting, clashing, hungry.

Then he pulled back, breathless.

"Essa," he said. "I have to tell you something. When I say I'm not a poet... I'm not a writer, either."

"And I am not a rider," I said fiercely. "I am nothing. I have nothing. I feel nothing. Except when I'm with you..."

I shook my head. Words failing. Instead, I went in for another kiss, but he held me back, shaking his head.

He shut his eyes, bared his teeth with frustration. "I want you, Essa. I want you like I've never wanted anything. But... I really am your enemy."

"Then conquer me," I breathed.

For a second, he hesitated, his eyes wild with want, his chest rising and falling.

Then he was on me, pushing me backward. He caught my head in the crook of his arm, protecting me from the impact as we landed together upon the floor. Our teeth clashed, our lips nipping and sliding together. He sucked my lower lip in a way that sent a hot tingle between my legs. I bit his until I tasted blood. In response, he pressed me to the floor, his weight bearing into me. I felt his desire pressing against me, wringing a groan of longing from my chest. I reached for him and squeezed, making him gasp with want.

"Take me," I breathed. "Now."

His hands were on my bodice, untying, unlacing, finally tearing with frustration, then his mouth was on my breasts. Kissing. Sucking. I arched my back, a tiny squeal of desire coming from the back of my throat as I wrapped my legs around him, pulling him closer. Even through the layers of clothes, I felt him throbbing, and I pulled him closer still, making him groan in pain and longing.

"Essa," he gasped. "I want you. God, I want you."

"Yes," I growled, my hand on his belt.

"But we can't," he hissed.

My hand found him. I stroked, feeling him hot against my palm. His mouth opened in a silent cry.

"Yes, we can," I whispered.

He gave the faintest nod. Then he was shoving my skirt aside, reaching for his belt buckle. I shifted, opening my legs —and my foot hit something. There was a clink, then the sound of shouts from below.

I craned my neck to see the wine bottle had tipped, its contents spilling, drizzling through the grate—onto the dancers below.

Kit and I locked eyes, an identical look of open-mouthed shock on our faces. They were followed an instant later by peals of uncontrollable laughter. Quickly, Kit righted the bottle and we both scooched back from the grate and the many eyes that now peered up at it with ire.

"Oops," he whispered. And we were both laughing again. I didn't even notice our hands were entwined until I looked down at them. It felt so natural, so right, being tangled up with him.

"They'll be looking for a culprit. We should run," I said.

"Or lock the door," he smiled, pulling me to him. He looked at me for a moment, his gaze so full of feeling it almost brought tears to my eyes. Then he kissed me. It was a kiss filled with everything. Want and need and—and something else I feared to put a name to. But I felt it, as real and as alive as the beating of my own heart.

Then there came a sound. A low, sonorous blast that every Skrathan instantly felt in their very bones.

"The Theyrune horn," I whispered. "Battle..."

We stood up fast, righting our clothes. Below, the music had stopped. Another sound came from outside the door— the tramping of feet coming up the stairs—toward us.

"There's another door. Quick!" I said, taking Kit's hand and tugging him behind me. The second door led to a short stair down to a hallway that ran along the upper edge of the ballroom. More grates looked down on the space below, which was clearing out fast. We traversed a short maze of halls and staircases, then finally emerged into one of the palace's many courtyards, still hand-in-hand. The bells in the tower were clanging, and the drone of necromancer engines hung in the distance. Airplanes. An attack.

It couldn't be... Enemy planes regularly attacked at the front lines. But they'd almost never ventured as far as Issastar. And they almost never attacked at night.

I turned to face Kit. "I'll find Othura. You return to your room. Go!"

He looked at me like he wanted to protest. Instead, he gave a single nod.

"Be careful," he said.

And we ran.

33
ESSA

My thoughts raced as I sped toward the barracks. How could this be happening? And why did it have to happen now?

A series of booming sounds rattled the ground beneath my feet, and I looked up to find smoke rising from the direction of the Hatchery.

Othura? I reached out for her with my mind.

Under attack, she shot back. I could feel her adrenaline, her fury, and I ran faster. At the palace's central square, I faced a conundrum. Continue to the barracks, where riders were supposed to gather when the horn sounded, or hurry directly to the Hatchery, where flashes of light and fire now illuminated the sky. I looked down at myself and cursed at the absurdity of my outfit. A ball gown! Who invented such things? I might as well be wearing a circus tent. With a snarl, I reached down and tore the puffy skirt away. That was better. At least I could run properly. But the lace and taffeta would be of no protection in battle, and I was unarmed. I should go back to the barracks and change into my flight armor. And yet, the urgency of Othura's fear and rage drew me toward her. I plunged into a narrow alleyway between the palace tanner and the armory, running so hard I felt lightheaded, so hard I was barely looking ahead of me, so hard I turned a corner and ran right into—

Braimar.

He caught me by the arm and held me, as if inspecting me.

"What are you doing?" I said. "We're supposed to be at muster."

"And yet, you're running away from the barracks," he pointed out.

"I'm running to the Hatchery to find Othura. Come on. We're missing the battle."

I tried to shrug out of his grasp, but he held onto me, his hand squeezing painfully into my upper arm.

"You forget, my dragon is wounded. I can't fly. But I can still be useful."

"Yes. By letting go of me," I said, trying to squirm out of his grasp again—and failing. I silently cursed myself for going to the dance unarmed.

"The nobles have been very concerned about your behavior, Essa. *I've* been very concerned. You should have exiled yourself when I gave you the chance."

From the shadows behind him, two more riders emerged—a pair of brutes I recognized as Braimar's friends.

"What I do is none of your business," I snarled.

"On the contrary. The behavior of a princess is the business of everyone in the kingdom, Essa. If you won't step aside willingly, there are only two ways. Either we kill you, or we render you unfit for the queenhood. You're lucky. I'm choosing the merciful way."

More explosions boomed in the distance, rattling the world. Shadows veiled Braimar's face, but the light of the explosions illuminated his eyes, and I saw the depth of madness in them.

"Braimar," I whispered. "You're not yourself. I don't know if it's because your dragon was injured or..."

He shook his head. "It's not that, Essa. I've been scrying with my uncle. I've seen the future..."

With a sudden, violent motion, he shoved me down. I fell on my back, skinning an elbow on the cobblestone.

"Hold her down," Braimar snarled, and his friends fell on me, pinning me to the ground.

Braimar's hand was unbuckling his belt as he strode toward me, an inhuman grin on his face. And I understood what he meant by rendering me unfit for queenhood. A queen was supposed to be pure...

The burning hunger in his eyes confirmed my fear. "I always wanted to do this," he said.

Just as he knelt, I rocked back on my shoulders and kicked. My heel caught him in the mouth, causing him to stumble back. When his hand came away from his lips, blood drizzled down his chin. It glistened as he laughed.

"Oh, Essa. I would take a thousand blows for the chance to come inside you."

Then he was on me again. I fought, but his friends fell on me, twisting my arms painfully. I screamed, but my voice was lost in another volley of explosions.

Othura! I cried out.

Her voice, when it came to me, was weak and distracted. *I can't get to you. Fight, Essa!*

I did, rocking back and forth violently and kicking with both legs. But Braimar's friends only twisted my shoulders harder, pinning me down. Braimar got past my feet and knelt between my legs, staring down at me with those insane, fiery eyes.

"Give in, Essa," he snarled through a bloody mouth. "Enjoy it."

"I don't think she will," a voice said.

The heads of my three attackers snapped up to see a man step out of the shadows, brandishing a small metal object. It took me a moment to recognize what he was holding; I'd never seen a URA gun up close before. And then my attention moved from the weapon to the man's face.

"Kit," his name came out a sob.

Braimar tilted his head, his bloody mouth contorting into a grin.

"Ah, here he is. The enemy in our midst. Are you here to make some more notes to give to my uncle? You know that's what he's doing, don't you, Essa? He's no reporter. He's a spy."

"He has more honor than you'll ever dream of having," I snarled—hoping it was true.

Kit's thumb pulled the gun's hammer back until it clicked.

"Let her up," he said.

Braimar laughed. "Please. You're a scribe and a petty spy. You're no killer."

"Find out," Kit said.

There was such ice in those two words that they sent a chill through me. Othura's intuition pulsed in my mind. *He is a killer. He's a killer many times over.*

"Maybe I'll start with your friends," he said, turning the weapon on one of the men holding me, who let go and scrambled to his feet. As soon as my hand was free, I brought it to the other man's face, raking his eyes with my fingernails. One finger hooked in his eye socket for a moment before he screeched and rolled away from me.

I kicked off of Braimar's chest and rolled backward, staggering to my feet.

Braimar looked from his friend cowering against the wall with his hands up to his other friend, who now lay face down on the stone, cradling his bloody face.

Then he stood, dusting his hands off on his tunic.

"Very well. I'll let Essa go—for now. But I challenge you to a duel. Three days hence. In the palace square. With swords. Noon. All of you are witnesses to this challenge." He sneered. "Unless you want to take the coward's way out and shoot me with that necromancer weapon of yours."

"Kit—" I started to shake my head.

Kit's jaw was clenched, his eyes like burnished steel, the hand holding the weapon untrembling.

"I'll fight you," he said. "With pleasure."

"Kit, you can't—" I started, but Braimar clapped his hands.

"Very well. Until then..." Smiling a bloody smile, he turned and strode away into the darkness. His friend cowering against the wall hesitated for a beat, then hurried after him, glaring daggers at us as he went. The third, they left behind, face down in the gutter, holding his face and crying.

34
CHARLIE

I followed Essa down a series of streets and alleyways to the barracks. The battle was already over, the droning of plane engines fading into the night. Dragons and their riders were returning from battle, some injured and snarling with pain, others merely lying down in exhaustion, still others stalking around the space, growling with lingering anger. I watched Essa spin a circle, her eyes wide and searching for Othura. When she didn't find her, she said, "Come on," and we started running again.

As we passed through the courtyard, I could hear the riders shouting updates to the command crew on the ground.

"They left."

"They were attacking the Hatchery."

"We drove them back."

For now, I thought. Quite likely, this was only a probing attack designed to see what sort of defensive response they would receive—to determine whether their target was vulnerable. A target I'd suggested in the last message I'd given Kortoi ...

Guilt pulsed through me at the sight of the wounded dragons and the flaming buildings we passed. But that was foolish. Yes, I'd acted friendly with these people. But I was not their friend. In the right circumstance, they would kill me and everyone I love—just as I would kill them. I must not forget the game I was playing. This was war. To lose meant death.

Yet as we hurried toward the Hatchery, I couldn't deny feeling relieved to find it still standing. Several small craters pocked the ground leading up to it, and in numerous places, the stone of the structure itself had been blasted clean of lichen and accumulated dirt. But the ziggurat still stood. Several dragons were upon its rooftop, some sniffing at the stone as if inspecting the structure. Others stood like prairie dog sentries, watching the skies in case the enemy planes returned. Several more flew above, circling like colossal, protective buzzards.

As we neared, a gray dragon bounded down the slope of the temple rooftop and leaped down, coming toward us.

"Othura!" Essa called, and the two ran together, Othura wrapping her long neck partway around the princess in a sort of embrace.

"You're hurt," Essa said, pulling back to inspect her dragon.

Othura's wing was crooked at an odd angle. As she turned, I saw a gout of dark liquid running down the beast's shoulder and side.

A hollow, aching feeling opened up in my chest. The generals had read my intelligence report and attacked. Now, Othura was hurt. Essa had only the barest chance of beating

Laynine on a healthy dragon. Now she was truly doomed—
and it was my fault.

The sound of hoofbeats rose behind us, and I turned to
see a rider on a gray horse coming our way with a sword in
his hand. Ollie.

"Blast it, Essa!" he shouted, reining in and dismounting.
"I'm meant to protect you. How can I if you disappear
on me?"

"Sorry, Ollie," she said. "Kit and I were..." she trailed off.

Ollie glanced at me, then at her again, and his expression softened.

"Well. I hope it was worth the heart attack you gave me.
I was in the ballroom searching for you when I heard the
horn. Then the explosions started. I rushed to the barracks,
and when you weren't there..." he shook his head.

"Braimar attacked her," I said.

Ollie's face twisted into a frown of disbelief, but when
he looked to Essa, she nodded.

"Why?" Ollie demanded.

"He wanted to despoil me, to make me unfit to be
queen," Essa said. "He's gone mad."

Ollie's face grew red. The sword in his fist trembled.
"That goat-prick. Make me your champion. Let me challenge him. I'll—"

"He's already challenged Mr. Rowley," Essa said.
"Swords."

"Kit...?" Ollie looked me up and down. "Can you fight?"

"With a sword?" I grimaced. "There's a first time for
everything."

"Braimar is not a great opponent to practice on," Essa
warned. "He has been the sword champion of the Skrathan
these past four years."

"I'll teach you," Ollie gave a decisive nod.

"But we have other concerns now," Essa said, her arm around Othura's neck. "The enemy's aces have never made it so close to Charcain. And they've never hit the Hatchery before."

"How did they get past the patrols?" Ollie wondered aloud.

Perhaps because they knew the patrol routes and timing... which I had observed and taken notes on while confined to my room.

"From what I saw riding through the barracks, an unusually large number of dragons were wounded in the attack," Ollie said. "And how did they know to target the Hatchery?"

"Someone has been feeding them information," Essa concluded. The coldness in her tone made the hairs on the back of my neck stand up.

"A spy," Ollie nodded grimly—echoing Braimar's words.

Essa looked at me. Surely, she wouldn't believe that lunatic Braimar's accusations about me, even if they were true...

I opened my mouth to speak, then stopped. I had no idea what to say. Essa's eyes met mine. For a second, they brimmed with all the feelings we'd shared in that room above the ball. Then, I watched the feeling disappear, like a door slamming shut.

"I'll take Othura to the infirmary. Ollie, you will take Mr. Rowley back to his room," she said, her voice cold as steel. "See that guards are posted there—to keep him safe from Braimar and his friends. Then bring your horse and meet me at the north gate. Bring food for a day's ride. We'll learn the truth about this attack."

Ollie looked ashen. "You don't mean to...?"

She gave him a fierce look. "You have your orders," she said. "Now go."

"Essa," I started, but she was already mounting Othura.

Instead of flying, the wounded dragon folded her wings and took off in a gallop, moving far faster than any horse could ever run.

There was nothing left for me to do but to follow Ollie back to my prison cell.

35
KITTY

Edward arrived, as usual, in the dead of night.

Kitty arose naked from her bed and slipped on a silk robe to find him at the door. The brim of his fedora tilted low over eyes shadowed already by his prominent brow, so that they looked like black holes. That did nothing to lessen the appeal of his chiseled face, however, or his broad shoulders, or his smell, which was unlike the scent of any other man. He smelled of cloves and cinnamon and... something else Kitty had never smelled before. Whatever it was, it sent a prickling of gooseflesh across every inch of her body.

"Well, look who that cat dragged in," she teased.

He did not smile. One thing Edward did not have was a sense of humor. That was normal for an officer of the Secret Intelligence Bureau—the SIB—they were famous for lacking personalities. Edward took that to a new extreme. But she'd learned over the past year she'd been working with him, Edward had other positive attributes.

"Aren't you going to invite me in?" he asked.

"I'm thinking about it," she said. He bared his teeth a little—but she didn't think it was a smile. "By all means, come in," she said dryly.

He brushed past her, set a briefcase down on the dining table, and clicked open the clasps. Kitty sauntered to the counter where a glass carafe of whiskey sat.

"Drink?" she asked, already pouring.

He sat at the table, opened a manila envelope, and examined the papers inside.

She turned to him, holding two glasses expectantly.

When he continued to ignore her, she stepped up to him and threw the drink in his face.

For a moment, he remained perfectly still. She started to laugh. How bedraggled he suddenly looked, his tie sopping, a drip of liquor hanging from the end of his nose. But when he slowly turned his head to look at her, the coldness in his eyes made the laughter die in her throat.

"Don't come into my home and ignore me," she said, and she downed the other drink, feeling it burn all the way down her throat and into her belly.

Slowly, Edward took the handkerchief from his pocket and dabbed at his face.

"To what do I owe the pleasure of your visit today, Mr. Langford?" she asked.

He just watched her. Something about his stillness made her think of a tiger crouching in long grasses, watching its prey. The thought chilled her and turned her on at once.

"Can I offer you something to eat?" she asked. "I have some leftover steak. So rare it's bloody."

"I don't eat steak," he said slowly.

"Then what do you need?" she asked.

He just kept staring at her with those predator's eyes, and her heart began to flutter.

"I've done everything you asked," she said. "I've done photos with that new Silver Wraith. I've written the articles you told me to. What now?"

He drummed his fingers on the table, each click of his fingernails like the tick of a clock.

"There have been plans made across the ocean that are now approaching completion," he said at last. "A trap is about to be sprung. If anyone makes it out of the Maethalia capital alive, it will be a miracle."

Kit frowned. "What about Charlie? You said his messages have been helpful. You'll ensure his safety, won't you?"

Suddenly, Edward did smile, but it was far from a comforting sight. An expression of happiness on his austere, perfect face seemed about as natural as seeing his skin turn inside out.

"It is a very dangerous world, Kitty Rowley," he said. "It's impossible to ensure anyone's safety. Even yours."

Suddenly, he was on his feet, standing with preternatural speed, his chair screeching back.

Kitty felt lightheaded with excitement—and fear. The last time Edward had spent the night came back to her as a blurred, warped, fragmented memory, half fantasy, half nightmare. The pleasure and the terror of that night had been so extreme that she'd told herself ever since that it must have been a dream. But here he was again. Terrible memories bubbled up from her subconscious, so vivid she wanted to scream and run. Edward, holding her down with impossibly strong arms. Biting her. Licking her own blood off her breasts. Doing other things. Horrible things. But at the same time, she felt a pulse of hot longing between her legs, throbbing in time with her heart, as strong and insistent as a drumbeat.

"The hour of destruction is coming," he told her. "I must be strong. I must feed. And you must *become*."

"I don't... know if... I want to..." Kitty was trembling too hard to speak.

In the next instant, he was on her, so fast she didn't even have a chance to cry out. He lifted her and bore her into her bedroom. She hit the sheet, breathless as he ripped her robe from her body. His mouth was open, like that of a snake preparing to strike, and he nuzzled his lips across her skin, across one hard nipple, down her taut stomach as she writhed with longing, down to her slick core. His tongue slid up her once, so slow a groan wracked her whole body. She rolled her hips, pressing against him, moaning. Then his teasing mouth slid up her stomach, over her navel, up to her neck.

His pants unzipped, and he entered her, so hard and deep and huge she felt impaled, and she cried out in pain as much as pleasure. Then his face was next to hers, and she saw his snarling mouth. His fangs.

Not a dream. Not a dream, she thought, panicking. She squirmed, trying to get away, then in the next moment her hands were at his hips, pulling him deeper into her. Pleasure throbbed through her, her mouth falling open.

Then he bit into her neck. Pain went through her like fire, and she screamed. But in the next instant, the pain was gone, replaced with an intense, radiating feeling of euphoria that was indescribable—like nothing else.

"Stop," she whispered. "Stop... Never... Never stop."

And so, he went on. Drinking her, filling her, until the pain and pleasure of it swallowed all meaning, and she was lost.

36
ESSA

"This is a bad idea," Ollie said as we stepped onto the narrow stone footbridge that led to the temple.

I glanced down. The black depths on either side showed no sign of a bottom. "You're right. They might've at least put up a railing,"

"No," Ollie snapped. "I mean visiting the oracle."

We'd ridden the entire day to get here along a winding road that led up into the Yrdam mountains. Travelling this path via dragon back was far simpler, but Othura needed to rest and recover from her wound. And so, we slogged along on horseback down an ancient path that snaked through valleys and gulches, across gurgling streams and among trickling rills, moving steadily upward until the air grew thin and the trees grew sparse. It was an ancient and treacherous road, trod by pilgrims since before the days of recorded history. And it led to the place where I might find the answers I needed: the temple of the Oracle.

Many of Maethalia's most famous tales featured the

Oracle. Her words had influenced countless historical events over the centuries, and her track record could be summarized in a single sentence: she was always right, but her advice often turned out badly.

That, more than the alarmingly narrow footbridge, was the reason for Ollie's reticence.

And yet, my mother and the queens before her had made this journey for generations for a reason. If there was a simple way to learn the truth about Kit, this was it. And I had to know the truth.

We staked the horses and crossed the chasm.

On either side, crows looked down at us like sentinels, perched on the heads of statues so ancient their faces had been erased by time. Like a child on a balance beam, I hurried ahead, my arms spread in an uneven T. When I reached the far side, I turned back to find Ollie less than half of the way across.

"Oh, come on, Ol," I said.

"I don't relish heights," he said through gritted teeth. "You know that."

"Well, it's a good thing I'm the rider and you're the Torouman, isn't it?" I said.

His breath was ragged now, sweat beading on his brow.

"Say something... to distract me," he said. "Where were you? During the ball, when I was looking for you?"

"I was tangled up naked with Kit. We're madly in love."

Ollie looked at me, wide-eyed, and his arms windmilled as he nearly lost his balance.

"Kidding!" I said as he righted himself. "We were in that room above the ballroom. Remember? Where I used to hide out when we were kids."

"In the secret room? *Doing what*?" he said, balancing the

last few steps, then leaping to me. I grabbed him and steadied him.

"Oh, Ollie. I love you." I said wistfully. He'd always been like a protective brother to me. That was the nature and the role of the Torouman. To follow and counsel and defend their charge, to cross every chasm, even unto death. I knew Hoatan was loyal to Mother that way, too. It was a profound thing to have a person like that in one's life. I tried not to take it for granted ever, but in this moment especially, I felt suddenly overwhelmed with gratitude for him.

He studied me. "You joke. But you do care for him, don't you?"

"Oh, I..." I looked away, trying to deflect. But there was no explaining away the blush on my cheeks or the smile that was creeping onto my lips. I forced myself to meet Ollie's eyes. "He believes in me," I said at last.

Ollie smiled. "As he should."

One of the crows looking down on us gave a raucous call, breaking the moment.

"Come on," I said, leading Ollie onward.

A rough staircase had been cut into the stone cliff face rising before us, so ancient and weathered that it looked almost as if it were a natural part of the rockface. We climbed it using our arms as well as our legs, for it was so steep it was nearly a ladder.

At the top, we found ourselves face-to-face with two female warriors, golden masks over their faces, blade-tipped spears in their white-gloved hands. They guarded a set of stone doors carved top to bottom with runes and strange ancient glyphs. My hand went to the hilt of my sword, but neither guard moved nor spoke as we stepped toward them. I would have thought they were incredibly lifelike statues except I could see their eyes shift behind their masks as they tracked our movement.

I stood tall and spoke in my most official-sounding voice. "I am Essaphine, Princess of Maethalia, and this is my Torouman, Ollyvar. We seek audience with the Oracle."

For an instant, no one moved or spoke. Then, there came a low *boom* that sounded as if it came from deep inside the mountain itself, and the doors swung open, revealing a dark passageway cut into the living stone of the mountain, lit with flickering torchlight. It sloped downward ominously, and Ollie and I exchanged a glance as we passed the sentries and entered. After we'd gone a few steps, the doors boomed shut behind us.

I expected the passage to lead into a black cavern. Instead, a glow emanated ahead, and we soon passed through an archway and into daylight—and I stopped and stared in wonder. A mountaintop crater formed a sort of courtyard, nearly the size of the main courtyard back at the palace, and it was filled with the richest garden I'd ever seen. Butterflies flitted. Lazy bees hummed from flower to flower, and lush grasses formed a carpet under our feet. A stream of clear water flowed through it all, and even from here, I could see the silvery scales of fish flashing past. It made me want to lie down and stretch out on the grass and nap, letting my exhaustion melt away as the sun warmed my face. It was so completely at odds with the forbidding path we'd travelled to reach this place that the contrast was jarring.

"It's a paradise," said Ollie in wonder.

"Yes," I said, walking on. "But let's not let our guard down."

We followed a stone path, crossed a little bridge over the

stream, and found ourselves before a low stone building. White curtains hung to either side of the doorway, rustled by the breeze. Peering in the open door, we could see what looked like a cozy home lit by many windows and skylights with plush rugs on the floors and vases of flowers on the tables.

"Come in!" a friendly voice called from within.

"This is not what I was expecting," Ollie whispered. He was smiling, but one hand remained on the hilt of his sword as he followed me inside.

We found the oracle seated on a chaise with her bare feet up, sipping a cup of tea. She raised a hand to wave to us, and I saw a mark on her palm in the shape of a star—and it was glowing with a strange bluish light.

"Ah, the princess and her Torouman. I knew you'd come. Of course I did. I'm all-seeing and all-knowing, right?" she laughed, gesturing to a pair of chairs. "Come on. Have a seat."

I frowned. "You're..."

"Not super old and hideous? I know. I get that a lot."

She looked to be no older than my mother—in her mid-forties, perhaps. She had long, dark hair and wore a dress of airy, black fabric over a long, lean frame. The only adornment to her garb that hinted of anything special or supernatural was a thin silver tiara with a diamond dangling from it so that it lay upon her forehead.

Before her, approximately six feet wide and as high as

my knees, there stood a basin of dark stone. The water in it was black and utterly still, so that I thought for a moment it was a slab of polished metal—but of course it was a large scrying bowl. Ollie and I took chairs at its edge and looked to the oracle expectantly. Without haste, she poured us tea from a little cart at her elbow and handed the cups to Ollie and me.

It tasted bitter but filled me with an immediate warmth that made my head swim.

"This isn't the draught of the Gray Brothers," the oracle said, noticing Ollie's hesitation. "It isn't addictive, and it won't make you feel drunk. But it will facilitate visions. The psychogenic qualities come from an herb that's grown only here in the temple garden. Ope—that's a bit of a secret. The elder priestesses would probably be pissed off that I told you, so if you don't mind, try not to repeat it. But I was a teacher, once upon a time. I can't seem to help blabbing interesting facts."

She stopped, her eyes narrowing. "You look perplexed."

I shook my head. There were so many strange things about this oracle that I was having a hard time processing them all. First, there was her appearance. Then there was her accent, which was clipped and lazy in a way that reminded me of Kit's—but different. I hardly knew where to begin. "It's just... You were a teacher?" I said. "I thought you've been an oracle for thousands of years. And you look so young."

The oracle laughed. "Oh, that. It's another big secret. You see, there has been a changing lineup of oracles over the years. I showed up—oh, two or three years ago now. A sojourner on a search for knowledge. I found this place, and the oracle at the time decided I was a worthy apprentice."

She shrugged. "The rest is history. I find it quite addicting, though," she added, gazing down at the still black water. "Being able to see the past, present, and future. Being able to see what's happening on the other side of the world... this world, anyway."

She seemed a little sad as she trailed off.

Ollie and I exchanged a glance, and he cleared his throat. "Since you seem to be so forthright," he began. "They say there's a danger to using the oracle. That the visions come from the demons of the void. That the information contained in them can backfire on those who receive it."

With effort, the oracle tore her eyes from the dark water to level them back on us. "It's true," she said. "I'm still studying how the visions are created and where they come from. I do think there is an intelligence—or intelligences—behind them, and I'm not sure they're entirely benevolent. But everything seen when scrying is real and true. It's up to the seer to interpret their visions and act rightly. Which brings us to you. Unless I'm wrong, your question is urgent, and time is short. So tell me, what would you like to see?"

I hesitated, gathering my thoughts, unsure where to begin. "There's a man," I said.

"There always is," the oracle gave a wistful grin.

"He came to us from the United Republic of Admar."

"Ah, the enemy state," the oracle nodded knowingly.

"He was a reporter, coming to do a story on our country. But his plane crashed, and—anyway, I need to know if he's who he says he is. Is he a reporter? Is he trying to help me? Or is he a spy?"

"Say no more," the oracle said, waving away my words. As she did, I again noticed the glowing star on her hand. It illuminated the water as she reached out and touched it with one finger, sending ripples across its surface.

"I find it is always best to start with the present. So let us begin by seeing where your dashing foreigner is now. Ask the water and it will show you. Be direct and use his full name."

Eyeing the black water with foreboding, I took a steadying breath. *Kit is true,* I told myself. *And he is good, even if he is from the URA. And he... he cares about me. Nothing this demon water can show me will change that.*

And yet, I was afraid.

The oracle seemed to sense my thoughts. "The truth can be scary," she said. "But we must have knowledge to name the thing that truly scares us—and defeat it."

I nodded, steeling myself.

"Void," I said. "Show me Kit—"

"Kitty," Ollie reminded me.

"Show me Kitty Rowley."

For a moment, the ripples the oracle had made in the water calmed down. Then, they increased again in a rhythmic beat, as if the footsteps of some great beast approached, disturbing the water. Then, suddenly, the water went still again. But nothing was there. Or... no, there was something. When I looked beyond the surface, into the depths, I could make out a face, growing clearer by the moment. But it wasn't Kit's face. This was a woman, very pretty, with short blonde hair. The salt tracks of dried tears trailed from her makeup-smeared eyes. Rivulets of blood trailed from two wounds on her neck, but she paid the injury no mind, instead staring upward as if entranced by the ceiling of the bedroom she was in.

As we watched, she blinked and seemed to come back

from her stupor. She looked to her left. A handsome man lay in the bed next to her, so unnaturally still that I thought he must be dead. His chest did not rise or fall with breath. But somehow, I knew he remained alive. *No, not alive,* some part of me corrected, *but not dead, either.*

"That isn't him," Ollie protested.

"Shhh," I hushed him, watching with rapt attention as the woman cautiously rose from the bed, wrapping a torn robe around herself to cover her nakedness. She moved out of the bedroom into what appeared to be a sitting room. From the stark, utilitarian style of the furnishings, I could tell she was clearly not in Maethalia. This had to be taking place in the URA. The woman went to a table, where a brief-case stood open. With a wary glance at the open bedroom door, she opened a folder, picked up a scrap of paper, and looked at it.

"Let me see the paper," I told the water. I didn't know if such a command would work, but instantly the paper was near enough to read, as if brought closer with my own hand.

But the figures on the page were unfamiliar, although the URA used the same letters as Maethalia did. I should have been able to understand...

"It's a cipher," Ollie said.

"Let us read it," I told the void.

The figures on the page blurred, rearranged themselves, and suddenly the writing became familiar.

The woman's lips whispered the words at the same time we read them.

"The crates are in place beneath the city. At the appointed time, send all the squadrons. The time to end the war is nigh."

"Crates beneath the city..." Ollie mused, rubbing his chin.

"Show us the crates," I commanded.

The vision in the water blurred and shifted. When it reconstituted, it showed a vast catacomb filled with countless wooden crates.

"Those are the catacombs beneath Issastar," Ollie said, frowning.

As we watched, a long-haired figure in a black robe strode up to one of the crates, inspecting it.

"Prelate Kortoi," Ollie whispered.

The prelate began to lift the lid off the crate, and Ollie and I leaned closer, ready to see what lay within.

Then, suddenly, the water went black again. The Oracle released a pent-up breath, as if some great exertion on her part had ended.

"That's it," she said. "That's all it will show us today."

My mind was spinning. "Kortoi. Could he be in league with whoever that was in Admar?" I asked.

Ollie shook his head. "And what could be inside those crates? Weapons? Explosives?"

"Whatever they are, the city is in danger," I said. "We'd better get back."

"I agree. But we still haven't seen Kit," Ollie protested. "I don't understand why it showed us this woman instead."

The oracle pursed her lips. "You asked to see Kitty Rowley. The scrying is never wrong. The woman you saw *is* Kitty Rowley."

Ollie rubbed his furrowed brow. "That means Kit..."

"Is not Kit," I finished, a sick feeling opening up like a wound in my belly.

"So, who is he?" Ollie said.

"That is what I mean to find out," I said, rising from my seat and nodding to the oracle. "Thank you. You've been most helpful."

She shrugged. "But don't thank me yet. Remember, you have to be very careful with how you respond to these visions. The void isn't our friend. And the visions can be confusing. Some of the things they show us have already come to pass. Some are happening now. And some will happen in the future—but only if conditions remain as they are now."

I nodded. "Thank you all the same."

"Come see me again sometime," the Oracle said. "It gets lonely sitting here on this mountaintop drinking tea all day with these uptight priestesses."

I smiled. I liked this strange Oracle. "I will," I said.

"Until then, I'll be watching—and I'll be rooting for you," the Oracle said.

As I went to turn and go, my eyes wandered once more to the scrying basin, and I thought I saw something in the dark water. It was Kit, striding alone through a city of Issastar that was devastated and in flames. Tears shone in his eyes as he screamed my name.

Essa! Essa! ESSA!

Then, in a blink, the vision was gone.

37
CHARLIE

The dragon had taught himself to fly.

Since six AM, Parthar had been climbing up on objects and gliding off them. As a result, though the sun was only just lighting up the sky in the east, I was already wide awake and cranky. I would have loved to go down to the kitchens and beg some biscuits and tea, but the door was locked and I heard low, rumbling voices outside in the hallway. I was under guard again. Under suspicion. And soon enough, I'd be fighting Braimar to the death.

Things were going great.

I'd learned some bayonet techniques, as well as elementary hand-to-hand combat tactics, in basic training. Then, for about eight months, I'd been assigned to train for the Iron Lions, an elite special forces infantry unit. I'd learned a lot of fight techniques there, including how to fight with a knife. And I'd gotten a hell of a lot stronger and tougher. But then, I'd been selected for pilot's training and left. I still remembered what I'd learned in fight training, but it was unclear how well any of it would translate to a sword fight.

And against the best swordsman out of the entire
Skrathan? I didn't like my odds.

Essa is a dead girl, I'm a dead man. And yet, I didn't even
have the pleasure of her company...

How many times had my mind slipped back to those
moments spent together above the ballroom? Each time
they did, I felt my blood pulse and my heartbeat quicken. I
wanted Essa. If I was being honest, I wanted her in
every way.

When my thoughts wandered to Kitty, all I saw was that
picture of her kissing that imposter Silver Wraith. And I felt
nothing at all. Whereas when I thought of Essa...

But where was she? Could she really believe that I was
a spy?

"Oof!"

Parthar had leaped off the bed canopy to glide into my
lap, nearly knocking the wind out of me. He was getting
heavier.

"Watch it," I groused.

He squeaked an apology and licked my nose with his
hot, gritty tongue. His scaly cheek nuzzled my cheek. The
damned little beast was as sweet as he was irritating...

A key clicked in the door.

Wardrobe. Quick!

I thought the words rather than saying them aloud, but
Parthar obeyed, jumping off my knees and gliding to his
place in the wardrobe. I got the doors shut just as the door
to the room swung open.

I expected to see Rohree. I'd failed to tell Essa about
Parthar before her midnight deadline. Maybe the sprite had
told Essa. Maybe this was the end... but instead of Rohree,
Ollie and Clua entered, each with a sword strapped at their

waist. Ollie held another sword in a sheath. He tossed it to me, and I caught it.

"We're here to prepare you for your duel with Braimar," the Torouman said. The cold formality of his tone gave me pause.

I glanced past them to the hallway. "Where's Essa?"

"Not coming," Clua said.

"Why? Is she okay? Is she mad at me, or...?"

Ollie gestured to the doorway. "Please, Kit. Time is short, and we've been given the rather difficult task of saving your life."

They led me out of the city to a clearing in the middle of a pine forest. A stream ran through one edge, and wildflowers dotted its banks. It would have been a lovely scene to relax in—if it weren't for the high stakes of my situation.

"You have only today to train, and you must fight a man who has trained his whole life," Ollie said. "Braimar is the greatest swordsman among the Skrathan."

"Yes. You mentioned that," I said.

"I will be your master at arms," Clua said. "Since Ollie is more the size of Braimar, he will be your sparring partner. How much sword training have you had?"

"None."

My two instructors exchanged a glance. Clua sighed. "Well, at least you're holding the right end of the sword. Now put it down."

"What?"

"We won't begin with swords, even these dull practice ones, unless you fancy getting your head split open," Clua said. "Find yourselves a couple of sticks and we'll begin."

I glanced around the clearing. "Will Essa be joining us later?"

"Do you wish to live?" Clua snapped. "Then forget the princess and find some sticks."

They began at the bottom—with my feet—with Clua instructing me on how far apart they should be and which direction my toes should be pointing. In the second hour, I was finally able to take a step, with Clua slapping me on the ass every few minutes to remind me to bend my knees. Soon, my legs were aching and trembling—and all they'd taught me was how to take one shuffling step forward and back.

"Is this really necessary?" I griped. "I can box a bit. I know how to handle myself in a scrap. Can't you give me a few tips and let me... I don't know... wing it?"

"When you're building a tower—" Clua began, but Ollie stopped her with a gesture.

"Let's try it your way," Ollie said, brandishing his stick. "Go ahead and *wing it.*"

Trying to remember what I'd been taught so far, I raised my weapon and began circling Ollie. He circled with me, but otherwise remained as still as a cocked mousetrap. With a quick step forward, I gave his stick a smack. He met my blow and we both continued circling.

See? This isn't that hard, I told myself. Feeling more confident, I struck again, lunging in and slashing toward Ollie's neck. His stick found my hand, smacking it so hard I dropped my weapon. In a smooth, continuous motion, he whipped his stick back around—and broke it over my face.

"Agh," I groaned, one hand pancaked over my stinging cheek.

Clua stood watching with crossed arms. "Ah. So that's how they wing it in the URA. Good to know."

I felt Parthar in my mind. He was mentally sniffing me to see if I was okay. When he found me hurt, I felt his growl.

"It's okay. I'm fine," I muttered. I looked down at my hand and was relieved to see it wasn't bloody, though my face stung and throbbed like hell.

"You're fine now," Clua groused. "But if that had been Braimar, the top half of your head would be at your feet right now."

Ollie looked at the broken-off stick in his hand and tossed it aside.

"Find me a new stick, poet, and we'll start again."

The drills continued.

Eventually, we took a break for lunch. But even as we sat and ate, both my companions were quiet and cold toward me. *I am a spy, and they know it,* I thought. *They will probably be relieved when Braimar kills me tomorrow...*

I could hardly blame them. But it surprised me how much it bothered me. I'd come to think of them both as friends.

I cleared my throat, breaking the tense silence. "So. How did you two learn your sword skills?" I asked.

Ollie didn't look up from the chunk of bread in his hand. "I have been practicing swordplay since I was four years old. It is part of the Torouman training. We are not only councilors to the royals we bond with; we are also bodyguards. Which is why it should have been me with Essa after the ball—and why it should be me fighting Braimar, not you."

That explained Ollie's attitude toward me, at least.

"I apologize. It wasn't my desire to take your place."

Ollie sighed. "No. I'm glad you were there with her. Otherwise..." he shook his head. "It's Essa's fault for giving me the slip."

I looked to Clua. "How about you?"

"My father was a warrior," she said. "He trained me from the time I started to walk. The ax is the traditional weapon of dwarves, and he did teach me to wield it, but I'm not as stout as my brothers. The sword always suited me better. My hope was to become a soldier, like my brothers, but my father—may his soul fly—was loath to see his only daughter in the trenches of Dorhane, so he apprenticed me to the blacksmith before I could enlist. I still train, though, every day. And one day, I will fight."

"Meanwhile, she picks fights with soldiers at the taverns," Ollie laughed.

"Only the ones who deserve it," Clua muttered, but she was smiling.

"Many a young man who has mistreated a barmaid has been humbled by Clua the Terrible," Ollie said. "I've seen it happen. She's a tremendous fighter."

A smile dawned on Clua's face, and she gave Ollie a grateful nod. "High praise, considering the Torouman are known to be among the deadliest warriors in the kingdom. Thank you. I do enjoy seeing the shock on their faces when they realize they're being bested by a lady dwarf."

I laughed. "Well, I'm certainly glad the two of you are on my side. Otherwise..."

My hand went to my swollen cheek, and the humor that had animated my companions a moment before drained away. The birds still chirped, and the sky was still clear, but it felt as if a cloud had passed over the sun.

They know I'm a spy. And they know at this time tomorrow, I'll be dead.

Will Essa even be there to watch?

Clua took a sip from her waterskin and rose. "We'd best get back to work."

What followed was four hours of vigorous, sometimes excruciating, training. I learned to circle, lunge, retreat, parry, thrust, and slash. The concepts were basic, elementary, even. But I understood why we were drilling them. Like flying a plane in a dogfight, the small details of how things were done were critical. Proper tension in the sword arm when parrying a strike meant you lived; improper technique meant you died. And there were a hundred little details to remember, details Braimar would have drilled into his muscle memory since childhood. Still, by the end, Ollie and I had graduated from sticks to blunted swords. We were sparring vigorously, and I was holding my own.

"Good. Now retreat. Bend those knees!" Clua called as I weathered a blistering attack from Ollie, then countered, nearly catching him with a thrust. As he circled away from my attack, his foot caught on a root, and he fell. He caught himself with his sword arm, and I took advantage of the moment and lunged in, my blade at his throat.

"Yes!" Clua crowed, clapping.

Ollie chuckled. "Well done."

I felt a wind on my face and looked up to see a dragon swooping down on me. I spun to face it, my blunted sword raised. Othura landed, and Essa slipped off her back. An outcropping of rock overlooked the clearing, and I realized she and Othura must have been sitting up there. I couldn't help but smile with relief knowing that she still cared enough to check in on my training.

"How long have you been watching?" I asked.

"Long enough to know your chances against Braimar," she said without humor. She held a hand out toward Ollie. "Give me that sword and leave us."

"But—" Clua started to protest.

"Thank you for training him, Clua. You did well. Now go, all of you."

Ollie rose and handed Essa the sword, then he and Clua departed. Othura also gave us a glance, then took wing, retreating to the rocky promontory above.

The footsteps of the Torouman and the dwarf receded. The dragon's wingbeats were lost to the wind.

We were alone. Me, Essa, and a pair of swords. And from the look in her eyes, she was ready to use them.

38
ESSA

K it—or whatever his name was—faced me alone in
the clearing. I felt his discomfort at the intensity
of my stare, but I refused to look away. Maybe I
wanted to see him squirm, to see him break. But he didn't
look away, either.

"Have you been honest with me?" I said at last.

He blinked. "What?"

"You heard me."

His jaw clenched. "Essa, from the moment I saw you, I
have been on your side…"

"I didn't ask if you were *on my side*, I asked if you've been
honest."

He hesitated for an instant, glancing away—an evasion
my dragon instincts picked up on.

"Of course," he said. A lie.

I felt a protective wall inside myself going up. The oracle
was telling the truth. He wasn't who he said he was.

"We're leaving," I said.

"Where?"

"I'm taking you home."

His mouth fell open. "What?"

"We can ride Othura. We'll stop by the palace to get your things," I turned to call Othura down from her perch.

"No," he said, taking my arm and turning me back around. "I'm not missing your challenge against Laynine."

"I'm trying to save your life, idiot."

"I'm not leaving before I fight Braimar, either. After what he tried to do to you..."

"He did nothing."

"Because I stopped him!"

"Right," I said. "You stopped him with your necromancer weapon. With swords, in a duel, you don't stand a chance."

Anger flared in his eyes. "I think you're underestimating me."

"You're a poet!"

"A... reporter!" he corrected. "But I'm more than that."

"What are you, then? And tell me the truth."

I realized in my fury I'd gotten in his face, so close our lips were nearly touching.

"I'm a man," he whispered. "Who will never let anyone hurt you."

At those words, I felt as if my heart cracked open, so much pouring out of it that I could hardly breathe. Why was the one person who would say such things to me, the one person I felt *so much* for, also the one person I couldn't trust?

I gave a bitter laugh. "If you're so tough, then show me. Show me you can beat Braimar."

I took a step back and raised my sword.

He cocked his head at me. "That wouldn't be fair."

The softness I'd felt inside for him a moment before

turned to steel. "Why? Because I'm a girl? Because I have one arm?"

"Because you're far better and more experienced than me," he said.

I threw my head back, appealing to the heavens in my frustration. "Then how can you expect to beat Braimar?"

"Because when I'm defending you, there's no one in the world who could stop me."

"Stop saying things like that!" I shouted, and I attacked him.

He barely got the sword up in time to deflect the first strike, a blow that surely would have split his scalp open. He side-stepped my follow-through with surprising dexterity and countered with a slash so quick, I barely got my blade up for it. Snarling, I launched a barrage of blows at him, each swing of the blade harder than the last, driving him backward. He retreated with patience, then circled to my left.

"So, you *were* paying some attention to Clua's lessons," I said.

"I'm a quick study," he replied breathlessly, darting in for a counterattack.

His style was unusual, his attacks coming in at odd angles, low, then high, then circling in from the side; they were surprisingly difficult to defend against, even for someone as seasoned as I was. But despite my anger, I remained patient.

I kept my distance, circling and retreating, and watched as his fatigued arm grew slower. Finally, I lured him in and waited for him to lunge. When he did, I hit him with one of my favorite ripostes, stepping sideways and slashing at his forearm.

The blade smacked him, causing him to snarl in pain, and the sword fell from his grasp. I stepped in, hooking his leg with mine and barreling into him with my shoulder, taking him to the ground. When we landed, I was straddling him, my blade pressed to his throat.

"You're dead," I said.

"Then why is my heart beating so fast?"

"Shut up!" I shouted. "You are the most infuriating person alive!"

"Ah," he grinned. "So you concede: I'm still alive."

"But at this time tomorrow, you won't be. So are you ready to let me take you back to Admar?"

"After I've defended your honor against Braimar and after your challenge, you can do whatever you want with me. I'm not leaving until then."

"Whatever I want?" Angry as I was, I couldn't help flirting. I gave a twist of my hips, grinding myself against him. His lips parted, a low groan grating out of him.

No. Stop. I told myself. *What's wrong with you?*

I forced myself to get off him and stand.

"Seriously, I have no time to debate this with you," I said, pacing. "There are other matters that require my attention."

I thought of the vision I'd received from the Oracle—the crates in the catacombs. As soon as darkness fell, I had a plan to investigate, and it was edging toward twilight now. I had no time to remain here, arguing with a stubborn, lying enemy spy, handsome as he might be.

I called Othura with my mind. She swooped down, looking a bit lopsided with her injured wing. Kit seemed to notice her wobble as she landed.

"You okay, Othura?" he asked. I was surprised; it was the first time he'd addressed her directly.

"She's okay," I said. "The healers said her wound was shallow. They stitched her up. Dragons heal fast."

In reality, I wasn't sure Othura could handle flying all the way to Admar. Maybe part of me had known Kit would refuse to go... But there were other dragons who could take us if necessary.

"Last chance, Kit," I said. "Come with me. Please. Don't make me watch you die."

"I'll make a deal with you," he said. "I promise I'll survive my duel if you promise to survive your challenge."

I sighed in frustration. "You know I can't promise that."

"And I can't leave."

I shook my head, climbing up Othura's tail and dropping into my saddle. "You're the most infuriating person I've ever met," I said.

"But you're still glad you met me," he pointed out.

At my urging, Othura began jogging ahead.

"Really? You're not giving me a ride back to the palace?" he called after me.

"Consider the walk part of your training," I shouted over my shoulder, and I kept going.

39
CHARLIE

B ack in my room, I sat on the floor, watching Parthar wrestle his own tail on the rug. I hated to admit it, but the little beast was growing on me. He reminded me of a pup I'd had growing up, Spottie. But I could already see Parthar was far more intelligent than any dog.

"I don't know. I think that tail is tougher than you are, buddy," I said, giving one of his wings a playful tug. He left off playing with his tail and came over, sitting on his haunches in front of me and gazing into my eyes with an intensity that made me a little uncomfortable. I chuckled, glancing away, but his tail snaked up and touched my chin, directing my face toward him once more. There was such earnestness in his expression...

"Come on," I said. "I don't even gaze into Essa's eyes like this..."

And yet, I didn't feel I could look away, either.

You have to fight soon... Parthar said. The communication

came to me not in words, but in feeling, *knowing* what he was trying to communicate. I was lost in the fiery depths of his eyes, plugged into him in a way I'd never been with another creature in my life. Then, suddenly, he retched, then retched again, like a cat about to cough up a furball. I scrambled backward, not wanting to get vomited on—or hit with fire. With a third belch, Parthar bowed and vomited clear fluid onto the floor. In the midst of the puddle was an object, reddish orange and oval in shape, a little larger than a human eye.

"What the...?"

I leaned over to get a closer look at it. The object emitted a faint glow, shining with an inner light that shimmered and swirled beneath its surface. I grabbed my wash rag from the basin, picked the object up out of the slime and washed it off.

Its surface was smooth beneath my fingers and surprisingly hot. It was like the stone in the necklace Essa wore, I realized. A dragon stone. I looked at Parthar.

Keep it, he said in my mind. *And I'll always be with you.*

Late that night, the door to my room swung open without warning.

Parthar had taken to sleeping in the same bed with me. He was hell to sleep with, all claws and spines and scales with a tail that regularly wrapped around my leg or arm like a snake and squeezed when he was having a dream. But the body of a dragon runs hot, and his warmth kept the chill of the castle at bay. And besides, I felt I could protect him better in the night when he was right next to me. He was a baby, after all.

When that door swung open, though, I cursed myself for my laxity, tugging the blanket up over Parthar's head and jerking my ankle free of his tail as I stood blinking in the lanternlight.

The wavering illumination revealed the ugly face of the queen's guard, Trag. The white strips of his scars almost seemed to glow in the dark as he eyed me. "Get dressed and come."

"The queen?" I asked.

"The prelate," Trag corrected. "He wishes to have one last chat before young Braimar sends you to your maker. I'll let you dress."

The big man turned and exited, the door clapping shut behind him.

I pulled on my boots and went to the desk, where my notebook and pen sat—filled with my attempts at writing an article that would convince the queen I was truly a reporter. They were all terrible; writing was far more diffi-cult than I imagined.

Opening to a blank page, I scribbled my final message of my spy career and tore it loose. When I turned, I found Parthar's head poking out of the blanket.

Hungry?

Hush, you! It's the middle of the night. Go back to sleep.

Hungry.

I'll give you all my bacon in the morning. Now stay quiet.

I tugged the blanket back over the dragon's head and

pushed him down so he lay flat against the bed just as the door swung open again.

"Coming," I said, and I let Trag usher me out into the night.

The keep of the Gray Brotherhood at night was one hell of a spooky place. The walls and ceilings groaned, and windows seemed to whisper, although there was hardly a breeze outside. As we walked down the long corridor to the prelate's audience chamber, I kept seeing movements out of the corner of my eyes, but when I turned my head to look, there was never anything there. The numerous candles that lent tenuous light to the space flickered constantly, as if on the verge of blowing out. The shadows seemed to have shadows.

I'd have given anything to be back in my room, curled up in the bed with Parthar. Or better yet, with Essa.

Then I remembered the look on her face the last time we'd met. My lies were unravelling. She'd sooner put a piece of steel in my chest than kiss me again. It would be better to put her out of my mind—as if that were possible. To run away from her and this place and never look back. And yet more and more, she was all I could think about. Even now...

We found the prelate in a library filled with ancient, musty-smelling books, seated in a chair before a hearth.

"The foreigner," Trag said with a bow.

The prelate watched me with those strange eyes of his. They were both dark and bright at once, like polished obsidian, and the smile on his face reminded me of the grin of a skull.

"Ah, our intrepid friend has returned. How has your sojourn in the land of magic been going, Charlie?"

"I'll tell you at this time tomorrow," I said.

The prelate chuckled. "Well spoken. Come, sit. Are you familiar with Zaynat?" Kortoi gestured to a small table before him. On it sat a glass dome, like the cover for a cake plate, and beneath the dome a pair of rats, one white, one black, tussled with one another.

I shook my head. "Never heard of it."

The prelate twiddled his fingers excitedly, his many rings glinting in the dim light. "It's a form of divination. Watch."

The rat battle was coming to a close. The black rat had the white one by the neck and was gnawing it ferociously. The poor white one scrabbled with its pink feet but was unable to get free. After a few moments, it went still, blood pooling beneath it, but the black rat continued, tearing a mouthful of stringy flesh and fur free and gobbling it down. I looked away.

"Ah," the prelate said, nodding. Taking a quill pen, he jotted a few words down in a notebook. "You see, it doesn't only matter which rodent wins. It also matters *where* the victory happens—on which square. And after it dries, we'll look at the pattern of blood on the board."

I looked again and saw that the rats had indeed been killing one another on a sort of chessboard, each uneven square marked with strange runes.

"You'll learn something from that?" I nodded at the rats in disgust.

"I've learned everything," the prelate said, an unsettling

gleam in his eyes. "But I wouldn't want to tell you about it. It would spoil the surprise. Oh, where are my manners? I have coffee and cigarettes. And I managed to get a package of those delicious chocolate cookies from the URA. Jollies. Enjoy!"

He gestured to another table in the corner. Though the thought of those treats and the prelate's highly addictive coffee tugged on my desires, I shook my head.

"I can't stay long. I have a big day tomorrow. I just wanted to give you this."

I handed him the rolled-up page I'd torn from my notebook. He took it with a flourish of his long nails and unrolled it, held it at arm's length.

"You don't have to read it now," I said. "In fact, maybe wait until—"

"I am writing," the prelate read in a theatrically loud voice. "To share that this is my last communication. I have a duel tomorrow. Most likely, I won't survive, but if I do, my days as a spy are over. In my time in Maethalia, I've learned many things. Foremost is this: not all magic is evil. Some of it is wonderful. And not all Maethalians are evil. Some are the most spectacular people I've had the honor to meet. Even dragons can be good. I already regret the information I've shared and the damage it has caused. And I regret the killing I've done. My last wish for both Admar and Maethalia is peace."

The prelate looked up at me, his eyebrows raised in mocking surprise. Back by the door, Trag laughed. I hadn't realized he was still in the room, but it suddenly struck me as odd that the head of the queen's guards would be running errands for one of her chief rivals in the middle of the night.

"Well, perhaps you're a writer after all," the prelate teased, carefully rolling the paper up once more and placing it in his pocket. He leaned over his dead rat, placing his hands on the glass dome, and locked his eyes on me.

"Do you know what the Zaynat told me?" he asked. "You may be finished with this war, Ace. But the war is not finished with you."

I chose to ignore the ominous glee in his tone.

"I'm not finished... So you're saying I'm going to live tomorrow?"

He laughed. "It is not only the living who participate in events, Ace. The dead, the denizens of the void—they will have their say, too. They are beneath us now. And all around us. And their time is coming. Soon."

As if to emphasize his words, the shadows around us seemed to writhe in exaltation. It sent a chill through me, a terror that extended far deeper than my mind to shiver my very soul.

"I'll die, then," I said.

"Live. Die," the prelate shrugged. "You will fulfill your role, just as we all must."

"Very philosophical," I growled with a glance at Trag. "Tell me something, Kortoi. Whose side are you on?"

He reached out toward me. My impulse was to shy away, but I refused to show him that he scared me. His long fingernails brushed my cheek; instantly, the spot he touched felt numb.

"I'm on your side, Charlie, of course," the prelate soothed. "Now go. Get your sleep. And know that everywhere, in the shadows, the lords of the void are working toward our triumph."

I rose, all too eager to leave that place. But before I

turned to go, I glanced back down at the rat board. The black rat had completely consumed the white one, all except its wormlike tail, which it slurped into its mouth now like a strand of pasta. All that was left of the white rat then was a blotch of blood. On the square it stained there lay a rune which looked, to me, like a flying dragon.

40
ESSA

We stood together in one of the palace wine cellars—Rohree, Ollie, Clua, and me.

"I'm *not* sending her in alone," I said. "Even if what the oracle said wasn't true, I would never send a friend down into the catacombs alone at night."

"She's a peri," Ollie argued.

As a sprite, Rohree had the ability to become nearly invisible; all her kind could. To the trained eye, she'd appear as the faintest shimmer in the air. To everyone else, she'd be undetectable. Ollie was quite right that she had the best chance of any of us of sneaking in and out without being caught if whoever had brought those crates down there had posted sentries. Still, I hated the idea of sending her in alone.

"If she's holding a torch, people will still see her," Clua pointed out. "And she has to hold a torch or she won't be able to see."

"I have a glowstone," Rohree said, holding up a smooth, palm-sized rock that gave off an eerie, bluish light.

Glowstones weren't so rare. They were the most common vestiges of elven artifacts still around. Most curiosity shops had at least one or two for sale, although they didn't come cheap.

"See? If someone is about to grab her, all she has to do is put the stone in her pocket and step to one side, and they'll never find her," Ollie said. "The rest of us can't do that."

"I'm going with her," I said again, with growing irritation. The smell of the barreled wine and curing cheese and hanging sausage around us was making me hungry—and irritable.

The entrances to the catacombs were all supposed to be locked and guarded as part of the palace's security protocol. But I had grown up in the castle, and I knew there were dozens of entrances that the palace guards probably weren't even aware of—like this one. A hole that led to the caves beyond could be accessed by pulling back a loose wall panel next to this wine rack. We'd had to roll three barrels of pickles aside to access it, so it was no wonder it had escaped the guards' attention. The hole had seemed big enough when I was a child, but as I looked at it now, I saw that a large man would never fit through. Even for a smaller man like Ollie, it would have been a tight squeeze. But a sprite could fit easily.

Rohree stepped in front of me and put a hand on my arm. "Essa," she said gently. "Ollie is right."

"I usually am," he shrugged.

"I'm the one most likely to get in and out unnoticed," Rohree pressed. "You have your challenge in just two days, and Kit's duel is tomorrow."

"The poet's fight has nothing to do with—"

She gave me a sharp look. "It has everything to do with

you," she said. "You're distracted. You're stressed. And besides, the tunnel is a tight squeeze, at least until it reaches the catacombs. I'm quite sure I'm a faster crawler than you."

I looked down at the stump of my right arm. She was right. Crawling wasn't my strong suit.

"I *am* a bit of a three-legged table," I said, giving everyone a tense laugh.

"Then let *me* come," Clua said, putting a hand on the mace at her belt. "I'm small. And I'll smash anyone who hassles you into fish-bait."

"But you can't turn invisible," Rohree said. "You can fight, sure. But if someone spotted you, it would put us both in danger."

Clua smoldered, but she couldn't argue with Rohree's point.

Rohree was far more than just a handmaid. She'd done spy work before—for me as well as my mother—and as much as I hated sending her in alone, I knew she could handle herself.

"Great. Then it's decided," Ollie pulled the wood panel back further, ushering Rohree toward the blackness beyond.

"We'll wait for you here," I said.

"No," Ollie replied. "I'll stay."

"But—" I started to protest.

"If I'm found down here, I can say I'm grabbing a bottle of wine you requested. What will we say if a princess is found down in the storerooms?"

"I get my own wine plenty," I huffed.

"The gods know you do," Ollie said. "But it's more suspicious. If I'm seen down here, no one will raise an eyebrow."

I sighed. "You are all so vexing. Especially when you're

right. Fine, Rohree. Go. But be careful. And come back to my chambers the moment you're finished."

The sprite gave a dutiful nod, then turned, dropped to her knees, and crawled into the hole. When she'd disappeared, Ollie slid the wall panel back in place.

"If she calls for help or if anything happens—"

Ollie's hand went to the hilt of his sword. "I'll take care of her, Essa. Now go. Before someone sees you."

Grudgingly, I took Clua's arm, and together we made our way out of the cellar. As we went, I grabbed a dusty bottle of Easastar Red.

"To pass the time while we wait," I explained.

She grabbed a wheel of cheese. "I'll do you one better," she said, and together we let the flickering light of our candle lead us back up the steps.

41
ROHREE

For what seemed like an hour, Rohree crawled through the claustrophobic, cobweb-swagged shaft, until her knees were scuffed and her wrists ached. At last, the tunnel opened up into a wider space, and she was able to get to her feet.

The things I do for Essa, she thought as she stretched the kink out of her aching back. But in the next instant, her regrets only grew. In the glowstone's pale light, she saw she was in an arched passageway. Stone shelves lining the walls bore haphazard stacks of bones. The black, empty eye sockets of skulls stared at her. Gray femurs and jumbles of ribs made her think of the bodies they had once supported, now broken and scrambled. The quiet was so deep it seemed to have dimension, like a well one could drop a stone into, and from in its depths tiny sounds came. Slithering. Scratching. And something else. Voices.

Drawing the short dagger at her waist, Rohree followed the sound. As she went, she made herself invisible. Activating that power always gave her a strange feeling, like the shiver just before a sneeze, but she was grateful to have the ability, especially in moments like these. The blood of the ancient fairies flowed in her people's veins, so it was said, and allowed them to hide from mortal sight. It was a handy thing for times like these, although Rohree would have much preferred being in her cozy bedroom, sitting in front of her little hearth and reading a book.

By the light of the glowstone, she made her way forward until the tunnel opened up to a larger chamber. Wall-mounted torches cast a quavering orange light, and she slipped the glowstone into her pocket and took in the sight before her. The chamber was round and large, perhaps two hundred spans across. And the whole space was filled with large, wooden crates of various sizes. Some were no longer than she was tall. Others were large enough to fit a team of horses. And there were thousands of them.

At the far end of the chamber, workers in dark cloaks were bringing in more crates, grunting and grumbling as they did. She recognized their robes. They were Gray Brothers.

What are they up to? she wondered, knowing it could be nothing good.

Forward she went on stealthy feet, but before she reached the workers, another set of voices caught her attention to her left. One voice sounded familiar, though she couldn't make out what it was saying. More torchlight glowed in that direction, and she took off toward it, weaving her way through a labyrinth of wooden boxes as silently as possible.

At last, she rounded a final corner and saw two men speaking. One wore the robes of the Brothers, but his was a midnight black. She immediately recognized his long hair and galling baritone voice. Prelate Kortoi. The other man wore a cloak with his hood up over his head.

"We're sure the numbers are sufficient?" the cloaked man was asking. "Present overwhelming force, and the royal knights will see the odds are insurmountable and lay down their arms. But if they think they have a chance, they will keep fighting. The losses could be immense."

"Fear not. There are over two thousand here now," the prelate said. "And another five hundred in ships in the bay. When the blow comes, it will be like a sharp sword to the neck. Painless."

The cloaked head nodded.

"But let me show you this one," the prelate said. "The workmanship of the sylphs and their goblin artisans is quite impressive."

Using a crowbar, the prelate pried open a large crate and pushed up the lid.

Both men looked down into the crate. The cloaked man shook his head in astonishment. "Incredible..."

Rohree knew she should stay back, but curiosity burned in her. What was in the crates? Whatever it was, it was clearly of utmost importance and pointed toward a conspiracy of the highest magnitude. She'd have to tell Essa right away, of course. But in order to give a full report, she had to know what was inside. Forward she crept, until she was at the side of the crate the two men were staring into. Then she grabbed the top of the crate's wall, and, quiet as she could be, pulled herself up to peer into it.

Inside was a dragon—or something like a dragon. It was dragon-shaped, but skeletal. And yet, it wasn't just a skeleton. It looked as if someone had taken the bones of a dragon, rearranged them a bit, and covered them in clay.

"And you're sure you and your priests can animate them?" the cloaked man asked.

"Believe me, the lords of the void have been waiting to manifest for thousands of years," the prelate said. "When we give them their chance, they will come."

Rohree's arms were beginning to tremble, but she couldn't take her eyes off the thing in the crate.

"And afterward, you can banish them again?" the cloaked man asked.

The prelate chuckled. "As easy as snapping my fingers."

Without warning, he dropped the crate lid. It bashed down on Rohree's fingers, and she dropped off the crate with a cry of pain, cradling her throbbing hands against her chest.

She heard a sword ring free of its sheath.

"What was that?"

The cloaked man stepped around the side of the crate, pulling back his hood to listen—and Rohree saw his face.

Hoatan. The queen's Torouman!

Could he really be conspiring with the prelate? Plotting to release a secret army?

I must get out of here. I must tell Essa.

A sprite's invisibility was effective, but a person looking closely could spot a telltale shimmer. And these men were no fools. They were staring right at her. Heart thundering in her chest, she rolled to her feet and dashed off between two crates.

"A peri! After it!" the prelate shouted behind her.

Between the crates she ran, darting left, now right, now sprinting straight, trying to make her way back the way she'd come. Her legs burned; her heart pounded. And still the bootfalls of her pursuers thudded behind her. Coming closer.

It was no use. She was a handmaid, not a Skrathan, and many moons had passed since the summers of her youth when she could run through the fields for hours. She felt she couldn't go on a moment more or her heart would burst. And so, she turned aside, ducking into a gap between two containers, and threw herself down.

The footsteps of her pursuers passed her by, but after a moment she heard their voices.

"Wait. Stop. We've lost her."

"I heard her a second ago. She must be close."

She listened, straining to control her labored breathing, as their footsteps turned and went back the way they came. As soon as they were well past, she was on her feet again, first creeping, then running. She burst free of the maze of crates, looking around. Where was the tunnel she had entered from? There were five tunnel entrances on this side, and they all looked the same. She'd been too taken with the sight of the crates and the Gray Brothers to note which tunnel she'd come out of.

Curse you, Essa, for sending a stupid handmaid to do the work of a scout, she thought bitterly. She looked at the tunnels again, from one to the next, but she truly had no idea which she'd emerged from. Choose wrongly, and she might be wandering these catacombs forever.

Whispering a prayer to the Earth Mother, she shut her eyes, trying to feel which path to take. She'd heard tell of minor gods who held sway over luck, and she prayed to these, too.

But don't take all day, she told herself. *Those two will be back —and with their Gray Brothers.*

And so, with a wary glance over her shoulder, she chose the nearest tunnel entrance and entered at a jog. The further she went, the better she felt. The tunnel did look familiar. Here were the shelves of bones. There was the dead rat she'd stepped over. Unless all the tunnels looked identical, she'd chosen the right one. Hope took wing inside her as she imagined herself telling the princess what she'd seen. Essa hadn't been such a fool to send her after all. Maybe she'd even be brought in to report to the queen!

There! On her right was the low tunnel she'd entered through. She raced for it, dropped to her knees to crawl through—and felt cold steel on her neck.

She turned her head slowly, and in the light of the glow-stone she saw—

"Ollie?"

It was him, his expression unreadable in the dimness. She dropped her invisibility with a sigh of relief and went to rise, but the dagger point pressed into her neck, bringing her up short.

"Sorry, Rohree. But I can't let you go back," he said. "Not after what you've seen."

Surely, he was joking... but no hint of humor showed on his face.

"Ollie... what are you—?"

"Here!" he shouted.

Rohree turned to see torchlight bobbing toward them. Hoatan and Kortoi rounded a corner, with a half-dozen Gray Brothers behind them, their curved daggers glinting in the torchlight.

"Good. You caught her," Hoatan said when he saw them.

Rohree turned to Ollie. "Traitor. You've betrayed Essa. Betrayed me..."

It was Hoatan who answered. "No, my sprite friend. A Torouman will never betray his charge."

Kortoi's smile was unsettling. "But he *will* make sure she's on the winning side."

"Essa will be safe," Ollie said coldly. "And so will you," he added with a glance at Hoatan.

"Certainly," Hoatan nodded.

"But we can't have you blabbing what you've seen to the entire court, either," Kortoi said, nodding to his Brothers.

Two of them grabbed Rohree's arms and started dragging her down the passage.

"Ollie!" she shouted, giving him a pleading look—but he was already turning away.

42

CHARLIE

Birds chirped furiously in the flowering trees around us, morning dew still sparkled on the cobblestones of the courtyard, and the sky was a clear azure, a perfect day for flying. It was a fine morning to die.

I wasn't sure what was worse: that the entire court was assembled, filling the courtyard to watch me fight—or that I was expected to read the article I'd written first. All eyes were upon me, some nobles watching with curiosity, others openly sneering as I took my place before the queen's high chair and bowed low, as I'd been coached to do.

"You may begin reading," the queen said.

I straightened up, shuffling the papers in my hands. "Ah... I don't suppose I could do it after my duel, Your Majesty?"

Some quiet laughs and whispers made their way through the assembly. I was keenly aware of the joke, of course. They all assumed there would be no *after the duel*—not for me.

"In Maethalia, it is expected that a queen asks the questions," Synaeda said, her words cold but not without a touch of amusement. "Indeed, there have been quite a few unorthodox activities you have taken part in these last few weeks. Helping my daughter train for her challenge. Attending balls. Getting challenged to a duel."

"I am a man of many interests, Your Majesty," I said, eliciting more smiles of amusement from the crowd.

I spotted Essa, then, off to the queen's left. She was shaking her head at me, but the faintest smile touched her lips. She looked pale. Nervous.

"I regret to point out," the queen said, "This may well be the court's last chat with you. And we don't want to miss out on the chance to hear the article you've been working on directly from the lips of the author. I expect it will be quite the opus since you've had so long to work on it."

I gave a nod and glanced down at the papers. My hands were shaking, which was absurd. How was I more nervous to read what I'd written than to fight to the death?

There were different kinds of terror, I supposed. I'd been in hundreds of dogfights, and the battle-fear gave me power. But this... this was another sort of fear altogether.

I cleared my throat. "Essa always calls me a poet, but... Princess Essaphine, I mean..."

I gave the papers a shake, straightening them, and began reading.

"Three and a half weeks ago, I was sent on assignment to the land of the enemy. Maethalia. I expected to find a land of hostile people. A land of superstition and false magick. A land of evil and... uh... badness," I glanced up to see a lot of frowning faces. "But I learned a lot. The economy of Maethalia is thirty-five percent agricultural. Twenty-five percent of the economy consists of what we would refer to as light industrial—the forging of weapons and tools, weaving of baskets, coopering of barrels, et cetera. Five percent, I was surprised to find out, consists of nothing but magick, the sale of spells, potions, and scrying, which is a sort of long-distance viewing magic Maethalian people use..."

I looked up again to find the nobles glancing at one another in open irritation.

"I just got most of those facts from a book..." I muttered, shuffling to a different page.

"Um... let me see.... Maethalia contains at least five diverse races of people."

I shuffled the papers again, then spied what I was looking for.

"Ah! Dragons. We Admites think of dragons with fear and worry, but really, in Maethalia they're no different than cars or steam engines or airplanes. Except imagine a steam engine that could speak to the conductor in his mind. *Feed me more coal,* it would probably say." I looked up from my paper, hoping to see laughter, but there was not so much as a grin on the face of any of the nobles. I cleared my throat. "In truth, I imagine most Admites would find dragons charming, as long as they were not being eaten by one."

I glanced up again to find the queen scowling at me. I shuffled papers again.

"Um. Let's see. The palace is very nice. It's extremely large, and—"

"You mean to tell me," the queen interrupted in a booming voice. "That you, the foremost bard of your people, have been here for weeks, have enjoyed our hospitality, have toured every corner of our capital, have witnessed the wonders of our magick and the majesty of our dragons, and this is the best you can do?"

I glanced over to find Essa watching me with concern. Then I forced myself to meet the queen's royal glare and took a deep, steadying breath.

"I do have one more..." I said, shuffling the papers once again. When I found the right page, I cleared my throat and read:

"I began as her captive
    She bound both my hands
    And carried me home
    To the strangest of lands

By oath I'd have killed her
    By duty, made war
    But I felt with her
    Things I'd never before

How to describe her?
    Like mist after rain?
    Like mirth after sorrow?
    Like joy after pain?

She can be cruel as winter
    And gentle as spring
    Brighter than summer
    I'm falling, I think.

. . .

She showed me sky
    And drank me the wind
    The fire of dragons
    The rightness of sin

They say she is broken
    That she'll fall in defeat
    But I know her power
    She makes me complete.

Perhaps she will slay me
    Perhaps let me die
    Some days she hates me
    And soon I must fly

But though soul and body
    May soon pass away
    With Essa forever
    My heart shall remain."

The silence dropped in the wake of my words like a hammer on an anvil. Tears stood in Essa's eyes. Her lower lip trembled, and I longed to kiss it with all my being. The queen stood pale and stiff as a marble effigy.

"Well," she said, her commanding voice now breathless. "It seems you have been busy after all."

She looked to her head guard, Trag, and nodded.

"Let us begin our next order of business."

The trumpet sounded. All eyes turned toward the gates. Down from the battlements Braimar came, swooping in on his dragon. The beast looked lopsided now, its left head intact, the shoulder area where its right head would have been a bandaged lump. Laynine was with him, her dragon coming to rest beside Braimar's. Both riders sprang down from their mounts and strode into the center of the court-yard to bow before the queen.

I had to admit, it was a pretty impressive entrance.

"So," the queen said. "Braimar, you have challenged our royal guest Kit Rowley to a duel, is that right?"

"It is, Your Majesty."

"And what is the reason for your quarrel?"

"He attacked me with a necromancer weapon," Braimar said.

Whispers and muttering ran through the court.

"Um, for the record, I didn't attack him," I said. "I threatened him. Because he was trying to—"

The queen held up a hand. "Silence. You are in our nation, you will follow our customs. In Maethalia, the challenger explains the grievance."

Her sharp eyes went back to Braimar. "And it is a mortal challenge."

Braimar gave a single nod.

"Would you reconsider? This man is a guest in our court. Although the use of necromantic weapons is a grave offense, I would not willingly breach our duty of hospitality by sending him home a corpse."

"With respect, my queen, it is my right to challenge him, and it must be a mortal challenge," Braimar said.

The queen took a long, slow breath, then exhaled. "Very well. And who is your second?"

"Laynine," he said, and she stepped up beside him.

"And who is your second?" the queen asked me.

"I have none," I said, giving the answer Clua had coached me to give. A second was expected to vouch for the honor of the first in a duel, and to fight and avenge him if he were killed due to trickery. No Maethalian could be expected to do that for me.

"Very well, then—" the queen went on, but a voice called from the crowd.

"I am his second."

Essa stepped out from among the nobles, looking, to me, like an avenging goddess. She wore her flight armor, and there was wind in her hair and fire in her eyes.

"Essaphine—" the queen scolded in a low voice. But the look from her daughter squelched whatever objection she was about to make. She scowled, nodding. "Very well. Take your places. And may the Star Father grant victory to the righteous."

A gust of air whooshed across the courtyard, ruffling dresses and causing guards to stumble as Braimar and Laynine's dragons departed—for as Ollie had explained to me, Skrathan were not permitted to have their dragons present at a duel.

Guards were now pushing the courtiers back and creating a square arena bounded by a red ribbon. Braimar and Laynine retreated to the far corner while Essa grabbed my arm and tugged me into a corner of our own.

"Thank you," I said. "You didn't have to—"

"Of course I had to, idiot. You're here because you defended me—when I should have defended myself."

We reached the corner, and she turned me around, looking me up and down like a mother about to send her child off to school. I wore a suit of armor Clua had provided. It was not dragon skin like the armor of the Skrathan—only riders were allowed to wear dragon-skin armor— but it was of thick boiled leather reinforced in places with steel plates and swaths of chainmail, made by Clua herself. She'd said it would be light and easy to move in and would turn aside most attacks—though not nearly as well as Braimar's armor would. Essa frowned as she looked at it, though.

"His armor is better than yours," she said. "This should be able to repel most slashes, but beware of thrusts."

"Sure," I said. "Easy."

Her eyes narrowed as if my flippant attitude displeased her.

"And listen. I don't know if Clua and Ollie talked to you about dragon stones?"

I shook my head.

She reached up to her neck and took out the necklace I'd tried to touch during our tour of the city. A gray-blue, teardrop-shaped gem hung on a chain of silver. "Once they've bonded, dragons sometimes give their riders stones. It allows them to channel their dragon's power. If Braimar feels threatened, he may use his. It would manifest in the form of fire coming from his hands."

"So I don't just have to worry about Braimar's superior sword skills, I also have to avoid being roasted by dragon magick?" I said. "Perfect."

She slapped me on the chest. "Be serious."

"If I didn't know better, I'd say you were worried for me," I teased. "You look a bit pale."

She glared at me, adjusting my armor at my neck. "If you

must know, I didn't sleep well. I sent Rohree on an errand for me last night. She didn't come back."

The sudden feeling of unease in my gut betrayed how much I'd come to care for the sprite. "Do you think she's okay? Should I help you look for her?"

Essa rolled her eyes. "First things first, don't you think? Show me your sword."

I drew the weapon Clua had given me. I didn't know much about swords, but it seemed like a good one.

"Clua said it's a century-folded steel blade with a dwarf-iron hilt, made by her mentor," I said.

Essa took the weapon and gave it a test swing.

"It's a nice sword, but..." She dropped it and drew her own weapon. "Here. Use mine."

She put the sword into my hand. It was a gorgeous weapon, with a long, graceful broadsword blade and a silver hilt that branched like a stag's horns. The guard was encrusted with gems of a sort I'd never seen before. They were like diamonds, but every facet seemed to have a different color. It must have weighed half of what the other sword did, and there was something else about it, too. It seemed to sing in my hand, giving off a vibration that made my whole arm tingle.

"That is the Oodantan. The heir sword of Maethalia, made by the daughters of the Star Father when the world was new," she said, with a satisfied nod.

I looked with wonder at the blade. "Essa... I can't..."

"What chance would a poet have against a Skrathan without a magick sword?" she teased.

"I told you, I'm no poet," I said. "I think I just proved that in front of everyone."

"On the contrary. I think you've been a poet all along," she said. "Perhaps you just didn't know it yet."

I laughed, but it gave way to a feeling of deep longing and melancholy as I looked at her face. How I wanted to touch her cheek. To feel my lips brush against hers, even here, with everyone watching. I might never get the chance again. But the way she looked at me wasn't the same as it had been in the room above the ballroom. Her smile looked as if it were filled with the same ache I felt.

As we spoke, we'd been unconsciously moving closer to one another. Now, I found that my forehead was nearly against hers. She exhaled, and I felt her breath on my lips, sending a shiver of want through me.

"Essa... after this is over, I have something to tell you," I said. "It may change how you feel about me."

Her eyes met mine. They reminded me of the gems in her sword—so changeable, so bright.

"Nothing will change how I feel about you," she said. Her hand closed on the front of my armor, and she pulled me to her, our lips meeting in a breathless clash.

Gasps and murmurs rustled around us, but the world fell away as I shut my eyes and surrendered to the kiss. Her scent, her lips, her tongue, her breath. It was like heaven. Like falling into a dream.

A blast of trumpets cut through the morning stillness, and Essa and I parted like two swimmers coming up for air.

"Essa—" I began to speak, but she put a finger to my lips.

"Stay alive so you can tell me after."

I love you. The words roiled inside me, ready to boil over. But I didn't say them aloud. Instead, I let their fire fill me, a fever in my mind, an inferno in my veins. And I

turned, ready to face death, ready to kill and ready to live—
for Essa.

A deep hush fell over the assembly as Braimar and I made
our way to the center of the courtyard. The only sounds
were the thudding of my own heart, the flapping of the
banners atop the palace walls, and the thumps of our boots
on the flagstones as we strode inexorably toward one
another. Crows already circled above, like they knew there
would soon be a corpse to feast on.

My thoughts suddenly went to the boys from my
squadron. I imagined the taunts they'd be hurling at
Braimar and the bets they'd be making with one another if
they were here now. They'd never believe ol' Charlie was
about to get into a sword fight...

What a surreal world I'd fallen into. What a heaven.
What a nightmare. And soon, for better or worse, it would
come to an end.

Braimar stopped perhaps thirty yards away from me and
spun his sword with an impressive flourish, watching me
with eyes as electric as the green of his hair. There was
madness in those eyes. And hunger, the bloodlust of a
dragon. Strike me down, and he'd probably take a bite out of
me. And he might very well strike me down...

In the next few minutes, one of us would be dying—that
was certain. The thought should have been terrifying, but
the high of adrenaline that had filled my veins a moment
before was ebbing now, fading into the steel-cold resolve

that took over whenever I was in a dogfight. The world slowed. Seconds became minutes. My attention sharpened. Every detail around me stood out with incredible clarity. I could have memorized the pattern of the scales on Braimar's dragon up on the parapet or counted the queen's eyelashes. But this was no magick. No supernatural gift. I'd always been a man who didn't give a shit if I lived or died. That had been my superpower. Now, I had Essa to live for. To kill for. And I refused to let her down.

I brought the blade up in front of my face in salute as Ollie and Clua had taught me, but Braimar didn't repeat the gesture. He just shouted a battle cry and charged, coming at me with a barrage of overhead strikes so forceful they nearly knocked me to my knees.

In an instant, the crowd came alive, screaming and whistling and shouting Braimar's name. Somehow, I managed to block those first few blows and disengage, circling to my right.

"I've already decided what I'm going to do when I kill you," Braimar said as we orbited one another. "I'm going to cut off your head and bury it inside Zamar's mouth. A head for a head. One last piece of Admar flesh for my dragon boy to feast on." He gave a mad laugh.

I leveled a probing slash at his face, but he dodged it without even bringing up his sword.

"After Laynine kills Essa, perhaps I'll bury her head there, too," he snarled. "A shame, though. It is a pretty head. And such delicious lips..."

I lunged in with an attack. Thrust, left, right, overhead, circling, now a swipe at Braimar's leg. The Skrathan met every motion of my blade smoothly and effortlessly. When I stepped back to catch my breath, he nodded approvingly.

"I see you've done some training. That's good, poet. It's good form to put on a bit of a show for the court before the blood gets spilt."

He feigned low, then slashed high. His blade raked across my chest, sending links of chainmail tinkling across the cobblestones.

I glanced down to see a tear in my armor and a crimson glint of blood.

"Oh, that armor won't stop my sword," Braimar said. "This is an ancient blade, in my family for fifteen generations. Steel from the bones of the original Star Children. It's imbued with magick and luck beyond reckoning."

He swooped in, slashing for my throat. I brought my blade up fast, blocking his strike and circling away.

"You move well for a poet," Braimar said. "You're sure you haven't fought before?"

I could have told him about the hours I'd spent at the window above this courtyard, watching the young knights and Skrathan train when I had nothing else to do. I could have told him of the strategic parallels I'd noticed between swordplay and dogfighting. The feigns and attacks. The approaches and retreats. The two arts had a surprising amount in common... But instead, I decided to show him.

While circling right, I suddenly shuffled left, then lunged in, slapping his blade aside and catching him with the tip of my sword in the meat of his hip. Essa's blade bit through the armor, and Braimar's mouth fell open in a silent cry of pain and shock before he stumbled backwards, his sword raised defensively.

A few cheers went up, and I glanced over to find Lure, Pocha, and Dagar jumping up and down. The rest of the crowd had gone ominously silent.

Braimar was circling me now, limping slightly, his mocking grin replaced with a rictus of pain and fury.

"You're no poet," he snarled. "Who are you?"

I shook my head. "Nobody noteworthy."

"Liar!" Braimar shouted. "My dragon can smell your lie."

At the mention of a dragon, I felt Parthar in my mind. *Careful. He's crazy!*

Go to sleep, Parthar. Don't distract me.

I help you.

Braimar shot in and swung his sword upward at an awkward angle, clipping my left elbow. Pain shot through my arm, and I stumbled backwards, trying to keep space between Braimar and me. It was the advantage he'd been waiting for. His blade seemed to come at me from all directions, a barrage of slashes and stabs and feigns that showed me just how much he'd been holding back so far. His speed and power were overwhelming; I was no match for them. It was like a Sackman Comet versus a mail plane.

I blocked, blocked, blocked, then my heel hit a cobblestone and I fell. With a mighty clash of blades, Braimar dashed the sword from my hands. I rolled right and started to stand, but before I could get upright, his blade thumped into the muscle between my shoulder and my neck. Pain sent a veil of black across my vision, and I fell again, landing on my belly and rolling to get clear of him. He was too fast. His thrust glanced off my armor—and perhaps one of my ribs—and I cried out.

I thought I heard Essa shouting for me, but I didn't want to look at her. Not while I was losing, letting her down.

The blade's tip slipped past me and into a crack between two flagstones. And with all Braimar's force behind it, it stuck there. He yanked, trying to free it, and I seized the moment, windmilling a kick upward. It caught him in the elbow, and I heard a crack.

He growled in pain, staggering away with his injured arm held to his side. In a second, I was back on my feet, scanning the ground for Essa's sword. I spotted it perhaps ten yards away and dashed for it, but Braimar caught me first, hitting me from behind with a tackle that sent us both sprawling.

He came up on top, his uninjured elbow grinding my cheek, pinning me down.

All decorum had left the court now; their shouts and shrieks and jeers were as loud as those of a drunken crowd at the Ironberg Forum during a heavyweight title fight. They were eager for Braimar to finish me, but neither of us had a sword now, and I knew how to fight hand-to-hand. Braimar landed a couple of short hooks to my head, but before he could land a third, I kicked up with my legs and caught his head in the crook of my knee. I straightened my body, pushing him off me, then rolled onto my belly and scrambled to get on top of him.

I almost flopped right onto his knife blade. He'd pulled the weapon from somewhere and had it ready, and I saw it at the last second. Only by catching his wrist and reeling back was I able to avoid being skewered. For a moment, we were frozen in an arm-wrestling stalemate, the knife blade trembling between us as I tried to force it down towards him and he tried to force it up into me. He may have been stronger, but I had gravity on my side. Slowly, the blade began inching downward, toward his left eye.

I watched him, grunting, snarling, red-faced and trembling, as the knife blade came closer and closer to ending the fight. The screams of the crowd were deafening. Then, something changed. I smelled hot metal and saw that the knife blade was beginning to smoke and glow red. Then it burst into flame, along with Braimar's entire hand.

The dragon stone power.

The flames scalded my hands, forcing me to let go of his wrist. Quick as a snake strike, Braimar punched the knife up toward my neck. I rolled in time to avoid being stabbed in the throat, but the blade caught my upper chest, sending a bright flash of pain through me as I rolled away.

I didn't get far.

Braimar was on me again in a second. He grabbed my armor with burning hands as I writhed to get away. The stink of searing leather filled my nostrils, and pain washed over me.

Through my burning and panic, I somehow heard Parthar's voice in my mind.

I help you, Charlie.

The thing that struck me most was that the little dragon knew my name. I'd never told it to him. I'd never told it to anyone here. And yet he knew me.

Perhaps that realization caused some psychic wall inside me to come down, for in that moment, I felt a power fill me. My vision seemed to grow suddenly sharper. Strength flooded my limbs. And my hands suddenly felt hot. Not flaming like Braimar's, but hot enough to scald.

Without another thought, I shoved my hand up and clapped it to Braimar's face. It sizzled. As my forefinger and thumb pressed against his eyelids, he screamed and tried to roll off me, but I rolled with him, coming up on top and pinning him to the ground. Smoke rose from his burning face as he screamed.

Shouts came from the crowd around me.

"Treachery!"

"What is this?"

"A foreigner—doing magick!"

"Stop him!"

I glanced at the queen and saw her watching me, stone-faced.

Essa stood near her, her shoulders raised with tension, watching with her hand cupped over her mouth.

Then a great wind buffeted me, and I looked in the other direction to see Zaman swooping down from the battlements to alight before me.

The rules of single-combat prevented a dragon from interfering in the duel—but judging from the outraged shouts, everyone seemed to think I'd cheated. And now, cries of *eat him* rang out from all around.

The beast's jaws opened, a cavern ringed with jagged white teeth. The sound of its roar almost knocked me sideways as it swung its head toward me. I threw up my hands defensively and fell backward—as if that could protect me from the jaws of this monster.

It loomed closer, saliva dripping, teeth ready to stab the life out of me.

But an instant before those deadly jaws closed on me forever, something red streaked down from above—something with sprawled wings and scrabbling claws. It hit the massive dragon's left eye.

Zamar roared in pain and shook his head, dislodging the attacker.

The small red dragon tumbled to a stop just in front of me and wheeled to face the much larger dragon, snarling like a protective dog.

"Parthar," I whispered, glancing up at the window of my room high, high above.

Told you. I protect you, Charlie, Parthar said in my mind.

I felt an unaccountable swell of emotion. I'd resigned myself to die. For years, I'd been ready for it at any moment. On any mission. In any dogfight. But the idea that this little creature would fight for me. That Essa would care for me... tears could almost have blinded me, but I set my jaw. Essaphine's sword lay at my feet, and I stooped and picked it up, its steel ringing off the flagstones as I rose.

Braimar, too, was back on his feet. He'd retrieved his sword and was striding toward me, a demonic glint in his eyes. His face looked grotesque, a handprint of bloody red and singed black. Behind him, Zamar reared up, wings spread, fanged mouth gaping, body so huge it eclipsed the sun.

"Let's carve these bastards up," I told Parthar, raising my sword, and I strode forward to finish the fight.

"Halt!" the queen shouted.

The command in her voice was enough to make even Zamar freeze. All turned to face her as she stepped carefully off her dais and came toward Parthar and me. As deafening as the crowd had been moments ago, it was terribly silent now as the queen approached us and stopped.

"What is this?" she demanded, her gaze ranging from me to Parthar and back again.

It took a moment to catch my breath before I could speak.

"It's a baby dragon, Your Majesty."

"I can see that," the queen said. "How is it here?"

I gave a wary glance at Essa, who shook her head at me, eyes wide, as if to ask *what the hell?*

I grasped for a plausible lie to tell, but I was too weary to think of one. And in any case, it was time to face the truth. I was no spy. I was a fighter.

"I took an egg from the Hatchery," I said. "Just to have a closer look at it. It was to be destroyed anyway. I didn't think it would do any harm. But while it was in my room, it hatched."

A ripple of murmurs passed through the court.

For the first time, I saw Prelate Kortoi among the onlookers. He watched me with narrowed eyes, looking decidedly displeased.

"A dragon egg from the Hatchery... hatched?" the queen asked.

I nodded.

She looked away, clearly thinking hard. The rest of the court seemed to be doing the same calculus. It was a question I'd been wrestling with for weeks. The eggs of the Hatchery were all infected with fungus. How was it that the one I rescued had hatched?

Though I could see her struggling with this question, the queen didn't ask it aloud. Instead, she turned back to me, a regal coldness in her eyes.

"We will get to the bottom of this situation," she said. "But for the moment, there is a question of justice to decide. Taking a dragon egg from the Hatchery is forbidden. And for a foreigner to bond with a dragon..."

Just the words made the queen go so pale she looked as if she might vomit.

"Your Majesty, let us finish the duel," Braimar said. "I will serve this foreigner the justice he deserves."

"Silence," Synaeda snapped. "The duel was ended when your dragon interfered. You have dishonored yourself."

Zamar hung his massive head, chastened, but Braimar only looked more furious than ever.

One of the elder nobles came forward, a man in a crimson cloak with a long, black beard streaked with silver. "Your majesty, speaking for the nobles, the law here is clear. No one except the Skrathan or the Gray Brothers may attempt to rear a dragon, certainly not a foreigner. He must be executed immediately."

A clamor of agreement went up from the court. The queen lifted her hand, and they went quiet.

"Your advice is noted, Lord Natath. But I will remind you, it is still the queen's purview to dole out justice, not that of the Noble Council."

"Then do it!" the noble said, to a cheer from the crowd.

The queen looked as if she might draw her dagger and carve up this Lord Natath herself, but before she could respond, Essa came to her mother's side.

"Mother. This man may be a deceitful trickster, an enemy, a liar... he may be repugnant in every way..." She shot me a look like a flaming arrow. "But you are merciful. Exile him. Send him back to his people. I can take him—"

"Silence, Essaphine," the queen hissed. "Your lack of judgment is pitifully obvious. I will not be taking counsel from you."

The queen's steely gaze ranged over the entire court-yard. "There are many in this court who will have to account for the events that have unfolded today." She gave a sharp look to Prelate Kortoi, then to Essa. Finally, her stare zeroed in on me. "But as for the question before me, there can be only one verdict. I sentence the Admite, Kit Rowley, to death."

43
ESSA

The unfolding events felt fractured, like scenes in a dream. The guards chaining Kit's wrists and taking him away... The Gray Brothers throwing a net over the little red dragon and carting it off... Healers fussing over Braimar's wounds, then leading him toward their temple... Mother and her entourage making their way back inside with a flourish of trumpets... My friends pausing to check on me, then departing when their words were met only with my stunned silence... Finally, Laynine and I were the only ones left in the courtyard.

"Tomorrow that will be us, cousin," she said. "Only our dragons will not be able to step in and save us."

From her demeanor, I couldn't quite gauge how she felt about it. Was she sorry we'd have to fight or gloating about it?

"No one will need to save me," I shot back, and I turned to follow Mother's procession inside, leaving her alone in the windswept courtyard.

I caught up to Mother in her throne room and grabbed her arm, turning her around.

"Mother," I said. "A word in private."

The anger in her eyes gave way to a dismissive eye roll. "Oh, Essaphine. I'm tired. Let it wait until—"

"Now," I said.

The command in my voice was sufficient to make her look at me. Our eyes locked for a moment, a silent struggle taking place between us, then she nodded to her courtiers.

"Leave us."

Muttering in irritation, the nobles filed out until the only ones left were four guards, Trag and Hoatan.

I looked at them. "I said alone."

"By the Goddess, Essaphine! You know these two don't leave me..."

"Perhaps they should," I said. "There is treason among us, Mother, if what just happened hasn't made that clear."

"If there is treason, Princess," Hoatan said calmly. "One imagines it might come from the girl who is clearly smitten with one of our enemies."

Me? In love with Kit? Ha! I hated him for his lies—*he'd bonded a dragon behind my back?*—and yet when I tried to speak, the denial caught in my throat.

"I'm not talking about Kit," I finally managed to say.

Mother sighed as if I were an exasperating child.

"Trag, guards, leave us. Hoatan will stay."

Trag's ugly, scarred face remained impassive as he bowed and strode from the room, guards at his side. Mother took her place on her throne, and Hoatan took his on a stool just behind her, looking for all the world like an old bird on a perch.

"Say what you will, Essaphine," Mother said wearily.

"The oracle told us—"

The words roused Mother from her torpor like a slap of cold water.

"What? You saw the oracle?"

"Yes," I said. "And she told me—"

"Visiting the oracle is forbidden to any but the queen," Hoatan said, red-faced.

"I went, and she granted me an audience," I snapped. "Perhaps you'd like to know what she said?"

This shut them both up.

"I saw crates under the city, Mother. Hundreds and thousands of them being moved into the catacombs."

"Crates?" Mother said. "Filled with what?"

"I don't know," I said. "I sent Rohree to investigate last night. She never came back."

At last, I had Mother's full attention. She rubbed a finger thoughtfully over her lips, her brow furrowed.

"The Admites' doing, no doubt..." she muttered.

"If it's even true, Your Majesty," Hoatan said. "You know how unreliable the Oracle can be."

"Those crates could be filled with the Admites' vile explosives," Mother mused. "Or they could be moving in troops in some clandestine fashion, ready to jump out at a signal and spring a trap. Invade us from within."

"Impossible," Hoatan said calmly—though he looked a shade paler than usual. "Such a thing could not have happened without our noticing. But it is an easy enough lie to suss out. I can send men to the catacombs now to learn the truth of it."

"Good," the queen said. "Do it."

"But don't send the Lacunae," I said.

Hoatan glared at me. "The Shadow Knights are our best warriors, Princess. If there is truly a danger—"

"They are of the Gray Brotherhood," I said. "Which brings up the next question. How did the egg Kit stole survive?"

"Rather, we might ask how he was able to steal an egg and raise a dragon while he was supposed to be under your watch," Hoatan replied, but Mother raised a hand, silencing him.

"The Gray Brothers are supposed to be experts on dragon rearing," I went on. "They've been telling us for years that fungus-infected eggs can't hatch. They've been destroying them. But what if that's not true? What if the eggs they've been destroying are good, viable eggs?"

"Ridiculous!" Hoatan said. "Why would Kortoi and his men destroy perfectly healthy dragon eggs?"

"Let's think it through," I shot back, turning Torouman rhetoric back on him. "What would the result of such an action be?"

"We've had fewer dragons," Mother mused. "The Skrathan's numbers have remained low. The riders have been weakened. We've had to rely more and more on the prelate's Lacunae. And the war has dragged on for decades..."

"In that time, the Gray Brothers have built up their foreign contacts," I continued, picking up her thread of thought. "We rely on the Brothers and their connections with the sylph for critical trade. And we rely on the nobles convincing their tenant farmers to become soldiers. All of that reliance has served to weaken the crown and empower the Gray Brothers—and the nobility. What little power we have is all bent on fighting the URA for the one piece of land where dragon eggs still hatch, because without it, the strength of the Skrathan would slip away completely. They have made us weak, Mother. What would be the endgame of the Gray Brothers weakening the royals?"

"This is absurd—" Hoatan sputtered.

"Taking the crown," Mother said. Her eyes met mine, and she surged to her feet, wheeling on Hoatan.

"Send men to investigate the catacombs. *Not* the Lacunae—*OUR* men."

"Your Majesty—" Hoatan began, but she cut him off.

"And send our knights to the Hatchery as well. Expel the Gray Brotherhood, bar the doors, and bid the Skrathan and their dragons to guard the remaining eggs until we get this sorted out."

Though it seemed to pain him to do it, the Torouman bowed in acquiescence. "Yes, Your Majesty."

"Now, about Kit," I began.

Mother held up a hand, stopping me.

"Your council has been wise, Essaphine. We shall see how much truth is in your words. But that doesn't mean your impertinence is forgotten or forgiven, and it doesn't erase the foreigner's crimes. He has bonded a dragon. For that, he must die. And once the dragon has been studied to see how it survived the fungus, it must die, too. It would be far too dangerous to allow a dragon bonded to one of our enemies to live."

Another protest boiled up in me, but I could see from the look in Mother's eyes that I'd might as well shout at a slab of granite.

"You have a challenge to prepare for," she went on. "In less than twenty-four hours, daughter, you will be able to bend my ear again as Irska of the Skrathan. Or else you will be in Prelate Kortoi's dominion—a shade of the void. I suggest you prepare. I'm sure your aunt will be expecting a visit from you to conduct one last training session—now that your foreign tutor is indisposed."

"And you will be preparing Laynine," I said, unable to keep the bitterness out of my voice.

"As our tradition demands," she said. "You're dismissed."

I bowed and went to leave. After I'd gone only a few paces, Mother's iron voice called me back. "Essa."

I turned to her.

"Whatever happens tomorrow... I love you."

Her words hung in the air between us. I tried to remember the last time she'd said those words to me—if ever. Part of me wanted to say them back to her, those three words and so many more. So much had gone unsaid between us for so long. And this might be our last chance. If I lost tomorrow...

And yet, I could find no way to capture all I was feeling. No way to begin. So, I merely gave her a nod and turned and strode from the room.

44
CHARLIE

The day of Essa's challenge came, the silvery light of dawn piercing the haze of a gray morning. Light rain drizzled from a blustery sky as I stood at my window, gazing out on the north wing of the palace and the city beyond. Below, in the courtyards, banners, tents, and bleachers were being assembled, for unlike the other Skrathan challenge events, this main attraction took place directly over the city and the palace. It gave the event a bit more of a dangerous thrill, I supposed, since in theory one of the dragons or their riders could fall onto the heads of the onlookers—not unlike the airshows back home.

Everyone loves a thrill.

But I felt more or less dead inside.

Yesterday, after the duel, I'd been brought back here. It was the same chamber as before, but it had been transformed into a true prison cell now. Guards had stormed through and removed anything that could be used as a weapon—fire irons, firewood, chairs and tables, my trusty oilskin bag, even the sheets and canopy from the bed.

Healers had come, stitching my wounds and declaring without much enthusiasm that I would be fine; Braimar's worst strikes had either glanced off a bone or simply not been very deep—a lucky outcome. The healers had patched me up, then left, locking me in.

I'd paced, kicked the stone walls, even dropped and tried to do a few painful push-ups, anything to burn the pent-up energy I felt. All night, I thrashed in my sheets, unable to sleep from the smoldering anxiety that burned its way through my gut. Yet I must have slept at some point, for I arose shivering in my cold, fireless room, feeling as listless as I'd felt passionate the night before, as if I were a candle that had burned down to nothing.

Today is the day. Essa will live or die. The thought reverberated through my mind over and over in an endless loop.

Whatever happened to Essa, I would be dead. Executed. There could be no reunion for us, no romantic denouement, no happy ending. I thought I could at least write a letter to tell her how I felt—but they'd taken the damned paper and pen, too.

And how do you feel about Essa? Some coy inner voice asked me. I knew. But something kept me from uttering that truth, even to myself.

I'd never told Kitty I loved her, even when we got engaged. She was not the *I love you* type. The closest we'd come was a flirty, *you're alright, kid.*

But comparing my feelings for Kitty to my feelings for Essa was like holding a flashlight next to the sun. It wasn't just that the picture of Kitty kissing the counterfeit Silver Wraith had soured me on her. I'd never truly loved Kitty. I didn't even know what love was before Essa.

If I could just see her one more time. The things I would say to her. The things I would do...

Essa wasn't the only loss that pained me. Worry for Parthar plagued me as well. What would they do with him, now that they knew he existed? Would they fling him from the cliffs as they'd done to the eggs? Kill him for bonding to a foreigner? Or would they try to retrain him somehow, brainwash him to forget me?

Whatever their plan, he wasn't dead yet. I could feel him when I reached out with my mind, but his only response was a lonely, distant whimper that I hardly found reassuring.

I was a fighter. An ace. I'd killed five dragon riders in one night, once. I'd been admiringly called a cold son of a bitch on more than one occasion. And yet here I was, my heart breaking in two ways at once.

Maybe this is a magical place. It's changed me. It's ruined me, I thought as I paced.

Out the window, the preparations for the challenge continued below. It would take place at noon. What time was it now? Curse this place and its lack of clocks...

The door opened and I spun to face it, eager to see Rohree and to get a bit of news. But it wasn't the sprite, just a pair of guards, a stocky male guard holding a tray of food and a blonde female who stayed by the door, sword drawn.

"Excuse me, can you tell me what time it is? How long until the challenge begins?" I asked.

The stocky guard set the food tray on the floor and stood, glaring at me. "Just be glad you're alive to see it, Admite," he said, glancing to the window. "Normally, a prisoner would be placed in the dungeon, but our merciful queen wanted you to have a front row seat—so you can watch the traitorous princess you corrupted drop out of the sky."

I stepped forward, ready to throttle both of them, but they'd already backed out of the room, the door banging shut and clicking locked behind them. I heard the two laughing as they departed down the hall.

Grumbling curses, I knelt over the tray. The breakfast fare, too, was that of a prisoner and not a guest: a slab of dry, hard bread and pale, tepid tea in a tin cup. I rose, crunching and sipping, not at all hungry but knowing I should face whatever was coming with a bit of food in my stomach.

Back at the window, I ate and drank, gazing out over the palace's opal battlements and the city beyond. It truly was a beautiful place. And so vast and varied and magical that Essa and I could have spent one hundred lifetimes exploring it together and still failed to unlock all its mysteries.

How unfair it felt to face death now. I felt like I'd only just learned to live.

I reached out to the window and tried to open the casing. I'd scaled down the tower once, after all. But someone had thought of that; the window had been sealed shut.

So accept your fate, I thought. All aces ended the same way, eventually. It was the nature of fighting gravity. What goes up must come down. When it's a plane, it usually does so fast and in flames... Death had always awaited me; I was just meeting it in a different way.

But Essa. She still had a chance. And if she could live, if she could somehow triumph, it would all be worth it.

As if in answer to my thoughts, that low, booming horn sounded, its blast ringing across the battlements. I looked down to see throngs of people filling the streets, finely dressed nobles taking their places on the courtyard bleachers below. At the sound of the horn, a shout of excitement seemed to rise from every corner of the city. I squinted beyond the palace walls to see the merchant buildings, houses, and stables squirming with bodies as scores of onlookers climbed up to watch from the rooftops.

And then, from the direction of the mountains, the dragons came, hundreds of them filling the skies, slicing the clouds with their wings, lighting up the heavens with their exuberant blasts of fire.

And in the midst of them, two dragons flew apart from the others, a great, dark blue akmerus, and a smaller, gray libran. Tryce and Othura. Riding them, I knew, were Laynine and Essa.

The final challenge was about to begin.

God, I hope Othura's wing holds up...

A restless energy still compelled me to pace, but I was loath to miss even a moment of what was to come. So I stood, restlessly drumming my fingers on the window frame, tapping my foot, biting my lower lip, as the two dragons alighted in the courtyard below. Words drifted up to me from beyond my windowpane. I couldn't make out what was said, but from the tone I could tell it was the queen speaking, and from the timbre of her voice I guessed she was reciting some prescribed speech wishing both riders good fortune—as any good, impartial monarch should. After a few minutes, the speech gave way to a roar of the crowd and the flourish of horns.

Far, far below, the two riders took their mounts. Perhaps I imagined it, but I thought I saw Essa's head tilt back to look up at my window.

"I'm watching. I love you," I blurted. I instantly felt foolish. Of course, she couldn't hear me from so many stories above her. Then, her voice was in my mind.

I love you, too.

I froze, feeling at once naked, exposed—and strangely connected. It only took me a second to understand what had happened. Now that she knew I was bonded with a dragon, we were able to communicate through our dragons, the way Skrathan did.

Though it was a bit like the game of telephone children play, the communication still felt surprisingly intimate. The inclusion of the dragons as intermediaries somehow made the messages more meaningful rather than less.

And now, in what were probably the last hours of our lives, why not be honest with our feelings?

We'll be together when this is over, I thought to her. *And I'll explain everything. I know there's a lot to explain...*

For a moment, she didn't answer, and my heart began to dip like a falling kite. Then she replied.

Yes. Yes. I fly for you.

Then the two dragons surged skyward, and I watched, gripping the window frame with both hands as if I were flying with her, as if I were hanging on to Essa for my own precious life.

45
ESSA

"The winner of this challenge will be the one still breathing. The winner will be Irska. The winner will lead all the mighty dragons of Maethalia. The winner will be heir to the Dragon's Eye crown," my mother called in a clear, flat voice, speaking in the old Elven tongue loud enough for everyone assembled to hear. "May the Earth Mother grant you wisdom. May the Sky Father grant you bravery. May the Fifty-Two grant you luck. And may the Lords of the Void grant you the peace to accept your fate. Now, challengers—fly!"

Othura crouched, ready to take flight, and next to us, Tryce, with Laynine on his back, did the same.

"Hold!" Lord Natath shouted, stepping forward. "On behalf of the council of nobles, I contest the princess's flying apparatus. She's using machines."

I glanced down at the clip on my arm and the lance Kit and Clua had created for me.

The look Mother gave Natath was venomous. "The

noble council has no jurisdiction over the inner workings of the Skrathan, Lord Natath."

"But we do," Natath said, brandishing a scroll. "Per the second Accord of Davit, the Noble Council shall act as judge in matters pertaining to the royalty where a majority of the nobles deem the Monarch is unable to render unbiased judgment for any of a number of reasons, including but not limited to—"

"Absurd," Hoatan began. "The Accord of Davit is—"

"Are you questioning my ability to preside over the Challenge of Irska—" Mother demanded. "Something my ancestors have done without disruption for twenty generations? And think well on your answer, Natath, because I call such a challenge to my power treason."

He took a step forward, and the swords of all Mother's guards rang from their sheaths. The noble knights, in turn, drew their weapons.

And into the midst of the two parties a single metal implement landed. My hand clip. All eyes settled on me.

"So much fuss over a little piece of metal," I said. "I don't need it."

"Essaphine," Mother said, her voice low. "Pick it up. You'll fall."

I'd wondered what she truly thought of the aid Kit was giving me. Now I had my answer, and it filled me with warmth and relief. It gave me hope that more goodness might lie hidden within her cold, royal exterior.

I turned to face the assembled nobles. "Isn't everyone here convinced I'll die either way?" I shouted. No one answered. In fact, I'd never in my life heard such a multitude of people stay so silent.

I'm watching. I love you.

I recognized the voice in my mind. It was coming through Othura, and for an instant, I was confused. Then I understood. Kit had bonded a dragon—and he was communicating with me the Skrathan way.

I was keenly aware of his lies and omissions, as aware of them as I was of the lance in my hand. And yet, in that moment of heightened emotion, I had an almost preternatural awareness of him—of both of us—as a pair of insects trapped in the same spider web, each tugging at the strings that held us, trying to crawl to one another. And the truth was, despite everything, I was glad to hear his voice. As alone as I'd felt a moment before, I suddenly felt the opposite feeling. Belonging. Desire. Purpose.

I love you, too, I said in his mind.

Somehow, we'll be together when this is over. And I'll explain everything, he said.

Yes, I told him. *I fly for you.*

Mother was watching me with those gray eyes of hers that seemed to perceive so much. Whatever she saw in me satisfied her, and she gave a small nod.

"Very well. The machine is removed. Therefore, the nobles, I assume, will withdraw their objection."

Lord Natath bowed in agreement, and his knights sheathed their swords and stepped back—a crisis averted.

"So be it, then," Mother said. "Challengers—fly!"

Othura's wing was hurting her. I knew because I could feel it, the faintest ache in my own left shoulder, but she launched from the ground now as if pain were nothing. There was no time now for pain, or love, or anything else.

The final challenge had begun.

The beginning of the challenge final was always the same, a tradition dating back thousands of years meant as a salute to the monarch and the assembly. Both dragons spiraled upward together until we were past the uppermost turret of the palace, then we broke apart, winging in opposite directions. It was a spectacle for those on the ground, and their applause and cheers rose, faint on the wind as we flew away from Laynine and Tryce, then banked around for our first lance pass.

I could feel Kit in my mind—not his words, for he knew better than to distract me—but his nervousness. I could feel Mother, too, a presence more aloof but equally probing. I clapped my mind shut just as I'd closed the wind visor on my helmet, locking their thoughts out. But there was another presence there. Laynine.

I'm sorry to do this to you, cousin, she said.

And I'm sorry for what I must do to you, I thought back.

What a world we live in, where young people are forced to destroy each other, she lamented.

But I could ill afford to be distracted by her philosophies. I blocked her out, just as I'd done with Kit and Mother, and Othura winged toward her and Tryce, picking up speed. The lance Kit and Clua made me felt good, light in my hand and firm under the crook of my arm. But I was keenly aware of my missing clip. It meant however tightly I clenched my legs, any hit from Laynine's lance could easily send me tumbling out of my saddle—to my death.

Closer we came. My eyes locked on Laynine's chest. Closer. Closer...

And there was her lance point, veering for my face. At the last instant, Othura brought up her wing, deflecting the lance. I felt the blow jostle me, but then we were past, and I was still in my saddle.

Heart thundering in my ears, I looked down at my left shoulder to see the armor there scraped from Laynine's lance tip. Three inches lower and to the right, I'd have been finished. And my lance hadn't come close to hitting Laynine.

Nice wing block, I told Othura.

Of course, she said. *Take her head off next time.*

A challenge started off with three lance passes. I'd survived the first...

The second came before I was ready for it.

We turned, and Laynine and Tryce were already there—she must have pulled him into a tight turn just after our first clash. Already her lance was streaking toward my chest. I had no time to defend myself or aim my lance. All I could do was throw myself backward in the saddle until my back rested against Othura's spine and watch Laynine's weapon rip through the air above me—where my body had been an instant before.

I sat up with a groan, my back and stomach muscles protesting the sudden, unnatural movement.

Of all the dishonorable... Othura snarled, looking over her shoulder as she winged ahead, putting some distance between us and Laynine.

There are no rules in challenges, I reminded her. *Just traditions.*

Still... Othura huffed.

Let's make her regret it, I thought, and lifted myself in the saddle, an unspoken way of urging Othura to climb higher.

Excellent idea, she said, understanding my intent. Up we climbed, ranging outside the castle walls, moving toward the mountains.

Running already? Laynine asked in my mind, mockery in her voice.

Come and get me, I shot back.

But at that moment, I felt Othura falter. Probably someone who didn't ride her every day wouldn't have felt it —but I knew the rhythms of her wings as well as the beating of my own heart. And they were off.

Your hurt wing—

It's nothing. Concentrate on the fight.

Climbing would normally have been a good strategy. Larger dragons had to expend more energy to gain altitude than smaller dragons did. By making Tryce climb, we could tire him out—then wheel and come down on them from above with the double advantage of height and greater speed. But Othura's injury changed that calculus. I didn't want to wear her out with a steep climb if she was in pain. Instead, I brought her around.

Tryce was there, following closer than expected, only perhaps five dragon lengths back and gaining. Laynine crouched in her saddle, taut and ready, her lance trained on my chest. I matched her posture, leaning forward, squeezing Othura with my knees and locking the lance under the crook of my arm.

Four lengths, three lengths...

Even this high, the roar of the crowd rose like the rush of the sea.

Othura snapped her wings once more and pinned them

back, making herself like a javelin. It was the most aggressive jousting posture, giving us the advantage of surprising speed—but it also meant I wouldn't have the benefit of her wings to deflect Laynine's lance this time. It was kill or be killed.

Two lengths...

One...

At the concussion of the hit, the world blurred and spun. My body reverberated with pain like a struck bell. I didn't know what was happening. I might have been falling from the sky, or diving into a lake, or dreaming in my own bed. With effort, I came back to myself, sucked a ragged breath, refocused my eyes, and found I was still in the saddle, the splintered haft of the lance still gripped in my trembling hand.

Othura was banking, and I looked up and back. Laynine was there, banking and holding a broken lance of her own—like a mirror image of me.

We'd broken lances on each other. And even without my clip, I'd managed to keep my seat. I looked down at my aching chest and saw the front of my armor had a distinct check-shaped mark on it. It wasn't pierced, but the bruise underneath would probably be a record-breaker if I lived to examine it.

Well done, Dear Heart, Othura said. *Now the entwining.*

We'd survived the first phase of the challenge, and it was on to the next. If the joust was like boxing, the entwining was more like a wrestling match. Rider and dragon would come in close and meet in a clash of muscle and claw and tooth, while their riders did what damage they could with their sword or other short-range weapon of choice. This was another moment my clip would have come in handy. But I'd trained plenty holding on with only my knees. I'd just have to do it again now.

I would have to win the challenge here and end it—because the third phase, the one where the dragons used their powers, was one we couldn't survive.

I drew my sword and stood up in my stirrups, snarling into the wind.

In Tryce swept, buffeting us with air from his massive wings. The force of his body slamming into us probably could have knocked Othura out, but she veered away at the last second, causing the bulk of Tryce's body to miss us, and managed to bite onto the webbing of one of his wings with her teeth.

Yes! I cheered.

This was a textbook technique for a smaller dragon fighting a large one, something my auntie called *grab and grind*. Get in close, cling to a larger dragon, and you could negate many of the advantages of their longer limbs, heavier bodies, and stronger jaws.

Tryce flapped awkwardly with his free wing as he tried to keep the one in Othura's jaws still so it wouldn't tear. The problem: one wing wasn't enough to keep two dragons aloft. We fell, my stomach seeming to rise into my throat as we plummeted through the clouds. Screams rose from the onlookers below.

Othura clamped onto Tryce's belly with her back claws and slashed with her front ones, but trying to pierce Tryce's tough skin was like clawing through a stone wall.

The sun went black as Tryce brought his foreclaw up and swooped toward me, hitting both me and Othura. Before he could rip me off her back, Othura released her grip. We dropped off Tryce, and the dragons flew apart. But Othura had twined her tail with his. She used it now to swing us around to his back.

Suddenly, Laynine and I were helmet to helmet. Our swords flashed furiously, the blades clashing.

Teach her some respect! I called to Othura. She knew what I meant and spun, bringing her wing around and slapping Laynine so hard she reeled in the saddle— though somehow, she kept hold of her sword.

Now that both dragons had use of their wings again, we were locked together in a spiraling ascent. As I turned Othura again to get in sword range of Laynine, Tryce managed to get a good grip with their locked tails and tugged Othura downward, yanking me out of range.

I cursed as Othura disentangled herself and we wheeled, both dragons circling one another. The sight of Laynine drew a curse out of me. She might have been stunned by Othura's wing slap a moment before, but she was steady in the saddle now, and I knew I might not get her off balance like that again.

We were descending back toward the courtyard now. As we circled, the sound of the crowd came back to me, the entire city in an uproar over the show we were giving them. I imagined I could hear Kit's voice among them. But if he was trying to talk to me directly in my mind, I couldn't tell —I had to keep all communication with everyone except Othura blocked out until this was over. Any distraction could be the end of me.

We'd made it this far. Further than anyone had ever imagined... But time was running out. Two more passes, then Tryce would unleash his lightning on us, and it would be over.

We continued to circle, giving our dragons a moment to

recover and eyeing one another, watching for openings to attack.

Hit them with an invert, I said.

It was one of the moves I'd worked on with Kit. Charge the enemy dragon, flip over, and fly under them while Othura raked upward, slashing their underbelly with her claws. We'd practiced, and I had it mastered—when I was using the clip.

Othura huffed dismissively. *No.*

It will be the last thing they expect.

For good reason. Without the clip, you'll fall.

I can hang on.

And if you can't?

I took a slow breath. *Then I fall.*

Othura growled beneath me, showing exactly what she thought of my plan. It was a risk. The invert was never a move we practiced before Kit came to town, before I had a clip, when I was terrified to go upside down. In truth, I was still terrified. But...

Do you have any better ideas? I demanded.

Othura's growl grew sharper. *You're an idiot.*

But you love me.

Against my better judgement... she admitted. *Fine. Here we go.*

With a suddenness that jerked me in the saddle, she veered toward Tryce, jaws wide as if she were going to bite at Laynine. As Tryce raised his head to defend her, we dropped under him and rolled.

I felt myself go weightless for an instant as we flipped, and I tried with all my strength to clench with my legs and stay in the saddle. There came the familiar, grating sound of claw on scale, and I felt a spatter of blood—Othura's strike was working. But my legs were slipping. I had no choice but to drop my sword and grab the saddle horn, watching the blade spin into oblivion below me as I held on with all my strength with my one hand. But something was wrong. We'd jerked to a halt, and I looked up to see Tryce had caught us with one of his rear talons. We were stuck—upside down. Tryce's claws dug into Othura's haunch near her tail, squeezing until I saw blood. I felt Othura's pain, and she gave a roar of pain.

I had to help her. But my legs, my hand, everything was slipping. And the jostling as the two dragons clawed at one another only made it worse.

Use wind! I told Othura.

No powers... until after... the third pass, she replied, her thoughts broken as she grappled with her pain.

Curse dragons and their ethics...

I had to help her. But how? I was hanging on for my life.

Tryce's other claw swung down, raking Othura's face.

Whip your tail over to me, I told Othura.

I'm... a bit... busy... she snarled.

Just do it!

Her tail came, flopping over my shoulder like a snake.

I twined my handless arm with it.

Now take me up to Laynine.

What are you—?

Now!

I released my legs' grip on the saddle just as Othura's tail whipped me upward and dropped me on Tryce's back—just behind Laynine.

She spun her head around, startled to find me there, and I clamped my maimed arm around her neck, my dagger point to her throat.

"Tell Tryce to let Othura go."

"You miss the point of the game, cousin. It's a fight to the death," she said. And with amazing speed, she reached up and grabbed my wrist, wrenching my arm sideways. Pain shot through my shoulder, causing me to cry out, and the dagger tumbled from my grip. Then, the world seemed to drop out from under me. Tryce was rolling—and I fell.

46

ESSA

I was a child again. Breathless. Helpless. Falling.

Last time, I'd been saved by jaws and teeth, a rescue I often felt was worse than death itself would have been. But that wouldn't be my fate today. Othura was too high. Too far away. Too tangled with Tryce to break away.

I became aware of my body. Arms pinwheeling. Legs pumping in empty air. Wind ripping upward, pulling my helmet from my head, yanking at my cloak, whipping my hair across my face like a banner.

Wind.

A dragon's breath without fire wasn't much good, that's how the thinking went. But a little wind and a little luck could make a difference. It could make all the difference. And so I summoned Othura, summoned the wind.

Breathe.

I glimpsed her above, making an arrow of her body, shooting down at me as fast as she could—still too slow.

Her breathing wind would only push me down faster, make my death quicker.

But with the dragon stone...

Breathe. I told her. *I'll use it.*

Just a little. That's all I needed. A nudge, a change of course.

The ground was speeding up too fast. There was no more time to think, no time to explain.

But Othura listened. Breath issued from her mouth so fast it quickly became a whirlwind, shooting down to me and snagging me in a hot embrace that whipped me around like a rag.

Tame it. Use it.

In my dizziness and panic, I didn't know if the words came from me or from Othura—or from both of us, maybe. I focused on the stone hanging around my neck, urging it to activate. Instantly, I felt its heat against my chest.

A thought—a jerk of my head—and the whirlwind bucked, hurling me sideways, toward the palace wall. I saw one of the lower spires rushing toward me.

Slow me down!

The wind obeyed. It wouldn't have amounted to much more than a stiff breeze, maybe, but I felt it pushing upward against my feet, slowing my descent just enough. With the crook of my bad arm, I caught the flagpole atop the tower's conical roof and spun down it, my speed decreasing as I went, until my boots thudded against the slate of the roof.

Shouts of amazement came from below. Somehow, in the midst of it all, I heard a voice shouting:

"She used her power! The final phase begins. Now, Laynine!"

I thought I heard the voice aloud—but perhaps it was in

my mind. Either way, I knew who it belonged to. It was Auntie, my durrah, urging her daughter on. Urging her to kill me.

Somehow, that realization hurt more than any heartbreak or any injury I'd felt so far. Laynine was her daughter. Of course, in her heart of hearts, Auntie Dreya wanted her to win; it was foolish of me to imagine otherwise. Still, it was a bitter confirmation: I'd always felt alone—and I *was* alone.

Perhaps Kit cared for me. Perhaps my friends loved me. Certainly, Othura held me as dear as her own heart. But in that moment, none of it mattered. I would let myself die, or I would fight to live. Either way, I would do it for *me*, not for the sake of anyone else. Not for Mother, or Auntie, or even for Maethalia. I would fight for myself. Because I deserved to live. I deserved it as much as Laynine. As much as anyone.

And so, as my heartbeat slowed to a more normal pace, the death-terror drained from my mind, and I saw everything around me with clear eyes. Othura dropping toward me. Tryce behind her, talons extended like a hawk diving for a sparrow. And behind him, a dark and growing cloud of water vapor. We'd used our wind power. Now, Tryce was summoning his lightning. The last phase of the duel had begun...

Othura! Watch out! I called.

She rolled onto her back and looked up at the much larger akmerus bearing down on her—just as lightning began to crackle in the clouds surrounding him. His claws swooped toward Othura, just a dozen feet away now, in a trajectory that would have allowed him to strike her, then slam her down into me.

But at that moment, Othura released the wind. It was greater than any breath I'd seen come out of her before, a savage tornado so concentrated it hit only Tryce's left wing. The wing twisted, sending Tryce plummeting sideways.

As he fell, he swiped at me with his tail. The blow smashed into the roof of the tower, taking half of it out and sending a hail of sharp slate across the rooftop. Pieces pelted me as I tried to protect my face.

Then Othura was there, sailing past. I leapt onto her back just as the tower roof I'd been on a second before collapsed.

You're brilliant. I gave her neck a grateful squeeze.

But something was wrong. We were dropping again.

We tilted, and I caught a glimpse of Tryce below us, his jaws clamped onto Othura's tail, dragging us downward.

The four of us—dragons and riders—landed heavily in the courtyard, sending up a cloud of dust and leaving the crowd to scream and scatter. I stumbled to my feet, groggy, and felt it instantly—the telltale tingle of my hair standing on end.

Othura! Cover!

We dove together beneath the now-abandoned bleachers just as lightning cracked down all around us, a half-dozen bolts lighting the world up a blinding blue-white.

When my vision came back, the bleachers all around us were burning. Smoke began to roil off the flames, obscuring everything.

Out of the haze, I heard Laynine's voice.

"You put up a good fight, cousin. Worthy of a saga song. No one can say you dishonored your royal name. But don't you think it's time to end this now? Before the lightning causes any more damage?"

Peering through the stands, I caught sight of her coming toward us through the haze, a black shadow in the miasma.

Instead of answering, I drew my knife and crept to my right, along the bleachers.

"Stop playing games," she called.

She turned a circle, looking for me in the drifting smoke, then shouted into my mind. *Come out and fight!*

Tell me, I shot back. *What were you doing in the prelate's keep?*

What? Her response dripped with annoyance. But my dragon intuition detected something else, too. Defensiveness.

Perhaps I will submit to you, I said. *But not without knowing you're loyal to the crown and the Skrathan.*

Do you think dealing with the prelate is treachery? she mocked. *Don't be a fool, cousin. Kortoi controls trade. He controls the Lacunae. His strength is the only thing keeping the Admites at bay and keeping the nobles from open rebellion. Without Kortoi, there is no crown.*

So, she *was* working with Kortoi...

And what of the crates beneath the city, cousin?

I felt her hesitation—her guilt. *What crates?*

But she was only pretending not to know. I could feel it with as much certainty as I could feel the flagstones beneath my feet. Something terrible was in those crates. Kortoi had brought them here. And whatever was happening, Laynine was in on it... There was no way I could let her get the crown.

She stalked nearer. And behind her, Tryce loomed, massive and menacing.

I could still spare you, cousin, Laynine said, her tone more civil. *You could be my right hand. The way my mother has been to your mother. You could live...*

Don't trust her, Othura warned.

There came a creaking sound to my left, where Othura was hiding. I saw the first flaming brace fall, then watched, as if in slow motion, as all the bleachers there buckled and fell, revealing Othura.

Before I could move, before I could speak, Tryce opened his terrible mouth. Lightning flowed into it from the clouds around him and cracked forth—a dozen bolts at once—all hitting Othura.

No!

I didn't know whether I screamed aloud or in my mind as I surged toward her, leaping and clambering over burning wreckage. Embers filled the air, drifting like unmoored stars amid the smoke and soot. The crowd's cheers had dwindled to nothing, and a dense silence hung about us, thicker than the smoke. As I picked my way forward, I stepped around a chunk of flaming wreckage and caught sight of Othura again. She lay sprawled out on the ground, her hide steaming, her mouth slack, and her orange eyes shut. My heart constricted in my chest. Tryce loomed over her, mouth open, gathering lightning for a final blast. And closer, her back to me, Laynine stood, her drawn sword in her hand, watching. She didn't see me yet.

As silently as I could, I ran toward her, knife in hand.

But her dragon senses alerted her. At the last second, she turned, swiping my knife away with a slash of her sword. My momentum carried me into her, and our bodies crashed together. Her free hand grabbed my wrist, but her sword arm was pinned across her body between us. We stumbled together toward a jagged, burning piece of timber from the bleachers. I saw the white of Laynine's teeth as she snarled, trying to guide me into it. My legs wavered under me, exhausted from clamping onto Othura. But at the last second, I managed to hook my bad arm around Laynine's body. As we both fell, I turned her—and the chunk of timber plunged into her gut with a sickening thud.

I fell to the ground, my breath coming in ragged bursts.

A sudden blast of cold wind fluttered my cloak. It raked over everything, trembling the flames, stirring the ashes, blowing away the smoke, and revealing the crowd. When they saw Laynine, they gave a collective gasp.

I looked at her, too. My cousin. My rival. A person who had been in my life since before I could remember. We'd never been close, but she'd always been there, a presence as constant as the sky, as inevitable as winter.

Her eyes rolled, glassy and wide with terror, searching then settling on my face. Her mouth glistened with blood as it worked, trying to speak.

"I'm sorry," I blurted, crawling to her.

With effort, she forced her eyes to focus. Gods, they seemed to look right through me.

"No. I'm sorry," she panted. She took my hand and squeezed. "Beware. Beware the—"

Then breath seemed to rush out of her. She shuddered once, then again, then her head hung limp. Her fingers slipped out of my grasp. I knelt there, staring at her, my eyes and mouth both wide.

Then the earth shook with booming footsteps, and a shadow fell over me. Tryce was there, his snarling mouth crackling with lightning, a low growl rumbling from his heaving chest. His glare flicked from Laynine to me. Then, the pupils in his orange eyes constricted as the connection between him and his rider was severed. He reeled once, stumbled, then fell, his massive head booming into the cobblestones before me.

The wind gusted again, a cold, stiff breeze that caused the fires all around to flicker and dim. I felt the dragon stone hot against my chest and realized I was the one causing the wind. So, I made it blow harder, the breeze swelling into a gale that snuffed out the fires and made the whole palace shiver.

Then there came a new sound. Clapping. Whistling. Shouts.

I looked over like a person waking from a dream and saw the crowd—the entire city—was cheering for me.

The challenge was over. I had won.

47
CHARLIE

"Yes!" I shouted, spinning away from the window to rampage through the room in elation—and knocking a chair over in the process. My celebration didn't stop until I saw the guards in the doorway, watching me with frowns and drawn swords.

"There's a new Irska in town, my friends!" I shouted. They merely looked at me impassively. "One day, the three of us will sip whiskey together and laugh about this!" I called as they left, slamming the door behind them.

In the silence, more sober thoughts returned to me. Essa had lived, and I felt like a pile of bricks had been lifted off my heart. But I was still sentenced to death. And Othura...

I ran back to the window, pressing my face against the glass. I had to look down at an infuriatingly difficult angle to see what was happening, and I wished with all my being that I were down there, that I could sweep Essa into a hug. Far below, I watched as she approached Othura and knelt before her, pressing her face to the dragon's and wrapping her arms around her.

I'd pulled away from Parthar during the challenge, not wanting my heightened emotions to worry him, but I reached out again now. I could feel Othura's pain through him, somehow. The emotion that came through wasn't translatable into words; it was more like the low wail of a baby.

"She'll be okay," I soothed Parthar. Then I realized perhaps he might know Othura's status better than I. "... won't she?"

The little dragon's only response was a sorrowful sigh.

And so, I tried again to reach out to Essa through the dragons. She hadn't been open to communication during the challenge, and I hadn't pressed her. I might not be able to reach her now, either, especially if Othura was gone. But I reached out anyway.

Essa?

For a moment, there was nothing, no response, and the elation I'd felt moments before began to ebb.

Then I felt her. Like so many of my exchanges with Parthar, no words passed between us. But I felt the glow of her pride from her victory. I felt her bone-melting weariness. I felt her concern for Othura and her deep relief at discovering Othura was still breathing. Most of all, I felt her love, warm and bright as a summer sunrise, its scope so vast and so strong that it enveloped Othura and me and pulled us both in close. In every relationship I'd had before, even with my parents, there had been a sense of stoic reservation, of holding back. But when connecting through dragons, none of those layers of hesitation were there. I felt what she felt. Never had I felt so close to another being, so complete, so loved.

Through Essa I felt—rather than saw—Othura stir and

raise her head. She was injured and groggy, but with each second her wits and wellbeing returned, and she sat up to great cheers from the watching crowd. Parthar gave an enthusiastic coo.

I realized I'd fallen to my knees, and I reached up to find tears on my cheeks.

I rose and pressed my forehead to the window once more, looking down. Othura stood. She followed a step behind Essa, who went and knelt before her mother the queen.

Now she will become Irska. And someday, queen. And I will still die, I thought. *But at least I've lived long enough to see this.*

48
ESSA

I knelt before Mother.

Her face betrayed no emotion as she drew a beautiful longsword from its sheath. It was Lohath, the sword of the Irska—an ancient star steel blade which had been found with Paemalla's body—even more powerful than the royal sword I already carried. For a moment, she paused, her eyes moving up and down the length of the blade. Then she spoke in a loud, clear voice.

"Since the days of Aulucia the White, the royals of this house have served as lead dragon riders," she said. "Many times, there have been those who doubted that Torholt blood would be able to rise to the challenge and maintain the crown."

She glanced at Lord Natath.

"And many times, those doubters have been silenced. We will not forget Laynine. We loved her as a daughter. And yet, the providence of the Gods may not be denied. Let any who would challenge the right of this crown to rule—whether they be across the sea or closer to home—

take warning: all who challenge us will share Laynine's fate."

Her attention returned to me. Her words about Laynine —*we loved her as a daughter*—still rang in my ears. They stung, but it did not diminish the sense of pride I felt as Mother lowered the sword, touching its tip to my shoulder.

"Essaphine Torholt. You, who went from the hundredth flyer to the first, we applaud your feat. Just as you defeated Laynine to take power over the Skrathan, so you will destroy our necromancer enemies across the sea. It is therefore with pride that I name you Irska, first of the Maethalian dragon riders."

Mother touched the tip of the sword to my other shoulder, then to the top of my head, then she turned it around to offer me the hilt.

The wave of applause was bracing, but not nearly as loud as it had been while the battle was going on. The sight of Laynine's blood had turned the mood somber, and even the fiery sense of triumph I'd felt a moment before had cooled and hardened like a blade on an anvil.

Mother's words had me thinking of the future. I'd won the challenge. Now, I'd have to lead our flyers in battle with the URA aces and their death machines, a task even more daunting. And I'd have the lives of all the other Skrathan in my hands.

Perhaps I shouldn't take the sword. Perhaps I should just stand and walk away... But I had reasons to become Irska that went beyond duty and honor. The vision... those crates... Mother hadn't listened to her daughter, hadn't taken the danger seriously enough. But she'd have to listen to the leader of her dragon riders.

I reached out and took the sword.

Horns blew from the battlements, the signal that the challenge was over and the next phase of the event was set to begin—the feast. Commoners would return to their homes and share a festive meal. The nobility would move to the palace's great hall and enjoy a vast spread of food and drink to toast the new Irska. They'd already begun filing into the palace.

Mother also began to turn, nodding to her guards to lead the way inside, but I stopped her.

"Wait."

She turned back, wariness and annoyance on her regal face.

"My wish," I said.

It was customary for anyone accomplishing a great victory or receiving an honor from the queen to make a wish. Normally, it was for something like a chest of gold, permission to marry a sweetheart, or a title of nobility. And normally, the queen invited the wish, saying something like, *ask anything of me, and it shall be granted.*

I didn't doubt that her omission, in my case, had been deliberate.

Her smile was forced. "Name your wish, Irska."

The line of nobles that had been moving toward the palace paused, many of them turning to listen. Noticing them, Mother's smile slipped. She knew exactly what was coming next.

"Spare the life of the foreigner Kit Rowley," I said.

Her eyes flashed with displeasure.

"Essa..."

"That is my wish," I said. "Let me take him back to his homeland. You will not see him again. He will be separated from his bonded dragon, which is punishment enough. Just let him live."

"That I cannot do."

"Cannot or will not?" I demanded.

Mother's lips tightened. If I were a little girl, I'd have braced myself for a slap.

"We shall discuss this further in private," she said quietly. "Any reasonable request you have, ask it. But the life of Kit Rowley you shall not have. Tomorrow at dawn, he dies. Be grateful you still live."

She turned with a flourish of her royal skirts and made her way toward the palace, leaving no option but to follow.

On the way inside, Ollie pulled me into a tight hug.

"You did it, Essa," he whispered.

He tried to let me go, but I continued to hold onto him, bringing my mouth close to his ear. "Bring Lure, Pocha, Clua, and Dagar to my chamber after the feast. Armed and wearing dark clothing. Is Rohree back?"

"Not yet. But Essa..." He pulled back and locked eyes with me. "Your dream has just come true. Don't throw it away."

"My dreams are only beginning, Ollie," I said. "Come."

Rather than following the others into the castle, I turned from the flow of the crowd and went to Othura, who stood to one side, receiving accolades from those who had watched us today.

"Never have I seen such a small dragon fight so well," one was saying.

"Truly a noble beast," another agreed.

They all bowed and scattered as Ollie and I approached.

Othura. You okay? I asked, putting a hand on her snout.

I'll be fine. It's not the first time I've been scrambled by light-

ning, she reminded me. *They'll have a brace of roasted goats waiting for me at the Hatchery. I'll eat and have a good nap. That will set me right.*

Good. Will you be able to—?

But she was my dragon. I didn't even have to finish the question.

I'll be ready to fly tonight, she said.

At the feast, I suffered through endless speeches commemorating my battle prowess, toasts to my name, and even an impromptu song about me by one of the kingdom's foremost bards, the famous Lucian Burke—though most of the nobles, knights, and Skrathan around me seemed more focused on the fine food and drink spread before them than on me. I couldn't help but wonder what the response would have been if Laynine had won instead of me. Would the celebration have been more enthusiastic? Or less? No one would have been surprised if Laynine had slain the defective princess. And yet there were many whose faces looked sullen now who would have been happy to embrace Laynine as their leader.

I picked at my food, hardly able to eat, and drank big gulps of water while leaving my mead and wine untouched. Mother sat to my right in her throne, and I could feel her watching me. Beyond her, Prelate Kortoi and Hoatan sat, watching me less obviously but just as intently.

Would this be my last time sitting at this table, after

what I was about to do? Was Ollie right? Was I foolish to risk everything for Kit?

Probably. But there was no way I could let him die.

The feast went on with excruciating slowness. One by one, nobles came up before my table to express their congratulations. Skrathan paraded before me as well, saluting me as their new leader. Most were stone-faced. A few openly sneering. Only Lure, Pocha, and Dagar seemed truly pleased.

By the end, I felt ready to collapse on the table, though I wasn't sure whether it was the challenge or the party that exhausted me more. I forced myself to eat a few sweet cakes and drink a cup of tea, fortifying myself for the night ahead.

Lord Natath and Kortoi were among the last to come and pay their respects, and they came up together.

"An impressive victory, Princess," Natath said with a bow. "The nobility looks forward to working with you as the Irska of the Skrathan. And I, personally, look forward to honoring you as heir to the crown."

His lecherous grin made my skin crawl.

He stepped aside as Kortoi gave me a bow.

"Congratulations, Princess Essaphine," he said. "We are truly at the beginning of a new era. In my scrying, I have seen it. Many changes are coming to our capital—and the world. I hope the new epoch will find us aligned so we may work together to eliminate the enemies of our beloved kingdom."

I gave him a nod. "We are both survivors, Prelate Kortoi. I have no doubt whatever events your scrying has foretold, we will both meet it with ferocity, and the Brothers and the Skrathan will receive the glory and power they each deserve."

Kortoi flashed a crooked smile. "Spoken like a true diplo-
mat," he said. "One word of warning. Keep an eye on the
weather, Princess. There is a storm coming."

I had no doubt there was some deeper significance to his
smug pronouncement, but I couldn't tell what it was. Why
all mystics had such a tiresome penchant for speaking in
riddles was a question I didn't have time to consider.

"I'll keep a cloak handy," I said, trying to sound as
dismissive as possible, though his warning chilled me. The
two men bowed and moved along.

And so it went with toasts and compliments, congratulations and honors, gifts and oaths, until the final pour of
dessert wine was served and noble ladies were yawning and
being escorted from the room, ceding the space to the more
serious drinkers, who would not cease emptying the queen's
wine until someone took their cups away.

Only then did Mother see fit to release me from my duty.
"Essa, you must be tired," she said. "You have been kind to
share your glory with us. Go, if you wish. Wash up and sleep.
You will need what rest you can get, for your duties as Irska
begin tomorrow."

I rose, bowed, and let Ollie escort me from the room.

"Well, that was excruciating," I said.

"What?" Ollie asked. "Slaughtering your cousin, or
enduring all that praise?"

"Hard to say which was worse," I said. His words
brought forth a grotesque vision of Laynine, all that dark
blood, the way her body had spasmed... I couldn't believe
that she was gone, and that I had killed her. Nausea twisted
my gut, threatening to bring up what little food I'd eaten.

We were in the garden courtyard now, passing the Oerl
Stream. At its head, the waterfall called the Tears of Cheselie

rumbled in the darkness. Impulsively, I kicked off my boots and jogged off the cobblestone path, through the long grass, and into the water with a splash.

"What, are you drunk?" Ollie called after me, no hint of amusement in his voice.

I dashed my head under and let the frigid water wash over me for a count of ten. Then I burst back out, whipping my hair back and wiping the water out of my eyes with my hand. I strode back to shore feeling awake and invigorated again.

"Not drunk," I said, clapping a hand on Ollie's shoulder. "Just filthy and exhausted with no time for a bath or sleep tonight. Here, carry my boots. You gathered the others?"

His expression darkened, but he nodded as he followed me across the courtyard.

In my chambers, we found Lure and Pocha engaged in a game of Torzame. Dagar was eating a whole berry pie that looked to have been pilfered from the feast, and Clua was on the rug, doing pushups. I couldn't imagine a more appropriate milieu in which to find my friends, and the sight brought a smile to my lips. But sorrow came close upon its heels at the thought that I would soon leave them—and I might never be welcomed back.

"Let me guess," Lure said without looking up from the game board. "You've fallen in love with the foreigner, and you want our help rescuing him before they execute him tomorrow."

I put my hands on my hips. "No, actually. Rescuing a prisoner of the crown is a capital offense. I would never ask you to do that... I'm doing that myself."

Clua looked up at me with one eyebrow cocked. "What do you need from us, then?"

"I need you all to rescue his dragon."

By the time I'd laid out my plan, it was nearly midnight, and exhaustion was nipping at me like a hound. We all agreed to get a few hours' sleep, Pocha, Lure, and I jammed into my bed, Ollie on the lounge, and Dagar with his big frame stretched out on the floor.

The next thing I knew, my friends were bustling around me, strapping on weapons.

Pocha touched my shoulder gently. "I made them let you sleep a little longer. You needed it. But if we want to beat the dawn, we'd better go."

I threw off my blanket and rose, instantly awake and sharp at the knowledge of what lay ahead.

Clua tossed me a sweet roll from a basket she'd brought, and I caught it and took a bite. My hunger had caught up with me, and I wished I could take another crack at the feast that had been before me a few hours earlier, but there was little time to eat now. The few rations Clua had brought might have to last for days.

"Everyone know their roles?" I asked through a mouthful of bread.

There were nods all around.

I was grateful for these friends, for this crew of warriors —but it wasn't lost on me that my first act as Irska was to order them to commit treason. Not an auspicious start...

"So, after we get the dragon, we'll meet up with you and Kit?" Pocha asked.

I shook my head. "No. I have no idea how soon they're planning to execute Kit. First priority has to be getting him out of Maethalia. We'll worry about reuniting him with his dragon later."

When everyone seemed to be in agreement, I gave a nod. "Alright then. Let's go."

No one spoke as they filed grimly out, leaving only me and Ollie behind. When they were gone, he shut the door, locked it, and turned to me.

I crossed my arms. "Let me guess," I said. "You're going to tell me not to do it."

Ollie was ever the deep thinker, but the look in his eyes was a more complex one than I'd ever seen from him in a long time. There was sadness there. Regret, maybe. Anger. And some other zealous light I hardly recognized, almost like the spark of madness that had inhabited Braimar since his dragon's head died.

"I'm not going to tell you not to do it," he said. "I can already tell your mind is made up. I'm going to tell you not to come back."

I laughed, shocked. "What?"

But I could tell from his face that he was deadly serious.

"Why?" I demanded.

"I can't tell you. Don't ask. But if you trust me, Essa, if you believe I care about you, then I beg you to listen. Stay away for three days."

"Why?" I asked, my eyes narrowing. "Are the Torouman finally dealing with Kortoi?"

He put his hands on my shoulders. "In a manner of speaking."

"Don't be vague with me. If there's violence, I should be

here. Kortoi's Lacunae are powerful. You'll need the Skrathan. And the Irska must lead them."

Ollie shook his head. "No. It will be worse if you're here, believe me. Go. Drop your Kit off in his homeland. Then return to Maethalia and find someplace on the coast to hide out for a couple of days. A cave, an abandoned farm, anything. Rest. Keep out of sight. When you return, all will be well."

"But what are you—?"

"The less you know, the better, Essa."

My eyes locked on his for a long moment as I tried to plumb the depths of his thoughts. Hoatan and his Torouman were always cooking up some sort of political maneuver. Like all great Torzame players, they were ruthless and always looking two steps ahead. I didn't like following plans I didn't understand. And yet, for hundreds of years, the crown had survived by following the wise counsel of the Torouman. I would be foolish to defy them now.

"Fine. But have Lure and the others reach out through Othura to keep me updated. And keep them all safe. Promise?"

He nodded. I took his hands and squeezed. They were unusually clammy. He was more nervous than he was letting on...

He pulled me into a hug, then, so tight it almost hurt. I felt him trembling.

"Ollie, you're scaring me," I said.

"Don't be scared, Essa," he whispered, his lips pressed to the top of my head. "All will be well. Just remember, everything I do is for you."

49
CHARLIE

I knew. From the moment I glimpsed a silvery gray dragon winging through the night toward the tower, I knew. Perhaps that's why I had been standing in the window in the first place, staring out at the darkness, waiting. I knew Essa would come. I even had time to throw on my cloak and pull on my boots.

The window shattered, sending a sparkling of glass across the moonlit floor. Then Othura's tail whipped across the window's muntin bars, dashing them aside.

I leapt into the window frame and froze.

There was Essa, her hair windblown and wild, her eyes filled with starshine.

"Hi, poet," she said. "Come fly with me."

Despite everything, a smile lit my face.

The door behind me banged open. Guards were there—but not the normal royal guards. It was the Brotherhood's dreaded Lacunae—five of them. They gave a shout of alarm and charged, swords drawn, but I was already leaping, landing on Othura's back, wrapping my arms around Essa's waist, and holding on as Othura winged us off into the night.

"You lived," I whispered into Essa's ear. My lips traced down her neck, a trail of kisses.

"Stop." She shrugged me off. "You have a lot of explaining to do. But not now. I have to concentrate on getting us out of here."

"Wait. What about Parthar?"

"Who? Oh, your dragon. My friends are working on freeing him. I'll meet up with them later, and we'll get the two of you back together. First step is getting you out of Maethalia with your head still on your shoulders."

Knowing that Parthar would no longer be in the hands of those disturbing Gray Brothers, I felt a pressure release in my chest. Parthar would be okay... but our danger was far from over.

I looked back. No dragons were flying after us—yet.

"Can they catch up to us? When they realize I'm gone?"

Othura huffed beneath us. *I'm a libran. Not likely.*

I still wasn't used to hearing Parthar in my mind, much less another dragon, but I took comfort in her words. At that moment, the wind jostled us, shifting into a strong tailwind. Othura opened her wings and pumped them hard, propelling us forward like an arrow. Essa leaned down, laying her chest down against Othura's back, and I leaned with her, though my mind was less on escape and more on her body as it pressed back against me in the saddle. I pulled her tighter and she gave a teasing squirm, wresting a groan of longing from me. She flashed me a dark smile, then looked ahead once more, and we flew even faster toward the darkness as, behind us, the light of dawn began to seep into the horizon.

I lay my head against Essa's back and closed my eyes. For a fleeting moment, I felt completely content, grateful, and at peace—even as thunder rumbled in the distance.

We feared dragons pursuing us. But as the wind picked up and the first raindrops began pelting down, it soon became clear that the greatest danger lay not behind us, but ahead. Fast-moving thunderheads swept in, dousing the stars and blackening the moon. The angry clouds flashed from within, unleashing booms so powerful they stuttered my heart. Shards of forked lightning cut like jagged, glowing veins across the night. For a while, we climbed, Othura trying to gain enough altitude to get us above the storm, but I doubted we'd get there. A storm of this magnitude probably topped out over 40,000 feet, far higher than dragons or airplanes could venture—especially a small, injured dragon like Othura. Sure enough, we soon stopped climbing. Othura glided, panting with exertion, her spread wings buffeted by the storm.

Kortoi warned me of a storm... Essa said, the words in my mind meant for me and for Othura. When she glanced back at me, I saw something in her eyes I'd rarely seen: fear. Then she was conferring with Othura but allowing me in on the conversation.

How far to Dorhane?

We're close. A few more leagues, maybe, the dragon replied.

I frowned. We'd never make it that far in a storm like this.

Can you control the wind? I asked. *Make it calm down?*

Othura grunted in annoyance at my question.

We can direct a gust, but not a storm like this, Essa said. *It's too big.*

Then we need to get to five thousand feet, I said. *Descend.*

Essa turned and gave me a sharp look.

Are you telling me how to fly my dragon?

I'm telling you how to save us. Five thousand feet is the best altitude for penetrating thunderstorms, Princess. Trust me.

She might have argued. But the wind hit us again, blasting us in the face so hard our forward progress nearly stopped, leaving Othura wobbling. Then a second draft came, along with a change of air pressure, and we dropped so fast that even I felt a nervous flutter in my belly.

Without further argument, Othura angled us into a descent. We squinted ahead, rain spattering our faces, wind blasting and buffeting us, and for a while it seemed as if the storm was only worsening.

Then suddenly, we broke through. The winds that had assaulted us diminished, and our wobbling flight path steadied, though rain still stung us and thunder still rumbled ominously above.

You're a very knowledgeable poet, Essa said. Speaking mind-to-mind as we were, I could feel the wonder, the relief, and also suspicion in her thought.

I would have to tell her the truth as soon as we landed. And before...

Before we parted.

It hit me with the force of a bullet: I didn't want to be parted from Essa. I *couldn't* be parted from her. Somehow, I had to—

There!

It was Othura's voice in my mind. Below us, through the gauzy gray clouds, I could just make out a shape against the vast expanse of dark water. A horn-shaped land mass.

Rograd Point, Essa said with relief.

Here it was, the epicenter of the battle between our two nations, a piece of land that held both the world's last viable dragon hatchery and vast stores of valuable petroleum. The Isle of Dorhane. Off to our left, where the point widened out to the larger landmass, light flashed through the fog. Mortar explosions. Muzzle flares. Flashes of fire magic. I knew what lay there. Miles of trenches and scorched fields, the blood and misery of war. The Front. Dorhane had once been a paradise, it was said, but decades of war had left it a scarred hellscape, a place few sane people had the courage to visit willingly—and yet tonight it was our only refuge. And so, we veered toward it, descending through the storm.

We dropped out of the maelstrom and into the only shelter we could find—an old underground dragon's den.

It was perhaps a twelve-foot drop from the opening down into the cave itself, and we rode Othura in. Once inside, the opening turned and extended for another twenty-five feet or so, giving the cavernous space the shape of a sock.

There was some dry grass and pine boughs scattered about—dragon nesting materials—which we gathered together. In moments, I had a fire going. In its tremulous light, Kit walked, tracing his fingers over the smooth, glassy walls, a look of wonder on his face.

"It's a dragon den," I explained. "They dig them out, then melt the earth with fire, making dragon glass. This is a small den. It probably belonged to a libran like Othura who had one of their fire-breathing friends finish the walls."

"Where are the dragons now?" Kit asked with a wary glance toward the entrance.

"Gone," I said. "Some serve with the Skrathan. The wild ones hunt in the Yrdam Mountains and beyond. They come here to roost four times a year because the conditions are right for the eggs to develop. The rest of the time, the dragons are gone. Migrating. Hunting..."

"Wild dragons," Kit said in wonder.

We both took in the den's walls, which glinted in the shifting firelight.

"It's beautiful," he said, but his eyes were back on me when he said it. Despite everything, I felt a blush rise to my cheeks.

He ran a hand through his wet hair. "Essa, you did it."

I gave a faint laugh. "What? Rescued a prisoner of the crown?"

"You won the challenge. You lived."

My eyes drifted to the fire, its flames shifting and twisting. "Yes..." I said. Though living would do me little good. After this, I'd be branded a traitor. Mother might well strip me of the title I'd just earned, or exile me, or worse. Freeing a prisoner sentenced to death would be a capital offense. But there was no point in making Kit feel guilty.

"And you've won as well," I told him.

"My duel with Braimar? I'm afraid that was more of a draw."

I shook my head. "No. I mean, you ventured into the land of the enemy. Soon, you'll be home safe. And I'm sure you've gotten more than enough material to write a whole series of articles—maybe even a book."

He winced at my words. "Essa... I hope you know this is about far more than any article to me."

He squirmed under my glare, then sighed.

"I know... I have a lot to explain. First of all, I'm sorry for keeping the dragon egg a secret. I was just—"

I raised a hand, silencing him.

"You know what? Let's not talk of the world. Or tomorrow. Tonight, it's us. This cave. This fire. Let's pretend the world doesn't exist."

For a long moment, his eyes searched mine. Then he reached out a hand, his fingers gently wiping the raindrops from my cheek. "You're shivering," he said.

"It's these wet clothes..." I said, the words coming out a whisper.

His fingers traced down my neck to the clasp that held my cloak in place. He unclipped it and let it fall, then he pulled slowly at the knot that laced up my flight armor, pulling the string. It came free, and his hands were at the collar, pulling it down my shoulders. His eyes met mine, a question in them, and I nodded, shivering now from more than just the cold.

He glanced at Othura, but she was already asleep, giving off slow, quietly rumbling dragon snores.

Kit's jaw clenched, his eyes lit now with a fire like the one I'd seen during his battle with Braimar. A look of power and hunger.

He pulled again, and the flight armor slipped from my shoulders. Revealing the sheer, wet undershirt beneath. His hand trailed from my collarbone downward, tracing down my chest, brushing my achingly hard nipple, and making my back arch. He found the bottom of the shirt and lifted, pulling it off over my head. He paused then, his eyes roving hungrily over my bare breasts, then back to my face.

"God Essa. All this time, do you know how hard it's been to look at you?"

I was painfully aware of my missing arm. My hand went to the place where it had been severed, that smooth scar tissue.

But his eyes were on my lips. "You're so beautiful it hurts."

Gently, he took the hand that was covering up my injury in his and brought it to his lips. Then his other hand slipped down my shoulder to take my maimed arm and bring it to his face, too. He kissed it.

"You're perfect, Essa."

Tears blurred my vision.

"I'm not perfect," I said with a bitter laugh.

His arms were around me then, forceful. Strong. "Never say that again."

This was not a poet's ferocity. It was a warrior's. And I felt something stir deep within me. An ache in my belly, a throb between my legs.

"You think I'd let an Admite tell me what to do?" I said with teasing defiance.

"I think you'll let me conquer you," he said, his voice deep with longing.

I brought my face to his, nose to nose, forehead to forehead. "I beg you to try."

His hands were on my waist then, swinging me to the cave floor. His lips slipped over mine, soft but hungry, his teeth bit my lip just hard enough to make my toes curl, then our tongues met—how I wanted to taste him—all of him. His hands went to my wrist and my forearm, pinning me to the ground, his lips kissing beneath my jaw, down my neck, across my collarbone, and down my breast. His lips found my nipple and slipped across it—far too gently.

I moaned in longing and frustration. I wanted him—more of him—all of him. I couldn't wait another second.

"Take off your—"

"No," he said.

"No?" I countered, but my protest disappeared as his lips made an orbit of my areola, making my mouth gape in a silent shout of desire.

"No," he said. "We waited this long. We're going to make this last."

Then he took my nipple in his mouth and sucked, his tongue rubbing across as he did. I wrapped my legs around him, grinding my hips against him, the feeling between my legs turning from an ache to a fire.

I couldn't wait a second more. My hand went to my waist, pulling down my flight pants, and I wriggled out of them. Kit pulled his shirt up over his head, unbuckled his belt. Then he was yanking my boots off, pulling my pants from my feet. He brought one ankle to his lips and kissed it.

"Kit..." I said, a pleading, a warning. He kissed up my calf, my ankle on his shoulder, and ran his tongue slowly, slowly up the inside of my thigh.

"Now," I panted. "I just want you..."

But he kept kissing upward, his tongue tracing my skin with painful gentleness until it found the center of my desire. He kept it there, moving so, so slowly, I wanted to scream. I felt a burning rise in me, my muscles clenching, body throbbing, my nipples so hard they ached. Then his tongue was moving down, teasing over my slit. I could feel how wet I was. Dripping.

"God, Essa, the taste of you..."

His tongue went up again, moving faster now, with purpose. I put my hand on the back of his head and pushed him against me, my hips grinding and writhing, my teeth bared with feral need.

Then my whole body was clenching, waves of pleasure washing over me.

"Now, now!" I pleaded.

"Maybe," he said, teasing, smiling up at me with wet lips.

"Now!" I commanded. I was ripe, dripping, my whole body beating in time with my heart. I wanted him. Needed him.

No matter how wrong. How forbidden.

I grabbed his arm and hauled him upward, wrapped my legs around his waist.

His face was next to mine, his lips brushing my ear, his muscular body looming over me, dominating and powerful.

"You sure, Essa?" he whispered.

My hand found his ass and drew him to me. Into me.

I was already clenched, already peaking, but he pushed into me with a snarl of pleasure. I cried out, pulling him deeper into me, deeper, deeper, until I felt so full of him I would burst. We moved together, each thrust more forceful than the last, an animal dance that left me wild, feral with longing.

Time seemed to fold in on itself, to lose its meaning. There was only us, only ecstasy and the scent of smoke and the light of flames trembling on the cave walls and the waves of pleasure washing over me again and again like nothing I'd ever felt before.

Finally, I felt him explode inside me. We both cried out together as I peaked again, thumping shivers of aching euphoria washing over me.

When it was over, I felt completely limp and satisfied, like I'd been washed ashore on some warm beach.

My eyes opened. I found Kit staring down at me, looking so brutally handsome it hurt to look at him.

"God help me, Essa," he whispered. "I love you,"

I opened my mouth to respond. There was only one true answer I could give. My body sang with it. My heart ached with it. My soul had melted with it—so that I felt like my entire being was now a warm liquid he held in his cupped hands.

But somehow, my lips wouldn't say it. The feeling was complete, but my fear was still too much. And so, I didn't speak. Instead, I pulled him to me, his bare body warm against mine. I closed my eyes and tried to feel the beating of his heart through his skin, and I fell asleep smiling.

51
CHARLIE

We awoke tangled together, the scent of Essa's hair and skin filling me with peace, her taste still on my tongue. Behind us, Othura slumbered, her rumbling snores filling the den. A chill hung in the air, but with my body pressed to Essa's, I felt perfectly warm and more content than I ever remembered feeling. I could have stayed forever in that moment. I could have died and been a happy angel.

But a boom shook the ground, startling me fully awake. Then another came—far off but closer than the last—and Essa stirred and rose to one elbow.

"Good morning," I said, reaching to brush her hair from her face, but she raised a hand, shushing me.

"I smell smoke."

She was on her feet in a second, pulling on her flight armor, and I followed suit, dressing as quickly as possible. A few jagged stones protruded from the glassy, slick wall of the cave entrance, and we climbed up them and peered over the edge. I heard the buzz of airplane engines—Sackman

Bison, if I wasn't mistaken. They were similar to the Comets I flew, but heavier-duty. Bombers. Smoke rose in the distance. And nearer, three figures were moving toward us. Essa grabbed my arm and pulled me down before we were spotted.

When we peered out again, more cautiously, I saw the figures I had at first taken for people were not, in fact, human.

One was a sort of wingless dragon which had a wagon hitched to it. The other two were humanoid, with the arms and legs of a man and wearing the armor of a warrior. But their heads were not human. One appeared to have the head of an eagle, the other of a bear. But they didn't have fur or feathers—and the dragon didn't have scales, either. Their skin was gray and cakey. And their eyes—their eyes were black but glowed red around the edges, like burning coals. Something about those eyes and the twitchy way they moved sent a shiver through me.

Golenae, Essa whispered in my mind.

What's that?

Abominations. Dead bones with flesh of clay, animated with demonic souls from beyond the void.

The void... Who created them? The Gray Brothers?

Essa shook her head. *They would never. It's forbidden.*

But just then, two Lacunae in their black armor clambered out of a dragon den, each bearing a large basket. As we watched, they began loading dragon eggs from the basket into the wagon.

They're harvesting dragon eggs? I asked. *What would Lacunae want with dragon eggs?*

She shook her head, at a loss. *I don't know. But I intend to find out.*

But before we could clamber out of the cave, the sound of the plane engines grew louder. Other sounds, too. Shouts, the snap of gunfire, and a rumbling of the earth that could only mean one thing.

"Tanks," I said. "The URA army is coming."

The golenae heard it too, because they turned in the direction of the sound just as a squadron of seven Bison bombers broke the horizon. At the same moment, a line of tanks and soldiers burst from the scrub approximately a hundred yards away. The Lacunae drew their swords and raised their shields as bullets pinged off them. I saw each golena take what must have been dozens of shots without so much as flinching—but in the next instant, the bombers were over us. The first bomb fell near the golenae. The concussion bowled them off their feet, then sent a subsequent wave of flame washing over them, its heat so potent that even fifty yards away, I felt as if it would singe my hair off.

"Fire bombs!" I shouted. "Down!"

I grabbed Essa's arm, but she tried to yank herself free. "The dragon eggs!"

"No. There's no time." I pulled her arm harder, and we slid together down the slick glass side of the den—just as a sea of fire flowed over us. At the bottom, Othura was there, awake now, throwing her wing open to shield us. We huddled together, all three of us, eyes closed and bodies balled up. The heat flashed over us so intensely that for an instant, it felt like we were in an oven. Essa screamed, and I clutched onto her, as if there were anything I could do to protect her.

I realized I was shouting, "Stop, stop!" as if my comrades could hear me. As if there were anything at all I could do.

Then in the next instant, the heat was ebbing. I was trembling. Dripping with sweat. Essa and I looked at one another, and I knew the wild panic in her eyes must be mirrored in mine.

We have to get out of here, I said, but she was already clambering onto Othura's back. I jumped on behind her.

I saw with alarm that Othura's wing was still smoking. Dragon hide was generally fire-proof, but I still felt alarm as Othura galloped to the cave entrance and leapt, flapping us upward.

The first thing I saw as we emerged from the hole was the charred remnants of the golenae, the Lacunae, and their wagon. The dragon eggs inside it were scorched black. Soldiers jogged across the smoldering waste toward us. Then I spied the tank, its barrel trained on us, gaping like the mouth of a monster. It boomed, and I felt my whole body flinch.

We're dead.

But we were not dead. We were falling.

Something like a black spiderweb spread over my vision, and Othura dropped heavily back to earth, her wings tangled. We landed with a teeth-clapping bang, Essa and I both falling from Othura's back. I reached to brush something off my head and realized it was netting. The tank had hit us with a dragon net round, not an explosive one—thank God.

But two more tanks were rolling toward us, their treads vibrating the earth, and perhaps a hundred soldiers rushed forward alongside them, rifles leveled and bayonets glinting in the morning light.

Essa had her sword drawn and tore the netting aside with one slash. With a shake of Othura's head, we were free.

The dragon snarled and crouched, and Essa took a fighting stance. A hundred rifles pointed at her head.

"Whoa, whoa, whoa!" I shouted, stepping in front of her. "Stand down. Who's the ranking officer here?"

The door atop one of the tanks clanked open, and a mustached man emerged. He was perhaps forty, barrel-chested and red-cheeked, with salt-and-pepper hair. I recognized him from many briefings—and not a few nights spent carousing in Ironberg's show district. Colonel Billy Bloom.

"Charlie? Charlie Inman?" He gave a rumbling laugh. "Well, I'll be damned. Stand down, boys. He's one of us."

The soldiers eyed Othura uneasily, but they followed orders, lowering their guns.

"Kit, what's he talking about?" Essa whispered to me, her sword still at the ready.

Another head emerged from the next tank over. "What the hell's going on?" a short-haired female officer asked. I'd seen her around the base once or twice but didn't know her name.

"This here's Charlie Inman. One of our best aces. Why, I've even heard a rumor or two that he's the famed Silver Wraith," he gave a big, theatrical wink. "But information like that is highly classified, eh, Charlie? Way above my pay grade."

"So, what's he doing with a sorceress in the middle of enemy territory?" the female officer demanded.

"Spy mission," Bloom sniffed. "Brass told me to keep an eye out for him, and here we are. Ha! This guy. I tell ya, if a cat's got nine lives, old Charlie's got ten."

I looked at Essa to find her eyes burning into me. All color had drained from her face.

"Essa..." I whispered.

"So, what do we do with him?" the lady officer was asking.

"Escort him back to base. Those are the orders," Bloom said.

"And the dragon and rider?"

"I've got no orders on her. I'm guessing they're his contacts on the other side," he turned to me, though my attention was still on Essa. "Say, Charlie. What's the deal with the dame and her dragon? Friend or foe, eh?"

Then Essa spoke in my mind.

Is it true?

Essa...

Is it true?

The breath seemed to have drained from my lungs. *Yes, I am an ace. Yes, my name is really Charlie. I crash-landed in Maethalia and... I tried to tell you... Your people would have killed me if they knew.*

Bloom had dipped down into the tank. He emerged now, holding a sheaf of yellow papers—it looked like a carbon copy of briefing notes.

"Ah, here we go," he said, reading. "This is the girl you backed to become lead dragon rider, eh? The one-armed princess."

"I've heard nothing about this," the female officer said.

"He backed the weak one so the strong one would die," Bloom said. "Genius plan."

Essa hadn't taken her eyes off me. She lowered her sword now, the pain and vulnerability on her face terrible to see.

"Essa," I said quickly. "That's not... Listen to me." I touched her face, my hand trembling.

I could have wept. But she did not. As I watched, the hurt in her eyes changed, like water becoming ice.

"Essa…"

"He was found on the battlefield with an enemy combatant," the woman officer snapped. "Unless you can show me a written order to the contrary, we take them both in as prisoners."

Bloom banged a fist on the top of the tank and shook the papers. "How do you think we found the hatching fields today? Why do you think dragon kills are up fifteen percent? Because the aces now know where to shoot 'em. It's all this man's reports. He's a goddamned hero. I'm not taking him home in handcuffs!"

Is it true? Essa demanded once more, a horrible finality in her voice as it rang in my mind.

My thoughts reeled with all the lies I could tell, all the excuses I could make. But I cared about Essa too much to lie to her anymore.

It is true, Essa. But the truest thing of all is that I love you.

I touched her cheek with my hand, leaned close to her, tears rising to my eyes. She tilted her head back and put her arm around me, pulling my lips toward hers.

The next thing I knew, I was on my ass.

For a second, all I could see was blackness and swirling stars, but when I managed to squint up with one eye, I saw Essa leaping onto Othura's back. The dragon released a blast of wind that sent the soldiers around us scattering like chaff, then she was winging upward, her tail snapping like a whip as she sped off into the sky.

A few gunshots cracked skyward. The tank cannons turned to track the departing dragon, but they were all too slow.

I brought a hand to my face, and it came away slick with blood. My left eye was already swollen almost completely shut, my head throbbing.

Essa, my princess, my love, had headbutted the hell out of me. And now, she was gone.

5²
ESSA

I made it back to Charcain feeling frail as a leaf blown in on the wind.

I was alive. I was Irska. I was sole heir to the crown of Maethalia. Everything I'd dreamed of had been in my grasp—and I'd already thrown it away for the love of a man who had been deceiving me all along. The shame of it was so immense I'd considered pitching myself off Othura's back more than once as we crossed the narrow sea back to Maethalia. But I knew Othura would just pluck me out of the water again. And besides, I had to tell Mother about the golenae and the Lacunae stealing the dragon eggs.

Something ominous in the crates under the city... Viable dragon eggs being smashed on the cliffs... And now, golenae and Lacunae working together on Dorhane. It all had to be connected. I didn't know how it all fit together yet, but I was beginning to see a picture taking shape, a mosaic that looked to me like a diabolical conspiracy with the Gray Brothers at its center.

I would find out the truth. I would warn Mother.

But first, I was supposed to meet my friends and Kit's—no, Charlie's—dragon.

Othura alighted in the small pasture behind Clua's blacksmith shop—our appointed meeting place. Our landing sent horses whinnying and scattering, and Othura eyed them, no doubt hungry after our long flight.

Don't even think about it, I chided.

She huffed in rebuke as, together, we entered the stables. As soon as we were inside, she immediately curled up, eager to rest her weary wings.

I found Lure, Pocha, and Dagar sitting together around a rickety table, playing cards. When they saw me, they sprang up from their seats, all speaking at once.

"Essa!"

"Did you get him delivered safely?"

"Here, sit."

"What happened to your head?"

I reached up to find a goose-egg on my forehead from where I'd headbutted Kit—no. Charlie. Curse him—Charlie Inman. The ace. The *Silver Wraith*. My head spun with fury and shame and another feeling more like heartbreak—which, in turn, made my anger burn hotter.

I slumped into the chair they put beneath me and let my face fall into my hands. I felt a heat of tears rising to my eyes and quickly sat up, taking a steadying breath. There would be time to share my feelings later. For now, I had to get my update from them and then make my report to Mother.

"I delivered the poet back to his people," I said briskly. "He's gone."

"Oh, Essa," Pocha put a comforting hand on my shoulder.

I waved off her concern. "There's more to tell, but I don't

have time for it. Tell me of your mission. Did you get the little dragon saved?"

They all exchanged a look.

"We were going to try," Dagar started, "but..."

"Lure spotted a Lacuna going into the Hatchery," Pocha said. "So we hid and watched the place. There were hundreds of them there, Essa. Half an army. But they were trying to hide, as if waiting to spring a trap. We crept away before any of them saw us."

"I think they knew we were coming to rescue the dragon," Lure concluded, arms crossed. "Someone betrayed us."

I frowned, glancing around. "Where's Clua?"

"She's here. Finishing her chores," Pocha said.

"And Ollie?"

"Had to go back to the palace," Lure said. "To check in with Hoatan."

"Any sign of Rohree?"

All three shook their heads.

I bit my lip, thinking through what my friends were telling me. "So, the little dragon...?"

"Is still locked up in the Hatchery as far as we know," Lure shrugged. "Sorry, Essa."

It galled me that the baby dragon was being treated as a prisoner. Really, he should have been reunited with Kit —Charlie—even if he was a traitorous bastard. A bonded dragon separated from their rider so young often succumbed to madness. It would be difficult to rehabilitate the little dragon, but I or another experienced rider might have done it with months of careful effort. Locked up in the Hatchery, however, isolated and under guard, the poor thing didn't stand a chance. It was a terrible thing to waste a sweet young dragon like that, and I vowed to help the creature if I could. But I had bigger concerns now.

"What now, Irska?" Lure asked, putting special emphasis on my new title.

"Now I go to my mother. I have important information to relay to her. I saw some alarming things at Rograd Point. The Gray Brothers and their Lacunae are not to be trusted."

Lure snorted. "Did we ever trust those creepy shadow-worshippers?"

"No," I agreed. "But we have less reason than ever to trust them now. We'll find Rohree and free that little dragon. And I have much more to tell you. But first, I must fly and report what I've seen to my mother."

Pocha looked alarmed. "The queen will know by now that you rescued Kit. She's going to be furious, Essa. Why not wait a few days, let her cool down?"

I shook my head. "The news I have can't wait. You three get back to the barracks. Eat and rest. I have a feeling we may be needing your wings soon."

53
CHARLIE

Bloom radioed command, and orders came down that I was to be brought back to the Republic with all possible haste. I became a baton in a relay race, rushed by tank then airplane then car back to headquarters. Once arrived, I was escorted to the showers and given a fresh uniform and a razor. Once I was cleaned up, my escorts —a couple of young MPs— brought me to the commissary.

Fare from McNally Air Base was nicknamed McNasty, but I wolfed down the fried eggs, limp bacon and white toast eagerly, for although it couldn't compare to the spiced sausage and honey biscuits of Maethalia, it tasted like home, and part of me reveled in it—although the rest of me felt terribly broken, bereft, and full of regret.

Essa...

The thought of her name ripped through me like a knife blade. Would I ever see her again? I had to. I *had* to.

I closed my eyes and reached out to her with my thoughts for perhaps the hundredth time since we'd parted, but there was nothing. She'd shut her mind to me. Even

Parthar's presence was dim, his thoughts indecipherable. Perhaps I was just too far away.

I shoved my plate of food away half-eaten and nodded to my MPs.

"I'm ready to see the brass," I said.

Instead, I was escorted to the infirmary. A doctor and a nurse frowned at my eye—still swollen shut. They threw four stitches in my brow, examined the wounds I'd received from Braimar, which were apparently healing fine, then scratched some notes in a folder and sent me on my way.

Finally, I found myself sitting in General Peckham's office, coffee in one hand, cigarette in the other, listening to the ticking of a clock. I took a drag off the cigarette, feeling like myself for the first time in months—and at the same time like a total imposter.

The door burst open, and General Peckham stormed in. Behind him came his assistant, Michaels, pushing his glasses up on his nose, and behind him came two more men. One was a tall prick in a leather pilot's jacket I recognized from Flight Academy—Carter Blaize. The last fellow wore a black suit and had slicked-back blond hair, a pale movie-star's face, and dead blue eyes.

"Inman! Back from the dead," Peckham bellowed when he saw me. I stood and saluted, and he returned the gesture with obvious pleasure. "You're a hero, my man. Sit. Hell, put your feet up on my desk, if you like. You've earned it."

The general took the chair behind the desk and lit up a cigarette of his own.

"I know you must be exhausted," he said. "We'll give you a more formal debriefing later. But I wanted you to understand what you've done before all hell breaks loose."

"What I've done?" I asked numbly.

"The intelligence you sent back via that prelate fellow. Oh, he's been sending us stuff for years. But you—you're one of us. You knew exactly the information we needed to come out on top. Now that we've got it, by God, we're going to use it."

"Use it?" I muttered. "Like you used it to firebomb those dragon eggs? A thousand unborn dragons, roasted in their shells..."

If Peckham noticed that my teeth were on edge, he didn't show it.

"Exactly, my boy! We couldn't have done it if you hadn't given us the exact location of their hatching grounds there on Rograd Point. And setting up the queen's crippled daughter to take command?" he chuckled. "Genius. With her in charge, I doubt they'll even be able to mount an organized defense when we hit them tonight."

"*Tonight?*"

Peckham clapped me on the shoulder. "Absolutely, my boy. With everything we've got. Every squadron we have will be hitting their capital. Dragons will be falling from the sky like goddamn snowflakes!"

"Hell of an analogy, sir," Michaels chimed in.

Peckham glanced back at him and seemed to notice the men standing by the door, too.

"But that's nothing compared to what'll be happening on the ground, thanks to Mr. Langford and his efforts."

The pale man nodded an acknowledgement, but he didn't take his eyes off me. And I didn't like those eyes, not one bit. He didn't blink. It was like being stared at by a statue.

"I don't believe I know Mr. Langford," I said.

"Of course," Peckham said. "Charlie Inman, meet

Edward Langford of the Secret Intelligence Bureau. They stationed him here when you disappeared, to help bring you back, at first, then to manage communications with you. He's been the Maethalian prelate's contact for years. And, at his recommendation, we brought Major Blaize here to fill in for you while you were away."

"As the Silver Wraith," I said.

Carter gave me a cocky-ass grin.

"Seven dragon kills already," Peckham boomed, thumbing toward the man. "You might have some competition, Inman. We couldn't let the Wraith die, you understand. Would have been bad for public morale."

"Right..." I said.

"It's been fun being you," Blaize said.

From what I'd heard, he had been stationed at Portholm with the Second Air Force after flight school. He had a reputation as a hell of an ace—and a diva. I didn't like the idea of him being me. In fact, I kind of wanted to punch him in the face.

"Of course, nobody could fill your shoes, Charlie," Peckham went on. "We'll have you flying as the Wraith again in no time. I'll tell you, the accolades you're going to get from what you've done—we're talking a Presidential Medal of Valor at the very least."

"I agree," the spook, Langford, said. "We've been laying the groundwork for the downfall of the dragon riders for years. Your arrival came at the perfect time. And the work you've done has been excellent. Even if you were a marionette and I were pulling your strings myself, it could scarcely have happened more perfectly."

His words were complimentary, but his voice made me

think of coiling snakes. And God was he a cold customer. It didn't even look like he was breathing.

"Thanks," I told him drily.

The door swung open, and a young lieutenant stuck his head in and gave a rushed salute.

"Sir, the planes are ready."

Peckham's face lit up. "Here we go."

He glanced at his wristwatch, then grabbed the microphone sitting on a corner of his desk, hauled it in front of himself, and pushed the button. Outside, a series of bullhorns fixed atop poles squealed to life.

"All pilots and crews to battle stations, all pilots and crews to battle stations. Operation Silver Dawn begins now. Take off at your squad leader's signal."

The speakers squealed once more as the mic shut off. Outside, the familiar sound of many thumping boots filled my ears, setting my blood pumping. One by one, plane engines roared to life.

"Well, that's my cue," Blaize said, putting his flight helmet on and pulling his goggles down. "I'll finish what you started and shoot down the one-armed princess of yours," he said, a sadistic glee in his voice, then he turned and swept out the door. Langford followed, whispering in his ear.

I felt as if my blood had turned to slush. I started to rise from the table.

"Woah, woah, woah, easy there, Ace," Peckham said, dropping his heavy hands on my shoulders and pushing me back down. "Where do you think you're off to?"

"I'm going. I have to fly."

He gave me a pitying smile. "I knew you'd feel that way.

And I was planning to send you. But not with that eye. The medics have grounded you."

"But—" I faltered, one hand going to my swollen eye. Certainly, in normal circumstances, they'd have never let a fellow fly with his vision so severely limited. But I didn't give a damn about that.

"No *buts*, Charlie. We just got you back, and I'll be damned if I'm going to lose you now. You're grounded, that's an order. But I do have someone who might be able to console you," he turned and shouted over his shoulder. "Send her in!"

The door opened, and there was Kitty. I slowly rose from my chair at the sight of her.

Peckham clapped me on the shoulder once more. "I'll leave you two to get reacquainted," he said with a wink. Then bustled out the door with Michaels at his heels.

Kitty moved toward me, somehow making her hips prominent even in the suit dress she wore. Having been away for so long, I looked at her with fresh eyes. Her short-ish, curly hair was perfectly coifed. Her lips, the vermillion of fresh blood. Her face, as flawless as a painting of a twenty-year-old angel—though I thought she looked paler and thinner than she had when I left. She'd been cooped up in her apartment, worried about me, maybe.

"Well, look what the cat dragged in," she said, one corner of her red lips quirking up.

Outside, the engines of more and more planes were starting, becoming a deafening chorus. With each one, my heart beat faster.

She stared at me without blinking. "Well? It's been two months. Aren't you going to kiss a girl hello?"

She stepped forward, her heels clacking on the floor in a

way that made me think of a hammer driving nails. Then her lips were on mine, her lipstick smearing on my face.

When I didn't kiss her back, she pulled away, giving me a sharp look. "What's the matter? Didn't you miss me?"

I couldn't answer. My heart felt like a whirling propeller. The buzz of the engines outside was driving me mad, the song of a siren.

I should just relax. Stay. This was my home. My time in Maethalia was just a dream. I was a fool to think...

And yet...

Dragons will fall like snowflakes...

I'll finish what you started and shoot down the one-armed princess...

Essa...

Kitty's hands grabbed the front of my shirt, pulling me closer.

"I missed you, Charlie," she said into my ear. "Take me back to your apartment."

My first impulse was to recoil at her words. But a voice of reason inside me countered. I should just stay. This was my home. Kitty had been my girl. Everything in Maethalia had been amazing. But could anything that amazing last? Could anything that amazing be real? Kitty's lips slipped slowly down my neck.

"There's something I want to try with you, Charlie," she whispered. "I promise you'll love it."

I felt her mouth open, felt her teeth on the skin of my neck.

Suddenly, Parthar shouted in my mind—faint but urgent:

Run!

It was like being shaken awake.

I grabbed Kitty and shoved her back to arm's length. Something was different about her. Her skin? Her teeth...?

"Hey!" she said.

"I have to go," I muttered, brushing past her.

She grabbed my arm, stopping me short.

"You heard the general, Charlie. He ordered you to stay here. With me."

I tried to pull my wrist from her grasp, but she held on with freakish strength.

"I have to go," I said, yanking my arm again. There was a ripping sound as my shirt sleeve tore off. I left her holding it as I bolted from the room.

"Charlie. Charlie!" she called after me. But I didn't turn back.

Outside, the entire airfield was filled with planes. Normally, we sent out no more than a third of the squadrons on a single mission. But now, from the looks of it, they'd called up anything with wings. Peckham wasn't joking; this was going to be an all-out attack.

I scanned the runway for my plane—the Silver Wraith—and found it already taxiing up the runway for takeoff.

"Damned Carter," I snarled.

"Charlie!" Kitty burst out of the administrative building behind me, a pair of MPs in tow.

I ran. The planes were taking off now, wave upon wave of them taxiing forward and buzzing into the air as I sprinted into their midst. Wind from their propeller blades buffeted me, and wings whooshed over my head as I raced toward the back of the formation. At last, in the second-to-last row, I saw a plane with an empty cockpit. She was no Silver Wraith, just a ratty old patched-up Comet painted a drab army green—but she would have to do. The pilot was just clambering his way up when I grabbed him by the back of the jacket and yanked him down, snatching the leather flight helmet off his head.

"What the hell?" He wheeled and swung at me. I ducked it and slugged him in the side of the face, sending him to the dirt.

"Sorry, pal," I said, leaping over him and climbing into the cockpit. The wave of planes in front of us was already taxiing, and I put her in gear with a clunk. The smell of burning fuel filled my nostrils. The heat of the engine warmed my feet. I was home.

At the edge of the formation, Kitty and the MPs were still trying to get me, but there were too many whirling propellers blocking their way. And then I was picking up speed, the rumble of the engine becoming a roar as I went faster, faster, faster, then weightless, veering up into a tumultuous gray sky.

"I'm coming, Essa," I said. "I'm coming..."

54
ESSA

I burst into one of the sitting rooms adjacent to the throne room. A fire burned in the hearth, maps were spread upon the table, and Mother stood around them with Hoatan, Trag, and three of her generals.

"Leave us," I commanded.

The men glared at me but made no move to leave.

"Essa..." Mother began.

This time I shouted. "Leave us!"

Hoatan glanced at Mother, who nodded. He cleared his throat and began moving toward the door. One by one, the others followed suit. Mother watched me expectantly until the door was shut. Something about that look of hers, those sharp gray eyes, the line between her brows, a slight frown —as if I were a vexing cipher, too difficult to solve—made me feel like a little girl again.

"I...He..."

I tried to speak, but my throat clamped shut. My face twisted as tears filled my eyes. Embarrassed, I pressed my hand to my face and silently sobbed, falling to my knees.

"Whatever your punishment... I accept it..." I managed to say. "I deserve it."

Her hands were on me and I looked up, startled. She'd knelt down next to me and pulled me onto her lap. For a moment I resisted, then I gave in, falling into her arms and burying my face against her chest.

"Oh, Essa," she whispered.

"He betrayed me," I said. "All along he was betraying us. And I trusted him... I'm a fool."

She stroked my hair.

"Laynine died for nothing. I'm not worthy to be Irska."

"No," Mother said. "You fought well. I never could have imagined how well you fought. You earned your victory."

"But the moment I became Irska, I betrayed the kingdom by freeing a prisoner... a spy."

Mother gave me a sad, knowing smile. "I've known some who have done worse for love."

I looked at her, wiping tears from my cheeks.

"Have you been in love?"

She shook her head. "I'm not as brave as you. I knew I would one day be queen, and love was not a luxury a queen of Maethalia could enjoy. There were moments, but... I pushed them away. Still, I can imagine what it must have been like for you."

I shook my head. "He was spying. Stealing our secrets. He's an ace. The Silver Wraith, Mother."

This, at last, caused her eyes to widen in surprise.

I shook my head, tears filling my eyes again. "I'm a traitor. You'll have to have me killed."

Mother's brows knit. "Do you truly think I would do that?"

"But the law—"

"I am the law," she said.

I released a pent-up breath, relieved. Then I remembered the intelligence I had come to share.

"At the hatching grounds on Dorhane, we saw something, Mother. The Lacunae. They were working with golenae."

Mother frowned. "Golenae? From the old tales?"

"Yes, I swear. Creatures made of bone and earth and animated by the souls of demons," I said quickly. "Golenae. They were taking dragon eggs."

"And they were working with the Lacunae? Are you certain?"

I nodded. "We saw them."

"The prophesies... What is dead must not live again..." Mother looked away from me, and I saw the millstones of her mind grinding in thought. What I'd said could only mean one thing. Prelate Kortoi had broken the cardinal law. He'd used the spirits of the void to animate unliving matter. If he would do that, there was no telling what else he might be capable of.

"Did you ever investigate those crates in the catacombs?" I asked.

Mother's face had gone pale. "Kortoi sent his Lacunae. He said they found nothing. The prelate must be brought in for questioning. He must be arrested, before—"

A sound stopped her words, faint at first, like the whining of a mosquito, but growing louder and deeper with every second. It was a sound every Maethalian was intimately familiar with. The sound of plane engines. Mother and I both sprang to our feet and rushed to the window just as the Theyrune Horn blew a low, hair-raising blast. The sky was clear for now, blue and empty, but there could be no doubt about it—the Admites were coming.

Then, the floor was shaking under our feet. In the courtyard below, we saw a great fissure forming among the flagstones.

"What's happening?" I whispered. Mother's only answer was to place a hand on the hilt of her dagger.

The fissure widened until it was at least two spans across, then out of its black depths, figures began emerging. Monstrous figures—golenae. Some were humanoid with the heads of beasts, others shaped like dragons with mismatched body parts. Oversized heads, gigantic claws, limbs of different sizes—a grotesque and terrifying menagerie. Two guards charged at the first few that emerged with their spears leveled. In seconds, the golenae had reduced them to piles of splintered bones and shredded meat.

Mother spun from the window just as Hoatan burst in the door.

"Your Majesty—" he said breathlessly.

"I know," Mother interrupted him. "Wake my dragon. Today I ride with the Skrathan."

Mother went to find her dragon. I went to find mine.

Othura. Come to me!

For a moment, the only response was a whimper and a snarl.

We're trapped. The cowards have trapped us, she said.

Where?

In the Hatchery. Hurry, Essa. It's burning.

I remembered what my friends had said about Lacunae surrounding the Hatchery. They'd assumed it was some plan to catch them trying to rescue Kit's dragon, but obviously they'd been planning something far bigger than that...

I burst out of the palace, drawing my sword and sprinting across the courtyard. To my left and my right, golenae were emerging from the ground— claws, spiked heads, and toothy jaws bursting up like breaching leviathans. The royal guards were fighting them as they emerged, but I saw immediately how futile that was. One golenae—a human-shaped one with a head and claws like a lobster's—had seven spears protruding from its body and still fought ferociously. Another one shaped like a huge wolf continued to fight despite being covered in burning pitch. As I watched, it snarled and sprang onto two guards at once, pinning one down and clamping the other one's face in its jaws.

Cursing, I veered toward them.

With a shout of fury, I swung my sword with all my force at the wolf's foreleg, cleaving it just above the paw and freeing the man stuck beneath. He rolled free and stumbled to his feet, spear ready.

The flaming wolf turned to face us, its mouth covered in gore, its teeth still gripping the dead guard's torn-off head. Its coal-red eyes burned into me as it snarled and began padding forward. A normal wolf would have been limping from having a paw chopped off, but this one simply walked smoothly on the stump of its foreleg.

How can we defeat creatures that feel no pain? I thought, dread welling up in me.

The wolf pounced. I dove beneath its jaws, leaving it to snap at empty air.

As I rolled to my feet, I chopped at the same leg I'd cut off before, hacking it one, two, three times, until I'd exposed bone beneath the layer of clay. But I was only halfway through the muscular upper leg—and the beast leaped again, this time onto the other guard. The guard got his spear up in time, and it plunged into the golenae's chest—but when a living wolf would have recoiled at the injury, this one kept coming, driving the spear deeper into its own body until it was near enough to get its jaws around the guard's throat. The guard got his shield up just in time, but the wolf's mouth closed on it and crumpled it like an eggshell.

I whistled, charging, hoping to distract the thing from the defenseless guard. It turned its head toward me, the crumpled shield still in its mouth. Before it could spit it out, I was there, leaping and stabbing downward into the gole-nae's face. The blade entered the bottom of the thing's eye socket, and a shiver went through its body. With a scream of fury, I twisted my sword, prying upward. The beast stopped, twitching, and with a final effort, I wrenched my sword sideways.

The creature's eye came out, an oblong chunk of burning coal, and I stomped on it. It crumbled into smoldering dust, and the right side of the beast's body went limp. With a battle cry, the guard followed my lead, stabbing his dagger into the creature's other eye socket over and over. With each strike, smoking dust sifted out until at last the socket was nothing but a smoldering hole and the beast lay still on the ground.

The guard looked at me, wild-eyed. "Thank you," he breathed.

I saw his relief, but I didn't share it. All around us were hundreds—or thousands—more golenae. If it was that hard to kill just one of them, there was no hope of defeating them all.

I took a step forward and tripped on something. The arm clip I'd taken off and thrown down before the challenge still lay where I'd left it. Impulsively, I snatched it up.

"Go for their eyes!" I shouted at the guard, then I was running again.

Somehow, I made it through the menagerie of horrors the palace had become and fought my way to the Hatchery—but the sight that greeted me made my stomach clench.

The Hatchery's door and windows were covered by some black, shimmering substance—a magical barrier. And the entire structure, from foundation to peak, was licked with eerie blue flame. Normally, fire was no concern for a dragon; their hide was fireproof. But the carcasses of several large dragons littered the ground, their bodies wreathed in flame. They must have been outside when the fire began, tried to free their fellow dragons, and touched the flames in the process. And it had burned them.

Clearly, this was no ordinary fire. Every element of this attack was magical in nature—the dark magick of the void.

If I doubted Kortoi's involvement before, ample proof

stood before me. Row upon row of the Brotherhood's Lacunae knights stood lined up on their black horses, preventing anyone from reaching the Hatchery.

My Skrathan were gathering opposite them, staring in horror and bewilderment at the sight before them. A few sat astride their dragons, but most were on foot since their dragons, like Othura, were trapped inside. Off to the right, there lay a knot of mangled bodies where a group of Skrathan had clearly charged the Lacunae ranks and paid the price.

"The Irska!" someone shouted when they saw me.

"Irska Essaphine!"

"Our dragons!"

"What do we do?"

My fellow Skrathan looked to me, panic and fury on their faces. I saw Lure pushing to the front of the crowd, and Pocha and Dagar, too. Pocha was on dragon back.

Where the hell was Ollie? I wondered, but there was no time to dwell on that question.

"What do we do, Irska?"

"What are your orders?" several Skrathan shouted at once.

For a terrible moment, my mind was a perfect blank. What *could* we do? The golenae were so hard to kill, each of them could probably slaughter five of us before we could take out one. And the Lacunae were the strongest knights ever to live. Skrathan were trained to fight hand-to-hand, but we were far better on dragon back. A hundred of us couldn't take on five hundred Lacunae and hope to live— not without our dragons.

And where were the royal knights? I spun a circle,

looking for them, but there was not a single one to be found. Either they'd all been slaughtered already, or Lord Natath and the nobles had betrayed us, too.

My riders stared at me, desperate, expectant. If Laynine or Paemalla were here, they'd have a plan. They'd have an answer. But me... I could see no way out of the noose our necks were now in.

Unless...

Unless we could somehow free our dragons.

Defeat the Lacunae, quench the flames, reach our dragons...

I looked at the burning ziggurat, then off to the right. The falls of Cheselie ran down the cliff face, sending mist into the air. And beyond that, far above us, lay the dammed basin of the lake. *What if...?*

"Irska?" someone prompted.

I could see my Skrathan glancing at one another, skepticism and worry on their faces. I was losing their faith.

I stood up straight and shouted in the loudest, most commanding voice I could muster. "Form up ranks, but do not attack until my command," I said. "Pocha, you're giving me a ride up to the top of the falls. Let's go!"

I climbed behind Pocha onto the back of her teal-colored piscean, Razune, and she winged us up toward the cliffs. Almost immediately, a barrage of arrows streaked toward us from the Lacunae ranks below.

"Look out!" I shouted.

Pocha saw the danger and steered us to the right, out of range of the arrows. But they were far from our only concern. A half dozen flying golenae had spotted us as well and had taken flight, winging up toward us from the ground.

Golenae, I warned Pocha.

I see them.

Drop me off at the edge of the falls. Then you hold them off.

Yes, Irska, she said.

With a last effort from Razune, we emerged above the falls. She roosted on the edge of the cliff for a second, just long enough for me to jump off, then she turned and dove to take on the oncoming golenae.

I now stood atop an ancient, two-foot-thick stone dam. It held back the water from the spring, forming a basin perhaps a hundred spans wide. The falls plunged down from a twenty-foot-wide gap in the center of the dam. For a second, I was struck by how tranquil the water was, given the chaos taking place below. Then Razune rose into the air behind me, snarling, locked in combat with two golenae, and the illusion of calm dissolved.

Focus. How do I get the water from up here to down there?

In my mind, it had been easy. Break the dam, watch the water pour down. But now that I looked at it, I was impressed with how thick the dam was. And it had been in place for thousands of years. If it were easy to break, it would have broken already. I sure wasn't going to make any progress hacking at it with only my sword...

Frustrated, I turned away from the water, thinking.

As I did, I saw Razune hit one of the golenae with a blast

of ice, freezing the upper half of its body. As it began to fall from the sky, she wrapped her tail around the leg of a second golena and swung it into the first. When the two collided, the frozen one shattered, and both fell from the sky. It was an epic move. And it gave me an idea.

We need fire, I told Pocha.

She was distracted, preparing to engage two more golenae—a giant eagle and something that looked like a flying snake.

Someone with a strong dragon stone and fire power... Lure! Bring me Lure.

As you command, she thought back to me, and her dragon tilted and dove, slipping right between the two attackers who shrieked in irritation. The snake dove to pursue Pocha. But the eagle spotted me and began flying in my direction.

"No. No, no, no..." I fled, sprinting down the dam wall as the eagle's talons slashed the air just behind me. Water lay on one side of me, a thousand-foot drop on the other. Fall left, and the eagle could snatch me out of the water like zyrfish. Fall right, and I'd drop to my death. So, I tightroped my way ahead, clay beak snapping at me as I ran. I reached the grassy sward at the end of the dam and dove as the eagle screeched over me, talons raking the air where I'd been a second before.

I rolled to my feet and channeled Othura's power using my dragon stone. A stone's power was far more potent when the dragon itself was present. But I'd have to do this on my own.

I summoned the power, focused, and released. A blast of swirling wind hit the golena, twisting the thing's wings about itself and causing it to plummet over the edge of the cliff. I ran and looked down. The eagle fell halfway down the cliff face before righting itself and starting to fly up again. Three more flying golenae joined it.

But Kortoi's abominations weren't the only worry. The URA planes were arriving, too. Bursts of fire bloomed on the palace's east wing as bombs fell and exploded. The rattle of machine gun fire filled the air as five planes buzzed the courtyard, strafing the Skrathan there.

This is a disaster.

Where was Pocha?

There!

I caught sight of her weaving her way toward me among the golenae, dodging attacks from the biplanes. And Lure was on Razune's back with her.

Suddenly, two more golenae burst up from the edge of the cliff, screeching and flying toward me. I hit them both with another blast of whirlwind, and they dropped just as the eagle had—for now.

Then Razune was there, rising over the cliff's edge.

Lure, you heat the water near the outlet to the falls. Just don't get washed over.

Pocha, you cover Lure. Buy time. We want the water near the dam boiling. I'll try to draw the golenae over to me.

Yes, Irska, my friends replied.

Pocha deposited Lure atop the wall, and Lure's hands plunged into the water. Immediately, the nearest water began boiling and steaming. Razune turned, hovering, ready to take on the next wave of golenae. From my place off to the side, I ran to the cliff's edge and whistled. Two of the five onrushing golenae shifted their attack and came at me.

Are you coming anytime soon? Othura demanded in my mind.

Trying my best, I said, sprinting to draw the golenae away from Pocha and Lure. When I'd gone far enough, I wheeled and hit them both with a blast of wind, knocking them back. It worked—but channeling Othura's power through the stone was taxing. I wasn't sure how many times I could do it.

I spared a glance at the basin and saw that a large swath of water near the dam was now boiling.

Gods, Lure's fire ability was powerful...

What now? Lure demanded in my mind.

Keep it going, I shot back. *We need the rock of the dam to be as hot as possible.*

The buzzing of an engine grew louder as a plane swooped toward us, machine gun blazing as it fired at Pocha. A few shots hit Razune's tough hide before she barrel-rolled out of the line of fire. A blast of ice gushed from her mouth and froze the plane's propeller. It paused in mid-air, then started to fall. As it did, Razune grabbed it with her talons and steered it into a pair of attacking golenae, knocking all three from the sky.

Yes, Pocha! I cheered. I glanced over again to see the water abutting the dam roiling and steaming. That was hot enough. It had to be.

Now freeze the dam, Razune. Lure, run!

Obediently, Lure took off down the length of the dam as Razune spun and blasted the dam with ice.

For a second, nothing happened, and I felt like my heart dropped into my belly. Then, I saw a crack appear on the dam wall. Then a second. Then a third.

"Yes!" I shouted.

But the celebration was short-lived. A shape blurred toward me from the left, and I looked over just in time to see a golenae dragon swooping toward me, talons flared. As it

hit me, I dove and twisted, freeing myself from its grasp—
and falling into the basin with a splash. There was a sound
beneath the water. Crackling, then a *boom*. I surfaced,
gasping for air, and felt my body tugged along in a powerful
surge. The dam had broken. The water was gushing out over
the cliff's edge. And I was rushing with it.

55
ESSA

Glimpsed images flashed past as I flew along in the flowing water. Lure catching sight of me, shouting and pointing. The sky above, criss-crossed with dragons and monsters and airplanes, choked with drifting smoke. And finally, the edge of the basin, rushing toward me with inexorable speed. I swam frantically in the opposite direction, grasping for something to hold onto. But there was no resisting the powerful flow of the water, and nothing to grab. I sped toward the edge. Closer, closer.

Over.

For an instant, the palace and the city and the sea beyond were all laid out before me, a vivid tapestry. My home. My last sight.

I fell, a moment of horrible weightlessness that made me scream.

Then, I wasn't falling.

A chill burned through the entire right side of my body, so cold it hurt, and I looked down to find myself half encased in a wave of ice. Razune and Pocha winged up from below me, and I understood—they'd frozen the water and saved me.

Now, Razune descended to roost upon the ice chunk, and Pocha locked arms with me.

"Good timing," I said, barely able to find the breath to speak.

Pocha flashed a smile.

Razune whipped the ice outcropping with her tail. It shattered, freeing me, and Pocha pulled me onto Razune's back. As we retrieved Lure from the nearby bank, I noticed Lure's hand on their belly, blood on their fingers.

"Lure. What happened?" I asked, pulling them onto Razune's back behind me.

"One of the golenae," Lure grunted. "It's nothing."

But Lure's ashen face showed that was clearly a lie.

"Just hang onto me," I said.

Heavy with three riders, Razune spread her wings and soared us downward.

As we descended, I surveyed the chaos below. The Lacunae had attacked the Skrathan, their ranks pressing my riders back and into a waiting pack of golenae. The result was chaos, a desperate melee. Planes buzzed over it all, strafing mercilessly with their machine guns.

It's going to be a slaughter, Lure said in my mind.

But there was reason for hope. The water we'd freed had indeed inundated the Hatchery dome. Smoke had replaced the blue flames that had flickered there minutes before, but still, no dragons were emerging.

The fire is out, I told Othura. *See if you can get free.*

We're trying, but the magical barriers are too strong, she said.

I cursed.

The only way to save my Skrathan was to free the drag-ons. If I couldn't do it soon, there'd be no one left to save.

"Look out!" Lure shouted, pointing left as a biplane banked and flew toward us, machine guns blazing.

Razune tilted hard, shielding us, and I felt the thuds as bullets struck her body.

"Razune?" I shouted.

Fine, she replied in my mind.

But even without speaking aloud, she sounded breath-less. She was hurt.

"Just get us to the ground," I told her. But it would be easier said than accomplished—because the biplane was turning for another pass.

From over toward the palace, there came the boom of an exploding bomb, and I looked to see one of the citadel's opal walls collapsing in a sheet of rubble.

A wall that had stood for ten thousand years...

No.

Everything was slipping away. The palace. The crown. Kit. My Skrathan. Everything. I'd been Irska for less than twenty-four hours, and I was already losing it all.

The biplane buzzed past again, and we all flattened ourselves against Razune's back as bullets whistled past us. This time, she managed to dive out of range.

What do we do? Pocha asked, her words brimming with desperation.

Thinking, I told her.

A bright flash lit up the day. I looked to the palace, bracing for some new calamity, in time to see a billowing cloud of flame blast over the palace wall, leaving three planes and a golenae burning in its wake. Autan, the greatest stellhan to ever live. Mother's dragon.

Clearly, her hibernation had done its work, for she was a third larger than any dragon I'd ever seen. Her golden scales scintillated like diamonds in the firelight, and her majestic wings spread like the sails of a clipper ship upon the sea.

At the sight of her, planes and golenae alike veered away. Even the Lacunae paused in their attack.

Mother! I called in my mind. *The dragons are trapped in the Hatchery.*

Not for long, she said, and Autan pinned her wings and dove toward the Hatchery dome, lowering her horned head just before impact. The boom seemed to shake the world, and when the dust cleared, I saw that the top of the ziggurat was cracked open like an egg. Dragons poured out, leaping, clambering, soaring down to save their Skrathan and attack the Lacunae and golenae below, their furious roars rending the air.

"Yes!" I screamed.

But my excitement was short-lived, for just as we touched down on the ground, I felt Lure's arms slip off my waist. I turned to find their head reeling, eyes fluttering shut.

"Pocha. Get Lure to the healers," I slipped off Razune's back and to the ground.

Othura landed next to me, and I bounded onto her back.

"What are you going to do?" Pocha asked, shifting Lure so they were in front of her.

I looked to the smoke-streaked heavens. "Mother and I are going to tear every plane and monster out of the sky," I said, and we took flight.

56
CHARLIE

With every mile we flew, the tension had built in me, like the twisting of a watch spring. I'd never flown with this many planes before, and it felt both exhilarating and claustrophobic to have so many other fighters around me. The roar of their engines eclipsed everything, even my own thoughts. Being surrounded by all that power made me feel small and mighty at once, like a raindrop riding a thunderstorm.

How many rounds of ammunition filled the planes around me? How many tons of explosives? And all of it bent on the beautiful city of Issastar. And on Essa.

That was the thought that scalded most, that burned like a brand inside me. I could not let them hurt Essa. I *would* not allow them to hurt Essa.

But what would I do? Shoot down my friends and comrades? Would I do that for her?

Yes, God help me. I would. It was the only reason I was here now.

Did that make me a traitor?

Yes.

For her, I would be a traitor.

And the hell of it was, I didn't even feel bad. On the contrary, the thought filled me with purpose, with life.

And so, I pushed my plane's throttle until I could hear the engine's pistons pounding to keep up. Inch by inch, foot by foot, I wove my way forward in the formation, like a fish working its way to the head of its school.

What would I do when I got there? That was a question I couldn't answer yet. I sure as hell wouldn't be able to shoot down three hundred planes. But I knew I didn't want to arrive too late to be of any help. So, I pushed until the plane's engine manifold was rattling and the exhaust gave off the faintest whiffs of smoke.

"Come on, you whore. Hold together," I told the plane. Then, feeling superstitious, I added, "Be a good girl for me..."

I'd have loved to be flying my old Silver Wraith instead of this shit-trap Comet One with patches on the wings. But my beloved steed was at the bottom of the sea. And that bastard Blaize doubtless had the fastest, newest plane in the squadron...

Never mind all that. When I found him, I'd—

There! Up ahead at the front of the formation, I spotted silver wings glinting in the evening sun. And beyond, the walls of Issastar lay spread out before us. But something was wrong. We weren't even there yet, and already thick columns of smoke rose into the sky. Far below, I could see frantic movement in the streets, the glint of weapons. And creatures. Gray, strange, monstrous creatures...

My mind raced as I tried to understand what I was seeing.

But there was no time to ponder. Blaize was banking left

and diving, making for the palace complex. About a third of the squadrons followed him. Another third broke right, toward the city's south gate, and another third carried on straight—no doubt following a battle plan laid out long before I showed up back in the URA. I hesitated only a moment before banking to follow Blaize's squadrons. He was going toward the Hatchery, and that's where the Skrathan would be taking off from—where Essa would be.

As we dove, I leaned on the throttle until it topped out, the engine screaming in protest, and still I dove harder, tipping my plane's nose downward and passing beneath my squad mates to get closer to the front of the formation.

As the ground drew closer, I tipped the wings and hazarded a glance down. Below, the space outside the Hatchery was absolute pandemonium, a vast melee of fighting bodies and gray... what were those things? Beasts?

No... Those were the strange things Essa and I had witnessed on Dorhane. Golenae, she'd called them. What the hell was happening? Were URA forces fighting alongside monsters, now?

I tilted my wings again and squinted down for another look.

But there weren't URA forces down there. There were forces in black armor—Lacunae? It looked like they were fighting the Skrathan. But where were the dragons?

A sudden coolness brushed my face, and I glanced over to see I was passing the Cheselie Falls—which were now gushing far, far stronger than I'd ever seen them. With a jerk of the plane's stick, I banked left just as even more water gushed down where I'd been a moment before.

"What the—?"

I banked, coming around, and saw that the dam above

had been breached. At first, I thought, *Oh no.* Then I saw where the water was going. It was hitting the Hatchery, which was awash in blue flame. As the water hit it, the flames gave off great puffs of steam and flickered out.

I heard the cheers of the Skrathan.

So that's where the dragons were... trapped inside the Hatchery?

Othura? I probed, calling for the dragon, but what I felt where she should have been was an utter blankness, a silence that could only be deliberate. Essa had slammed the door on me.

And how could I blame her?

Parthar? I tried.

Charlie! His voice came back, faint but full of such eagerness and joy that it made my heart ache.

Where are you? I asked.

I don't know. It's dark here. I can't tell. Come find me!

I will, I vowed. *As soon as I can. I promise.*

But first things first. Judging from the movement of bodies on the battlefield below, the Skrathan were getting slaughtered. They needed their dragons, and they needed them now.

I banked and made a pass at the Hatchery dome, firing a burst of gunfire at it. But just as I expected, the bullets had no effect on the thick stone. I didn't want to waste too much ammo, so I banked again, scanning the sky for Carter Blaize. Something in my gut kept telling me to keep an eye on that prick...

No silver plane was in sight, but what I saw instead made my jaw drop. The biggest dragon I'd ever seen was emerging from the palace, its body glittering and golden, its horns as long and sharp as a pair of lances, its wings wide enough to span an entire squadron.

"Ho-ly..." I muttered, my breath hitching as the dragon flew over me, making for the Hatchery. I was traveling in the other direction, so I missed the moment of impact, but when I banked and came back around, I saw the huge dragon had cracked the ancient building's roof. Dragons emerged from it, thick and furious as hornets spilling from a nest.

"Yes!" I shouted, pumping my fist, until it occurred to me that these dragons would be just as likely to come for me as for anyone else.

But where in all this chaos was Essa? I wanted to scream her name. To land and search for her among the Skrathan fighting hand-to-hand on the ground. But if she were fighting down there, I would be of much more use to her in the air. I banked and dove, pointing my nose at the ranks of Lacunae knights.

Lacunae were prime enemies of the URA. If they were fighting against the Skrathan, too, then great. I could fight for Essa and not be a traitor after all...

I buzzed low over the battlefield and unleashed my cannons, strafing the Brotherhood knights and leaving a path of fallen warriors in my wake. But when I came to make another pass, I found myself face-to-face with a huge green dragon.

"I'm helping you, buddy!" I called and even tried to project my thoughts into its mind—but if it heard me, it paid no heed, instead opening its cavernous jaws and sending a jet of flame straight for me. I pulled up fast into a stall, then banked and dropped out of harm's way, leading the green brute toward a trio of planes that were making a pass to strafe the Skrathan below. The planes and the dragon engaged in a fiery battle as I turned and got out of the way.

I didn't have long to bask in my cleverness—because I spotted the Silver Wraith above and to my left. Three other fighters were shadowing it as it made for the huge, golden dragon. And at that dragon's wing flew another dragon. Smaller. Silver. Othura.

Essa.

More and more planes were falling in formation with Blaize, ten, fifteen, twenty, all pursuing the massive dragon. Their strategy was clear. Take down the biggest dragon, and enemy morale would crumble. Meanwhile, Big Gold veered out over the sea, no doubt intending to draw the planes away from their comrades and their city.

Blaize and his squadron followed.

And so did I.

57

ESSA

I n Skrathan training, we were taught to keep track of how many enemies were in each quadrant of the sky. It was to help us know at any instant what direction we might turn in order to attack or to flee. But now the foes were like stars in the night. There was no chance of keeping count. And more kept coming.

Luckily, we had Mother.

She and Autan had winged out over the bay, drawing our enemies away from the city, and I stayed with her, shadowing a short distance to her left. She drew heavy fire, but the ancient dragon's thick hide kept the bullets at bay—so far. When she'd gone far enough, she spun to face her attackers, sending a billowing blast of fire into their midst.

URA planes were fire-proofed, but fire from a dragon like this was another story, and six or seven fell burning toward the sea.

Attack! I told Othura, and she loosed a blast of wind. Dozens of enemy planes were in formation, firing at Mother, but the sudden gust knocked them off course, sending their shots wide.

Charge. Straight at them!

Othura obliged, pinning her wings back and diving to meet a low-flying biplane. We came at them from above, and Othura caught their upper wing with her back talons, then banked hard, swinging the plane around, then letting it go, slamming it into two more planes that were flying in formation next to it. All three tumbled from the sky, in flames.

Yes! I cheered Othura. This was how an Irska should battle, and I felt pride rising in me, warm and bright—until I glanced around and saw how many planes were still in the sky.

And it wasn't just planes, either.

A horde of winged golenae had followed us too, launching themselves from the castle walls like gargoyles and winging toward Mother.

Her dragon was fighting like a demon out of the pit, roasting planes with her flames, crushing others in her jaws, whipping more down with her tri-tipped tail, slashing others with her claws and leaving them to fall, tattered, into the sea.

But no matter how many she destroyed, more appeared, and her dragon was taking so many shots, especially from—

Him.

Every Skrathan in the kingdom knew the Silver Wraith and what he meant. Death. Every rider dreaded him—but only I had felt his lips on mine. Only I had lain, my body tangled with his in the cool morning air. And only I carried the fire of his betrayal like a torch burning in my heart.

Only I had loved him...

So, it was only right that I should be the one to bring him down.

He was fighting cleverly, staying out of range of Mother's dragon's tail and her fire, but still managing to hit her with his gunfire, more bullets thumping into Autan's hide with each pass. He was attacking her from below, several bullets striking the tender area beneath her wings, and I could tell from the way she winced that they were hurting her.

Let's go, I urged Othura, but she hesitated.

Are you sure?

Othura knew my feelings—perhaps better than I knew them myself. But this was not a time for emotion. It was a time for action.

"Go!" I said again, digging my heels into her side and leaning forward, flattening myself against her back as she dove. We closed on the Wraith.

Perhaps I don't have to kill Kit—Charlie, I thought. *Maybe if I just chase him away from Mother, he'll get the hint and move on...*

But as I closed in, he banked and nosed his plane up— toward me. Fire flashed from his machine gun, and I saw the flares as his bullets streamed in my direction. Only by dipping at the last second did Othura save me from having my head taken off.

For an instant, I sat hunched on her back, my heart thudding as I processed what had just happened.

He really just tried to kill me.

So that was how it was.

With a feral scream, I urged Othura forward again. I could feel her pulling a little unevenly through the air; her injured wing was bothering her, but I knew she wouldn't give up any more than I would. Straight at the Silver Wraith we flew, dragon teeth and a whirling propeller in a collision course.

Who would veer off first?

Not us.

But the machine gun was firing again, and Othura had to roll to keep me from being taken off her back.

Upside down, I felt myself leaving the saddle, weightless. But I'd put the clip back on, and it kept me securely in place. As we passed the Silver Wraith, Othura raked upward with her claws, slashing the underbelly of the plane and leaving its cloth fuselage in tatters. But as I looked back, I saw the damage was mostly cosmetic. The plane still flew fine. And already, the Wraith was banking for another pass.

Your mother, Othura said, and I looked over. The good news was that she'd managed to lure the bulk of our attackers away from the city. The bad news was, Autan was beset with dozens of golenae even as the planes continued to pelt them with machine gun fire. Autan was a powerful and ancient dragon, but she'd only just woken. She couldn't last forever against an attack like this...

We have to help them!

Othura turned, flying hard for Mother. As we drew close, Othura blew a hard blast of wind that knocked several golenae off Autan, but there were still dozens more. A human-like golenae had been riding one of its winged brothers and leaped onto Autan's back. As I watched, Mother hacked it with a mighty blow from her sword, nearly splitting the monster in half.

We swooped in, attacking one of the golenae clinging to Autan's flank, Othura snagging the monster's wing with a rear claw and ripping it off while I dispatched another with my sword.

But the thunderous chuckle of machine gun fire came from our left, and I looked to see the Wraith streaking toward us again. Another plane behind him was firing as well, but that pilot must have been inexperienced, because it looked like some of his shots actually struck the Wraith.

Chaos...

Then the unthinkable happened. One of the Wraith's bullets hit home. Autan unleashed a bellow of pain, and her wings began flapping lopsided.

With a battle cry, I broke off and sped toward Kit—Charlie—the Wraith—once more.

One of his wingmen got to us first, coming at us from above with blazing guns.

Wind! I called, and Othura let forth a blast of air. It jostled the plane just enough to disrupt its aim. As we closed on it, Othura rolled, grabbing its landing gear in her foreclaws and whipping it sideways. The plane fell in a spiral.

Behind us, another terrible roar issued from Autan, and I looked over to see the Silver Wraith once again pelting her with gunfire. Her wingbeats were slowing, causing her to lose altitude. He opened his mouth to breathe fire, and only a cloud of smoke came out—a bad sign. Charlie was taking another pass, his bullets mercilessly hitting the dragon's body—and from the worst angle too, from below and to the side. Blood spattered as bullet after bullet struck him, a trail moving along Autan's belly, onto her side, up her flank, up her back, and to—

Mother!

I saw the moment the bullet hit. Saw her go limp in the saddle.

Then she and the dragon were both falling.

Time seemed to falter. I could have counted the folds in Mother's cloak as she fell, or the bloody wounds in the dragon's body.

We dove, swooping into the line of fire to protect Mother and Autan. I felt Othura's body clench as two shots hit her.

Still we dove, shielding Mother and spiraling down to reach her. I felt torn between the need to save Mother and a burning desire for revenge—and I looked up to the Silver Wraith. Charlie was showing no mercy, still firing down at Mother even as she fell. I could see him in the cockpit, the leather flight helmet covering the hair that sometimes fell into his eyes— lifeless glass disks of his goggles covering those dark blue eyes I had so loved gazing into.

As I watched, a second plane, which must have been out of control, dove toward the Wraith, cannons blazing, and caused Charlie to veer off track, buying us a momentary respite.

I felt my balance shift as Othura dove more steeply. Her action spoke louder than words could have, and she was right. Save Mother now. Revenge could come later.

Down we dove.

And down Mother fell.

Down. Down...

I watched as Autan struck the water with an impact like a boom of thunder, her wings splayed, her huge body parting the waves and sending up a massive blast of spray.

The water seemed to open up for them, and I saw Mother upon the dragon's back, her body slack.

Othura dove even more sharply until we were almost in free fall, dropping so fast my scream was left somewhere behind me, so fast my tears were lost to the wind.

58
CHARLIE

One of us will die.

That was my oath for Carter Blaize as I unloaded my machine guns on him. But the slippery bastard banked out of my line of fire, breaking off his attack on the dragons to focus on me.

Seeing the queen fall, seeing Essa diving to save her mother, knowing the pain she must be feeling—those were stronger fuels than petrol could ever be.

But Blaize's plane was faster, newer, and more maneuverable. And I was already in trouble. Blaize turned faster than I could, accelerated, and managed to loop in behind me.

Now, he was on my tail. I banked left, he banked left. I banked right, he banked right. I climbed, the engine roaring with strain, then stalled and turned suddenly to get the drop on him—one of my favorite moves—but he knew that trick too well and broke right before I could get a good shot at him. Then he was coming around, behind me once again, his guns thundering, tracer rounds streaking past. I dove and tried to loop behind him, but he kept up, firing down on me and punching a hole in my fuselage.

This son of a bitch...

He was good. His reflexes. His anticipation. Better than any ace I'd trained with.

He was on my tail again—and closing. All I could do was jog back and forth, left and right, to keep him from getting a bead on me. It felt inevitable that he'd catch me sooner or later—but I still had a few tricks up my sleeve.

Closer. Come on, buddy. Just a little closer.

I let him feel like he was closing in on me, reeling me in like a fish.

Then I cut the engine and cranked the flaps, nearly stopping in the air and turning on a dime. It was a dangerous move. As my momentum stalled, I had no control; I only had to hope I'd spin far enough to get him in the bead of my guns.

I held my breath as the engine stopped. The world hushed, the wind whispering around me. *Turn. Turn. A little farther...*

The plane pivoted in the air, and he came in front of my crosshairs. *Now!* I opened fire and watched the flaming tracer rounds as they hit the Silver Wraith. Punching through a wing, pinging off the engine housing, then—click.

No!

I squeezed the trigger again and again, but nothing happened. The gun was jammed.

My plane, stalled and front-heavy because of the engine, nosed down and fell in a spiral. I grabbed the choke button and the throttle and tried to crank the engine up again. It coughed and grumbled, but didn't start.

I was vaguely aware of the Wraith firing on me, holes

bursting in the fuselage of the plane around me, canvas flapping.

I fired the engine again. Fired it again. Fired it again. Nothing.

The sea was spiraling up to meet me, a fatal impact. I was vaguely aware of Blaize peeling off, banking again to attack Essa and her mother down in the water.

"Come on, you dumb son of a bitch!" I shouted at the plane. The vast ocean spun up toward me. The engine heaved and coughed and stuttered as I tried to fire it again.

And again.

And again.

And one last time.

59
ESSA

Mother's dragon lay sprawled out on the water, floating, still, and wreathed in wisps of dissolving blood. I knelt on her back, holding Mother in my arms.

"You're going to be okay," I whispered, brushing her hair back from her face.

But it was a lie. Her face was white as bone. Her eyes stared into the sky, glassy and unfocused. I'd seen the ragged hole in her belly.

Othura sat hunched behind me, but there wasn't even time to get Mother onto her back. There was only time to say goodbye. Only I didn't have the words.

Mother was trying to speak, muttering through blood-soaked lips.

"What?" I leaned closer.

"It was... my fault," she said.

"No," I said, not understanding but trying to console her anyway. "It wasn't your fault. It's the prelate. And the nobles—Lord Natath—and—and Kit. We'll get revenge. I swear it. We'll—"

The deep rattle of a machine gun came again from overhead, and I saw a trail of splashes in the water, coming this way. I looked up to see the Silver Wraith strafing toward us. Kit. Charlie. How could he—? A well of hatred for him rose up in me, so potent that I could hardly keep from screaming. The gunfire came toward us, a trail of white splashes, inexorable death.

I wanted to cower, to hide. But there was nowhere to go. I looked up at the silver plane defiantly, as if Kit—Charlie— could see me. As if I could make eye contact with my traitorous poet, make him look me in the face as he killed me.

Closer, the bullets came.

Then seemingly from nowhere, another plane appeared, rising, it seemed, from the surface of the water and colliding with the Silver Wraith, shearing off one of its lower wings. Out of control, the Wraith tilted sideways and veered off to our right, looking as if it would crash somewhere on Dorhane. The second plane jittered off in the opposite direction, smoking and losing altitude as it went, leaving the twilit sky above us empty.

For the moment, the danger had passed.

Mother's hand found my shoulder, drawing my attention. Her fingers traced down to rest on the stump of my arm. It was the first time she'd ever touched it.

My eyes met hers. With effort, she seemed to focus on me.

"It was my fault," she said again. "I should never have let you fall."

I opened my mouth to reply, but found no words—only tears. So many tears. My chest heaved as I tried to keep from sobbing, to keep my eyes open, to memorize her face, words, this moment.

Then she shivered, sighed, and went still.

"Mother. *Mother?*"

I waited for her eyes to flutter open and held my breath, waiting for her to breathe.

It couldn't be over. There was so much more to say. I wasn't ready. I dug my fingers into the folds of her cloak, as if clinging on to her could slow down time, pull it back from the brink. I wasn't ready.

Water washed over Mother's face like a shroud. I felt water too, suddenly, its cold climbing up my waist, up to my chest, and still rising.

We're sinking. Othura warned.

Mother's mighty dragon fell away beneath us.

Mother fell, too, her cloak slipping through my fingers, her beautiful hair drifting like a banner in the wind, her royal crown glinting as she fell forever into the blackness of the deep.

60

CHARLIE

Black night smothered the world as I trudged through the fallen city, calling her name.

"Essa! Essaphine!"

The only response was a heckle of crows as they picked at the body of a fallen dragon.

The devastation was unbelievable. What a few hours ago had been a wonder of the world had been reduced to a hellscape of rubble. The only light came from fires that still burned, consuming the few remaining buildings. The palace's opaline towers had fallen. The walls lay in ruin. Bodies lay strewn in the dirt, twisted and torn. Nowhere did I see any living thing, not even a golena. The only movement was the curling and trembling of fire, the rush of smoke, and the occasional flutter of a tattered banner or a dead man's cloak.

Still, I trudged on, weary as a sleepwalker, calling her name.

"Essaphine! *Essa!*"

God only knew how I'd managed to coax my damaged

plane back to shore and find a level spot to put down before my fuel ran out—in a meadow I estimated to be six or seven miles north of the city. I'd hiked through the night to get here. My feet ached. My hands trembled. My stomach groaned with hunger. My eyes stung with spilled tears and smoke. But a fire burning within me drove me on.

I had to see her. To hold her. To know she was okay. To tell her I was sorry. To tell her I loved her.

"Essaphine!" I screamed into the desolation, my hoarse voice choking off the end of her name as my desperation got the better of me.

Something moved in the smoke. Lacunae. Or golenae, maybe. I didn't give a damn. I'd fight every one of them with my bare hands. I'd walk through this hellscape forever. And I'd never stop, never sleep, never rest until I found my Essa again.

61

ESSA

Through the darkness I stalked, sword in hand, Othura a few paces behind me. In the distance, the boom of artillery rattled the earth. The shouts of fighters and the screams of wounded men hung ghostly in the wind.

This was the Isle of Dorhane. No man's land. A scorched and bomb-pocked landscape scarred by trenches and blackened by fire and spilt blood. It was a place where generations of people from two nations had gone to die, and I could feel their suffering hanging in the air like a mist. It was a terrible place. The worst place.

And yet I felt at home here now, the coldest thing in a barren landscape, the deadliest thing in a land of death.

The silver plane had been badly damaged when it flew this way. It must have crashed here somewhere. *He* must be here somewhere.

Kit. Charlie. The Silver Wraith.

This would be a fitting place for my lover and me to

meet for the last time, I thought, squeezing the grip of my sword.

An image flashed through my mind. Mother dipping below the water, falling into darkness.

I'd lost so many people. I'd lost everything...

And I'd gained everything.

I was Irska.

I would be Queen.

The realization hit me like a wave of nausea: *I would be Queen.*

All the horrible duties and crushing responsibilities that came with the crown would be mine. It was a fate worse than death, a fate I never wanted.

Curse the one who orphaned me. Curse that betrayer. That deceiver.

And the worst part was, he'd made me love him.

Well. He'd felt the love of a princess. Now let him feel the wrath of a queen.

Steady, Othura urged. *There are enemies all around.*

As if to punctuate her words, a rattle of gunfire came from somewhere in the darkness off to our right, followed by more shouts and the concussions of explosions, their light flashing somewhere beyond the horizon. And yet I felt no fear. On I stalked, sword in hand. Through the smoke. Through the desolation. I would walk every inch of Dorhane if I had to. I would scour every hill and trench of no-man's land. Plumb every puddle, turn over every skull.

I would find Charlie Inman. And I would kill him.

*J. G. Gates here. I hope you loved Dragons and Aces Book 1! If you enjoyed it, **there are 3 things you absolutely need to do.***

1. Continue Essa and Charlie's story in book 2, Magick and Lead. Find it on Amazon!

2. Join my email crew, and you can get updates on all my upcoming books. Plus, you'll get a spicy bonus scene. *Remember that steamy encounter above the ballroom? Join my email list, and you'll get to read it from Charlie's point of view. TRUST ME, you don't want to miss that! Visit JGGates.com to sign up and download the chapter for free.*

3. Leave this book a review on Amazon, Goodreads, and wherever else you review books!

Did you find any typos in this book? I want to fix them! Please email them to me at: j@jgabrielgates.net.

Thanks again for reading! It truly means the world to me. Now, on to book 2...

THANK YOU!

Thank you to my amazing Kickstarter backers:
  Wallie Martinez-Vega
  Jarlyn Camacho
  A. Sturniolo
  Alexandra Corrsin
  Alyssa Heck
  Amanda
  Amy Frandsen
  Annarose Willhite
  Annette Wright
  April L. Miller
  AriStarry
  Arturo Gonzalez Argueta
  Ashley Mongold
  Ashley Summey
  Billye Herndon
  Brianna Bowling
  Brianna S.
  Brie Johnson

Caleigh Hayhurst

Casey Ward

Cassie Newell

Charlize Clémence Marin

Colleen Freeman

Courtney Pygott

Cristal and Flavio Juarez Lopez

Damion Brown

Danielle Fitzpatrick

Devon Hood

DeVonna Stephens

Emily B.

Enalia T.

Erin O'Connor

Ethan Brown

Gena Parker

Gregory Butt

Haven Bahr

Hermon Kirk Basone

Irinel Finco

Iris Juylyenne

Jacklyne & Daniel Jones

Jacob Savage

Jamie Brott

Jayson Legg

Jeff

Jennifer

Jennifer Nolan

Jess Micklethwaite

Jessica Hahn

Jillian Pehrson

Julia R.

Justise Briones

Karen Mishkin

Kat

Katelyn O'Leary

Katherine Malloy

Kela F.

Kerliza Foon

Kimberly Argana

Kristen M.

Kristen Staffieri

Krisy Grant

Krisztina Moore

Kyla G.

Kylee N.

Kylie Burrage

Laura C.

Laura Rodriguez

Lea Lemay

Leslie

Lily Roberts

Lorien Cord

M. Sommers

Maira O.

Marie Fisher

Meaghan Hughes

Michael H.

Michelle

Michelle and Perry Swenson

Mike McCue

Mom

Neola Kolentsis

Nic Mosman-Fischer

Nolalisse Han
Padonfane
Paige Desatoff McCarthy
Paige Reisenfeld
Phillip Sharp
Rachel Hoag
Rachel Temp
Rachel Walker
Renee KD Hurff
Rexi
Richie Hedges
Rosa Thill
Ruth
Shalana Battles
Shawn
Shayna Stockton
Sherry Mock
Somer Kemble
Stephanie
Stephanie Bugh
Stephanie Tebbs
Stephie L.
Susan Gates
Susan Stephens
Tammy Comerford
Travis Schirpke
V. Rankin
Andrea Hopkins
Sebastian Twardosz
Ashton Mackenzie
Megan E.
Calvin Smith

Devin Butler
Jackie Vandervest
Shannon Morris
Jessica Moslander
Safiyyah Rae Jensen
A.P. Beswick
Nicola
Morgan
Michelle Bragg
Robin Anderson
Dawn Link
Heyley Ingram
Elizabeth Rache

www.ingramcontent.com/pod-product-compliance
Lightning Source LLC
Chambersburg PA
CBHW020001120726
47903CB00004B/1085